A Death in
Cornwall

Also by Daniel Silva

DANIEL Silva

A Death in Cornwall

A NOVEL

HARPER

An Imprint of HarperCollins*Publishers*

A DEATH IN CORNWALL. Copyright © 2024 by Daniel Silva. All rights reserved. Printed in the United States of America. No part of this book may be used or reproduced in any manner whatsoever without written permission except in the case of brief quotations embodied in critical articles and reviews. For information, address HarperCollins Publishers, 195 Broadway, New York, NY 10007.

HarperCollins books may be purchased for educational, business, or sales promotional use. For information, please email the Special Markets Department at SPsales@harpercollins.com.

FIRST EDITION

Library of Congress Cataloging-in-Publication Data has been applied for.

ISBN 978-0-06-338420-0

24 25 26 27 28 LBC 5 4 3 2 1

*As always, for my wife, Jamie, and
my children, Lily and Nicholas*

Let me tell you about the very rich. They are different from you and me.

—F. Scott Fitzgerald

Preface

This is the fifth novel in the Gabriel Allon series to be set, in part, in the English county of Cornwall. Gabriel took refuge in the village of Port Navas, along the banks of the Helford River, after the bombing in Vienna that destroyed his first family. It was during this period that he befriended an eleven-year-old boy named Timothy Peel. Gabriel returned to Cornwall several years later—with his second wife, Chiara—and settled in a clifftop cottage in the parish of Gunwalloe. Timothy Peel, then a young man in his early twenties, was a frequent visitor.

PART ONE

The Picasso

1

The Lizard Peninsula

The first indication of trouble was the light burning in the kitchen window of Wexford Cottage. Vera Hobbs, owner of the Cornish Bakery in Gunwalloe, spotted it at 5:25 a.m. on the third Tuesday of January. The day of the week was noteworthy; the owner of the cottage, Professor Charlotte Blake, divided her time between Cornwall and Oxford. Typically, she arrived in Gunwalloe on a Thursday evening and departed the following Monday afternoon—three-day work-weeks being one of the many perquisites of academic life. The absence of her dark blue Vauxhall suggested she had decamped at her usual time. The glowing light, however, was an aberration, as Professor Blake was a devout environmentalist who would sooner stand in the path of a speeding train than waste a single watt of electricity.

She had purchased Wexford Cottage with the proceeds of her bestselling exploration of Picasso's life and work in wartime France. Her withering reappraisal of Paul Gauguin, published three years later, fared even better. Vera had attempted to organize a book party at the Lamb and Flag, but Professor Blake, after somehow getting wind of the project, had made it clear she had no wish to be fêted.

"If there is indeed a hell," she explained, "its inhabitants have been condemned to spend the rest of eternity celebrating the publication of someone else's latest waste of paper."

She had made the remark in her perfect BBC English, with the ironic drawl that comes naturally to those of privileged birth. She was not, however, from the upper classes herself, as Vera discovered one afternoon while stalking Professor Blake on the Internet. Her father had been a rabble-rousing trade unionist from Yorkshire and a leader of the bitter coal miners' strike in the 1980s. A gifted student, she had won admission to Oxford, where she had studied the history of art. After a brief stint at the Tate Modern in London, and an even briefer one at Christie's, she had returned to Oxford to teach. According to her official biography, she was considered one of the world's foremost experts in something called APR, or artistic provenance research.

"What in heaven's name does that mean?" asked Dottie Cox, proprietor of the Gunwalloe village store.

"Evidently, it has something to do with establishing a painting's history of ownership and exhibition."

"Is that important?"

"Tell me something, Dottie, dear. Why would someone be an expert in something if it wasn't bloody important?"

Interestingly enough, Professor Blake was not the first art world figure to settle in Gunwalloe. But unlike her predecessor, the reclusive restorer who had lived for a time in the cottage down by the cove, she was unfailingly polite. Not the talkative sort, mind you, but always a pleasant greeting and an enchanting smile. The consensus among Gunwalloe's male population was that the professor's author photograph had not done her justice. Her hair was nearly black and shoulder length, with a single provocative streak of gray. Her eyes were an arresting shade of cobalt blue. The puffy pillows of dark flesh beneath them only added to her allure.

"Smoldering," declared Duncan Reynolds, a retired conductor for the Great Western Railway. "Reminds me of one of those mysterious women you see in the cafés of Paris." Though as far as anyone knew, the closest old Duncan had ever come to the French capital was Paddington Station.

There had been a Mr. Blake once, a painter of minor note, but they had divorced while she was still at the Tate. Now, at fifty-two years of age and in the prime of her professional life, Charlotte Blake remained unmarried and, by all outward appearances, romantically unattached. She never had guests and never entertained. Indeed, Dottie Cox was the only inhabitant of Gunwalloe who had ever seen her with another living soul. It was last November, down at Lizard Point. They were huddled on the windblown terrace at the Polpeor Café, the professor and her gentleman friend.

"Handsome devil, he was. A real charmer. Had trouble written all over him."

But on that morning in January, with the rain falling in sheets and a cold wind blowing from Mount's Bay, the state of Professor Charlotte Blake's love life was of little concern to Vera Hobbs. Not with the Chopper still on the loose. It had been nearly a fortnight since he had struck last, a woman of twenty-seven from Holywell on the north Cornish coast. He had killed her with a hatchet, the same weapon he had used to murder three other women. Vera took a small measure of comfort in the fact that none of the murders had taken place during rainy weather. The Chopper, it seemed, was a fair-weather fiend.

Vera Hobbs nevertheless cast several anxious glances over her shoulder as she hastened along Gunwalloe's only road—a road with neither a name nor a numeric designation. The Cornish Bakery was wedged between the Lamb and Flag and Dottie Cox's Corner Market, which wasn't on a corner at all. The Mullion Golf Club was about a mile down the road, next to the ancient parish church. With the exception of an incident at the restorer's cottage a few years back, nothing much ever happened in Gunwalloe, which was just fine with the two hundred souls who lived there.

By seven o'clock Vera had finished baking the morning's first batch of sausage rolls and traditional cottage loaf bread. She breathed a small sigh of relief when Jenny Gibbons and Molly Reece, her two employees, hurried through the door a few minutes before eight. Jenny settled in behind the counter while Molly helped Vera with the steak pasties, a staple of the Cornish diet. A Radio Cornwall newscast played quietly in the background. There had been no murders overnight—and no arrests, either. A twenty-four-year-old motorcyclist had been seriously injured in a crash near the Morrisons in Long Rock. According to the weather forecast, the wet and windy conditions would persist throughout the day, with the rain finally ending sometime in the early evening.

"Just in time for the Chopper to claim his next victim," interjected Molly as she spooned meat-and-vegetable filling onto a circle of short-crust pastry dough. She was a dark-eyed beauty of Welsh extraction, a real handful. "He's past due, you know. He's never gone more than ten days without burying his hatchet into some poor girl's skull."

"Maybe he's had his fill."

"Got it out of his system? Is that your theory, Vera Hobbs?"

"And what's yours?"

"I think he's just getting started."

"An expert now, are you?"

"I watch all the detective shows." Molly folded the dough over the filling and crimped the edges. She had a lovely touch. "He might stop for a while, but eventually he'll strike again. That's the way these serial killers are. They can't help themselves."

Vera slid the first tray of pasties into the oven and rolled out the next sheet of short-crust dough and cut it into plate-size circles. The same thing every day for forty-two years, she thought. Roll, cut, fill, fold, crimp. Except Sundays, of course. On her so-called day of rest, she cooked a proper lunch while Reggie got drunk on stout and watched football on the telly.

She removed a bowl of chicken filling from the fridge. "Did you happen to notice the light burning in the window of Professor Blake's cottage?"

"When?"

"This morning, Molly, dear."

"Didn't."

"When was the last time you saw her?"

"Who?"

Vera sighed. She had a good pair of hands on her, did Molly, but she was simple. "Professor Blake, my love. When was the last time you actually laid eyes on her?"

"Can't remember."

"Try."

"Maybe yesterday."

"Afternoon, was it?"

"Could have been."

"Where was she?"

"In her car."

"Headed where?"

Molly inclined her head to the north. "Up-country."

Because the Lizard Peninsula was the most southerly point in the British Isles, everywhere else in the United Kingdom was up-country. But it suggested that Professor Blake had been bound for Oxford. Even so, Vera thought there would be no harm in having a look through the window of Wexford Cottage—which she did at half past three during a break in the rain. She reported her findings to Dottie Cox an hour later at the Lamb and Flag. They were sitting in their usual snug near the window, with two glasses of New Zealand sauvignon blanc between them. The clouds had finally broken, and the sun was dropping toward the rim of Mount's Bay. Somewhere out there beneath the black waters was a lost city called Lyonesse. At least that was the legend.

"And you're sure there were dishes in the sink?" asked Dottie.

"And on the countertop as well."

"Dirty?"

Vera nodded gravely.

"Rang the bell, did you?"

"Twice."

"The latch?"

"Locked tight."

Dottie didn't like the sound of it. The light was one thing, the dirty dishes quite another. "I suppose we should probably ring her, just to be on the safe side."

It took a bit of searching, but Vera eventually found the main number for the University of Oxford's Department of the History of Art. The woman who answered the phone sounded as though she might have been a student. A lengthy silence ensued when Vera asked to be connected to Professor Charlotte Blake's office.

"Who's calling, please?" the young woman asked at last.

Vera gave her name.

"And how do you know Professor Blake?"

"She lives down the road from me in Gunwalloe."

"When was the last time you saw her?"

"Is something wrong?"

"One moment, please," said the woman, and transferred Vera to Professor Blake's voicemail. She ignored the recorded invitation to leave a message and rang the Devon and Cornwall Police instead. Not the main number, but the special hotline. The man who answered didn't bother to state his name or rank.

"I have a terrible feeling he's struck again," said Vera.

"Who?"

"The Chopper. Who else?"

"Go on."

"Perhaps I should speak to someone a bit more senior."

"I'm a detective sergeant."

"Very impressive. And what's your name, my love?"

"Peel," he answered. "Detective Sergeant Timothy Peel."

"Well, well," said Vera Hobbs. "Imagine that."

2

Queen's Gate Terrace

It was a few minutes after 7:00 a.m. when Sarah Bancroft, still in the clutches of a turbulent dream, stretched a hand toward the opposite side of the bed and touched only cool Egyptian cotton. And then she recalled the text message that Christopher had sent her late the previous afternoon, the one about a sudden trip to an undisclosed destination. Sarah had been seated at her usual table at Wiltons at the time, partaking of a post-work Belvedere martini, three olives, Saharan dry. Depressed at the prospect of spending yet another evening alone, she had unwisely ordered a second. What followed was for the most part a blur. She recalled a rainy taxi ride home to Kensington and a search for something wholesome in the Sub-Zero. Finding nothing of interest, she had settled for a tub of Häagen-Dazs—gelato creamy fudge brownie. Afterward she had fallen into bed in time for the *News at Ten*. The lead story concerned the discovery of a body near Land's End in Cornwall, by all appearances the fifth victim of a serial killer the lesser tabloids had christened the Chopper.

It would have been reasonable for Sarah to blame her unsettled dreams on the second martini or the Cornish axe murderer, but the

truth was she had more than sufficient horrors buried in her sub-
conscious to disturb her nights. Besides, she never slept well when
Christopher was away. An officer of the Secret Intelligence Service,
he traveled often, most recently to Ukraine, where he had spent the
better part of the autumn. Sarah did not begrudge his work, for in
a previous life she had served as a clandestine operative for the CIA.
She now managed a sometimes-solvent Old Master art gallery in St.
James's. Her competitors knew nothing of her complicated past and
even less about her ruggedly handsome husband, believing him to
be a well-to-do business consultant called Peter Marlowe. Thus the
handmade suits, the Bentley Continental motorcar, and the maisonette in Queen's Gate Terrace, one of London's poshest addresses.

The windows of their bedroom overlooked the garden and were
streaked with rain. Not yet prepared to face the day, Sarah closed
her eyes and dozed until nearly eight, when she finally roused herself
from bed. Downstairs in the kitchen she listened to *Today* on Radio
4 while waiting for the Krups automatic to complete its labors. It
seemed the corpse in Cornwall had acquired an identity overnight:
Dr. Charlotte Blake, a professor of art history from Oxford University. Sarah recognized the name; Professor Blake was a world-
renowned specialist in the field of provenance research. Moreover, a
copy of her recent bestselling book about the turbulent life of Paul
Gauguin was at that moment resting on Sarah's bedside table.

The remainder of the morning's news was little better. Taken together, it painted a picture of a nation in terminal decline. A recent
study had concluded that the average British subject would soon be
less affluent than his counterparts in Poland and Slovenia. And if the
British subject were to suffer a stroke or heart attack, he would likely
endure a wait of ninety minutes for an ambulance to take him to the
nearest A&E ward, where some five hundred people were dying each

week due to overcrowded conditions. Even the Royal Mail, one of Britain's most revered institutions, was in danger of collapse.

It was the Conservatives, in power for more than a decade, who had presided over this state of affairs. And now, with the prime minister foundering, they were bracing for the prospect of a bruising leadership contest. Sarah wondered why any Tory politician would aspire to the job. Labour held a commanding lead in the polls and were expected to easily prevail in the next election. Sarah, however, would have no say in the composition of the next British government. She remained a guest in this country. A guest who moved in elite circles and was married to an SIS officer, she thought, but a guest nonetheless.

There was one piece of good news that morning—from the art world, of all places. *Self-Portrait with Bandaged Ear* by Vincent van Gogh, stolen from the Courtauld Gallery in a daring smash-and-grab robbery more than a decade ago, had been recovered under mysterious circumstances in Italy. The painting would be unveiled that evening during an invitation-only event in the gallery's newly refurbished Great Room. Most of London's art glitterati would be in attendance, as would Sarah. She had acquired an MA in art history from the Courtauld Institute before collecting a PhD from Harvard, and now served on the gallery's board of trustees. She also happened to be a close friend and associate of the Venice-based conservator who had knocked the Van Gogh into shape before its repatriation to Britain. He, too, planned to attend the unveiling—clandestinely, of course. Otherwise, his very presence might well overshadow the return of the iconic painting.

The ceremony was on the early side—six o'clock, with a cocktail reception to follow—so Sarah dressed in a striking Stella McCartney double-breasted blazer and skirt. The heels of her Prada pumps tapped a metronomic rhythm, forty-five minutes later, as she crossed the paving stones of Mason's Yard, a tranquil quadrangle of commerce concealed behind Duke Street. Isherwood Fine Arts, purveyors of museum-quality Old Master paintings since 1968, stood in the northeast corner of the courtyard, occupying three floors of a sagging Victorian warehouse once owned by Fortnum & Mason. As usual, Sarah was the first to arrive. After disarming the alarm, she unlocked the two doors, one fashioned of stainless-steel bars, the other of shatterproof glass, and went inside.

The gallery's office was located on the second floor. Once there had been a desk for a receptionist—the ravishing but useless Ella was the last occupant—but Sarah, in a cost-cutting move, had eliminated the position. The telephone, email correspondence, and appointment book were now her responsibility. She also handled the day-to-day business affairs and had veto authority over all new acquisitions. Ruthlessly she had shed much of the gallery's dead stock—manner of such-and-such, workshop of so-and-so—at bargain-basement prices. Even so, Sarah was the curator of one of the largest collections of Old Master paintings in Britain, enough to fill a small museum, if she were so inclined.

There were no appointments scheduled for that morning, so she tended to an outstanding billing matter, namely, a certain Belgian collector who seemed shocked to learn that he actually had to pay for the French School painting he had acquired from Isherwood Fine Arts. It was one of the oldest tricks in the book, effectively borrowing a painting from a dealer for a few months and then sending it back. Julian Isherwood, the gallery's founder and namesake, seemed to specialize in these types of arrangements. By Sarah's estimate, Isherwood Fine Arts was owed more than a million pounds for works that had already shipped. It was her intention to collect every last penny, beginning with the one hundred thousand pounds owed to the gallery by one Alexis De Groote of Antwerp.

"I would prefer to discuss this matter with Julian," the Belgian sputtered.

"I'm sure you would."

"Have him call me the minute he arrives."

"Yes, of course," said Sarah, and hung up the phone as Julian teetered through the doorway. It was a few minutes after eleven, considerably earlier than his normal arrival time. These days he typically dropped by the gallery around noon and by one o'clock was sitting down to lunch at one of London's better tables, usually with female company.

"I assume you heard about poor Charlotte Blake," he said by way of greeting.

"Awful," replied Sarah.

"A terrible way to go, the poor thing. Her death will undoubtedly cast a pall over tonight's proceedings."

"At least until the veil comes off that Van Gogh."

"Is our friend really planning to attend?"

"He and Chiara arrived last night. The Courtauld is putting them up at the Dorchester."

"How are they possibly managing?" Julian removed his mackintosh and hung it on the coat tree. He wore a chalk stripe suit and a lavender necktie. His plentiful gray locks were in need of a pruning. "What in heaven's name is that awful sound?"

"Could be the telephone."

"Shall I answer it?"

"Do you remember how?"

Frowning, he snatched up the receiver and raised it resolutely to his ear. "Isherwood Fine Arts. Isherwood himself speaking . . . As a matter of fact, she is. One moment, please." He managed to place the call on hold without disconnecting it. "It's Amelia March from *ARTnews*. She'd like a word."

"About what?"

"Didn't say."

Sarah picked up the phone. "Amelia, darling. How can I be of help?"

"I'd love a comment from you for a rather intriguing story I'm working on."

"The Charlotte Blake murder?"

"Actually, it concerns the identity of the mysterious art restorer who cleaned the Van Gogh for the Courtauld. You'll never guess who he is."

3

Berkeley Square

Where do you suppose she got the story?"

"It certainly wasn't me," said Gabriel. "I never speak to reporters."

"Unless it suits your purposes, of course." Chiara gave his hand a gentle squeeze. "It's all right, darling. You're entitled to a little recognition after toiling in anonymity all these years."

Gabriel's enormous body of work included paintings by Bellini, Titian, Tintoretto, Veronese, Caravaggio, Canaletto, Rembrandt, Rubens, and Anthony van Dyck—all while serving as an undercover operative of Israel's vaunted secret intelligence service. Isherwood Fine Arts had been complicit in his decades-long deception. Now, having officially retired from the intelligence trade, he was the director of the paintings department at the Tiepolo Restoration Company, the most prominent such enterprise in Venice. Chiara was the firm's general manager. Which meant that, for all intents and purposes, Gabriel worked for his wife.

They were walking in Berkeley Square. Gabriel wore a mid-length overcoat atop his zippered cashmere sweater and flannel trousers. His Beretta 92FS, which he had carried into the United

Kingdom with the approval of his friends in the British security and intelligence services, pressed reassuringly against the base of his spine. Chiara, in stretch trousers and a quilted coat, was un-armed.

She plucked a phone from her handbag. Like Gabriel's, it was an Israeli-made Solaris model, reputedly the world's most secure.

"Anything?" he asked.

"Not yet."

"What do you suppose she's waiting for?"

"I imagine she's hunched over her computer trying desperately to put you into words." Chiara gave him a sidelong look. "An unenvi-able task."

"How hard can it be?"

"You'd be surprised."

"May I offer a more plausible explanation for the delay?"

"By all means."

"Amelia March, being an ambitious and enterprising reporter, is at this moment fleshing out her exclusive story by gathering additional background material on her subject."

"A career retrospective?"

Gabriel nodded.

"What would be wrong with that?"

"I suppose that depends on which side of my career she chooses to explore."

The basic contours of Gabriel's professional and personal biogra-phy had already managed to find their way into the public domain— that he had been born on a kibbutz in the Jezreel Valley, that his mother had been one of early Israel's most prominent painters, that he had studied briefly at the Bezalel Academy of Art and Design in Jerusalem before joining Israeli intelligence. Less well known was that he had abruptly abandoned his service after a bomb exploded beneath his car in Vienna, killing his young son and leaving his first wife with catastrophic burns and acute post-traumatic stress disorder. He had placed her in a private psychiatric hospital in Surrey and locked himself away in a cottage in remotest Cornwall. And there he would have remained, broken and grieving, had he not accepted a commission in Venice, where he fell in love with the beautiful, opinionated daughter of the city's chief rabbi, not knowing that she was an operative of the very service he had forsaken. A twisted tale, surely, but hardly beyond the reach of a writer like Amelia March. She always struck Gabriel as the sort of reporter who had a novel hidden in the bottom drawer of her desk, something sparkling and witty and full of art world intrigue.

Chiara was frowning at her phone.

"Is it that bad?" asked Gabriel.

"It's only my mother."

"What's the problem?"

"She's concerned that Irene is developing an unhealthy obsession with global warming."

"Your mother only noticed this now?"

Their daughter, at the tender age of eight, was a fully fledged climate radical. She had taken part in her first demonstration earlier that winter, in the Piazza San Marco. Gabriel feared the child was now on a slippery slope to militancy and would soon be adhering herself to irreplaceable works of art or splashing them with green paint. Her twin brother, Raphael, was interested only in mathematics, for which he possessed an unusual aptitude. It was Irene's ambition that he use his gifts to save the planet from disaster. Gabriel, however, had not given up hope that the boy might take up a paintbrush instead.

"I suppose your mother thinks I'm to blame for our daughter's climate obsession."

"Evidently it's all my fault."

"A wise woman, your mother."

"Usually," remarked Chiara.

"Can she keep Irene out of jail while we're away, or should we skip the unveiling and go home tonight?"

"Actually, she thinks we should stay in London for another day or two and enjoy ourselves."

"A fine idea."

"But quite impossible," said Chiara. "You have an altarpiece to finish."

It was Il Pordenone's rather pedestrian depiction of the annunciation, which he had painted for the church of Santa Maria degli Angeli in Murano. Several other works in the church, all of lesser merit, were also in need of cleaning. The project was their first since assuming control of the Tiepolo Restoration Company, and already they were running several weeks behind schedule. It was essential the restoration of the church be completed on time, with no cost overruns. Still, another forty-eight hours in London might prove advantageous, as it would give Gabriel a chance to drum up a few lucrative private commissions, the kind that supported their comfortable lifestyle in Venice. Their enormous *piano nobile della loggia* overlooking the Grand Canal had diminished the small fortune he had accumulated during a lifetime of restoration work. And then, of course, there was his Bavaria C42 sailboat. The Allon family finances were sorely in need of replenishment.

He made this point to his wife, judiciously, as they turned into Mount Street.

"I'm sure you'll have no shortage of work after Amelia's article appears," she replied.

"Unless her article is less than flattering. Then I'll be forced to sell knockoff Canalettos to the tourists on the Riva degli Schiavoni to help make ends meet."

"Why would Amelia March write a hit piece about you, of all people?"

"Perhaps she doesn't like me."

"That's not possible. Everyone loves you, Gabriel."

"Not everyone," he replied.

"Name one person who doesn't adore you."

"The barman at Cupido."

It was a café and pizzeria located on the Fondamente Nove in Cannaregio. Gabriel stopped there most mornings before boarding the Number 4.1 vaporetto bound for Murano. And the barman, without fail, slid his cappuccino onto the glass countertop with a sneer of polite disdain.

"Not Gennaro?" asked Chiara.

"Is that his name?"

"He's quite lovely. He always adds little hearts to my foam."

"I wonder why."

Chiara accepted the compliment with a demure smile. It had been twenty years since their first encounter, and yet Gabriel remained hopelessly in the thrall of his wife's astonishing beauty—her sculptural nose and jawline, her riotous dark hair with its highlights of auburn and chestnut, the caramel-colored eyes that he had never succeeded in rendering accurately on canvas. Her body was his favorite subject matter, and his sketchbook was filled with nudes, many executed without the consent of his slumbering model. He hoped to explore the material further before tonight's gathering at the Courtauld. Chiara was amenable to the idea but had insisted on a long walk first, followed by a proper lunch.

She slowed to a stop outside an Oscar de la Renta boutique. "I think I'll let you buy me that delicious little pantsuit."

"What's wrong with the one you packed?"

"The Armani?" She shrugged. "I'm in the mood for something new. After all, I have a feeling my husband is going to be the center of attention tonight, and I want to make a good impression."

"You could wear a burlap sack, and you'll still be the most beautiful woman in the room."

Gabriel followed her into the boutique, and fifteen minutes later, bags in hand, they went out again. Chiara held his arm as they rounded the gentle curve of Carlos Place.

"Do you remember the last time we went for a walk in London?" she asked suddenly. "It was the day you spotted that suicide bomber headed for Covent Garden."

"Let's hope Amelia doesn't somehow find out about my role in that one."

"Or the incident at Downing Street," said Chiara.

"What about that business outside Westminster Abbey?"

"The ambassador's daughter? Your name got into the newspapers, as I recall. Your picture, too."

Gabriel sighed. "Maybe you should check the *ARTnews* website again."

"You do it. I can't bear to look."

Gabriel drew his phone from his coat pocket.

"Well?" asked Chiara after a moment.

"It seems my fears about Amelia March being an ambitious and enterprising reporter were well founded."

"What did she discover?"

"That I am regarded as one of the two or three best art restorers in the world."

"Who else does she mention?"

"Dianne Modestini and David Bull."

"Rarefied company."

"Yes," agreed Gabriel, and slipped the phone into his pocket. "I guess she likes me, after all."

"Of course she does, darling." Chiara smiled. "Who doesn't?"

———

They had lunch at Socca, a pricey bistro in South Audley Street, and walked back to the Dorchester through a sudden burst of brilliant winter sunlight. Upstairs in their suite, their lovemaking was unhurried, excruciatingly so. Exhausted, Gabriel toppled into a dreamless sleep and woke to find Chiara standing at the foot of the bed in her new suit, a strand of pearls around her neck.

"You'd better hurry," she said. "The car will be here in a few minutes."

He swung his feet to the floor and went into the bathroom to shower. His labors before the mirror were perfunctory. No miracle creams or ointments, just a subtle rearrangement of his hair, which was longer than he had worn it in many years. Afterward he dressed in a Brioni single-breasted suit and a regimental necktie. His accessories were limited to a wedding band, a timepiece by Patek Philippe, and a pistol by Fabbrica d'Armi Pietro Beretta.

Chiara joined him before the full-length mirror. In her stiletto-heeled pumps she hovered over him.

"What do you think?" she asked.

"I think your jacket must be missing its top button."

"That's the way it's supposed to fit, darling."

"In that case, you should probably wear a nice rollneck sweater underneath it. It's going to be quite chilly later."

Downstairs, the car was waiting, a Jaguar saloon model, courtesy of the Courtauld Gallery. It was located in the Somerset House complex on the Strand, adjacent to King's College. Amelia March, looking pleased with herself, stood outside the entrance along with several other reporters who covered the art world. Gabriel ignored their questions, in part because he was distracted by the sudden vibration of his mobile phone. He waited until he was inside the lobby before answering. He recognized the name of the caller, but the voice that greeted him seemed to have deepened an octave since he had heard it last.

"No," said Gabriel. "It's no trouble at all. . . . The quay in Port Navas? I'll be there tomorrow afternoon. Three o'clock at the latest."

4

The Courtauld Gallery

elf-Portrait with Bandaged Ear, oil on canvas, 60 by 49 centimeters, by Vincent van Gogh, stood atop a baize-covered pedestal in the center of the Courtauld's luminous Great Hall, veiled in white cloth and surrounded by a quartet of security guards. For the moment, at least, the painting was an afterthought.

"I knew it the minute I laid eyes on you," declared Jeremy Crabbe, the tweedy chairman of Bonhams' Old Master department.

"I rather doubt that," replied Gabriel.

"Do you remember that filthy wreck of a painting that you and Julian pinched from me during that morning sale about a hundred years ago?"

"Lot Forty-Three. *Daniel in the Lions' Den.*"

"Yes, that's the one. Eighty-six by one hundred and twenty-four inches, if memory serves."

"It doesn't," said Gabriel. "The canvas was a hundred and twenty-eight inches wide."

Jeremy Crabbe had been under the impression that it was the work of the Flemish painter Erasmus Quellinus, but any fool could see the brushwork belonged to none other than Peter Paul Rubens. Gabriel had cleaned it, and Julian had made a killing.

"I suppose he was in on your little secret, too," said Jeremy.

"Julian? He hadn't a clue."

Jeremy made to reply, but Gabriel abruptly turned away and accepted the outstretched paw of Niles Dunham, a curator from the National Gallery who was known for his usually infallible eye.

"Well played, my good fellow," he murmured. "Well played, indeed."

"Thank you, Niles."

"What are you working on?"

Gabriel answered.

"Il Pordenone?" Niles made a distasteful face. "He's beneath you."

"So I've been told."

"I might have something a bit more interesting, if you can find the time."

"You can't afford me, Niles."

"And if I were to double our usual fee? How do I contact you?"

Gabriel pointed out Sarah Bancroft.

"Is she a spy, too?" asked Niles.

"Sarah? Don't be ridiculous."

Niles cast a dubious eye toward tubby Oliver Dimbleby, a thoroughly disreputable Old Master dealer from Bury Street. "Oliver says that husband of hers used to be a contract killer."

"Oliver says a lot of things."

"Who's that stunningly beautiful creature standing next to him?"

"My wife."

"Well played," said Niles enviously. "Well played, indeed."

The next hand Gabriel grasped was attached to Nicholas Lovegrove, art adviser to the vastly rich. "The penny just dropped," he breathed.

"Did it?"

"That special winter auction at Christie's a few years back. There was something funny going on in the saleroom that night."

"There usually is, Nicky."

Lovegrove didn't disagree. "A client of mine is looking to unload his Gentileschi," he said, changing the subject. "But it needs a bit of retouching and a new coat of varnish. Is there any chance you might be willing to take it on?"

"That depends on whether your client has any money."

"Not at the moment. Messy divorce. But I think I can convince him to give you a piece of the final sale price."

"What did you have in mind?"

"Two percent."

"Surely you jest."

"All right, five. But it's my final offer."

"Make it ten, and you've got a deal."

"Highway robbery."

"You would know, Nicky."

Smiling, Lovegrove beckoned a tall woman with the flawless features of a fashion model. "This is my dear friend Olivia Watson," he explained to Gabriel. "Olivia runs a wildly successful contemporary art gallery in King Street."

"You don't say."

"You've met?"

"I've never had the pleasure." Which wasn't the case. Olivia had helped Gabriel destroy the external terrorism network of the Islamic State. Her gallery was payment for services rendered.

"We've just taken on an extraordinary young Spanish painter," she informed him.

"Really? What's his name?"

"*Her*," said Olivia with a knowing smile. "The opening is in six weeks. I would be honored if you would attend."

"Unlikely," replied Gabriel. Then he pointed out the man who had just entered the room, trailed by a security detail. "But perhaps he'll agree to come in my stead."

It was Hugh Graves, the British home secretary and, if London's chattering classes were to be believed, the next occupant of 10 Downing Street. He was accompanied by his wife, Lucinda, the chief executive officer of Lambeth Wealth Management. At last check the couple was worth in excess of one hundred million pounds, all of it Lucinda's. Her husband had never worked a day in the private sector, having launched his political career not long after leaving Cambridge. His ministerial salary would scarcely cover the cost of cleaning the windows at the Graveses' mansions in Holland Park and Surrey.

For the moment, at least, the arrival of the home secretary lessened the attention on Gabriel, a welcome development. "What brings the future PM to our little soiree?" he asked.

"Lucinda is on the Courtauld's board of trustees," said Lovegrove. "She's also one of the museum's biggest benefactors. In fact, I believe her firm underwrote tonight's ceremony."

"How much does it cost to remove a sheet from a painting?"

"You neglected to mention the champagne and canapés."

Hugh Graves was suddenly on the move. "Oh no," said Olivia through a frozen smile. "I have a terrible feeling he's headed straight toward us."

"Toward you, I imagine," said Gabriel.

"My money's on you."

"Mine, too," added Lovegrove.

The home secretary's advance was slowed by expressions of support by several well-heeled patrons. Finally, he alighted before Gabriel and thrust out his hand like a bayonet.

"It's a pleasure to finally meet you, Mr. Allon. As you might imagine, I've heard a great deal about your exploits. How long are you planning to stay in London?"

"Not long, I'm afraid."

"Is there any chance you might have a few minutes to drop by the Home Office? I'd love to hear your thoughts on recent developments in the Middle East."

"Since when are developments in the Middle East of interest to the Home Office?"

"It never hurts to broaden one's horizons, does it?"

"Especially when one is likely to be the next prime minister."

Graves hoisted a practiced smile. He was all of forty-eight, with the camera-ready good looks of a television news presenter. "We have a prime minister, Mr. Allon."

But not for long. At least that was the Whitehall scuttlebutt. London's political journalists were in agreement that Hillary Edwards, Britain's historically unpopular prime minister, would be lucky to survive the winter. And when the time came for her to go, it was widely assumed that ambitious Hugh Graves would be the one to show her the door.

"How about tomorrow afternoon?" he persisted. "Barring a crisis of some sort, I'm free for lunch."

"I'm retired now, Secretary Graves. I suggest you speak to the Israeli ambassador instead."

"He's a rather unpleasant fellow, if you must know."

"I'm afraid that's part of his job description."

The director of the Courtauld had made his way to a lectern next to the painting. Hugh Graves rejoined his wife, and Gabriel, after accepting a kiss from Olivia Watson, went discreetly to the side of Julian Isherwood. He was staring at his shoes.

"It seems the cat is finally out of the bag." Looking up, he fixed Gabriel with a stare of mock reproach. "And to think you deceived me all those years."

"Can you ever forgive me?"

"I'd rather tell the world that I was in on the joke all along."

"It might be bad for your reputation, Julian."

"You were the best thing that ever happened to me, my boy. And Sarah, of course. I don't know what I would do without her."

The director tapped the microphone, gaveling the proceedings to order.

"Where was it?" asked Julian.

"The Van Gogh? A villa on the Amalfi Coast."

"Who owned the villa?"

"Long story."

"Condition?"

"Remarkably good. I painted a copy while I had it in my studio. The esteemed director of the Courtauld Gallery, a Van Gogh expert himself, couldn't tell the difference."

"Naughty boy," said Julian. "Naughty, naughty boy."

The director's remarks were mercifully brief. A few words about the devastating impact of art crime, fewer still when introducing Gabriel. He declined an invitation to address the gathering but agreed to help remove the white shroud. He was assisted by Lucinda Graves.

Two curators hung the painting in its assigned place, and the waiters appeared with the hors d'oeuvres and the Bollinger. Gabriel and

Chiara each drank only a single glass; they had a nine o'clock dinner reservation at Alain Ducasse at the Dorchester. At half past eight they were rolling along Piccadilly in the Jaguar limousine.

"Was it my imagination," said Chiara, "or did you enjoy that?"

"Almost as much as my most recent visit to Russia."

Chiara gazed out her window at the brightly lit storefronts. "And the phone call you received as we were walking in the door?"

"A detective from the Devon and Cornwall Police."

"What have you done now?" she asked with a sigh.

"Nothing. He'd like my help with a murder investigation."

"Not that Oxford professor who was found dead out near Land's End?"

"Yes."

"But why you, of all people?"

"He's an old friend of mine, the detective." Gabriel smiled. "Yours, too."

5

Port Navas

Gabriel rose before dawn the next morning and fetched a Volkswagen from the Hertz outlet near Marble Arch. Chiara read the newspapers on her phone during the drive to Heathrow.

"It seems you're the talk of London, darling. There's even a lovely photo of you and Lucinda Graves unveiling the Van Gogh together. You look very dashing, I have to say."

"How are the reviews?"

"Quite positive."

"Even the *Guardian*?"

"Enraptured."

"About me or the Van Gogh?"

"Both." Chiara lowered the visor and regarded her reflection in the vanity mirror. "I look terrible."

"I beg to differ. In fact, I'm having second thoughts about letting you get on the plane without me."

"I'd love to come to Cornwall with you, but I have a church to restore and a mother who needs rescuing." Chiara raised the visor. "Do you think they remember us?"

"Who?"

"Vera and Dottie and the usual crowd down at the Lamb and Flag."

"How could they possibly forget us?"

Chiara fixed him with a stare of mild rebuke. "You were so very rude to them, Gabriel."

"It wasn't me," he said defensively. "It was only a role I was playing at the time."

"Giovanni Rossi. The temperamental but gifted Italian art restorer."

"His wife was quite lovely, as I recall."

"And much beloved by the villagers." Chiara returned the phone to her handbag. "It's a shame we didn't stay in Gunwalloe longer. If we had, we would have known Charlotte Blake."

Gabriel considered this notion as they approached the exit for Heathrow. "You're quite right, you know."

"I always am."

"Not always," said Gabriel.

"When have I ever been wrong?"

"Give me a week or two. I'll think of something."

"You should be asking yourself why Timothy Peel wants you to come to Cornwall to help with the investigation into Professor Blake's murder."

"He knew I was in the country."

"He follows news from the art world?"

"No," said Gabriel. "He follows news about me."

"Surely he must have given you at least *some* idea of what it was about."

"He said he didn't want to discuss it on the phone."

"What could it be?"

"Something art related, I suppose."

"Something Professor Blake was working on at the time of her murder?"

"An interesting theory," said Gabriel.

"Could there be a link?"

"Between Charlotte Blake's hypothetical research project and her subsequent murder by an axe-wielding maniac?"

"The Chopper uses a hatchet, you dolt."

"A most inefficient murder weapon, if you ask me. Effective, yes. But quite messy."

"You've never used one?"

"A hatchet? I'm quite certain that I have never once utilized a hatchet for any purpose whatsoever, least of all killing someone. That's what guns are for."

"I think I'd rather be shot than hacked to death."

"Trust me," said Gabriel. "A bullet is no picnic, either."

He drank coffee at a dingy café in Slough until Chiara's flight was safely airborne, then slid behind the wheel of the rental car and headed west on the M4. It was approaching noon when he reached Exeter. He skirted the fringes of Dartmoor on the A30 and during the drive down to Truro was pelted by downpours of torrential rain. The storm had passed by the time he reached Falmouth, and at half past two, when he arrived in the tiny Cornish hamlet of Port Navas, an orange sun blazed through a slit in the clouds.

The winding road down to the tidal creek was scarcely wide enough for a single car and lined by hedgerows. Gabriel had driven it countless times, usually at speeds that annoyed the neighbors. He had known them intimately—their names, their occupations, their vices and their virtues—and they had known him not at all. He was the foreign gentleman who inhabited the old foreman's cottage near the oyster farm. He had reconfigured it to suit his needs. Living quarters on the ground floor, a studio upstairs. No one in Port Navas, with the exception of an eleven-year-old boy, had the slightest idea of what went on there.

The boy was now a man of thirty-five and held the rank of detective sergeant in the Devon and Cornwall Police. He was standing at the stern of a wooden ketch tied up at the quay, his arm raised in a silent salute. The ketch, which had been painstakingly restored, had once belonged to Gabriel. He had bequeathed it to Timothy Peel the day he left Port Navas for the last time.

He climbed out of the car and walked down to the quay. "Permission to come aboard," he said.

Peel looked at Gabriel's suede loafers with disapproval. "Not in those shoes, you don't."

"I was the one who stripped and stained that deck, as I recall."

"And I've taken very good care of it in your absence."

Gabriel slipped off his shoes and stepped aboard. Peel handed him a crimson takeaway cup from Costa. "Tea with milk, just the way you like it, Mr. Allon."

"You mustn't call me that, Timothy."

"I thought you were out in the open now."

"I am. But I insist you refer to me by my given name."

"Sorry, but you'll always be Mr. Allon to me."

"In that case, I shall call you Detective Sergeant Peel."

He smiled. "Can you imagine?"

"I can, actually. You were always a natural snoop."

"Only where you were concerned. And Mr. Isherwood, of course."

"He speaks of you fondly."

"He called me a little toad, if I remember correctly."

"You should hear the things he says about me."

They sat down in the cockpit. The boat had been Gabriel's salvation during the lost years, the years after Vienna and before Chiara. When he had no painting to restore, he would sail out the Helford River to the sea. Sometimes he would head west to the Atlantic, sometimes south to the coast of Normandy; and each time he returned to Port Navas, Timothy Peel would signal him from his bedroom window with a flash of his torch. Gabriel, his hand upon the wheel, his mind ablaze with images of blood and fire, would flash his running lights twice in reply.

He looked at the foreman's cottage. "My old place seems to have been given a makeover."

"A young couple who work in the City of London," explained Peel. "After the pandemic hit, a lot of well-to-do Londoners suddenly discovered the joys of life in Cornwall."

"A shame, that."

"They're not so bad."

Gabriel looked at the ramshackle cottage where Peel had lived with his mother and her lover Derek, a whisky-soaked playwright with an anger-management problem.

"In case you're wondering," said Peel, "he's dead."

"And your mother?"

"Still up in Bath. She and her husband sold the cottage out from underneath me, so I got a place of my own in Exeter."

"Married?"

"Not yet."

"What are you waiting for?"

"A woman like Ms. Zolli, I imagine."

"She sends her regards."

"I hope she isn't angry with me."

"Chiara? Only at me," Gabriel assured him. "But that's usually the case."

A silence fell between them. Gabriel listened to the gentle slap of wavelets against the port side of his old boat. Memories of that night in Vienna were stirring. He held them at bay.

"All right, Detective Sergeant Peel, now that we've had a chance to become reacquainted, perhaps you should tell me why you dragged me all the way down to Cornwall."

"Charlotte Blake," said Peel. "Professor of art history from the University of Oxford."

"And the fifth victim of the serial killer known as the Chopper."

"Maybe, Mr. Allon. Or maybe not."

6

Port Navas

Detective Sergeant Timothy Peel, an eight-year veteran of the Devon and Cornwall Police, was assigned to the Chopper case after the second killing, joining a team of four senior officers. His first assignment was to identify and question everyone in southwest England, regardless of age or gender, who had recently purchased a hatchet. Late Tuesday afternoon he was crossing names from his list when a call came through on the dedicated tip line. It was from a resident of Gunwalloe.

"Which one?"

"Vera Hobbs. Who else?"

"What seemed to be the problem?"

A light burning in the window of Professor Blake's cottage. Admittedly, Peel didn't think much of it at the time, so he contacted a few more hatchet owners before ringing his colleagues at the Thames Valley Police. As it turned out, they were already looking into the matter.

"TVP had made entry into Professor Blake's home in Oxford and checked all the hospitals in its jurisdiction. There was no sign of her."

"What about her car?"

"I was the one who found it."

"Where?"

"The car park at the Land's End amusement center."

"If memory serves, there's a credit card kiosk there."

"The chit was displayed on her dashboard. The time stamp was 4:17 p.m. on Monday."

Gabriel cast his eyes to the west. "Less than a half hour before sunset?"

"Twenty-eight minutes, to be precise."

"Did anyone see her?"

"A receptionist arriving for work at the Land's End Hotel spotted a woman setting off along the coast path alone. We assume it was Professor Blake."

"At four seventeen in the afternoon?"

"It's a beautiful spot at that time of day. But under the circumstances . . ."

It made no sense at all, thought Gabriel. "The newspapers were a bit vague as to the exact location of the crime scene."

"An overgrown hedgerow north of Porthchapel Beach. It looked as though the killer tried to conceal the body. Which is interesting," added Peel. "The previous four victims were left where they had fallen, with the backs of their skulls split by a single blow. They were probably dead before they hit the ground."

"And Professor Blake?"

"He made a real mess of her. He also seems to have made off with her mobile phone."

"Did he take the phones of the other victims?"

Peel shook his head.

"Theory of the case?" asked Gabriel.

"My colleagues think Professor Blake must have heard the killer stealing up behind her. And when she turned around, she sent him into a rage."

"Which would explain the overkill."

"But not the missing mobile."

"She might have dropped it somewhere."

"We've swept the entire coast path and the area surrounding the hedgerow where the body was discovered. We found three old mobile phones, none of them belonging to Professor Blake."

"And it's not emitting a signal?"

"What do you think?"

"I think you should make sure she didn't leave it in the car."

"I know how to search a car, Mr. Allon. The phone is gone."

Gabriel smiled in spite of himself. "And what about you, Detective Sergeant Peel? What's *your* theory?"

He ran a hand over the gunwale of the ketch before answering. "We've always been a bit cagey about some of the details of the killings. The number of blows, the location, those sorts of things. It's standard procedure in a case like this. It helps us weed out the cranks and kooks."

"What about copycats?"

"Those, too. After all, how could someone imitate the Chopper if he doesn't know his exact methods?"

"Do you believe Professor Blake was killed by a copycat?"

"I'm willing to entertain the notion."

"I don't suppose you've shared this theory with your fellow officers."

"I didn't think it would be wise for me to rock the boat on such an important investigation. Not at this stage of my career."

"Leaving you no choice but to pursue the matter independently." Gabriel paused, then added, "With the help of an old friend."

Peel made no reply.

"Does the chief constable know that you've contacted me?"

"It's possible I neglected to mention it."

"Good lad."

Peel smiled. "I learned from the best."

The parish of Gunwalloe lay ten miles to the west on the opposite side of the Lizard Peninsula. They drove there through the gathering dusk in Gabriel's rental car.

"Do you remember the way?" asked Peel.

"Are you deliberately trying to annoy me, or do you come by it naturally?"

"A little of both."

They sped along the fence line of the Culdrose naval air station, then followed the nameless road that stretched from the heart of the Lizard to Gunwalloe. Beyond the hedgerows lay a patchwork quilt of dormant farmland. Then the road twisted suddenly to the left and the hedgerows fell away to reveal the sea, aflame with the last light of the setting sun.

Gabriel slowed as he entered the village. Peel pointed out the Lamb and Flag pub. "Shall we stop for a pint and a few laughs with your old friends?"

"Some other time."

"I've always loved that song," said Peel. "Especially the Bill Evans version."

"You have good taste in music."

"I owe it to you."

They rolled past the Corner Market, where Dottie Cox was ringing up the day's last customer. Across a sloping field of purple thrift and red fescue was the fishing cove. A single cottage, faintly visible in the dying twilight, stood atop the cliff.

"Do you ever miss it?" asked Peel.

"Yes, of course. But Venice has its charms."

"Better food."

"I've always had a fondness for Cornish cuisine, myself."

"Perhaps you can spend a summer here with Chiara and the children."

"Only if you let me borrow that beautiful sailing vessel of yours."

"Deal."

Gabriel turned through a gap in a wind-bent hedgerow of blackthorn. Behind it stood stately Wexford Cottage, the finest cottage in Gunwalloe. The windows were darkened, the shades tightly drawn. Adhered to the heavy wooden door was a notice declaring the premises to be an active crime scene. Detective Sergeant Timothy Peel thrust a key into the lock and led Gabriel inside.

7

Wexford Cottage

They pulled on shoe covers and latex gloves in the entrance hall and went into the sitting room. The furnishings were contemporary and sophisticated, as were the paintings hanging on the walls. Piled on the low coffee table were monographs and volumes of art history and criticism, including an essential compendium of Pablo Picasso's enormous body of work. *Self-Portrait with a Palette*, painted by the artist in 1906, graced the cover.

"Ever restored him?" inquired Peel.

"Picasso?" Gabriel looked up and frowned. "Once or twice, Timothy."

"I read not long ago that he's the most stolen artist in the world."

"Did you really?" asked Gabriel dubiously.

"And the most forged as well," Peel persevered.

"That's correct. In all likelihood there are more fake Picassos in existence than real ones."

"But you undoubtedly can tell the difference."

"Pablo and I are reasonably well acquainted," said Gabriel. "And I've enjoyed our time together despite the fact he doesn't think much of my craft."

"Espionage?"

"Restoration. Picasso disapproved of it. He thought cracking and natural aging gave his paintings a sense of character." Gabriel paused, then added, "But I digress."

It was an invitation for Peel to get to the point. The young detective responded by indicating the moisture ring next to the book. "We found a mug of tea when we made entry into the cottage. We assume Professor Blake left it there the afternoon she was murdered."

"And then, of course, there was the light burning in the kitchen."

"And the dirty dishes in the sink and on the counter. All of which suggests she was in a bit of a rush when she set out for Land's End."

"So stipulated," said Gabriel. "But where are we going with this?"

"Her office."

It was in the adjoining room. Entering, Peel switched on the desk lamp. The computer was an iMac with a twenty-seven-inch display, ideal for scrutinizing photographs of paintings or old exhibition records. Gabriel reached down and nudged the mouse. The computer awakened and requested a password for admission.

"Have you cracked it?"

"Not yet."

"Whyever not?"

"The territorial police forces in Britain no longer have the authority to obtain private data without the consent of a government oversight body connected to the Home Office. We are currently awaiting approval."

"If you like, I might be able to—"

"Don't even think about it."

Gabriel looked down at the books and papers scattered over the desktop. One of the volumes was *The Rape of Europa*, the indispensable account of Nazi art looting written by Lynn Nicholas. Beneath it was a copy of Charlotte Blake's *Picasso: The War Years*. Gabriel lifted the cover of a nearby manila folder. Inside, bound by a metal clasp, was a list of every known work of art stolen by the Germans during the Occupation.

Peel was now peering over Gabriel's shoulder. "It looks as though Professor Blake might have been conducting research on a painting."

"That's hardly surprising, Timothy. After all, that's what she does."

"A Picasso, if you ask me," said Peel, undeterred.

"Why would you assume that?"

"She highlighted every Picasso looted by the Nazis during the war."

Gabriel thumbed through the thick printout. It appeared to be the case.

"Were all those paintings stolen from Jews?" asked Peel.

"Most of them," said Gabriel. "They were brought to the Jeu de Paume for sorting and appraisal. Those works the Nazis found desirable were immediately crated and sent by train to Germany."

"And the rest?"

"The Nazis disposed of thousands of paintings on the French art market, thus giving dealers and collectors an unprecedented opportunity to enlarge their holdings at the expense of their Jewish countrymen."

"Where are those paintings today?"

"Some have been returned to the heirs of the rightful owners," said Gabriel. "But many are still circulating through the bloodstream of the art world or hanging on the walls of museums. Which is why a conscientious dealer, collector, or curator might retain the services of a renowned provenance researcher like Charlotte Blake before acquiring a painting with a murky past."

"He would want her seal of approval?"

"Correct."

"Is there another reason why someone might hire her?"

"Yes, of course, Timothy. To find a missing painting."

Smiling, Peel pointed toward the yellow legal pad lying on the corner of the desk. "Have a look. Tell me if you see anything interesting."

Gabriel adjusted the beam of the lamp and scrutinized the first page. "Sorry, but I'm afraid Sanskrit isn't one of my languages."

"It seems that penmanship wasn't the professor's strong suit."

Gabriel flipped to the following page, which was no more legible. The notation at the top of the succeeding page, however, was carefully rendered.

Peel read it aloud. "Untitled portrait of a woman in the surrealist style, oil on canvas, ninety-four by sixty-six centimeters, 1937."

"Picasso painted numerous such works that same year."

"How much would one be worth today?"

"A great deal."

Peel pointed out the next notation.

Galerie Paul Rosenberg . . .

"He was Picasso's dealer at the time," explained Gabriel. "His gallery was on the rue la Boétie in Paris. Picasso lived and worked in an apartment next door."

"Should we assume the painting was purchased there?"

"For now."

Peel's gloved fingertip moved down the page. "By this man?"

Bernard Lévy . . .

"Why not?" said Gabriel.

Peel's fingertip inched downward. "He doesn't seem to have kept it long."

Private sale Paris 1944 . . .

"Not a good year for someone named Bernard Lévy to part with a Picasso," said Gabriel.

Peel pointed out the final entry on the page. "But what could this mean?"

OOC...

Gabriel drew his phone. The three letters, when entered into the white box of his search engine, produced twenty-seven million pages of Internet mush. Adding the words *Picasso* and *Untitled* was of no help.

He snapped a photograph of the page, then looked at the slumbering computer.

Peel read his thoughts. "I'll let you know if it contains anything of value the minute we get authorization."

"If you like . . ."

Peel switched off the computer. "Don't even think about it, Mr. Allon."

Gabriel picked up the copy of Charlotte Blake's *Picasso: The War Years* and opened it to the acknowledgments. They were as spare and dry as a typical provenance. No expressions of heartfelt gratitude, no enormous debts due. One name managed to achieve an elevated prominence by dint of the fact that it was the last one mentioned. It was Naomi Wallach, the world's foremost expert on the wartime French art market.

8

Victoria Embankment

I t occurred to Samantha Cooke, while huddled on a frigid bench on Victoria Embankment, her hands numb with cold, that perhaps she had chosen the wrong line of work. She had been summoned to this spot by an anonymous text message. Polite in tone and precise in syntax, it promised documents of a politically explosive nature. The sender wanted Samantha to reveal the contents of these documents in her newspaper, which was the Tory-leaning *Telegraph*. Because she was the paper's chief political correspondent, and one of the most respected members of the Westminster press corps, she was accustomed to stories arriving over her transom—especially stories that could prove damaging to the opposition or, better yet, to a rival within one's own party. Most of the stuff was trivial and petty, but this approach felt different. It was something significant. Samantha was certain of it.

She had felt the same way about her most recent love interest, a divorced father of two called Adam who worked for the Department of Health. But Adam quickly came to resent the fact that she spent eighteen hours a day on the phone or in front of a computer. So had all of Adam's predecessors, including Samantha's ex-husband, who was long remarried and leading a blissful upper-middle-class existence in leafy Richmond. Samantha shared a flat in Primrose Hill with her cat and lived in fear that, given the precarious state of the journalism business, she might soon find herself out of a job. Her friends from university had all gone to work in the financial sector and made gobs of money. But Samantha had been determined to do something out of the ordinary. Now, as she watched the slow rotation of the London Eye, she could at least take comfort in the knowledge that she had achieved her goal.

The bench was located next to the Battle of Britain memorial. It had been chosen by the author of the text message, whom Samantha surmised was a well-educated man of late middle age, a description that applied to a significant portion of the British political establishment. He had instructed her to arrive at six o'clock. But Big Ben was now tolling the bottom of the hour, and there was still no sign of him—or the promised documents.

Annoyed, Samantha drew her mobile phone and typed, *I'm waiting.*

The anonymous leaker replied instantly. *Patience.*

Not my strong suit, answered Samantha. *Now or never.*

Just then she heard the clatter of high heels over paving stones and, glancing to her right, saw a woman walking toward her from the direction of Westminster. She was not yet thirty, blond, professionally dressed, quite pretty. Her head was turned toward the Thames, as though she were admiring the view, and in her left hand was an A4 envelope. A moment later the same envelope was lying on the unoccupied half of the bench. The young woman, having dropped it there, continued northward along the embankment and disappeared from Samantha's view.

Her phone pinged at once. *Aren't you going to open it?*

Samantha looked left and right along the embankment but could see no one who appeared to be watching her. The next message she received confirmed that, indeed, someone was.

Well, Ms. Cooke?

The envelope was lying face down on the bench. Samantha turned it over and saw the pale blue logo of the Conservative Party. The flap was unsealed, and inside was a sheaf of internal documents dealing with the Party's fundraising efforts—one large political contribution in particular. The documents appeared to be authentic. They were also political dynamite.

Samantha took up her phone and typed, *Are these genuine?*

You know they are, came the reply.

Where do you work?

A moment passed before he answered. *CCHQ.*

CCHQ was the Conservative Campaign Headquarters. It was located in Matthew Parker Street, not far from the Palace of Westminster.

Samantha typed her next message and tapped the send icon. *I need to see you at once.*

Not possible, Ms. Cooke.

At least tell me who you are. I promise not to reveal your identity.

You may refer to me as Nemo.

Nemo, thought Samantha. No one.

She returned the documents to the envelope and rang Clive Randolph, the *Telegraph*'s political editor. "Someone just gave me the means to bring down Prime Minister Hillary Edwards. Are you interested?"

9

Musée du Louvre

Gabriel spent the night at the Godolphin Hotel in Marazion and was back in central London by one the following afternoon. He dropped his car at Hertz and his gun at Isherwood Fine Arts and boarded a Eurostar train bound for Paris. Three hours later he was extracting himself from the back of a taxi outside the Louvre. Naomi Wallach, as promised, was waiting next to the pyramid. They had spoken only briefly while Gabriel was hurtling across the fields of northern France. Now, in the fading light of the Louvre's Cour Napoléon, she regarded him carefully, as though trying to decide whether he was a clever forgery or the real thing.

"You're not at all what I expected," she said at last.

"I hope you're not disappointed."

"Pleasantly surprised." She removed a packet of cigarettes from her handbag and lit one. "You mentioned that you were a friend of Hannah Weinberg."

"A close friend."

"She never spoke of you."

"At my request."

The late Hannah Weinberg had been the director of the Weinberg

Center for the Study of Anti-Semitism in France. Located on the rue des Rosiers in the Marais, the center was the target of one of the deadliest terrorist attacks carried out by the Islamic State. Naomi Wallach, a Holocaust restitution specialist focusing on issues related to art, should have been among the dead and wounded. But she was running late that morning and arrived to find the building ablaze and her friend Hannah lying in the ruins. A photograph of the two women, one brutally murdered, the other tearing at her garment in anguish, would become the atrocity's defining image. Consequently, when the director of the Louvre was looking for an outsider to at long last purge the museum's collection of looted works of art, Naomi Wallach was judged to be the perfect candidate.

She turned her head and expelled a stream of smoke. "Forgive me, Monsieur Allon. A filthy habit, I know."

"There are worse."

"Name one."

"Buying a painting that belonged to someone who perished in the Holocaust."

"A great many Frenchmen were afflicted with this habit during the war, including a curator from this very museum."

"The curator's name," said Gabriel, "was René Huyghe."

Naomi Wallach regarded him over the ember of her cigarette. "It sounds to me as though you know a good deal about the Nazi looting of France."

"I am by no means an expert on the subject. But I was involved in a case many years ago that led to the recovery of a considerable number of looted paintings."

"Where did you find them?"

"They were in the hands of a Swiss private banker whose only surviving child just happens to be the world's most famous violinist."

Her eyes narrowed. "Not the Augustus Rolfe case?"

Gabriel nodded.

"I'm impressed, Monsieur Allon. That was quite a scandal. But what brings you to the Louvre?"

"A favor for a friend."

"You can do better than that, can't you?"

"The friend is a detective for the Devon and Cornwall Police in England."

Her expression darkened. "Charlotte Blake?"

Gabriel nodded. "The detective asked me to review some papers that she left on her desk the afternoon of her death. It looked to me as though she was conducting provenance research on a Picasso."

"Untitled portrait of a woman in the surrealist style, oil on canvas, ninety-four by sixty-six centimeters?"

"You knew about the project?"

She nodded slowly.

"May I ask how?"

Naomi Wallach smiled sadly. "Because I was the one who asked her to find that painting."

———

They crossed the Place du Carrousel and set off along the Allee Centrale of the Jardin des Tuileries. The limbs of the plane trees lay bare against the evening sky. The dusty gravel footpath crunched beneath their feet.

Naomi Wallach raised her cigarette to her lips and drew. "I've told myself that I will find a new dreadful habit after I recover all the paintings that were stolen from the Jews of France during the war and return them to their rightful owners."

"You've set for yourself an unattainable goal, Madame Wallach."

"If I believed that, I never would have accepted the position at the Louvre. The collection contains seventeen hundred paintings that were either looted by the Nazis or acquired under dubious circumstances. It is my job to establish an unassailable provenance for each piece and then track down a living heir with a valid claim. A monumental task."

"Which is why you asked Professor Blake to conduct a provenance investigation on your behalf."

Naomi Wallach nodded. "I didn't have time to give the matter the attention it deserved. But there was also an ethical question involved. Since taking the job at the Louvre, I have refrained from conducting private inquiries. Especially inquiries as sensitive as the one involving Bernard Lévy."

"Who was he?" asked Gabriel.

"A successful businessman with an eye for modern and avant-garde art. Monsieur Lévy went into hiding with his wife and daughter after the Paris Roundup in July 1942. He was deported to Auschwitz in 1944 and gassed upon arrival. His wife was on the same transport."

"And their daughter?"

"She was taken in by a Catholic family in the Free Zone and managed to survive the war. She married a fellow survivor named Léon Cohen in 1955 and a year later gave birth to a child she named Emanuel. He was completing his medical training at the Sorbonne when she finally told him about her experiences during the Occupation." Naomi Wallach paused. "And about the small collection of paintings that had hung in her family's apartment in Paris."

"A collection that included a woman in the surrealist style by Pablo Picasso, which Bernard Lévy had purchased from Galerie Paul Rosenberg in 1937."

"Perhaps." Naomi Wallach dropped her cigarette to the footpath and ground it out with the toe of a stylish boot. "These cases are always complicated. Dr. Cohen had no photographs, receipts, or documentation of any kind to support his claim. He told me that his grandparents left everything behind when they fled Paris and went into hiding in the south."

"What did they do with the Picasso and the rest of the paintings?"

"Evidently, Lévy entrusted them to his lawyer in Paris." She picked up the cigarette butt and tossed it into a rubbish bin. "A certain Monsieur Favreau."

"And Favreau sold them?"

"Dr. Cohen believed that to be the case."

"What else did he believe?"

"That his grandfather's Picasso was inside the Geneva Freeport."

The Freeport was a six-hundred-thousand-square-foot storage facility located in an industrial quarter of Geneva. At last estimate, the complex contained more than a million paintings, including the largest collection of Picassos outside the Spaniard's heirs.

"It's a distinct possibility," said Gabriel. "But why did Cohen suspect that it was there?"

"He claimed to have seen the painting with his own eyes."

"In a storage vault?"

"*Non.* At a gallery that operates within the boundaries of the Freeport. There are several, you know. Dr. Cohen visited this gallery several months ago to see if there were any untitled Picasso portraits on the market. And guess what he saw there?"

"His grandfather's Picasso?"

She nodded.

"Did he ask to see the provenance?"

"Of course. But the dealer said the painting wasn't for sale and refused to let him see it."

"And the dealer's name?"

"Dr. Cohen refused to tell me."

"Why?"

"He thought it might taint my investigation if I knew the painting's whereabouts in advance. He wanted an unimpeachable provenance report from a leading expert that he could present in court."

There was a certain logic to it. "And when you told him that you weren't available?"

"He asked me for the name of someone who was up to the job. Charlotte Blake was the obvious choice. She was a world-class historian and provenance researcher, and her book on Picasso and the Occupation was extraordinary. She was also quite disdainful of the business of art, especially the so-called collectors who acquire paintings strictly for investment purposes and then lock them away in places like the Geneva Freeport."

They had reached the end of the Allee Centrale. Evening traffic was careening around the Place de la Concorde. They turned to the right and headed toward the Jeu de Paume.

"Scene of the greatest art heist in history," said Naomi Wallach. "Tens of thousands of paintings now worth untold billions of dollars. But it is important to remember, Monsieur Allon, that the Nazis were not the only perpetrators. They had willing accomplices, men who took advantage of the situation to line their pockets or adorn their walls. Those who retain possession of paintings they know to be looted are not blameless. They are accessories to a crime in progress. Charlotte Blake shared my opinion. That's why she was willing to take Emanuel Cohen's case."

"And when you learned that she had been killed?"

"I was shocked, of course, as was Dr. Cohen."

"I'd like to have a word with him."

"I imagine you would. But I'm afraid that's not possible."

"Why?"

"Because last evening, while walking home to his apartment in Montmartre, Dr. Emanuel Cohen fell to his death down the steps of the rue Chappe. The police seem to think he slipped somehow." Naomi Wallach's hand shook as she lit another cigarette. "Perhaps it wasn't an accident, after all."

10

Rue Chappe

The death of Dr. Emanuel Cohen, a widower with no children, went unrecorded by the Paris press. Naomi Wallach had heard the news that morning from a friend at the Weinberg Center and wasn't certain as to the details, including the precise location of Cohen's fall. Gabriel, after engaging his waiter at Café Chappe in a few minutes of small talk, discovered that the incident had taken place at the summit of the famous steps near the basilica. The waiter, whose name was Henri, had come upon the scene while walking home at the end of his shift.

"What did you see?"

"A couple of cops and EMTs looking down at a body."

"You're sure he was dead?"

"*Oui*. He was covered by then."

"Where was he?"

"The first landing. Next to the lamppost."

At the southern end of the rue Chappe, where the café was located, the street was typical of Montmartre, narrow and cobbled and lined with small apartment buildings. The steps began at the rue

André Barsacq. There were two separate flights, each with a pair of landings and an iron handrail down the center. The second flight, the one nearest Sacré Coeur, was the slightly steeper of the two. Gabriel paused on the uppermost landing and, crouching, examined the paving stones by the inadequate light of the streetlamp. If there had been blood the night before, there was none now. Nor was there anything to indicate there had been much in the way of a criminal investigation of the matter.

Rising, Gabriel climbed to the top of the steps. To the right was a small café, and beyond the café was the upper station of the Montmartre funicular. A group of tourists were gazing up at the floodlit domes of Sacré Coeur. Two young women were scrutinizing the counterfeit designer handbags arranged on a tarpaulin at the feet of an African migrant.

Gabriel turned and gazed down the steps of the rue Chappe. Something made him place a hand on the frigid lamppost. A fall, even a minor one, would doubtless result in serious injury. Still, most pedestrians managed to make the ascent without incident, especially lifelong Parisians and residents of Montmartre like Dr. Emanuel Cohen.

Gabriel moved away from the top of the steps and looked in both directions along the street. There were no surveillance cameras in sight, nothing to record how Cohen might have lost his balance. If there had been an eyewitness, he surely told the police what he had observed. Unless, of course, the eyewitness had been engaged in low-level criminal activity at the time of the incident and had therefore chosen to remain silent.

Gabriel walked over to the African street vendor, a towering figure, thin as a reed, with weary eyes that gazed out from an otherwise noble face. They exchanged pleasantries in French. Then Gabriel asked the African if he had been selling his wares on this spot the previous evening.

The weary eyes grew suspicious. "Why do you ask?"

"A friend of mine fell down the rue Chappe. I was wondering if you were here when it happened."

"*Oui*. I was here."

"Did you see anything?"

"Are you a cop?"

"Do I look like a cop?"

The towering African said nothing. Gabriel looked down at the counterfeit handbags lying at the man's feet.

"How much for that one?"

"The Prada?"

"If you say so."

"One hundred euros."

"My wife's cost me five thousand."

"You should have come to me."

"How about I give you two hundred euros instead?"

"Two hundred it is."

Gabriel handed over the money. The African shoved it into the pocket of his threadbare coat and reached for the bag.

"Forget about it," said Gabriel. "Just tell me how my friend fell."

"He got a phone call when he reached the top of the steps. That was when the guy pushed him." The African pointed toward one of the coin-operated telescopes on the opposite side of the street. "He was standing right there for several minutes before your friend arrived."

"Did you get a look at him?"

"*Non*. His back was turned the entire time he was there."

"And you're sure it wasn't an accident?"

"Left hand, center of his chest. Down the steps he went. He never had a chance."

"What happened to the man who pushed him?" Receiving no answer, Gabriel looked down at the African's inventory. "How about I buy another bag?"

"The Vuitton?"

"Why not?"

"How much would you like to give me for it?"

"I really don't like negotiating with myself."

"One fifty?"

Gabriel surrendered three hundred euros. "Keep talking."

"Another guy pulled alongside him on a scooter, and he climbed on the back. It was all very professional, if you ask me."

"And you, of course, told the police everything you had seen."

"*Non.* I left before they arrived."

"Did you at least try to help my friend?"

"Yes, of course. But it was obvious he was dead."

"Where was his phone?"

"On the landing next to him."

"I assume you picked it up as you were leaving."

The African hesitated, then nodded. "Forgive me, Monsieur. Those phones are worth a lot of money."

"Where is it now?"

"Are you sure you're not a cop?"

"When was the last time a cop paid you five hundred euros for two fake handbags?"

"I gave the phone to Papa."

"Great," said Gabriel. "Who's Papa?"

While loading his inventory into plastic rubbish bags, the street vendor introduced himself as Amadou Kamara and explained that he was from Senegal, the unstable former French colony on Africa's west coast where joblessness and public corruption were endemic. A father of four, he concluded that he had no choice but to go to Europe if his family was to survive. He attempted the typical Senegalese route north, an overcrowded fishing boat bound for Spain's Canary Islands, and nearly drowned when the vessel capsized in the treacherous waters off Western Sahara. After washing ashore, he walked to Morocco's Mediterranean coast, a journey of more than a thousand miles, and managed to reach Spain in an inflatable raft with twelve other men. He did backbreaking agricultural work for a couple of years in the blistering Spanish sun—for which he was paid as little as five euros a day—then moved to Catalonia to peddle counterfeit goods on the streets of Barcelona. After a scrape with the Spanish police, he made his way to Paris and went to work for Papa Diallo.

"The local distributor for Prada and Louis Vuitton?"

"And a lot of other luxury brands as well," replied Amadou Kamara. "The bags are manufactured in China and then smuggled into Europe aboard container ships. Papa is the biggest player in the Paris market. He's from Senegal, too."

"What else is Papa into?"

"The usual."

"Stolen iPhones?"

"*Mais bien sûr.*"

They were walking along the rue Muller, a dark and uninviting street rarely traversed by foreign visitors to the Eighteenth Arrondissement. Their destination was an immigrant quarter known as Goutte d'Or. Gabriel was carrying one of the contraband-stuffed plastic bags, an accessory after the fact. Not for the first time he wondered how his life had come to this.

"And what's your story?" asked Amadou Kamara.

"It is so insignificant compared to yours that I won't bore you with the details."

"At least tell me your name."

"Francesco."

"You're not French."

"Italian."

"Why do you speak French so well?"

"I watch a lot of French movies."

"What kind of work do you do, Monsieur Francesco?"

"I clean old paintings."

"Is there money in that sort of thing?"

"Depends on the painting."

"My daughter likes to draw. Her name is Alima. I haven't seen her in four years."

"Don't tell Papa about the five hundred euros I gave you. Send it to your family instead."

Goutte d'Or, otherwise known as Little Africa, lay to the east of the boulevard Barbès. Its densely populated streets were among the most vibrant in Paris, especially the rue Dejean, the quarter's bustling open-air market. Gabriel and Amadou Kamara threaded their way through the evening crowds, a mismatched pair if there ever was one.

There were more markets on the rue des Poissonniers, and a café called Le Morzine. Its windows were obscured by lotto ads and posters for African sports teams. Papa Diallo was holding court at a table inside, surrounded by several associates. He had biceps the size of stockpots. His spherical hairless head appeared as though it was mounted directly atop his torso.

A chair was procured from a neighboring table and Gabriel was invited to sit. Amadou Kamara explained the situation in a Senegalese dialect. At the conclusion of his discourse, Papa Diallo displayed two rows of large white teeth.

In French he asked, "Why do you want it so badly?"

"It belonged to my friend."

"Are you a cop?"

"Amadou and I have already covered that ground."

The two men exchanged a glance. Then Papa nodded at one of his associates, who placed the phone on the table. It was an iPhone. The screen had survived its collision with the steps of the rue Chappe intact.

"Original SIM card?" asked Gabriel.

Papa Diallo nodded. "I can get two hundred on the street. But for you, I'll make a special price."

"How much?"

"One thousand euros."

"That hardly seems fair."

"Neither is life, Monsieur."

Gabriel looked at Amadou Kamara, who had not seen his child in four years. Then he opened his billfold and peered inside. He had twenty euros to his name.

"I need to find a cash machine," he said.

Papa Diallo flashed a luminous smile. "I'll be waiting."

11

Queen's Gate Terrace

By the time Gabriel left the café with Emanuel Cohen's phone in his pocket it was too late to make the last Eurostar back to London, so he slept for a few hours at a dreary hotel near the Gare du Nord and was on the morning's first train. He rang Sarah Bancroft as he was approaching St. Pancras. Her voice, when at last she answered the phone, was heavy with sleep.

"Do you know what day this is?"

"I believe it's Saturday. Hold on, let me check."

"Asshole," she whispered, and rang off.

Gabriel redialed.

"What is it now?" she asked.

"I require the metal object, approximately two pounds in weight, that I left at your gallery yesterday afternoon."

"The Beretta nine-millimeter?"

"Yes, that's the one."

"It's resting on my bedside table."

"Mind if I drop by and collect it?"

"Since when do you ask before making entry into my abode?"

"It's the new me."

"I was quite fond of the old you."

Gabriel's train arrived at half past eight. He traveled by Tube from King's Cross to Gloucester Road, then made the short walk to Sarah's maisonette in Queen's Gate Terrace. She was drinking coffee at the kitchen island, dressed in stretch jeans and a Harvard pullover. Her blond hair was wound into an untidy top knot. The condition of her blue eyes was indicative of a late night.

"I foolishly agreed to have dinner with Julian and Oliver," she explained while massaging her right temple.

"Why?"

"Because it was a Friday, and I didn't want to spend it searching for something to watch on Netflix."

"Where's your husband?"

"Vanished to parts unknown. Haven't heard from him in days." She looked down at the Beretta, which was lying on the countertop. "Most men bring a girl flowers. But not Gabriel Allon."

He slipped the gun into the waistband of his trousers at the small of his back.

"Feel better?"

"Much."

Sarah yawned elaborately, then asked, "How was Paris?"

"Quite interesting. But if I had known about your dinner plans, I would have taken you with me."

"You brought me something expensive, I hope."

Gabriel placed the iPhone on the countertop.

"Since you don't use an Apple device, I'll assume that isn't yours."

"It belonged to a Parisian physician named Emanuel Cohen."

"Belonged?"

"Dr. Cohen fell down the steps of the rue Chappe in Montmartre two nights ago. The French police believe it was an accident, which wasn't the case."

"Says who?"

"Amadou Kamara. He sells counterfeit handbags on the streets of Paris for Papa Diallo. Amadou saw someone push Dr. Cohen down the steps."

"How did you get his phone?"

"I bought it from Papa Diallo. He made a special price for me. A thousand euros. That was in addition to the five hundred I gave Amadou for two fake handbags."

"How shrewd of you." Sarah drank some of her coffee. "I'm sure there's a perfectly reasonable explanation for all this."

"Untitled portrait of a woman in the surrealist style, oil on canvas, ninety-four by sixty-six centimeters."

"Picasso?"

Gabriel nodded.

"There are several untitled portraits, if memory serves."

"That's correct. And one of them belonged to Cohen's grandfather, a man named Bernard Lévy. He foolishly entrusted it to his lawyer during the Occupation."

"And the lawyer undoubtedly sold it."

"But of course."

"Should I assume that Dr. Cohen was looking for this painting at the time of his death?"

"Actually, he was convinced he'd found it."

"Where?"

"An art gallery in the Geneva Freeport. He asked the world's leading expert on the wartime French art market, a woman named Naomi Wallach, to prove that it was his grandfather's Picasso."

"Isn't Naomi Wallach working for the Louvre now?"

"Which is why she told Cohen she couldn't take the case. She did, however, suggest an alternative."

"Not Charlotte Blake?"

Gabriel nodded.

"But she was murdered by the Chopper."

"She was murdered with a hatchet," said Gabriel. "Whether it was wielded by the Chopper is unclear. In fact, there are inconsistencies with the previous killings."

"Do you think she was murdered because of the Picasso?"

"I do now."

"Any suspects?"

"A person of interest."

"The Geneva art dealer?"

Gabriel nodded.

"Which is why you paid a thousand euros for a stolen iPhone."

"And five hundred euros for two fake handbags."

Sarah rubbed her swollen eyes. "You're right. I really should have come with you to Paris."

———

During a recent and wholly unplanned visit to Tel Aviv, Gabriel's old service had issued him a new laptop computer containing the latest version of Proteus, the world's most formidable cell phone hacking malware. Ordinarily, Proteus attacked its target remotely over the owner's preferred cellular network. But because Gabriel had the target phone in his possession, it was as simple as connecting the device to his laptop. Proteus instantly seized control of the phone's operating system and, with a click of Gabriel's trackpad, began exporting every bit of data stored in its memory.

The process took several minutes, leaving Sarah sufficient time to undo the damage of the previous evening's ill-considered outing with Julian and Oliver Dimbleby. When she returned to the kitchen, she was wearing black trousers and a black cashmere pullover. Gabriel handed her a thumb drive, and she inserted it into her computer.

"Where should we begin?"

"The end," said Gabriel, and opened a directory of every voice call the device had initiated or received. The last entry was an incoming call, the call Dr. Cohen had received as he was approaching the summit of the rue Chappe.

"Perhaps we should dial it," suggested Sarah.

"What good would that do?"

"The owner might answer."

"And what exactly would we say to him? Besides, when was the last time you answered a call from a number you didn't recognize?"

"Just yesterday. I enjoy torturing the person at the other end."

"You must have a lot of time on your hands."

"I manage an Old Master art gallery, darling."

Gabriel turned his attention to the geolocation data that Proteus had extracted from Dr. Cohen's phone. It allowed him to track Cohen's every move, including a visit he had made to Geneva six months before his death. He had traveled from Paris by train, arriving at the Gare Cornavin at half past one. The taxi ride to the Ports Francs et Entrepôts de Genève, otherwise known as the Geneva Freeport, was sixteen minutes in duration. He made a single telephone call along the way.

"It's a Geneva number," said Gabriel. "I'm betting it's the gallery."

He copied the number into his search engine and added the words *art* and *Geneva*. There were more than six million results, but only the first seven were relevant. They were for an art gallery based in the Freeport called Galerie Edmond Ricard SA.

"Monsieur Ricard is a major player at the Freeport," said Sarah. "And slippery as an eel, or so they say."

"You've never done business with him?"

"Not me. But we know someone who probably has."

"Call him. See if he's free."

Sarah took up her phone and dialed. "Hello, Nicky. I know it's a Saturday, but I was wondering if you had a spare minute or two . . . A boozy lunch at Claridge's? What a marvelous idea. How does one o'clock sound to you?"

Sarah rang off. "We're on," she said.

"I gathered that."

She checked the time. "We have two and a half hours to kill before lunch. What shall we do?"

"How about a nice long walk in Hyde Park? It will do wonders for your hangover."

"Yes," said Sarah, rising. "Just in time for my next one."

12

Claridge's

The first raindrops fell as they were strolling along Rotten Row. They took shelter in the café on the Serpentine Lido and drank tea as the clouds blackened and the gentle shower turned to a downpour.

"Any other brilliant ideas?" asked Sarah.

"I'm sure there's a bright interval just around the corner."

"This is Britain, darling. There are no bright intervals at the moment. Only endless gloom." She held up her mobile phone. "Have you seen the *Telegraph* this morning? Your old friend Samantha Cooke got quite the scoop."

Gabriel had read the story during the train ride from Paris. It stated that the treasurer of the Conservative Party, the wealthy international businessman and investor Lord Michael Radcliff, had personally accepted a heavily laundered million-pound political contribution from a pro-Kremlin Russian oligarch named Valentin Federov. An internal Party memorandum obtained by the *Telegraph* indicated that Prime Minister Hillary Edwards had been aware of the contribution. The Downing Street press secretary, however, had issued a swift and blistering denial of the allegation, declaring that Lord Radcliff was solely to blame for the egregious lapse in judgment.

"Do you think poor Hillary can survive?" asked Sarah.

"Not in her current condition. She's too weakened to fight off a challenge."

"But how could Lord Radcliff be so foolish as to accept a contribution from a Russian oligarch in the middle of the war in Ukraine?"

"It's not the first time the Tories have accepted money from a dubious foreign source. Or a Russian source, for that matter. Their fundraising apparatus has been a mess for some time."

"The entire Party is a mess. So is the country, I'm afraid."

"Don't worry, the worst is yet to come."

"So much for the new you," said Sarah.

They left the café at half past twelve and headed for Claridge's. Nicholas Lovegrove, in a dark suit and open-necked dress shirt, occupied a green leather booth in the hotel's famed restaurant. He was contemplating the label of an excellent bottle of Montrachet, to which he had already done significant damage.

The maître d' showed Sarah and Gabriel to the table, and Lovegrove rose to greet them. He could not hide his disappointment that he would not be lunching alone with one of the London art world's most alluring and mysterious women. Still, he was quite obviously intrigued by Gabriel's presence.

"Allon," he blared, turning heads at a nearby table. "What an unexpected surprise."

They all three sat down and the waiter filled their glasses with the Montrachet. Lovegrove ordered another bottle, but Sarah requested a Belvedere Bloody Mary as well.

"That's the spirit," said Lovegrove.

"Dinner with Oliver and Julian last night," she explained.

"I heard." Lovegrove turned to Gabriel and regarded him warily for a moment. "Shall we discuss the newest exhibit at the Tate Modern, or am I allowed to interrogate you at length about your rather remarkable career?"

"I'm more interested in yours, Nicky."

"I'm afraid the dealings of an art adviser are more classified than those of a professional spy. My clients demand absolute discretion, and I've never betrayed one."

But Nicholas Lovegrove, one of the art world's most sought-after consultants, made demands of his clients as well, namely, a percentage of all transactions, be they sales or acquisitions. In return, he vouched for the authenticity of the paintings in question and, more often than not, their prospects for a profitable resale. He also served as a cutout between seller and buyer, ensuring that neither knew the other's identity. And if he happened to be representing both parties to a sale, Lovegrove could expect to double his commission. It was not uncommon for him to earn more than a million dollars on a single deal—or eight figures if the piece was something stratospheric. It was, as the old jazz standard went, nice work if you could get it.

"I have no interest in any of your clients," said Gabriel. "I'd just like to ask your opinion of a dealer."

"I've never met an honest one in my life." Lovegrove smiled at Sarah. "Present company excluded, of course. But what's this scoundrel's name?"

"Edmond Ricard. His gallery is inside the Geneva—"

"I know where it is, Allon."

"You've been, I take it?"

Lovegrove was slow in offering a response. "What is the nature of this inquiry of yours?"

"That's a rather difficult question to answer, actually."

"Try."

"It involves a Picasso."

"A fine start. Please continue."

"A Picasso that belonged to a French businessman who was murdered in the Holocaust."

"A restitution case?"

"More or less."

"Which means there's *more* to the story."

Gabriel sighed. The negotiations had begun. "Name your price, Nicky."

"The Gentileschi."

"I'll do it for five percent of the hammer price."

"Three percent."

"Highway robbery."

"You would know."

"All right, Nicky, I will clean your Gentileschi for a lousy three percent of the final sale price, though I will insist on reviewing all the paperwork to make certain you haven't fleeced me."

"My good fellow," muttered Lovegrove.

"In exchange, you will tell me everything you know about Galerie Edmond Ricard."

"Without divulging the identities of any of my clients."

"So stipulated."

"Or any paintings they may have purchased or sold through said gallery."

"Agreed."

"In that case," said Lovegrove, smiling broadly, "we have a deal."

The waiter placed the Bloody Mary in front of Sarah. She raised it a fraction of an inch in Gabriel's direction. "How shrewd of you," she said, and drank.

The client had a posh double-barreled name that did not accurately reflect the circumstances of his birth. His personal fortune, however, was princely and growing by the day. It was his wish to acquire an art collection that would confer instant sophistication and thus grant him entrée into the upper levels of British and Continental society. With the esteemed Nicholas Lovegrove looking over his shoulder, he filled his stately Belgravia mansion with a dazzling assortment of postwar and contemporary paintings—postwar and contemporary being Lovegrove's strong suit. The price tag for the yearlong shopping spree was a mere one hundred million pounds, ten million of which flowed directly into Lovegrove's pocket.

"What sort of work does your client do?"

"I refer you to the terms of our arrangement, Allon."

"Come on, Nicky. Show a little leg."

"Suffice to say, he knows little about the paintings hanging on his walls and even less about the wicked ways of the art world. I chose the pieces for the collection and handled the negotiations. All the client did was write the checks."

Which was why it came as something of a surprise when the client, quite out of the blue, asked Lovegrove to accompany him to Geneva to inspect a painting being offered for sale by Galerie Ricard.

"The artist?" asked Gabriel.

"Let's say for argument's sake that it was Rothko. And let us also say that after careful inspection of the canvas and the provenance I had no qualms about its authenticity."

"Was Galerie Ricard the owner of this work?"

"Heavens no. Ricard calls himself a dealer, but in point of fact he's a glorified broker. A middleman, pure and simple. The owner of record was a company called OOC Group, Limited."

"OOC? You're sure?"

Lovegrove nodded. "Evidently, OOC stands for Oil on Canvas. I assumed it was a shell company of some sort. They're all the rage, you know."

"What was the asking price?"

"The equivalent of seventy-five million dollars."

"Seems a tad high."

"I thought so, too. But Ricard wouldn't budge and the client had his heart set on it, so he signed the sales agreement and wired the money from his account at Barclays."

At which point Lovegrove received a second piece of unexpected news. It seemed his client had no interest in hanging the Rothko in his Belgravia mansion. Instead, he wished to leave it in the Geneva Freeport in the care of Edmond Ricard.

"He controls a large portion of the Freeport's storage space. For a reasonable fee, he agreed to hold the painting for as long as my client wished."

"Sounds to me as though your unsophisticated client was getting sophisticated financial advice from another source."

"The thought crossed my mind," said Lovegrove. "But I didn't question the decision at the time. Several of my clients store paintings in that facility. It's perfectly legal."

"And your commission on the deal was a perfect seven and a half million."

"A substantial portion of which I handed over to His Majesty's Revenue and Customs."

A scant six months later, Lovegrove continued, he made a second visit to Galerie Ricard, this time with a client who was in the market for a de Kooning.

"And guess what we saw prominently displayed?"

"The Rothko?"

Lovegrove nodded.

"You're sure it was your client's Rothko?"

"Oh yes. And it was being offered for sale."

"By whom?"

"I didn't ask."

Lovegrove did, however, raise the matter with his client upon his return to London. And the client admitted that he had sold the painting to another party within the tax-free zone of the Freeport just two months after the original purchase.

"A rather short turnaround," said Gabriel.

"Not by today's standards, especially in the Geneva Freeport. But certainly suspicious. More important, it was a violation of our arrangement. If he in fact sold that painting, I was owed ten percent of the sale price."

"Did your client agree to pay up?"

"Immediately."

"How much?"

"He wrote me a check for six point two million pounds."

"The equivalent of seven and a half million dollars," said Gabriel. "Which means your client sold the painting for the exact same price he paid for it."

"He did indeed. The question is, why on earth would he do such a thing?"

"Perhaps you should ask him."

"Can't," said Lovegrove. "He dropped me the next day."

13

Fondamenta Venier

The church of Santa Maria degli Angeli stood at the western end of the Fondamenta Venier on the island of Murano. Gabriel unlocked the outer door and carried his overnight bag inside. Because it was a Sunday, the official day of rest in the Italian restoration community, he had the church to himself. Il Pordenone's towering altarpiece was adhered to a purpose-built wooden armature in the center of the nave. Gabriel switched on an electric space heater and a pair of standing halogen lamps and inspected his trolley. His brushes, pigments, and solvents were as he had left them four days earlier, or so it appeared. He had it on good authority that Adrianna Zinetti, the finest cleaner of altars and statuary in Venice, regularly tampered with his things, if only to prove that it could be done without detection.

He slid Christian Tetzlaff's recording of the Brahms violin concerto into his paint-smudged portable CD player, a faithful companion during countless restorations past, and allowed his eyes to wander over the canvas. Thanks to a period of uninterrupted work before leaving for London, he had removed nearly all of the surface grime and old varnish. It was possible he might complete the task today, tomorrow at the latest. Then he would commence the final phase of the restoration, the retouching of those portions of the painting that had flaked away or faded with age. The losses, while consistent with sixteenth-century Venetian paintings, were hardly catastrophic. Gabriel reckoned it would take no more than a month to repair the damage.

Only the upper left corner of the altarpiece was still in need of cleaning. Gabriel hoisted himself atop the platform of his scaffold and wound a swatch of cotton wool around the end of a wooden dowel. Then he dipped it into his solvent—a carefully calibrated mixture of acetone, methyl proxitol, and mineral spirits—and twirled it gently over the surface of the canvas. Each swab could clean a few square centimeters before becoming too soiled to use. Then Gabriel had to fashion another. At night, when he was not reliving nightmarish moments from his past, he was scrubbing yellowed varnish from a canvas the size of the Piazza San Marco.

He worked at a steady pace, pausing only once to insert a new CD into the player, and by noon the platform was littered with several dozen wads of soiled cotton wool. He sealed them in a flask, then, after locking the door of the church behind him, set off along the Fondamenta Venier to Bar al Ponte. Within seconds of his arrival, a coffee and a small glass of white wine—Venetians referred to it as *un'ombra*—were placed before him.

"Something to eat?" asked the barman, whose name was Bartolomeo.

"A *tramezzino*."

"Tomato and cheese?"

"Eggs and tuna."

The barman slipped the triangular sandwich into a paper bag and placed it on the countertop. Gabriel handed over a banknote and indicated that no change was required. Then he asked, "Do you know Bar Cupido, Bartolomeo? That pizzeria on the Fondamente Nove?"

"The one by the vaporetto stop? Sure, Signore Allon."

"There's a fellow who works there. I believe his name is Gennaro."

"I know him well."

"Really? What's he like?"

"Nicest guy in the world. Everybody loves Gennaro."

"Are you sure we're talking about the same Gennaro?"

"Is there a problem, Signore Allon?"

"No," said Gabriel as he plucked the paper bag from the bar. "No problem at all."

He ate the *tramezzino* while walking back to the church and listened to *La Bohème* while removing the last of the surface grime and yellowed varnish from the altarpiece. The stained-glass windows were black by the time he finished. He recorded the true condition of the painting with his Nikon, then locked the door of the church and walked to the Museo vaporetto stop. Ten minutes elapsed before a Number 4.1 finally appeared. It ferried him southward across the *laguna*, past San Michele, to the Fondamente Nove.

As he approached Bar Cupido he saw Gennaro at his outpost behind the counter. Ordinarily, Gabriel frequented the establishment only in the morning, but on a frigid night like this, its bright interior was warm and inviting. And so he went inside and in pitch-perfect Italian placed his order, a coffee and a small glass of grappa, thus signaling that he was a Venetian and not some interloper. Five minutes later he went out again and set off toward the Rialto Bridge, wondering why the nicest guy in the world, the one everybody loved, seemed to despise him. The answer came to him as he was climbing the stairs toward his apartment, drawn by the savor of his wife's cooking. "Yes, of course," he muttered to himself. It was the only possible explanation.

———————

Perhaps I should have a word with him," said Chiara.

"I'm sure he would love nothing more."

"What are you suggesting?"

"That Gennaro the barman has designs on my wife."

"You were obviously listening to opera while you were working today." Chiara poured a generous measure of Barbaresco into a wineglass and placed it on the kitchen island. "Drink this, darling. You'll feel better."

Gabriel settled atop a stool and gave the wine a swirl. "I'll feel better when you tell me that I'm wrong about you and your friend from Bar Cupido."

"It's only a harmless little crush, Gabriel."

"I knew it," he murmured.

"I'm old enough to be his mother, for heaven's sake."

"And I'm old enough . . ." He left the thought unfinished. It was too depressing to contemplate. "How long has this been going on?"

"Has *what* been going on?"

"Your affair with Gennaro the barman."

"You know, Gabriel, you really should wear a mask when you're using solvents. It's clear the fumes have taken a terrible toll on your brain cells."

Chiara removed the lid from the stainless-steel Dutch oven resting on the stovetop. The mouthwatering aroma of its contents, a rich duck ragu seasoned with bay leaves and sage, filled the kitchen. She sampled the dish, then added a pinch of salt.

"Perhaps I should taste it as well," suggested Gabriel.

"Only if you promise never to raise the subject of Gennaro the barman ever again."

"Is it over between the two of you?"

Chiara spooned some of the ragu onto a crostino and ate it slowly, the expression on her face one of sexual satisfaction.

"All right," said Gabriel. "I surrender."

"Say it," insisted Chiara.

"I will never mention Gennaro's name again."

"Who's Gennaro?" asked Irene as she wandered into the kitchen.

"He works at Bar Cupido on the Fondamente Nove," replied Gabriel. "Your mother is having a torrid affair with him."

"What does torrid mean?"

"Ardent and passionate. Scorched with heat."

"It sounds painful."

"It can be."

Chiara prepared another ragu-smothered crostino and pointedly handed it to Irene. The child was wearing a World Wildlife Fund pullover that Gabriel had never seen before.

"Where did you get this?" he asked, tugging at the sleeve.

"We adopted a tiger."

"Will he be sharing your room or Raphael's?"

"It's a symbolic adoption," said Irene, rolling her eyes. "The tiger remains in the wild."

"I'm relieved. But since when did you became an animal rights activist as well as an environmental extremist?"

"Do you know how many species are threatened because of climate change?"

"I haven't a clue. But I'm sure you're about to tell me."

"More than forty thousand. And with each degree of warming the problem will only get worse." Irene climbed onto Gabriel's lap. "How was your trip to Paris?"

"Who told you that I went to Paris?"

"Mama, silly."

"But I never mentioned it to her."

"I saw the charges for your train tickets and hotel on your credit card," explained Chiara. "I also noticed a rather large withdrawal from an ATM machine in the Eighteenth Arrondissement, which seemed odd. After all, you had plenty of cash in your wallet when I left London. Nearly a thousand euros, in fact."

Gabriel plucked the ragu-covered crostino from his daughter's hand and devoured it before she could object. "Paris was interesting," he said. "I went there to see someone named Naomi Wallach. She works at the Louvre."

Chiara reached for her phone and typed, then handed it to Irene. "She's very beautiful," said the child.

"All of your father's female friends are beautiful. And they all adore him to no end." Chiara reclaimed the phone. "Tell your brother that dinner will be ready in ten minutes."

"I want to stay here."

"I need to have a word with your father in private."

"About Gennaro the barman?"

Chiara squeezed the bridge of her nose between her thumb and forefinger. "Irene, please."

"I'm very torrid," she said, and left the kitchen in a sulk.

Chiara dropped a handful of bigoli pasta into a stockpot of boiling water and gave it a stir. "You're incorrigible, you realize."

"You're one to talk."

She took up her phone again. "It's funny, but she looks like a Naomi."

"How does someone named Naomi look?"

"Like a beautiful historian who's trying to purge the Louvre of looted paintings." Chiara set the phone aside. "But why did you go to Paris to see her? And, better yet, why did you withdraw one thousand euros from an ATM machine in the Eighteenth?"

"Because you were right about Professor Blake's murder."

"Of course I was, darling." Chiara smiled. "When have I ever been wrong about anything?"

14

San Polo

How much will you earn for Nicky's Gentileschi?"

"Barely enough to cover the cost of my solvents and cotton wool."

"Your work will be effectively pro bono, you mean?"

"Yes," said Gabriel. "Rather like my work for you."

Having dealt with the dishes and supervised the bathing of the children, they had repaired to the loggia overlooking the Grand Canal. The bottle of Barbaresco stood on the table before them. A butane outdoor heater, purchased over Irene's tear-streaked objections, burned the cold from the air. Gabriel wore no coat, only a zippered woolen pullover. Chiara was wrapped in a quilted down duvet.

"And to think that none of this would have happened if you hadn't attended that ceremony at the Courtauld."

"You're wrong about that."

"Me? Impossible."

"Charlotte Blake would still be dead, regardless of whether I had showed my face at the Courtauld. And so would Emanuel Cohen."

"I was referring to your personal involvement in this matter," said

Chiara. "Therefore, I was in no way wrong. And I resent the implication that I was."

"Can you ever forgive me?"

"That depends on whether Irene tells her teacher and her friends about my torrid affair with Gennaro the barman."

"So you admit it, after all?"

"Yes," she answered. "I've been tending to your boundless sexual needs as well as his. And in my spare time, I've been running the most prominent restoration firm in the Veneto and raising two children, not to mention a tiger." She emptied the last of the wine into Gabriel's glass. "But back to the matter at hand."

"My boundless sexual needs?"

"Your latest investigation."

"I should probably tell the British and French police everything I know."

"With all due respect, darling, you *know* very little. In fact, you can't even prove that Emanuel Cohen was murdered."

"I have a witness."

"The Senegalese seller of counterfeit handbags?"

"He has a name, Chiara."

"Obviously I meant no disrespect. I was just pointing out that your friend Amadou Kamara is less than reliable."

"What possible motive did he have to mislead me?"

"Fifteen hundred euros."

"You think he made up the story?"

"It did seem to get better every time you gave him money."

Gabriel admired the view of the Grand Canal from his loggia. "He needs it more than we do."

"You're beginning to sound like your daughter."

"Is she an immigrant-rights activist as well?"

"She's troubled by the way many Venetians refer to African street vendors, as is her mother. I see them every day in San Marco with their blankets and their handbags, the wretched of the earth. The way the police chase them away is disgraceful."

"And what about the retailers or the makers of real luxury goods? Do they not have rights?"

"I agree that the piles of counterfeit bags on our streets are unsightly and that the vendors are engaging in criminal activity and undercutting the profits of fabulously wealthy corporations. But it is not a life to which anyone would aspire. People like Amadou Kamara sell fake handbags because they are desperately poor."

"Which makes his story no less credible. He saw what he saw."

"A murder made to look like an accident?"

Gabriel nodded.

"Who do you suppose hired the killers?"

"Someone with a great deal to lose if that Picasso were ever to be discovered inside the Geneva Freeport."

"How much is it worth?"

"A hundred million, give or take."

Chiara considered this. "A hundred million isn't enough to justify two professional hits. There has to be more to this than just a single painting."

"All the more reason to go to the police."

"A dreadful idea."

"What would you suggest?"

"Finish the restoration of the Pordenone."

"And then?"

"Find the Picasso, of course."

"In the Geneva Freeport?" asked Gabriel. "One of the world's most heavily guarded storage facilities for art and other valuable objects? Why didn't I think of that?"

"I'm not suggesting that you break into the Freeport and go vault to vault. You have no choice but to go into business with this Ricard fellow. Not you personally, of course. You're far too famous for that now. You'll need a cutout."

"A collector?"

Chiara nodded. "But you can't invent one out of whole cloth. Ricard is far too crafty. You'll need a real person. Someone with a considerable fortune and, preferably, a whiff of scandal in her past."

"Her?"

Chiara allowed a moment to pass before answering. "Don't make me say that woman's name aloud. I've had enough unpleasantness for one evening."

"What makes you think she'll do it?"

"Because she's still madly in love with you."

She was perfect, of course. She was enormously rich, she was an international celebrity, and she was the keeper of a substantial collection of paintings that had belonged to her disgraced father. Still, Gabriel could not shake himself of the nagging fear that his wife was trying to get rid of him for a few days.

"This doesn't have anything to do with—"

"I wouldn't, if I were you."

He decided a change of subject was in order. "Is she buying or selling?"

"Your girlfriend? Selling, I imagine."

"I thought so, too. But that means she's going to need paintings."

"Dirty paintings," said Chiara. "The dirtier the better."

"How many?"

"Enough to move the needle."

Gabriel made a show of thought. "Six feels about right."

"Estimated market value?"

"How does a hundred million sound?"

"Not as sweet as two hundred," replied Chiara. "Or two fifty, for that matter."

"In that case, I'll need a couple of heavy hitters."

"What do you have in mind?"

"A Modigliani would be nice." Gabriel shrugged. "Maybe a Van Gogh."

"How about a Renoir?"

"Why not?"

"Cézanne?"

"A fine idea."

"You should probably give your girlfriend a Monet, too. Nothing moves the needle quite like a Monet."

"Especially a Monet with a murky provenance."

"Yes," agreed Chiara. "The murkier the better."

For the next ten days, Gabriel was the first member of the restoration team to arrive at the church each morning and the last to leave. Typically, he granted himself two brief intermezzi, both of which he took at Bar al Ponte. Bartolomeo, on a windblown Wednesday, quite unexpectedly raised the subject of Gennaro Castelli, the much beloved counterman at Bar Cupido.

"He's wondering why you haven't been stopping there lately. He's concerned you might be angry with him."

"Why would I be angry at a barman?"

"He didn't go into specifics."

"And anyway," said Gabriel, "how does he even know who I am? I've never told him my name."

"Venice is a small town, Signore Allon. Everyone knows who you are." Bartolomeo indicated a platter of *tramezzini*. "Tomato and cheese or tuna and egg?"

Gabriel returned to the church to find that Adrianna Zinetti had rearranged his work trolley and stolen his copy of Schubert's *Death and the Maiden* string quartet, a piece she loathed. She surrendered the CD that evening during the vaporetto ride from Murano to the Fondamente Nove. As they walked past Bar Cupido, she smiled at Gennaro Castelli through the glass.

"Friend of yours?" asked Gabriel.

"I should be so lucky. He's quite luscious."

"Signore Luscious has a thing for my wife."

"Yes, I know. He told me."

"And you, of course, told Chiara."

"I might have," Adrianna admitted. "She found it quite amusing."

"What are young Gennaro's intentions?"

"Harmless, I'm sure. He's terrified of you."

"He should be."

"Come on, Gabriel. He's the nicest guy in the world."

Gabriel saw Adrianna to the door of her apartment building in Cannaregio, then walked to the Rialto and caught a Number 2 to San Tomà. Over dinner that evening, Chiara did not speak the name of her not-so-secret admirer from Bar Cupido, despite the apologetic text message she had undoubtedly received from Adrianna minutes before Gabriel's arrival. Instead, she requested a progress report on the altarpiece and, satisfied with Gabriel's update, suggested he take Raphael to his math lesson the following afternoon.

"I'm rather busy at the moment."

"You're nearly finished, Gabriel. Besides, I think you'll find it interesting."

The lesson took place in a study room at the university, where Raphael's tutor was a graduate student. Gabriel sat outside in the corridor with Irene, listening to the murmur of voices within. His son, having already mastered basic algebra and geometry, was now wrestling with more advanced inferential and deductive concepts. Though Gabriel understood little of the material, it was obvious that he had somehow sired a genius. His pride was tempered by the knowledge that minds such as Raphael's were prone to disorders and disturbances. He was already troubled by his son's profound remoteness. His thoughts always seemed to be elsewhere.

During the walk home, the boy declined Gabriel's invitation to discuss what he had learned that afternoon. Irene walked a few paces before them, pausing every now and again to jump into a puddle.

"Why is she doing that?" asked Raphael.

"Because she's eight."

"It's a composite number, you know."

"I didn't."

"It's also a power of two."

"I'll have to take your word for it." They followed Irene over the Rio de la Frescada. "Do you enjoy it, Raffi?"

"Enjoy what?"

"Mathematics."

"I'm good at it."

"That's not what I asked."

"Do you enjoy restoring paintings?"

"Yes, of course."

"Why?"

"You wouldn't understand."

"What's an additive inverse?" Raphael looked up from the paving stones of the Calle del Campanile and smiled. The boy had been cursed with Gabriel's face and his jade-colored eyes. "Why are you asking me these questions?"

"Because I want to make certain you're happy. And I was wondering whether you might be interested in studying something other than math."

"Like painting?" The child shook his head.

"Why not?"

"Because I'll never be able to paint like you."

"I felt the same way when I was your age. I was certain that I would never be as good as my mother and grandfather."

"Were you?"

"I never had a chance to find out."

"Why don't you try again?"

"I'm too old, Raffi. My time has come and gone. I'm just a restorer now."

"One of the best in the world," said the boy, and chased his sister across the Campo San Tomà.

If need be, Gabriel was one of the fastest art restorers in the world as well. He completed the retouching of the Pordenone in five marathon sessions, then covered it in a fresh coat of varnish. Chiara came to the church two days later to supervise the return of the enormous canvas to its marble frame above the high altar. Gabriel, however, was not in attendance; he was on a train headed north through the Italian Alps. He waited until he had crossed the Austrian border before phoning the world's most famous violinist.

"Have you finally come to your senses?" she asked.

"No," he answered. "Quite the opposite."

15

Philharmonie am Gasteig

The Philharmonie am Gasteig, Munich's modern concert hall and cultural center, stood on Rosenheimer Strasse near the banks of the river Isar. Gabriel, in a dark suit and tie, the shoulders of his cashmere overcoat dusted with snow, presented himself at the will-call window and in perfect Berlin-accented German requested his ticket for that evening's sold-out performance of Mendelssohn's E-minor violin concerto and Beethoven's Seventh Symphony.

"Name?" asked the woman behind the glass.

"Klemp," he replied. "Johannes Klemp."

The woman drew a small envelope from the box before her, then, after reviewing the attached sticky note, reached for her phone.

"Is there a problem?" asked Gabriel.

"Not at all, Herr Klemp."

She spoke a few words into the phone, her hand shielding the mouthpiece, and rang off. Then she handed Gabriel the envelope and pointed toward the doorway at the far end of the foyer.

"The backstage entrance," she explained. "Frau Rolfe is expecting you."

The door had opened by the time Gabriel arrived, and a smiling young woman with a clipboard was standing in the breach. "Right this way, Herr Klemp," she said, and they set off along a gently curving corridor. Beyond the next door was the backstage area. The Philharmonie am Gasteig was the home of the Bavarian Radio Symphony Orchestra, widely regarded as one of the world's finest. Tonight it would be under the baton of Sir Simon Rattle, who at that moment was chatting with the orchestra's first concertmaster.

Gabriel's young escort paused before the closed door of a dressing room. The placard indicating the name of the occupant was unnecessary. She was readily identifiable by the matchless liquid tone she was drawing from her Guarneri violin.

The escort raised a hand to knock.

"I wouldn't, if I were you," said Gabriel.

"She left strict instructions."

"Don't say you weren't warned."

The woman's knock was tepid. Instantly the violin fell silent.

"Who goes there?" asked a voice within.

"Herr Klemp has arrived, Frau Rolfe."

"Please show him in. And then go away."

Gabriel opened the door and went inside. Anna sat before her dressing table, the Guarneri beneath her chin. The garnet-colored evening gown she wore was shimmering and strapless. Her catlike eyes were fixed on the reflection in the lighted mirror.

"As much as I would like to be kissed by you, I will insist that you somehow restrain yourself. It took several hours of intense effort to get me looking like this." With her bow she indicated a chair. "Sit, peasant. Speak only when spoken to."

Anna laid the bow on the strings of the Guarneri and, closing her eyes, played a silken E-minor arpeggio over three octaves. She had played the same simple exercise for hours on end during the six months and fourteen days they had lived together at her villa on Portugal's Costa de Prata. It was Gabriel, after first stuffing his possessions into a duffel bag, who had ended the relationship. The lines he recited that day were shopworn but entirely accurate. It was his fault, not hers. It was too soon, he wasn't ready. Tempestuous Anna had endured his performance with uncharacteristic forbearance before finally hurling a ceramic vase at his head and declaring she never wished to speak to him again.

Within a few short months she had wed. The marriage ended with a spectacular divorce, as did her second. There followed a succession of highly publicized affairs and liaisons, always with rich and famous men, each more disastrous than the last. During a recent visit to Venice she had made it clear that Gabriel was to blame for her tragic plight. If only he had married her, had toured the world with her while she basked in the adulation of her fans, she would have been spared a lifetime of romantic misfortune. It occurred to Gabriel, as he sat in Anna's dressing room, that this was the life she had imagined for them. She was not about to allow the evening to go to waste.

Her bow went still. "Did you have a chance to talk to Simon? He's quite anxious to meet you."

"Why would Sir Simon Rattle want to meet lowly Johannes Klemp?"

"Because Sir Simon knows Herr Klemp's real name."

"You didn't."

"I might have, yes."

She played the opening melody of the concerto's andante second movement. It sent a chill, like a charge of electricity, down the length of Gabriel's spine, as she had known it would. He nevertheless adopted an expression of mild boredom.

"That bad?" she asked.

"Dreadful."

Frowning, she lit a Gitane in violation of the concert hall's strict no-smoking policy. "You made quite a splash in London last week."

"You noticed?"

"It was rather hard to miss. But why the silly pseudonym tonight?"

"I'm afraid that Gabriel Allon can't be seen with Anna Rolfe in public."

"Whyever not?"

"Because he needs Anna's help. And he doesn't want his target to know that they are acquainted."

"We were more than acquaintances, my love. Much more."

"It was a long time ago, Anna."

"Yes," she said, contemplating her reflection in the mirror. "I was young and beautiful then. And now . . ."

"You're no less beautiful."

"I'd be careful, Gabriel. I can be quite irresistible when I want to be." She played the same passage from the concerto's second movement. "Better?"

"A little."

She took a pull at her cigarette, then crushed it out. "So what do you require of me this time? Another dreary fundraiser or something a bit more interesting?"

"The latter," said Gabriel.

"No Russians, I hope."

"We should probably talk about this after your performance."

"As it happens, I'm free for dinner."

"A marvelous idea."

"But if we can't be seen together in public, our options are somewhat limited. In fact," said Anna playfully, "it seems to me that the only place where we can be assured of absolute privacy is my suite at the Mandarin Oriental."

"Will you be able to control yourself?"

"Unlikely."

There was a knock at the door.

"What is it now?" Anna demanded to know.

"Ten minutes, Frau Rolfe."

She looked at Gabriel. "You're free to wait here, if you like."

"And miss your performance?" Gabriel rose to his feet and draped his coat over his arm. "I wouldn't dream of it."

"What time shall I expect you?"

"You tell me."

"Stay for the Beethoven. It will give me a chance to change into something a bit more comfortable." She lifted her check to be kissed. "You have my permission."

"Somehow I'll resist," said Gabriel, and went out.

Alone in her dressing room, Anna laid her bow upon the strings of the Guarneri and played a G-major scale in broken thirds. "Don't smile," she said to the woman in the looking glass. "You never play well when you're happy."

———

The seat to which the young escort led Gabriel was in the first row, slightly to the left of Simon Rattle's podium and not more than two meters from the spot where Anna delivered a spellbinding performance of Felix Mendelssohn's masterpiece. At the conclusion of the final movement, the twenty-five hundred members of the audience rose to their feet and showered her with rapturous applause and shouts of "Bravo!" Only then, with a mischievous smile, did she acknowledge Gabriel's presence.

"Better?" she mouthed.

"Much," he replied with a smile.

He adjourned to the foyer for a glass of champagne during the interval and returned to his seat for a memorable performance of Beethoven's stirring Seventh Symphony. By the time Sir Simon stepped from his podium, it was a few minutes after ten o'clock. Outside, there were no taxis to be had, so Gabriel set off for the Mandarin Oriental on foot. As he was crossing the Ludwigsbrücke, a Mercedes sedan drew alongside him and the rear window descended.

"You'd better get in, Herr Klemp. Otherwise, you'll catch your death."

Gabriel opened the door and slid into the back seat. As the car rolled forward, Anna threw her arms around his neck and pressed her lips against his cheek.

"I thought we were meeting at your hotel," he said.

"I got tied up backstage."

"By whom?"

Anna laughed quietly. "I miss that sense of humor of yours."

"But not the smell of my solvents."

She made a face. "They were atrocious."

"So was the sound of your endless practicing."

"Did it really bother you?"

"Never, Anna."

Smiling, she gazed out her window at the snow-covered streets of Munich's Old Town. "It wouldn't have been so terrible, you know."

"Being married to you?"

She nodded slowly.

"It was too soon, Anna. I wasn't ready."

She leaned her head against Gabriel's shoulder. "I'd watch your step, if I were you, Herr Klemp. My suite is full of vases. And this time I won't miss."

16

Altstadt

A nd what, pray tell, is the young man's name?"

"Gennaro."

Anna placed a finger thoughtfully to the end of her slender nose. "I could be mistaken, but it's possible that I had an affair with a Gennaro once myself."

"Given your track record," replied Gabriel, "I'd say the chances are rather good."

They were seated at opposite ends of the couch in the sitting room of Anna's luxurious suite, separated by a buffer zone of rich black satin. Her Guarneri violin, enclosed in its protective case, was propped on an opposing Eames chair next to her Stradivarius. A wall-mounted television flickered silently with the latest news from London. Lord Michael Radcliff, the Conservative Party treasurer who had accepted a tainted million-pound contribution from a Russian businessman, had bowed to pressure and resigned. Prime Minister Hillary Edwards, her support within the Party crumbling, was expected to announce her own resignation within days.

"A friend of yours?" asked Anna.

"Hillary Edwards? We've never met. But I was quite close to her predecessor, Jonathan Lancaster."

"Is there anyone you *don't* know?"

"I've never met the president of Russia."

"Consider yourself fortunate." Anna switched off the television and refilled their glasses with wine. They were drinking Grand Cru white burgundy by Joseph Drouhin. "I think we should have another bottle, don't you?"

"It was eight hundred and forty euros."

"It's only money, Gabriel."

"Says the woman who has an endless supply of it."

"You're the one who lives in a palazzo overlooking the Grand Canal."

"I happen to own a single floor of the palazzo."

"Poor you." Anna rang room service, then carried her glass of wine to the window. The view was westward across the Old Town toward the spire of St. Peter's Church. "Come here often?" she asked.

"To the Mandarin Oriental?"

"No," said Anna. "To Munich."

"I avoid it whenever possible, if you must know."

"Even now?" Anna smiled sadly. "It took me an age to get the story out of you."

"Actually, it took you about a day and a half."

"You *wanted* to tell me about your past. My God, you were a wreck back then."

"So were you, as I recall."

"Still am. You, on the other hand, seem deliriously happy." She drew the curtains. "You mentioned something about needing a favor. But I have a terrible feeling it was a rather transparent ruse on your part to get me into bed. If that was indeed the case, your plan worked to perfection."

"You promised to behave yourself."

"I said no such thing." Anna returned to the couch. "All right, you have my complete and undivided attention. What do you want from me this time?"

"I would like you to dispose of six of the paintings that you inherited from your father."

"What a wonderful idea!" Anna exclaimed. "To tell you the truth, I've wanted to sell those wretched paintings for years. But tell me, which six did you have in mind?"

"The Modigliani, the Van Gogh, the Renoir, the Cézanne, and the Monet."

"That's only five. Furthermore, I own no works by any of the artists you mentioned." She regarded him over her wineglass. "But then you already knew that. After all, you were with me the morning I found the last sixteen paintings from my father's collection of looted Impressionist and modern art."

"It turns out there were six additional paintings that we didn't know about."

"Really?" Anna raised a hand to her mouth, feigning astonishment. "And where were they hiding?"

"In a bank vault in Lugano. The Rolfe family lawyer told you about them after the scandal over your father's wartime conduct had died down. You instructed the lawyer to smuggle the paintings out of Switzerland and deliver them to your villa in Portugal."

"How naughty of me. Are they still there?"

"Yes, of course."

"In that case," said Anna, "I'm obligated to report them to the Swiss government immediately. Otherwise, I will face stiff fines. You see, Canton Zurich taxes the wealth of its residents annually. Each year I must submit a detailed list of my possessions, including an inventory of the paintings I own. And each year the government pockets a not insignificant portion of my net worth."

"What is it these days, if you don't mind my asking?"

"It's possible it starts with the letter B."

"And the number before the B?"

She delivered her answer with raised eyebrows. "Could be a two."

"I never realized there was that much."

"I am the only surviving heir to the Rolfe banking fortune. I've also earned a considerable sum of money throughout my long recording and concert career. But the last thing I would ever do is conceal my wealth to avoid paying taxes. That's the sort of thing my father did."

"It turns out that you're more alike than you realized."

Anna frowned. "If you keep talking like that, my love, you will never get me into bed. But let's get back to the matter at hand. When, exactly, did my father acquire these mysterious paintings?"

"In the fifties, mainly in France. They don't appear in the Lost Art Database or any other registry of looted artwork. But given your father's deplorable wartime conduct, most reputable dealers and collectors would steer clear of them. Which is why you're going to place them with a certain Edmond Ricard in the Geneva Freeport."

"And why would I do that?"

"Because Monsieur Ricard was recently in possession of a Picasso that was stolen from a man named Bernard Lévy during the German occupation of France. With your help, I'm going to find it and return it to Lévy's rightful heirs."

Anna nodded contemplatively. "If there's anything else I should know about this little scheme of yours, now would be a fine time to tell me."

"Two people linked to the painting have been murdered."

"Only two?"

"For all I know, there might be others."

"He's not going to kill me, is he?"

"Ricard? I can't imagine."

"Because the last time you and I got involved in looted art—"

The bell sounded before Anna could finish her thought. Rising, she went into the entrance hall and admitted a pair of room service waiters. They arranged the food on the table without commentary and hurriedly withdrew.

Anna sat down and laid a napkin across her lap. "Perhaps I've been going about this the wrong way."

"Going about what?" asked Gabriel as he removed the cork from the second bottle of white burgundy.

"Convincing you to leave that gorgeous wife of yours and marry me."

"Anna, please."

"Will you at least hear my proposal?"

"No."

"I'm prepared to be generous."

"I'm sure you are. But I'm not interested in your money. I'm desperately in love with Chiara."

"What about the reckless affair she's having with this Giacomo fellow?"

"Gennaro," said Gabriel. "And it isn't real."

"Of course it isn't. After all, why would she be involved with a coffee boy when she's married to you?" Anna lowered her eyes toward her plate. "In case you were wondering, the answer is yes. I'll help you find that Picasso."

"What's your schedule like?"

"I'm in Oslo next week and Prague the week after."

"And then?"

"I'll have to check with my assistant."

"Please do," said Gabriel. "And then get rid of her."

"Why?"

"Because I'm going to give you a new one."

"What's she like?"

"Pure trouble."

"Sounds like my kind of girl," said Anna. "All I need now are the paintings."

"I'll take care of those, too."

"How?"

Gabriel, with a movement of his hand, indicated that he was going to paint them himself.

"A Modigliani, a Van Gogh, a Renoir, a Cézanne, and a Monet?"

He shrugged.

"And the sixth?"

"I'll leave that to you."

"Is Toulouse-Lautrec part of your repertoire?"

"No sheet music required."

"Perfect," said Anna. "Toulouse-Lautrec it is."

17

Mykonos

The all-electric BMW i4 sedan slid into a parking space outside Café Apollo on the island of Mykonos at two o'clock the following afternoon. The woman who emerged from behind the wheel wore a leather jacket against the blustery February weather and a pair of stretch jeans that flattered her slender hips and thighs. Her shoulder-length hair was the color of toffee and streaked with blond. Her eyes, concealed behind a pair of fashionable Yves Saint Laurent sunglasses, were pale blue.

She entered the café and sat down at a table against the window. It looked eastward toward the sun-bleached terminal of Mykonos International Airport. A friend was arriving on a flight from Athens. He had given her little notice of his travel plans—and no explanation as to why they included a midwinter visit to a popular Greek island. She was confident it was not a social call. Her friend, the former director-general of Israel's secret intelligence service, was a very busy man.

That was certainly not the case for the woman, a citizen of Denmark named Ingrid Johansen. She had spent the better part of that winter holed up at her luxurious villa on the island's southern coast with no company other than her Hegel audio system and a stack of Henning Mankell and Jo Nesbø novels. Her Israeli friend was to blame for her present circumstances. Two months earlier, he had sent Ingrid into Russia to acquire the only copy of a secret Kremlin plan to wage nuclear war in Ukraine. The operation was her introduction to the world of espionage, but hardly the first time she had stolen something of value. A professional thief and skilled computer hacker, Ingrid had purchased her villa on Mykonos with the proceeds of a summerlong crime spree in Saint-Tropez. A single pair of Harry Winston diamond earrings, plucked from a hotel safe in Majorca, had paid for the BMW.

The Russia operation had resulted in a windfall profit of $20 million, more than enough money to allow Ingrid to retire. Regrettably, her lifelong clinical compulsion to steal, an affliction that surfaced when she was a child of nine, remained as powerful as ever. For that reason alone, she was looking forward to her friend's visit. He needed her for something; she was certain of it. Her fingers were already tingling with anticipation.

A waiter finally wandered over to Ingrid's table, and in passable Greek she ordered coffee. It arrived as an Aegean Airlines Airbus was dropping out of the cloudless sky. Twenty minutes went by before the first passengers trickled from the door of the terminal. Ingrid's friend was the last to appear. He turned his head to the left and right. Then, looking mildly annoyed, he stared straight ahead.

Ingrid's phone rang a few seconds later. "*Pronto?*" she said.

"Is that you I see sitting in that café?"

"Where else would I be?"

"Am I alone?"

"We'll find out in a minute."

He set off toward the café with the phone pressed to his ear. Ingrid, after determining that he was not under surveillance, aimed her remote at the BMW and pressed the unlock button. He tossed his overnight bag into the boot, then dropped into the passenger seat.

"Nice sled," he said.

Ingrid killed the connection and hurried out of the café, with her angry waiter in close pursuit. She handed him a twenty-euro banknote and, begging his forgiveness, slid behind the wheel of the BMW.

"Smooth as silk," said Gabriel. "Very impressive, indeed."

"Exactly the way I planned it." She started the engine and reversed out of the space. "What brings you to Mykonos, Mr. Allon?"

"I was wondering whether you might be interested in renewing our partnership."

"Where are you planning to send me this time? Tehran? Beirut?"

"Somewhere a bit more dangerous."

"Really? Where?"

"The Geneva Freeport."

———

The villa was white as a sugar cube and perched atop the cliffs rimming Saint Lazarus Bay. There were four bedrooms, two soaring great rooms, a fitness center, and a large swimming pool. They shared a bottle of Greek white wine outside on the terrace while watching the sun sinking into the Aegean. The evening air was blustery and cold, but there was not a butane gas heater in sight. Ingrid, like Gabriel's young daughter, was a climate alarmist.

"*The* Anna Rolfe?" she asked.

"I'm afraid so."

"She's a friend of yours?"

"You might say that."

"Do tell."

"It's possible that Anna and I had a brief romantic entanglement about a hundred years ago."

"What happened?"

Gabriel reluctantly provided Ingrid with a heavily redacted version of the story. It was better she heard it from his lips, he reckoned, than from Anna's.

"How could you?" asked Ingrid at the conclusion of his account.

"Wait until you get to know her better."

"Is she as difficult as they say?"

"Much worse. She fires her personal assistants almost as frequently as she changes the strings on her violins. I'm confident, however, that you'll be able to handle her."

"When do I start?"

"Anna would like you to meet her in Oslo on Thursday. You will then accompany her to Prague for the final three appearances of her winter tour, after which you will assist her in the sale of six paintings at Galerie Ricard in Geneva."

"Six paintings that will be forged by you?"

"*Forged* is an ugly word, Ingrid."

"You choose one instead."

"The paintings will be pastiches of existing works, and I will make no attempt to profit from their sale. Therefore, I am not, technically speaking, an art forger."

"*Pastiche* is a much nicer word than *forgery*, I'll grant you that. But it doesn't change the fact that Anna Rolfe will be engaged in criminal activity. And so will I."

"When have you ever worried about that before?"

"I happen to be wanted for a number of rather large scores in Switzerland. And if your little charade goes sideways, I might have to spend the next several years in a Swiss prison cell."

"Your scores, as you call them, are nothing in comparison to the stunts I've pulled on Swiss soil. I nevertheless have powerful friends in the Federal Police and security service. For that reason, I'm confident that you won't spend more than a year or two behind bars if you are charged as my accomplice."

She laughed quietly. "So how good *are* you, Mr. Allon?"

"With a paintbrush? Better than I am with a gun."

"Based on personal experience, I find that hard to believe. But there is an easier way to get that Picasso back, you know."

"Steal it?"

"*Steal* is an ugly word."

"I've been inside the Freeport on two separate occasions," said Gabriel. "A heist isn't possible. The only way to get that painting is to convince Monsieur Ricard to give it to us."

"You seem to be forgetting that I pinched a top-secret directive from the personal safe of the second most powerful man in Russia." Ingrid watched the sun slipping below the horizon. "You never told me how many of those border guards you killed that morning."

"I believe it was five."

"And how many shots did you fire?"

"Five," said Gabriel.

"While running downhill through knee-deep snow? That was rather impressive, Mr. Allon. But how did you get me across the Finnish border?"

"You don't remember?"

"No," she answered. "I don't remember anything that happened after the Range Rover crashed into that tree."

Gabriel gazed at the darkening sea. "Lucky you."

18

———

Great Torrington

The Chopper struck again later that same evening, this time in the town of Great Torrington, his first foray beyond the borders of Cornwall. The victim, a twenty-six-year-old employee of the Whiskers Pet Centre in South Street, was set upon sometime after 10:00 p.m. while walking home from the Black Horse pub, where she had been drinking with friends. She was felled by a single blow to the back of the head. Her assailant made no attempt to conceal the body.

Two of the friends with whom the victim had been drinking were male. Both had remained behind at the Black Horse after the victim departed, but both fell within the contours of the altogether useless psychological profile developed by a consultant to the Devon and Cornwall Police. Timothy Peel therefore questioned the two men at length before eliminating them as suspects. Their only misdeed, he concluded, was allowing an inebriated young woman to walk home alone after dark.

Peel also interviewed the victim's female drinking companions, her distraught parents, and her younger sister. The information he developed compelled him to pay a late-night call at the residence of a physically abusive former boyfriend. The interview established that the thirty-two-year-old mechanic was not a hatchet owner and that he wore a size eleven shoe, a size and a half larger than the footprints discovered at the crime scene. They had been made by a pair of Hi-Tec Aysgarth III walking boots. Police Constable Elenore Tremayne discovered two sets of identical prints—one incoming, the other outgoing—traversing Bastard's Lane, a narrow road on the town's northeastern fringe. It suggested to Peel that the killer had hiked into Great Torrington across the surrounding farmland and, after finding his prey, had departed by the same route.

It was nearly 5:00 a.m. when Peel toppled into his bed in Exeter. He slept for an hour, then drove out to Newquay to reinterview one of his favorite hatchet owners—a forty-eight-year-old schoolteacher, never married, slight of build and physically fit, who lived alone in a semidetached cottage in Penhallow Road. He had purchased his hatchet, a Magnusson Composite, twenty-five pounds plus VAT, at the B&Q in Falmouth. Peel caught him on his way out the door. They went inside for a cup of tea and a quiet chat.

"Why do you need a hatchet?" asked Peel as he looked out upon the treeless rear garden.

"You asked me that question the last time you were here."

"Did I?"

"Home defense," said the schoolteacher.

"Where were you last night?"

"Here."

"Doing what?"

"Grading papers."

"That's all?"

"A film on television."

"What was it called?"

"*The Remains of the Day.*"

"Are you sure you didn't pop over to the Black Horse in Great Torrington for a pint?"

"I don't consume alcohol."

"Ever take long walks in the countryside?"

"Most weekends, actually."

"What sort of boots do you wear?"

"Wellingtons."

"Do you happen to own a pair of Hi-Tecs? Size nine and half?"

"I'm a ten."

"Mind if I have a look in your closet?"

"I'm late for work."

"I'll need to see that hatchet of yours as well."

"Do you have a warrant?"

"I don't," admitted Peel. "But I can get one in about five minutes flat."

———

Peel left Penhallow Road at half past eight with the hatchet sealed in an evidence bag. While driving back to headquarters, he listened to the news on Radio 4. Not surprisingly, the Great Torrington slaying was the lead story. There was mounting pressure on the Metropolitan Police, which held legal jurisdiction throughout England and Wales, to take control of the investigation. Were that to happen, Peel would return to normal duty at the CID. His typical caseload consisted of narcotics investigations, sexual and physical assaults, antisocial behavior, and burglaries. The Chopper case, for all its gore and long hours, had been a welcome break in the monotony.

The headquarters of the Devon and Cornwall Police were located in Sidmouth Road in an industrial section of Exeter. Peel arrived a few minutes before ten and headed straight for DI Tony Fletcher's office. Fletcher was the lead detective on the Chopper investigation.

"How much time do we have left?" asked Peel.

"The announcement will be made at noon, but the lads from London are already on their way down here." Fletcher looked at the evidence bag in Peel's hand. "Where did you get that?"

"Neil Perkins."

"The schoolteacher from Newquay?"

Peel nodded.

"Does he have an alibi?"

"A lousy one, but he's a size ten."

"Close enough for me."

"Me, too."

"Type up your notes," said Fletcher. "And be quick about it. As of noon, we're officially off the case."

Peel sat down at his desk and updated Perkins's existing file with a description of the morning's interview and search. By 12:00 p.m. the file was in the hands of a ten-person team of detectives and forensic analysts from the Metropolitan Police, along with a Magnusson Composite hatchet and a copy of a sales receipt from the B&Q in Falmouth. So, too, was the blood-soaked clothing worn by Professor Charlotte Blake on the night of her murder near Land's End. The professor's Vauxhall, having been swept for evidence, was locked up in the Falmouth auto pound, but her mobile phone remained unaccounted for. Also missing was a yellow legal pad discovered on the desk in Professor Blake's cottage in Gunwalloe. Peel told DI Tony Fletcher that he must have mislaid it.

"Did it contain anything interesting?"

"Some notes about a painting." Peel shrugged his shoulders to indicate the matter was of no relevance to the investigation. "Looked like it might have been a Picasso."

"Never cared for him."

You wouldn't, thought Peel.

"For the life of me," Fletcher continued, "I don't understand why that woman was walking around Land's End after dark when there was a serial killer on the loose."

"Neither do I," said Peel. "But I'm sure the mighty Metropolitan Police will have it figured out in no time."

Fletcher pushed a case file across his desk. "Your new assignment."

"Anything interesting?"

"A rash of burglaries in Plymouth." Fletcher smiled. "You're welcome."

19

Cork Street

As Detective Sergeant Timothy Peel set off for Plymouth that February afternoon, the man who had asked him to accidentally misplace Charlotte Blake's legal pad was walking past the parade of luxury shops lining Burlington Arcade in Mayfair. He had returned to London on pressing business, namely, to recruit the final member of his operational team. The negotiations promised to be arduous and the price steep. Unlike Anna Rolfe, Nicholas Lovegrove never performed for free.

The prominent art consultant suggested lunch at the Wolseley, but Gabriel insisted they meet at his office instead. It was located in a redbrick building in Cork Street, two floors above one of London's most important contemporary art galleries. Lovegrove's receptionist was not at her desk when Gabriel arrived. His two underlings, both Courtauld-trained art historians, were likewise absent.

"As requested, Allon, it's just the two of us." They withdrew to Lovegrove's inner sanctum. It was like an exhibition room at the Tate Modern. "What is this all about?"

"A friend of mine is looking to unload a few paintings and requires the assistance of an experienced, trustworthy consultant. Naturally, I thought of you."

"What sort of paintings?"

Gabriel recited the names of six artists: Amedeo Modigliani, Vincent van Gogh, Pierre-Auguste Renoir, Paul Cézanne, Claude Monet, and Henri de Toulouse-Lautrec.

"Where are the paintings now?"

"They will soon be at the owner's villa on the Costa de Prata."

"Do you at least have photographs?"

"Not yet."

Lovegrove, with his well-tuned ear for art world gobbledygook, was dubious. "Does the owner have a name?"

"Anna Rolfe."

"Not the violinist?"

"One and the same."

"Don't tell me the paintings belonged to that awful father of hers."

"I'm afraid so."

"That means they're toxic."

"Which is why you're going to dispose of them with the utmost discretion at Galerie Ricard in the Geneva Freeport."

Lovegrove regarded Gabriel speculatively across the expanse of his desk. "I suppose this has something to do with that Picasso?"

"What Picasso, Nicky?"

"There is no Picasso?"

"Never was."

"And the six paintings by six of the greatest artists who ever lived?"

"They don't exist, either." Gabriel smiled. "Not yet, at least."

Lovegrove tugged at his French cuff while Gabriel explained the plan. The briefing contained no glaring omissions of fact or intent. Nicholas Lovegrove, a major figure in the art world, deserved nothing less.

"It might actually work, you know. It does, however, contain one serious flaw."

"Only one?"

"If everything goes according to plan, no money will change hands."

"That would be a crime, Nicky."

"No money, no commission. You see my point?"

"I was hoping you might agree to help me out of the goodness of your heart."

"You have me confused with someone else, Allon."

Gabriel sighed. "I will restore your Gentileschi for a flat fee of one hundred thousand euros. But only if we're able to recover the Picasso."

"You will receive fifty thousand for the Gentileschi, regardless of whether we find that painting."

"Deal," said Gabriel. "But I'll need the money in advance to cover my operational expenses."

Lovegrove took up a pen. "Where shall I send it?"

Gabriel recited the number and routing information for his much-depleted account at Mediobanca of Milan.

"It will be there by the close of business tomorrow afternoon."

"You have my gratitude, Nicky."

"What I want is your word that my role in *l'affaire Picasso* will never come to light."

"You have that, too."

Lovegrove screwed the cap onto his pen. "When would you like me to contact Monsieur Ricard?"

"There are six things I need to take care of first."

"The paintings?"

Gabriel nodded.

"In that case," said Lovegrove, "I suggest you get busy."

The crime of forgery requires more than raw artistic talent. The forger must know everything there is to know about the painter he is attempting to imitate—his technique, his palette, the type of canvases and stretchers he preferred. Plenty of forgers used contemporary canvases stained with tea or coffee, but Gabriel insisted on age-appropriate supports. A canvas from the 1950s wouldn't do for, say, a Cézanne or a Monet. Nor would Gabriel ever dream of using Italian or Dutch linen when forging a painting by a French artist. Yes, finding such canvases could be a time-consuming and costly endeavor. But using the wrong support was how a forger became a convict. Besides, Gabriel had his standards.

Equally challenging for the forger was the creation of a believable provenance that would explain the reemergence of a previously unknown work by a prominent artist. Gabriel also wished to leave the impression that the six paintings might have been seized from their rightful owners during the occupation of France. Therefore, a certain expertise was required. Fortunately, he knew an art historian who specialized in the wartime French art market. They met that evening at a brasserie on the rue Saint-Honoré. The historian insisted on sitting outside in the frigid night air so she could smoke her wretched cigarettes.

"Six fictitious provenances for six forged paintings?" asked Naomi Wallach. "Are you forgetting, Monsieur Allon, that I am currently employed by the French government?"

"I have no intention of profiting from my crime. I will use the forgeries only to make my approach to Galerie Ricard and recover the Picasso."

She drew a pen and notebook from her handbag. "I'll need the names of the artists, the titles, and the dimensions."

"I can't tell you anything about the motifs or dimensions until I acquire the canvases."

"What about the artists?"

Gabriel recited six names: Modigliani, Van Gogh, Renoir, Cézanne, Monet, and Toulouse-Lautrec.

Naomi looked up from her notebook. "Can you really—"

"Next question."

"Where did the paintings end up after they left France?"

"Zurich, I imagine."

"Private collection?"

"As private as it gets."

"And now?"

"Thence by descent to present owner."

———

Gabriel acquired his first canvas, a meritless nineteenth-century French School still life, the following morning at an antiques shop near the Jardin du Luxembourg. His second canvas, a landscape, also nineteenth century, he found early that afternoon in the sprawling Paris Flea Market. He placed the paintings in the back of his rented Volkswagen estate car. Then, after a stop at the Sennelier artists' supply shop on the Quai Voltaire, he headed south to Avignon.

He spent the night at the Hotel d'Europe and in the morning purchased his third canvas, another still life, at an art gallery on the rue Joseph Vernet. An all-too-brief visit to nearby Aix-en-Provence yielded a fourth canvas—a large but uninspired seascape—and a stop for lunch in Fréjus resulted in the unexpected acquisition of a lovely canvas by an unknown French flower painter.

He found his sixth canvas, a truly terrifying portrait of an elderly Provençal woman, at a gallery in Nice and arrived in Venice shortly after 2:00 a.m. The children awakened him at half past seven and insisted he walk them to school. Returning home, he removed the six canvases from their frames and ordered six faux antique replacement frames from Girotto Cornici of Milan. Then, scraper in hand, he reduced the work of six long-dead French artists to a pile of paint flakes.

Five of the canvases he covered in ground and underpaint, but the sixth he left unprimed, as that was Cézanne's preference. The master's usual palette contained eighteen paints. Gabriel used the same combination of paints—by the same paint maker, Sennelier of Paris—when executing a pastiche of one of Cézanne's many Provençal landscapes. He thought his brushwork was a touch hesitant, the telltale mark of a forgery, so he scraped the image from the canvas and swiftly executed another. Chiara agreed it was in every respect superior to the first.

"And you wonder why your son has no desire to become a painter."

"I can teach him everything he needs to know."

"Talent like yours can't be taught, darling. You were born with it."

"So was he."

Gabriel loaded his brush with peach black—so named because it was made with charred peach pits—and stretched his hand toward the bottom right corner of the canvas.

"Shouldn't you practice it once or twice?" asked Chiara.

Frowning, Gabriel executed Cezanne's signature as though it were his own.

"Freak," she whispered.

With his Nikon camera Gabriel documented his crime, lest his handiwork ever leak onto the legitimate art market. He emailed one of the photographs to Naomi Wallach, and an hour later she sent him her first fictitious provenance. The last line read "Thence by descent to present owner."

Gabriel waited until 8:10 p.m. before ringing the owner's latest personal assistant. She took the call in a backstage dressing room at the Oslo Concert Hall, where she was alone with a multimillion-dollar Stradivarius violin. Her first day on the job, she said, had gone much better than expected.

"I have to say, she's not the monster you made her out to be. In fact, she's really quite charming."

Gabriel killed the connection and, annoyed, cleaned his brushes and palette. Surely, he told himself, she had been referring to a different Anna Rolfe.

20

Venice–Zurich

For much of the following week, Gabriel remained a prisoner of his studio. His face was unshaven, his mood was brittle, never more so than when he was working on his Van Gogh, a pastiche of the blue-green olive trees that Vincent painted while living at the Saint-Paul Asylum in Saint-Rémy-de-Provence. When the work was finished, Gabriel added a signature to the bottom right corner, underlined and at a downward angle, and sent a photo to Naomi Wallach in Paris. She replied an hour later with a fake provenance. The salutation to her email read "Bravo, Vincent!"

He painted his Modigliani, a seated nude, in a single afternoon, but required three days to produce a suitable Renoir and another two until he was satisfied with his pastiche of Monet's *Low Tide at Pourville*. The Toulouse-Lautrec he saved for last, choosing for his subject matter the female form, which the artist had studied at length during his frequent visits to a brothel on the rue d'Amboise. An alcoholic with an adult torso mounted atop deformed child-sized legs, Toulouse-Lautrec often worked while under the influence of a concoction he called the Earthquake Cocktail, a potent mixture of absinthe and cognac. Gabriel made do with Cortese di Gavi and Debussy and used Chiara as the model for his prostitute. Naomi Wallach, upon receipt of the photograph and dimensions, declared it the finest Toulouse-Lautrec she had ever seen.

He secured the six paintings to their new frames and shipped them to Anna's villa on the Costa de Prata. A week later, with the help of Carlos and Maria, her longtime caretaker and housekeeper, he hung them in her music room. He met with Nicholas Lovegrove at his office in Cork Street the following afternoon, once again with no staff present. Lovegrove examined the photos in silence for several minutes before rendering his verdict.

"You are a truly dangerous man with a paintbrush in your hand, Allon. These really do look authentic. The question is, how much scientific scrutiny can they withstand?"

"Very little," Gabriel admitted. "But Ricard will be inclined to accept them as genuine because of the source."

"Anna's father?"

Gabriel nodded. "A well-known collector with a taste for looted art."

Lovegrove turned his attention to the six provenances. "They're full of holes. No reputable dealer would ever touch them."

"But you're not offering them to a reputable dealer. You're offering them to Edmond Ricard."

Lovegrove reached for his phone and dialed. "*Bonjour*, Monsieur Ricard. Listen, I have a very special client with six incredible paintings to sell, and yours is the first name that popped into my mind. Is there any chance we can stop by the gallery Thursday afternoon? . . . Two o'clock? See you then."

Lovegrove rang off and looked at Gabriel. "When do I get to meet this very special client of mine?"

"You're having dinner with her Wednesday evening at her home in Zurich. But don't worry, I'll be joining you."

"Is she as difficult as they say?"

"Anna?" Gabriel frowned. "Evidently not."

Next morning Nicholas Lovegrove received an email from Anna Rolfe's personal assistant, a certain Ingrid Johansen, with an itinerary for his trip to Switzerland. She had taken the liberty, she explained, of booking his air travel—first class, of course—and hotel accommodations at Zurich's exclusive Dolder Grand. Ground transportation would be handled by Anna's longtime personal chauffeur. "If there's anything else you require," she wrote in conclusion, "please feel free to contact me."

The chauffeur, as promised, was waiting in the arrivals hall of Zurich's Kloten Airport when Lovegrove's flight arrived late Wednesday afternoon. It was a drive of twenty minutes to the Rolfe family's imposing granite-colored villa, which stood atop the wooded hill known as the Zürichberg. Lovegrove climbed the steep front steps to the portico, where a startlingly pretty woman in her mid-thirties waited to receive him.

"You must be Ms. Johansen."

"I must be," she said with an enchanting smile.

Lovegrove stepped into the soaring entrance hall. From somewhere deep within the grand house came the liquid sound of a violin. "Is that really her?" he asked quietly.

"Yes, of course." The woman relieved Lovegrove of his overcoat. "Mr. Allon arrived a few moments ago. He's anxious to see you."

Lovegrove followed the woman into a formally furnished drawing room. The paintings adorning the walls included an arresting portrait of a handsome young Florentine nobleman. Gabriel was standing before the canvas, a hand to his chin, his head tilted slightly to one side.

"Manner of Raphael?" asked Lovegrove.

"No," replied Gabriel. "Raphael Raphael."

Lovegrove indicated the painting hanging next to it. "Rembrandt?"

Gabriel nodded. "Her Frans Hals is in the next room, along with a Rubens and a couple of pictures by Lucas Cranach the Elder."

Lovegrove lifted his eyes toward the ceiling. "I can't believe that's actually her," he said, sotto voce.

"You don't have to whisper, Nicky. She can't hear a thing when she's practicing."

"So I've read. But is it really true that her mother—"

"Yes," interjected Gabriel.

"In this very house?"

Gabriel nodded toward a row of French doors. "Outside in the garden. Anna was the one who found her."

"And her father?" asked Lovegrove.

"You're standing on the spot where it happened."

Lovegrove took two steps to the left and listened to the silken sound of Anna's violin. "You never told me how you know her."

"Julian arranged for me to clean a painting for her father."

"Which one?"

Gabriel pointed toward the Raphael. "That one."

———

Anna insisted on preparing dinner, so they gathered around her in the kitchen and held their collective breath while she attacked a large yellow onion with a razor-sharp knife.

"What are we having?" asked Gabriel warily.

"Boeuf bourguignon. It's a French country stew beloved by peasants like you."

"Perhaps I should handle the parts involving Swiss-made weaponry."

"Absolutely not!" She looked him straight in the eye as the knife reduced a carrot to perfect orange disks. "A man of your talent should never handle sharp objects."

"Anna, please."

"Shit!" she whispered and thrust her left forefinger into her mouth. "Look what you've done."

Gabriel hastened to his feet. "Let me see it."

Smiling, Anna showed him the undamaged appendage. "Works every time."

Gabriel relieved her of the knife and finished chopping the vegetables.

"Not bad," she said, looking over his shoulder.

"I happen to be married to a world-class cook."

"That was cruel." Anna snatched a slice of carrot from the cutting board. "Even for you."

Fortunately, Anna's butcher had already cubed the beef. Thirty minutes later, browned and seasoned and drenched in a bottle of excellent burgundy, it was simmering in a 350-degree oven. They shared another bottle of the wine in the half-light of the drawing room while Anna led Nicholas Lovegrove on an hour-long guided tour of her family's scandalous past. She omitted several episodes in which Gabriel had played a starring role.

"You can be sure that Monsieur Ricard is well aware of the many skeletons in my closet. I will do my best to convince him that I am just as unscrupulous as my father. It shouldn't be difficult. As you might have heard, I can be quite unpleasant at times." She looked at Gabriel. "Wouldn't you agree?"

"I'll withhold my answer until after I've devoured at least two servings of that boeuf bourguignon."

They ate at the table in the kitchen while listening to Radio Swiss Jazz on an old Bose. Anna was at her most charming, regaling them with uproarious tales of her untidy love life late into the evening. Lovegrove finally left around eleven and headed to the Dolder Grand. Ingrid saw to the dishes while Gabriel, in the drawing room, gave his asset a final operational briefing.

"And where will you be while we're inside the Freeport?" she asked.

"Here in Zurich. But don't worry, I'll be able to hear everything."

"How?"

He opened his laptop and tapped the trackpad. A moment later came the sound of water splashing in the basin. In the background was Franco Ambrosetti's lovely version of "Flamenco Sketches."

"What's the source of the audio?" asked Anna.

"Your new assistant's mobile phone."

"Have you been listening in on me?"

"Every chance I get."

Gabriel closed the computer. Anna allowed a silence to settle over the room before speaking. "Do you remember the night you found that photo in my father's study?"

"There were two, as I recall."

"But only one that mattered." It was the photograph of Anna's father standing next to Adolf Hitler and Reichsführer-SS Heinrich Himmler. "What does one do with such knowledge?" she asked. "How does one live one's life?"

"One fills the world with music until she can no longer hold a bow."

"That day is fast approaching. These young violinists run circles around me."

"But none of them *sound* like you."

Anna went to the French doors and peered into the garden. "That's because they didn't grow up in this house."

21

Geneva Freeport

The ancient city of commerce and Calvinism known as Geneva lay at the western end of Lac Léman, three hours by motorcar from Zurich. Its most recognizable landmark was not its medieval cathedral or elegant Old Town but the Jet d'Eau, which burst suddenly to life as Anna's Mercedes sped across the Pont du Mont-Blanc. She was seated behind her driver, with Ingrid at her side. Her art adviser had been relegated to the passenger seat. Having spent most of the drive on the phone to clients, he now extolled the geyser-like fountain's virtues as though he were reading from a tourist guidebook.

"It's quite an engineering marvel, if you think about it. The water leaves the nozzle at two hundred kilometers per hour and rises up to a hundred forty meters. At any given moment, more than seven thousand liters are airborne."

Ingrid was unable to restrain herself. "And do you know how much electricity that ridiculous fountain uses each year? A megawatt. All of it wasted."

"You're concerned about global warming, I take it."

"Aren't you?"

"Oh, I suppose so. But what can we do about it at this point besides hope for the best?" Lovegrove checked the time. It was already two fifteen. "Perhaps I should ring Ricard and let him know we're running late."

"You will do no such thing," declared Anna. Then she looked at Ingrid and said, "Unless our friend believes otherwise."

Ingrid consulted her messages before answering. "He doesn't, Madame Rolfe."

"Great minds think alike."

Ingrid returned the phone to her handbag as the Hôtel Métropole slid past her window. The elegant lobby bar, with its wealthy clientele, had once been one of her favorite hunting grounds. Her last visit had yielded an attaché case stuffed with more than a million dollars in cash. Ingrid, as was her custom, had given half of the money to charity. The rest she had entrusted to her account manager at Banca Privada d'Andorra.

She had experienced similar success at the Grand Hotel Kempinski, much beloved by grotesquely rich Gulf Arabs, and along the private bank–lined pavements of the rue du Rhône, a pickpocket's paradise. She had never, however, had occasion to visit the infamous Geneva Freeport. The very thought of being inside the facility—repository of untold billions' worth of paintings, gold bars, and other assorted treasures—had set her ablaze with the familiar craving. It had been building all day. Now she felt feverish with anticipation.

Anna's voice was a welcome diversion. "Are you feeling all right, Ingrid?"

"I'm sorry, Madame Rolfe?"

"You look unwell."

"I'm just a touch carsick, that's all. But not to worry." Ingrid pointed toward a row of featureless gray-and-red buildings looming before them. "We have arrived at our destination."

The enormous facility was several hundred meters in length and surrounded by a screened fence topped with razor wire and security cameras. A stubby gray annex, home to numerous small firms doing business within the boundaries of the Freeport, jutted from the southernmost end. Edmond Ricard's gallery was located on the third floor. Immaculately groomed and attired, he waited in the ill-lit corridor, visibly annoyed that Lovegrove and his mystery client had committed the unpardonable offense of arriving late for a business appointment in Switzerland. The dealer's countenance changed the instant he recognized the client's famous face. He nevertheless greeted her with Freeport discretion.

"Madame Rolfe," he said quietly. "It is an honor to have you in my gallery."

Anna nodded once but declined Ricard's outstretched hand. Unnerved, he turned to Ingrid.

"And you are?"

"Madame Rolfe's assistant."

"A pleasure to meet you," said Ricard, and led them into the gallery's small foyer. Ingrid scarcely noticed the vibrant painting by Frank Stella hanging on the wall; she was far more interested in the lock on the outer door. It was Swiss-made, mechanical, and purportedly unpickable, which was not the case.

The next room they entered was windowless and white-carpeted and furnished with matching Barcelona chairs. A single painting hung on each wall—a Matisse, a Pollock, a Lichtenstein, and an enormous canvas by Willem de Kooning.

"Good heavens," breathed Ingrid. "Isn't that the painting that fetched—"

"Yes, it is," said Ricard, cutting her off. "The owner has placed it on consignment with me. It can be yours for two hundred and fifty million, if you're interested."

He led them through a second exhibition room and into his office. The desk was black and spotless save for a modern lamp and a laptop computer. Two bottles of mineral water, one sparkling, one still, stood in the center of a small conference table. Anna, after taking her seat, declined Ricard's offer of refreshment and likewise fended off several attempts by the dealer to engage her in small talk.

Ricard finally turned to Lovegrove. "You mentioned something about six paintings."

Lovegrove opened his attaché case and removed a manila folder. Inside were six large photographs, which he laid on the table before Ricard. The dealer examined each image at length, then looked up at Anna without expression.

"I take it these paintings belonged to your father."

"They did, Monsieur Ricard."

"It is my understanding that his estate relinquished all the Impressionist and Postimpressionist paintings that he acquired during the war."

"That is true. But my father purchased these paintings several years *after* the war."

Lovegrove laid the six provenances on the table, and Ricard turned deliberately through the pages. "They are far from pristine," he said at the conclusion of his review. "But I've seen worse."

"I ran them through the relevant Holocaust databases," said Lovegrove. "There are no claims against any of the six paintings."

"I'm relieved to hear that. But it doesn't change the fact that they were in the hands of a rather notorious collector." Ricard turned to Anna. "Forgive my candor, Madame Rolfe, but your father's connection to the paintings will significantly reduce their value on the open market."

"Not if you conceal my identity from the buyers, Monsieur Ricard."

The art dealer did not dispute the point. "Where are the paintings now?"

"Not in Switzerland," replied Anna.

"Does the Swiss government know you have them?"

"It does not."

"May I ask why not?"

"I didn't know about the existence of the paintings until several years after my father's death. As you might imagine, I had no wish to relive the drama of the Rolfe affair."

"Still, the fact that you have failed to declare the paintings is a complicating factor. You see, Madame Rolfe, if I sell them on your behalf, you will have to explain the windfall profit to the cantonal tax authorities in Zurich, which will alert them to your previous misconduct." Ricard lowered his voice. "Unless, of course, we were to conceal the sale as well."

"How?"

"By structuring the transaction in a way that it takes place offshore and anonymously. Here in the Geneva Freeport, such sales are, as the Americans like to say, par for the course." Ricard smiled at Lovegrove. "But then your art adviser already knows this. Which is why you both are here today."

Lovegrove interceded on his client's behalf. "And what if Madame Rolfe were interested in a transaction that didn't involve an overseas bank account or shell company?"

"What sort of transaction?"

"A trade of her father's paintings for something a bit more, how shall I say, pristine in provenance."

"A trade will not solve your client's tax problems."

"It will if the new paintings remain here at the Freeport."

"Also par for the course," said Ricard. "Many of my clients leave their paintings here for years in order to avoid taxation and duty.

And oftentimes when they elect to sell a painting, the shipping process involves nothing more than moving a crate from one storage vault to another. The Freeport contains the greatest art collection in the world, much of which is for sale. I'm sure we can find something of interest to Madame Rolfe."

"She prefers contemporary works," said Lovegrove.

"Does she like de Kooning?"

"Madame Rolfe would like to carefully consider her options before making a decision."

"Of course," said Ricard. "In the meantime, however, there is the small question of the gallery's commission."

"Because Madame Rolfe cannot write you a check to cover the cost of your fee, you will have to structure the deal in such a way that takes your own interests into consideration."

It was an invitation to weight the transaction in the gallery's favor. Ricard quite obviously found the suggestion to his liking. "That leaves the six paintings," he said, glancing down at the photographs. "We need to move them from their current location here to the Freeport. And we have to do it in a way that involves a transaction. After all, the Freeport is not a public storage facility. All of the paintings and other valuables locked away here are technically in transit."

"It has to be done in a way that protects Madame Rolfe's identity."

"Not a problem," said Ricard with a dismissive wave of his hand. "I do it all the time. Galerie Ricard will be the buyer of record. Once the paintings are admitted into the Freeport, I will place them in a vault controlled solely by Madame Rolfe. Her name, however, will appear nowhere in my files, and the Freeport authorities will know nothing of our connection."

"It all sounds a bit like my father's bank," said Anna.

"With one important exception, Madame Rolfe. The Freeport

never gives up its secrets." Ricard's pen was hovering over his note-book. "You were about to tell me where to send the shippers to collect the six paintings."

Anna recited the address of her villa on the Costa de Prata.

"How does Tuesday sound?"

It was Ingrid, keeper of the schedule, who answered. She did so while looking down at her phone. "Tuesday would be fine, Monsieur Ricard."

22

Geneva Freeport

Anna and Ingrid traveled from Zurich to the Costa de Prata to supervise the ritual crating of the six paintings. The works arrived in Geneva the following Thursday and were cleared into the Freeport early Friday morning. "One of the greatest finds in living memory," declared Edmond Ricard during a midday phone call to Nicholas Lovegrove in London. The Swiss dealer nevertheless wanted his experts to give the canvases a thorough going-over before moving forward. Gabriel spent five anxious days in Venice awaiting their verdict, which was favorable. Ricard set the valuation at an astonishing $325 million, and Lovegrove provided the dealer with a list of stratospherically expensive artists that were of interest to his client. It did not include the name Pablo Picasso.

Another forty-eight hours would go by before Ricard, with apologies for the delay, sent Lovegrove a list of paintings for his client's consideration. Included were the Pollock and de Kooning that had been on display in Ricard's gallery, along with works by Gustav Klimt, Mark Rothko, André Derain, Georges Braque, Fernand Léger, Wassily Kandinsky, Andy Warhol, Robert Motherwell, and

Cy Twombly. Lovegrove called it a promising start, and three days later he was back in the Geneva Freeport with his client and her assistant in tow. For two hours they roamed the corridors and vaults of the facility, with Gabriel monitoring the proceedings from Venice via Ingrid's phone. Lovegrove's client was on her best behavior, but far from dazzled.

"Is there something specific you're looking for?" asked Ricard when they were back in his office.

"I'll know it when I see it," said Anna.

"The de Kooning would be a fine investment, Madame Rolfe. The Pollock as well. I'm prepared to take your six works in trade for both canvases and call it a day."

"Put it in writing," interjected Lovegrove. "In the meantime, we'd like to see what else is on the market."

The next viewing took place the following week. It included additional canvases by Pollock and Rothko, yet another de Kooning, a Basquiat, a Bacon, and a Jasper Johns—none of which Lovegrove's client found to her liking. Frustrated, Ricard suggested they have a look at one final painting—an extraordinary opportunity, or so he claimed, that had just come onto the market. It was stored in Building 2, Corridor 4, Vault 39. When Ricard opened the locked metal shipping container, Madame Rolfe drew a sharp intake of breath. A photograph of the painting, snapped by her assistant, appeared instantly on Gabriel's computer screen in Venice.

They were getting warmer.

———

The work in question, a streetscape of Barcelona, was painted by Pablo Picasso during the three-year phase of his career that would come to be known as the Blue Period. Ricard expressed surprise at Madame Rolfe's reaction to the painting. He was under the impression, he said, that she had no interest in the Spaniard's work.

"Wherever did you get an idea like that?"

"Your art adviser."

Anna gave Lovegrove a withering look. "An oversight on his part, I assure you."

"There are more than a thousand Picassos stored here at the Freeport," explained Ricard. "I know of at least a hundred that are currently on the market."

"I'd like to see every one of them."

Ricard showed them three more Picassos after lunch and four others the following Tuesday. Two of the canvases were from the Rose Period, two were Cubist works painted during the First World War, and two were later works executed by Picasso shortly before his death. The last canvas they viewed was a surrealist work—a woman seated before a window—painted by Picasso in 1936 while he was living on the rue la Boétie in Paris. Anna told the Swiss art dealer that it was her favorite of the lot.

"The Cubist pieces are quite fine as well," the dealer pointed out.

"But this one is special."

"They are not easy to come by, Madame Rolfe. I know of one other similar work here in the Freeport, but it's unlikely the owner will agree to part with it."

"Is there any way he might allow us to at least see it?"

"The Freeport is not an art gallery. Collectors keep their paintings here for a reason."

They were back again three days later, but the canvases Ricard showed them were all from the postwar period. They broke for the weekend—Anna and Ingrid spent it in Zermatt, Lovegrove at his weekend home in Tunbridge Wells—and the following Wednesday they viewed fourteen stunning Picassos. None were surrealist works from the thirties, leaving Anna predictably underwhelmed.

"What about the other surrealist canvas you mentioned?" she asked.

"I spoke with the owner's representative last evening."

"And?"

"I'm not sure I can convince him to sell it. But if I can, he will drive an extremely hard bargain."

"I have a gift card worth three hundred and twenty-five million dollars that was left to me by my father. Needless to say, money is no object."

They were the four most dangerous words to utter in front of an art dealer, especially a dealer who plied his trade inside the Geneva Freeport. "If you have a few minutes," he said, glancing at his watch, "we can have a look at it now."

"I'd love nothing more," replied Anna.

The painting was stored in a crowded vault in Building 3, Corridor 6. The markings on the metal shipping crate contained no clue as to the contents—a portrait of a woman, oil on canvas, painted by Picasso in his studio on the rue la Boétie in 1937. They all four gazed at the painting for a long moment in silence.

"Dimensions?" asked Lovegrove at last, as though it were the least of his concerns.

"Ninety-four by sixty-six centimeters," replied Ricard.

Lovegrove looked at Anna. "What do you think?"

"Give him whatever he wants," she said, and walked out.

The negotiations commenced late the following morning after Lovegrove had settled into his office in Cork Street. As promised, the owner of the Picasso—Ricard claimed not to know his identity, or even whether the owner was an individual or a consortium of investors—played hard to get.

"He wants the Modigliani, the Van Gogh, the Cézanne, and the Monet."

"For a single Picasso? I'm sure he does," replied Lovegrove. "But he's not going to get them."

"Perhaps you should put the offer to your client before you say no."

"I won't allow her to make a foolish deal, no matter how badly she wants that painting."

Forty-eight hours passed before Lovegrove heard from Ricard again. It seemed the owner of the painting had refused to move off his opening position. The ball, said Ricard, was on Lovegrove's side of the net.

"The Modigliani and the Van Gogh," he said.

"There's no way he'll go for it."

"*Who* won't go for it, Monsieur Ricard?"

"The man at the other end of the line. Never mind who he is."

"Put the offer to him. I'll wait to hear from you."

The Swiss dealer waited until five thirty the following afternoon to ring Lovegrove with the response. "The owner still wants all four paintings, but I think he might do it for the Modigliani, the Van Gogh, and the Cézanne."

"Why wouldn't he? It's the deal of a lifetime."

"Is that a yes, Monsieur Lovegrove?"

He indicated, grudgingly, that it was. By ten o'clock the next morning they had an agreement in principle.

"That leaves the Monet, the Renoir, and the Toulouse-Lautrec," said Ricard. "How does Madame Rolfe wish to spend the balance of her so-called gift card?"

"The Pollock."

"Done."

Lovegrove immediately rang Gabriel with the news. "We have a deal, Allon."

"Yes, I know."

"How?"

Gabriel rang off without answering. Lovegrove, after having a celebratory martini with Sarah Bancroft at Wiltons, walked over to Regent Street and bought himself a new phone.

23

Venice–Geneva

Ricard required seventy-two hours to draw up the sales agreement, hardly unusual for a transaction involving nearly a billion dollars' worth of art. He suggested they meet again at the Freeport the following Thursday at 4:00 p.m. to sign the documents and exchange the eight paintings. Lovegrove insisted the deal was contingent on a final authentication of the Picasso and the Pollock, as both artists were among the world's most frequently forged. Ricard saw nothing unusual in the request.

"When would your connoisseur like to see the paintings?"

"Thursday afternoon would be fine. He won't require more than a few minutes to make a determination."

"One of those, is he?"

"You might say that."

Lovegrove's connoisseur, whom he did not identify, passed those three days in Venice. He went to the church of Santa Maria degli Angeli in Murano each morning, avoiding a certain bar on the Fondamente Nove, and busied himself with the lesser paintings adorning the nave. On Tuesday he took delivery of an art carrying case—one large enough to transport a painting measuring 94 by 66 centimeters—and on Wednesday he accompanied his son to his math lesson at the university. That evening he sat at the kitchen counter drinking Brunello while his wife prepared dinner.

The BBC's *Six O'Clock News* issued from the Bluetooth speaker. Prime Minister Hillary Edwards, facing a rebellion within her Cabinet, had announced her resignation as leader of the Conservative Party. She would remain a caretaker prime minister until a new leader had been chosen. The Party's powerful 1922 Committee, hoping to avoid a protracted succession fight, had put in place rules that would limit the field of candidates to just three.

"Who are we rooting for?" asked Chiara.

"Someone who can stabilize the country and get the economy back on its feet."

"Is that Hugh Graves?"

"His colleagues appear to think so."

"He seems rather fond of you."

"Unlike your boyfriend from Bar Cupido," remarked Gabriel.

"I guess you're not hungry tonight." Chiara muted the newscast and changed the topic of conversation to Gabriel's impending trip to Geneva. "You don't really think he's going to let you walk out of the Freeport with the Picasso, do you?"

"Gennaro?"

"Edmond Ricard," sighed Chiara.

"I don't intend to give him much of a choice."

"And if he decides to call the authorities?"

"Then things will get very interesting for all the parties involved."

"Especially your girlfriend."

"Not to mention her assistant," added Gabriel.

"And if everything goes according to plan?"

"I will destroy my six forgeries so Ricard can't slip them onto the market. Then I will personally deliver the Picasso to Naomi Wallach in Paris. She's already searching for Emanuel Cohen's rightful heir."

"Someone is about to become extraordinarily rich."

"And someone else is going to be rather miffed."

"The owner of the Picasso?"

Gabriel nodded.

"One wonders why he agreed to sell it in the first place," said Chiara.

"We made him an offer he couldn't refuse. Three paintings of extraordinary value and a guarantee that the Picasso would remain locked away in the Freeport for the foreseeable future."

"And to think you wanted to go to the police."

"Yes," said Gabriel as he held his wineglass up to the light. "How could I have been so foolish?"

He awoke early the following morning and dressed in a pair of black trousers, a black pullover, and a gray cashmere sport jacket. Anna and Ingrid collected him at Geneva Airport at half past three. They stopped at an office supplies store long enough for Gabriel to purchase a retractable utility knife, then headed for the Freeport.

"You're not fooling anyone in that ridiculous man-in-black outfit," said Anna. "You can be sure that Monsieur Ricard will know exactly who you are the minute you walk into his gallery."

"Which will make the proceedings go much more smoothly."

"You're not going to strike him, are you?" Anna looked at Ingrid and whispered, "He can be quite violent when he loses his temper."

"I find that difficult to believe."

"You don't know him as well as I do. At least I hope not."

"She doesn't," interjected Gabriel.

"I'm relieved. After all, she's still a child."

"But hardly an innocent."

"Yes," said Anna. "Ingrid told me all about her lifelong struggle with impulse control."

"And you, of course, reciprocated with a tragic tale of your own."

"How did you guess?"

Anna's driver parked outside the office block at the southern end of the Freeport, and Gabriel and Ingrid followed her into the lobby. The guard at the security desk consulted a clipboard, saw that Madame Rolfe and her party were expected at 4:00 p.m., and directed them to the lift. Upstairs on the third floor, Ingrid pressed the intercom button next to the entrance of Galerie Ricard but received no response. Anna gave it a try and met with the same result.

"Perhaps we should phone him," she said.

Gabriel dialed the gallery's number and after several rings was invited to leave a message. He killed the connection and rang Ricard's mobile. There was no answer.

"He must be with another client," suggested Anna.

"As far as Edmond Ricard is concerned, you're the only client in the world that matters right now." Gabriel tried the door but it was locked tight. Then he glanced at Ingrid and asked, "I don't suppose you have a magic bump key in your handbag?"

"Personal assistants to world-famous musicians don't carry bump keys, Mr. Allon."

Gabriel drew a pair of lockpick tools from the breast pocket of his coat. "I suppose these will have to do."

Ingrid shielded the view from the security camera while Gabriel inserted the tools into the barrel of the lock. Anna was beside herself. "What happens if the alarm goes off?" she whispered.

"A global icon will be arrested for breaking into an art gallery in the Geneva Freeport."

"Along with her assistant," murmured Ingrid.

Gabriel moved the lockpick in and out of the barrel, expertly manipulating the pins.

"How much longer is it going to take you?" asked Anna.

"That depends on how many more times you interrupt me."

He turned the lock to the right and the latch gave way.

"Not bad," said Ingrid.

"You should see him with a gun," replied Anna.

"I have, actually."

Gabriel opened the door. There was no audible alarm.

"Perhaps there's hope for us yet," said Anna.

"Unless the alarm is silent," Ingrid pointed out. "Then we're totally busted."

Gabriel followed the two women into the gallery's vestibule and allowed the door to close behind them. Anna cheerfully called out Ricard's name and received only silence in reply.

"Perhaps you should play him a partita instead," remarked Gabriel, and entered the first exhibition room. The same four paintings were on display, including the Pollock, which in Gabriel's hurried opinion was authentic. Two of his six forgeries, the Van Gogh and the Modigliani, were propped on the baize-covered easels in the second room. The other four works—the Renoir, the Cézanne, the Monet, and the Toulouse-Lautrec—were leaning against the walls. There was no sign of an untitled portrait of a woman in the surrealist style, oil on canvas, 94 by 66 centimeters, by Pablo Picasso.

Ingrid tried the latch on the door to Ricard's office.

"Don't tell me it's locked," said Gabriel.

"It appears so," she replied, and moved aside.

Gabriel went to work, and the lock surrendered in less than thirty seconds. His hand hovered motionless over the latch.

"What are you waiting for?" asked Anna.

"Do you really want me to answer that question?"

Gabriel turned the latch and slowly opened the door. The familiar odor hit him at once, metallic and rusty, the smell of blood. It had spilled from the bullet holes in the man slumped behind the sleek black desk. Lying before him was a blood-soaked sales agreement bearing the name of the world's most famous violinist, and on the carpeted floor was an empty frame. Gabriel didn't bother taking the measurements. Any fool could see that the dimensions of the missing painting were 94 by 66 centimeters.

"Your Picasso?" asked Anna.

"No," answered Gabriel. "It *was* my Picasso."

"I suppose this means we're busted."

"Totally."

PART TWO

———

The Heist

24

Place de Cornavin

The headquarters of the NDB, Switzerland's small but capable internal security and foreign intelligence service, were located at Papiermühlestrasse 20 in the tranquil Swiss capital city of Bern. Christoph Bittel, the NDB's newly appointed director-general, was presiding over a meeting of his division chiefs when, at 4:12 p.m., he received a call on his personal mobile phone. After seeing the name displayed on the screen, he excused himself to conduct the conversation in the privacy of his office. Later he was glad he had.

"This might come as a surprise," he said, "but I'm inclined to hang up and return to my meeting."

"I wouldn't, if I were you, Bittel."

"Let's hear it."

The explanation was less than thirty seconds in length and involved a missing painting, a dead art dealer, and perhaps the most famous woman in Switzerland. Bittel was nevertheless certain he was getting only a small part of the story.

"Don't even think about leaving that gallery. I'll get over to Geneva as quickly as I can."

Criminal matters were not the province of the NDB—not unless they involved espionage or a threat to the Confederation's security, which this incident, at least for the moment, did not. It did, however, represent a potential threat to Swiss business interests, if for no other reason than the crime had occurred inside the Geneva Freeport. The facility had already been the source of several embarrassing scandals, including one involving a notorious Italian dealer of looted antiquities. If the truth be told, Bittel was not fond of the Freeport or the global superrich who hid their treasures there. Still, it was in his interests, and Switzerland's, to contain any damage.

And so Christoph Bittel rang the chief of the Police Cantonale de Genève and to the best of his ability explained the situation. And the chief, who was justifiably dubious as to the accuracy of what she was being told, agreed that discretion was called for. She immediately rang the head of the *sûreté*, the criminal division of the force, and at 4:27 p.m. the first detectives entered the stubby office block at the southern end of the Freeport. On their way to the lift, they instructed the security guard on duty in the lobby to lock all of the building's doors and remain at his post until further notice. They did not bother to tell him where they were going or why they were there.

Upstairs, they knocked on the glass door of Galerie Ricard and were admitted by a man of medium height and build dressed mostly in black. He was accompanied by two women, one the detectives recognized instantly and one they did not. The victim was in his office along with an empty frame. In one of the gallery's two exhibition rooms were six paintings by six of the most famous artists who had ever lived, or so it appeared to the detectives. Curiously, all six of the works had been cut to ribbons.

In short order they established that the gentleman clad largely in black was in fact the legendary former intelligence operative Gabriel Allon, that the older of the two women was indeed the renowned violinist Anna Rolfe, and that the second woman, a Danish citizen named Ingrid Johansen, was Madame Rolfe's assistant. Subsequent questioning revealed that they had arrived at the gallery at 4:00 p.m. to conclude a transaction involving several valuable works of art, including a 1937 surrealist painting by Pablo Picasso. The former intelligence operative had gained entry to the gallery by picking the lock, whereupon he discovered that Monsieur Ricard had been slain and the Picasso stolen.

"Do you have any idea who might have done it?"

"I'm betting it was the person who arrived at the gallery a couple of hours before we did. The security guard downstairs undoubtedly got a good look at him. In fact, if I had to guess, he might even have some video."

One of the detectives headed down to the lobby to have a word with the guard. Yes, Galerie Ricard had had a visitor earlier that afternoon, a sturdy German in his late thirties. He had arrived at 2:17 p.m. and was carrying an art transport case. He was carrying the same case when he left the building approximately ten minutes later.

"Name?"

"Andreas Hoffmann."

"Did you have a look at his ID?"

The guard shook his head.

"Where do I get the video?"

"The central security office."

It was located in the Freeport's main administration building. But as it turned out there were no images of a sturdy German to be found there. Someone, it seemed, had hacked into the Freeport's computer network and erased six months' worth of saved video. At which point the murder of Edmond Ricard, gallerist at the Geneva Freeport, became a matter for Christoph Bittel and the NDB.

It was approaching 8:00 p.m. when the Swiss intelligence chief finally arrived in Geneva. He headed not for the Freeport but the headquarters of the Police Cantonale in the Place de Cornavin. The world-renowned violinist and her assistant were in the staff canteen, surrounded by several admiring officers. The former intelligence operative was in an interview room, where he had been questioned at length by the head of the *sûreté*. Because the session was recorded, the subject had been less than truthful. But the version of the story he gave Christoph Bittel, a trusted friend and partner from his previous life, was for the most part accurate.

"Do you know how many crimes you committed?"

"None, actually."

"The shipment of those six paintings from Portugal to the Freeport was a violation of Swiss law."

"The paintings weren't genuine, though."

"Yet another crime on your part," said Bittel. He was tall and bald and bespectacled, with the cold demeanor of a Zurich private banker. "Needless to say, it is illegal to traffic in forged paintings here in Switzerland."

"But I made no effort to profit from my work. Therefore, I engaged in no unlawful activity."

"What about the sales agreement on Monsieur Ricard's desk?"

"I was never going to allow Anna to sign it. The transaction was a ruse on my part to find the Picasso."

"Which is now missing again."

Gabriel made no reply.

"You should have come to me in the beginning," said Bittel.

"And what would you have done?"

"I would have referred the matter to an investigating magistrate here in Geneva, and the magistrate would have conducted a thorough probe."

"Which would have taken years, allowing the owner of the Picasso plenty of time to move it elsewhere."

"We have laws, Allon."

"And those laws make it next to impossible for the rightful owners of looted Holocaust art to reclaim their property."

Bittel did not offer a retort, for there was none. He did, however, suggest that this case might have been different.

"Why?" asked Gabriel.

"Our tax and customs authorities have been concerned about the scale and legitimacy of Monsieur Ricard's activities for some time now. Regrettably, there was little appetite to do anything about it."

"I'm shocked to hear that."

Bittel shrugged his shoulders to indicate dismay or resignation or something in between. "This is the business of Switzerland, Allon. We cater to the needs of the global superrich. The Geneva Freeport alone brings billions of dollars of wealth to our little landlocked country each year."

"Which is why you and your friends from the Police Cantonale are desperately trying to find a way to cover up the fact that someone hacked into the Freeport's computer network and stole a painting worth more than a hundred million dollars. Otherwise, the global superrich might decide to store their paintings and gold bars in Singapore or Delaware instead of Switzerland."

"An all too real possibility."

"How are you going to handle it?"

"The same way I've dealt with every other mess you've made in Switzerland."

"I wasn't there?"

Bittel shook his head. "And neither was your friend Anna Rolfe."

"How do you intend to explain the dead art dealer?"

"The Police Cantonale will explore several possible theories, none of them involving a Picasso once owned by a Parisian Jew who was murdered at Auschwitz. You, however, will continue searching for the painting—and for Monsieur Ricard's killer, of course. And you will report your findings to no one but me."

"And if I were to decline your generous offer?"

"The Police Cantonale will have no choice but to arrest Anna Rolfe's assistant. Evidently, she bears more than a passing resemblance to the suspect in a robbery that occurred not long ago at the Hôtel Métropole."

"With good reason," said Gabriel.

"They say she's a top-notch professional thief."

"You should see her with a keyboard."

"Do you think she can get inside the computer network of the Geneva Freeport?"

Gabriel smiled. "I was afraid you were never going to ask."

25

Rue des Alpes

Late that Thursday evening, the Police Cantonale de Genève announced that the prominent art dealer Edmond Ricard had been shot to death inside his gallery at the Geneva Freeport. The brief statement went on to say that nothing had been stolen and that at no point were any of the valuables stored within the vaults of the facility in any danger. Police described the suspected perpetrator only as a German-speaking man in his late thirties. Investigators said they were acting under the assumption that his weapon had been fitted with a sound suppressor, as there were no reports of gunfire. They also assumed that the name the man had given to the security guard in the lobby was false and therefore had no interest in making it public.

Curiously, neither the police nor the Freeport authorities released video or still images of the suspect. Also absent from the initial statement was any mention of how the dealer's body had been discovered or even the approximate time the murder had taken place. Subsequent attempts by reporters to question the security guard who had been on duty that afternoon proved unsuccessful after he was hastily reassigned to a post deep within the bowels of the facility. The visitor log would vanish without a trace.

Had the document resurfaced, it would have revealed the name of the renowned Swiss violinist who had called on Galerie Ricard at 4:00 p.m. on the day of the murder—and on several other occasions during the weeks preceding it. A blood-soaked sales agreement discovered on the art dealer's desk would have laid bare the reason for those visits. But the agreement, like the logbook, seemed to disappear into thin air. So thorough was the cover-up that it extended to the headquarters of the Police Cantonale itself, where all evidence of the renowned violinist's brief visit, including selfies and autographs, was deleted and destroyed. Her departure, at 9:40 p.m., was carried out in a manner befitting a head of state.

Gabriel and Ingrid slipped out of the building a few minutes later. Owing to Ingrid's past conduct in Geneva, they steered clear of the luxury hotels and settled into a service flat on the rue des Alpes instead. Its amenities included a daily change of linen and bath towels and, more important, unlimited Wi-Fi service. Later, the IT department at the Geneva Freeport would mistake the apartment's Internet Protocol address for one in Râmnicu Vâlcea, a region of Romania known for the quality of its computer hackers.

Ingrid worked in her bedroom with the door tightly closed and Scandinavian jazz flowing from the speakers of her laptop. Tord Gustavsen, Marcin Wasilewski, Bobo Stenson, the Maciej Obara Quartet—essentially the entire ECM Records catalogue. Gabriel sent her a text message offering assistance and was told that he was clueless when it came to computers and therefore could only impede her progress. A part of him was tempted to remind Ingrid that he had once been the director of one of the most technologically proficient intelligence services in the world—and that he had overseen a number of high-profile hacking operations, including several targeting the nuclear weapons program of the Islamic Republic of Iran. That did not mean, however, that he had fully grasped the digital wizardry involved in the attacks. Indeed, he would have been hard-pressed to explain how the microwave oven in the apartment's kitchen heated the milk for his coffee.

Ingrid drank hers black with dangerous amounts of sugar. Gabriel left it on a tray outside her door. He left her food as well, but she never touched it. She didn't sleep, either. She would sleep, she said, when she found the man who had killed Edmond Ricard and stolen the Picasso.

Twenty-four hours after their arrival, she strayed from her room long enough to brief Gabriel on her progress. "I'm inside the Freeport's network," she explained. "But I'm having trouble cracking the password for the security system."

"I find that hard to believe."

"Shocking, I know."

"And when you do?"

"I'll have a look at the backup folder to make sure the video isn't sitting there in plain sight."

"You should assume the hackers deleted the contents of the backup folder on their way out the door."

"But as you well know, nothing is ever really deleted. They didn't shut down the system completely, which means the cameras were rolling and the hard drive was recording. That missing video is there somewhere. I just have to find it and bring it back from the dead."

"How much longer will it take?"

"Would you like me to give you the precise time that I will find and retrieve six months' worth of surveillance video from one of the world's most secure storage facilities?"

And with that, the door closed and the music started up again—an album of contemplative solo compositions by the French jazz pianist

Benjamin Moussay. "How about Schubert or Chopin instead?" asked Gabriel, but he received no reply other than the clatter of Ingrid's keyboard.

He saw her again at one the following afternoon, when she announced that she had finally cracked the password and gained access to the Freeport's security system. Another two hours would elapse before she was able to confirm that the hacker had drained the backup folder as well, at which point her search became forensic in nature. Her keystrokes became more intense, her choice of jazz more traditional. "Kind of Blue" by Miles Davis. "A Love Supreme" by John Coltrane. A beautiful album of standards by Keith Jarrett and the bassist Charlie Haden.

Shortly after 8:00 p.m., both the music and her keyboard fell silent. Gabriel allowed another hour to pass before entering her room. He found her stretched out on the bed, eyes closed, twitching with nightmares. In her hand was a flash drive.

Gabriel gently removed the device from her grasp and slid it into the USB port of his own computer. A request for a password appeared on his screen. He tried several combinations of letters and numerals without success. Then he entered the word *Aurora*, the code name of the secret Russian plan that Ingrid had stolen in Moscow, and a folder appeared. Inside were several hundred still images and a single video thirteen minutes in length.

"Gotcha," whispered Gabriel, and clicked the play icon.

The video commenced at 2:17 p.m. when the subject, a well-dressed man with pale blond hair, alighted from a Peugeot 508 sedan that paused briefly on the Route du Grand-Lancy. He removed a rectangular art transport case from the car's boot, then made his way toward the entrance of the stubby office block. Three different cameras observed his brief interaction with the security guard, and a fourth recorded his fifteen-second elevator ride to the third floor. He pressed the call button at Galerie Ricard at 2:21 p.m. and was admitted at once. Clearly, thought Gabriel, he was expected.

He remained inside the gallery for eight minutes, long enough to shoot Ricard three times and to remove the Picasso from its frame. He placed a brief phone call during the ride down to the lobby and breezed past the security desk without a word or glance. The same Peugeot was waiting in the Route du Grand-Lancy when he emerged from the building. He placed the art transport case in the boot and dropped into the passenger seat. The car shot forward, and at 2:33 p.m. it disappeared from view.

Its most likely destination was France. The nearest border crossing was at Bardonnex, a drive of approximately twenty minutes. Gabriel rang Christoph Bittel and gave him the make and model and registration number of the car. The Swiss intelligence chief got back to him in less than an hour.

"They crossed into France at two forty-nine. And by the way, the man in the passenger seat had black hair."

"And a Picasso worth a hundred million dollars."

"There was no Picasso, Allon."

"Never was," he agreed, and killed the connection.

26

Quai des Orfèvres

Gabriel and Ingrid left the apartment on the rue des Alpes at ten fifteen the following morning and made the short walk to the Gare Cornavin. Their Paris-bound train departed at eleven. After settling into her seat in first class, Ingrid opened her laptop and attached it to the Internet with a mobile hot spot. Gabriel glanced at the screen and saw line upon line of computer code.

"I'm afraid to ask."

"I copied a few files last night before logging off the Freeport's network." She opened a new document and turned the computer in Gabriel's direction. "Including this one."

"What is it?"

"A list of every individual or entity with a vault in the Geneva Freeport."

"I'm quite certain my friend Christoph Bittel didn't give us permission to pinch a document like that."

"What your friend doesn't know won't hurt him."

Gabriel scrolled through the list of names. Not surprisingly, nearly all of the Freeport's users were hidden behind anonymous shell companies. Each entry included the address of the company's vault—building, corridor, and number—and the date the vault had been acquired.

"Is the document searchable?"

"Yes, of course. What are you looking for?"

"A company called OOC Group, Limited."

Ingrid entered the name, then shook her head. "Nothing."

"Do you happen to recall the address of the vault where you saw the Picasso?"

"Building Three, Corridor Six, Vault Twenty-Nine."

"Search it."

Ingrid entered the address. "The vault is rented by a company called Sargasso Capital Investments. It appears that Sargasso controls six other vaults as well."

Gabriel entered the name of the company into his phone's search engine and was presented with more than ten million meaningless results. Then he looked at Ingrid and asked, "What else did you steal in violation of my agreement with the chief of Swiss intelligence?"

"A list of all employees of the Geneva Freeport, a log containing the names of everyone who has been cleared into the complex during the past two years, and five years' worth of customs declarations and shipping documents." She tapped the trackpad, and the lines of code reappeared on the screen. "I also grabbed all the user data for everyone who's been on the Freeport's computer network for the past ten days. One of those users, of course, was the hacker."

"My hackers always hid their identity or created a false one."

"I did the same thing when I hacked into the Freeport. But a fake persona and IP address don't hold up for long. I'm confident I'll be able to geolocate and identify him."

"Is there any chance you can find us a hotel in Paris first?"

Ingrid sighed and pulled up a popular booking website. "Where would you like to stay?"

"The Crillon is nice."

"During my most recent visit there, a number of women misplaced valuable pieces of jewelry. Therefore, I strongly suggest we choose another establishment."

"How about the Ritz?"

"Can't," she said.

"The George V?"

"I'm afraid not."

"Is there a single luxury hotel in Paris where you *haven't* committed a crime?"

"The Cheval Blanc."

"In that case," said Gabriel, "I suppose we have no choice but to rough it at the Cheval Blanc."

———

The hotel was located on the Quai du Louvre, a few steps from the museum. Their adjoining rooms were on the fourth floor. Gabriel stayed long enough to drop off his luggage and download two photographs of Edmond Ricard's killer to his phone. He poked his head into Ingrid's room before leaving.

"Are you sure you can restrain yourself?"

"Quite," she answered, and opened her laptop.

Outside, Gabriel crossed the Pont Neuf to the Île de la Cité, then made his way to a brasserie on the Quai des Orfèvres. Seated alone at a table in the back was a darkly handsome man in his early fifties who might have been mistaken for a French movie idol, the sort of fellow who looked good with a cigarette and spent his afternoons in the bed of a beautiful young woman before returning home to his equally beautiful wife. In truth, Jacques Ménard was the commander of the Central Office for the Fight against Cultural Goods Trafficking, which is how the French referred to their art squad. His office was located a few paces up the street at 36 Quai des Orfèvres, the iconic headquarters of the criminal division of the Police Nationale.

Ménard had taken the liberty of ordering a bottle of Sancerre. "A little something to celebrate your latest coup," he explained.

"The Van Gogh? All I did is clean it, Jacques."

"You don't really expect me to believe that, do you?"

Gabriel smiled. "Perhaps we should try the wine."

"Be my guest."

He drank some of the Sancerre. It was otherworldly.

"Well?" asked Ménard.

"I think we should have lunch together more often."

"I couldn't agree more. In fact, I was beginning to think I would never see you again."

Gabriel had made Jacques Ménard's acquaintance while researching the authenticity of a painting acquired and sold by Isherwood Fine Arts. The resulting scandal had ruined lives and reputations from Paris to New York. But not Ménard's. He had been fêted in the French press, and his department had seen a marked increase in its funding. Which explained the warm welcome and the exceptional bottle of Sancerre.

"When was the last time you were in town?" he asked.

"You tell me, Jacques."

"I think you were here about a month ago."

"Was I?"

The Frenchman nodded. "A few days before that as well."

"Sounds to me as though you're monitoring my movements."

"Should I be?"

"If you had any sense."

The waiter reappeared to take their order. Gabriel glanced at the menu and selected the mushroom tarte and the sole meunière. Ménard, after a moment's deliberation, chose the same. When they were alone again, Gabriel awakened his phone and showed the Frenchman the two photographs.

"Who is he?"

"The professional assassin who killed that art dealer in the Geneva Freeport the other day. I was hoping you might be able to help me find him."

"Why am I receiving this request from you and not the Police Cantonale de Genève?"

"Because the head of Swiss intelligence has asked me to investigate the matter quietly on his behalf."

"Why you?"

"We're old friends. For some reason, he still trusts me."

Ménard looked down at Gabriel's phone again. "What can you tell me about him?"

"He called himself Andreas Hoffmann. He and his driver headed for France after leaving the Freeport. The Bardonnex crossing. The Swiss say they cleared the checkpoint at two forty-nine p.m."

Ménard drew a small leather-bound notebook from the breast pocket of his suit jacket. "Vehicle?"

"A Peugeot 508. French registration."

"Number?"

Gabriel recited it and Ménard wrote it down. "Is there anything else you can tell me about him?"

"I have a feeling he flew from Dublin to Paris on Tuesday, January seventeenth. I also have a hunch he murdered a man named Emanuel Cohen two nights later in Montmartre."

Ménard laid down his pen. "Why would he have done a thing like that?"

"The Picasso, Jacques."

"What Picasso?"

"The one he stole from that gallery in the Freeport. It belonged to Emanuel Cohen's grandfather, a man named Bernard Lévy. You're going to help me find it and return it to his rightful heirs."

Ménard took up his pen again. "Subject matter?"

"A portrait of a woman in the surrealist style."

"Dimensions."

"Ninety-four by sixty-six."

"Oil on canvas?"

"*Oui.*"

27

Cheval Blanc

When Gabriel returned to the Cheval Blanc, there was no sign of Ingrid in her room. Ninety minutes went by before she finally reappeared, clad in sweat-drenched spandex. She had been working out in the hotel's fitness center.

"How was your meeting?" she asked.

"It went about as well as could be expected. The only way I was able to get what I needed was to offer him your head. Your execution is scheduled for tomorrow in the Place de la Concorde."

Frowning, she closed the communicating door between their rooms and worked late into the night. She was back at it early the next morning, when she hacked into the Freeport's network to run a few diagnostic programs. By one o'clock she was ready for a lunch break, so they walked along the Seine to Chez Julien. Gabriel's phone vibrated the minute they sat down at their table.

"Your friend Inspector Clouseau?" asked Ingrid.

"My wife."

"Does she know where you are?"

Gabriel typed a brief message and tapped the send icon. "She does now."

"She doesn't mind the fact that you're staying in a fancy Paris hotel with a beautiful young woman?"

"No."

"Why not?"

"Because fancy hotels and beautiful women were always part of my job."

"Care to explain?"

"Office doctrine," said Gabriel. "I never operated alone in a city like Paris or Rome or Zurich. I was always accompanied by a female escort officer."

"And they were always pretty?"

"The prettier, the better. My wife was one of those officers. That's how I met her."

A waitress appeared and Gabriel ordered a bottle of Chablis.

"Speaking of pretty girls," said Ingrid quietly.

"Was she? I didn't notice."

"You notice everything, Mr. Allon." Ingrid lowered her eyes toward the menu. "Have you figured it out yet?"

"I'm leaning toward the risotto with truffles."

"I was talking about the Picasso. How did the killer know it was going to be in Ricard's gallery on Thursday afternoon?"

"Ricard must have mentioned it to the wrong person."

"Who?"

"I'm guessing it was the owner of the Picasso."

"But the owner agreed to the trade."

"Maybe he did, maybe he didn't."

"Are you saying Ricard made the deal with Anna without telling his client?"

"Stranger things have happened, Ingrid. The art world is a murky swamp. And with a few notable exceptions, dealers are the slimy green scum that floats on the surface."

The waitress returned with the wine, and they placed their orders. An hour later, after finishing their coffee, they went into the cloudy afternoon. The Cheval Blanc was to the right. Ingrid turned to the left instead. She made another left into the rue Geoffroy l'Asnier and slowed to a stop outside the entrance of the Mémorial de la Shoah.

"I'd like you to take me inside," she announced.

"Why?"

"Because I want to know what happened to the man who owned that Picasso."

"He was murdered at Auschwitz along with more than a million other innocent Jews, including my grandparents."

"Please, Mr. Allon."

They entered the memorial along a luminous white passageway inscribed with the names of more than seventy-six thousand men, women, and children. The exhibition rooms told the story of their detention, deportation, and murder. In the crypt, where a flame burned in their memory, Ingrid clung to Gabriel's arm and wept.

"Maybe this was a mistake," he said quietly.

"I'm fine," she sobbed.

"Should we leave?"

"Yes, I think so."

Outside in the street she scrubbed the tears from her face. "I never knew."

"About what?"

"The Paris Roundup of 1942. *Jeudi noir.*"

"Most people don't."

"They were arrested by the French police? Thirteen thousand people on a single day?"

Gabriel was silent.

"Where did it happen?"

"All over Paris. But most of the Jews who were arrested lived a short distance from here. I can show you, if you like."

They walked through the shadows of the rue Pavée and turned into the rue des Rosiers. Once the heart of Jewish life in Paris, it was now one of the most fashionable streets in the arrondissement. Chic clothing boutiques lined the pavements. Gabriel pointed out the apartments on the upper floors.

"The French police went door to door on the morning of July 16, 1942. They had a list of names. A few were shown mercy and allowed to escape, but not many. Just five days later, three hundred and seventy-five of them were murdered at Auschwitz. Nearly all the others would be dead by the end of the summer."

"What about the children?"

"There were about four thousand in all. They were separated from their parents and loaded into cattle cars. The number who perished during the journey to Auschwitz is not known. Those who somehow survived were gassed upon arrival."

Gabriel slowed to a stop outside a boutique that specialized in designer jeans. It had once been a famous kosher restaurant called Jo Goldenberg. Gabriel had dined there a single time, on a dark and rainy afternoon, with a colleague from his service. They had been discussing a woman whose grandparents were arrested on *jeudi noir*. Her name was Hannah Weinberg.

Gabriel's phone disturbed the memory. He drew it from his coat pocket and stared at the screen.

"Your wife?" asked Ingrid.

"No," said Gabriel. "Inspector Clouseau."

Gabriel dropped Ingrid at the Cheval Blanc, then headed across the Seine to the Île de la Cité. This time he met Jacques Ménard in a café in the Place Dauphine. The French detective had brought along a manila envelope filled with photographs. He laid the first on the table. It depicted a fire-blackened Peugeot 508.

"They ditched it off the D30 in the Haute-Savoie. There were no traffic cameras nearby. They must have switched to another vehicle."

"I don't suppose the forensic team found the charred remnants of a Picasso in the boot."

"I didn't ask."

Ménard reclaimed the photograph and laid another in its place. It was the man from the Freeport navigating passport control at Charles de Gaulle Airport. The time stamp read 11:52 a.m. The date was Tuesday, January 17.

"How did you know?" asked Ménard.

"He murdered an Oxford professor named Charlotte Blake in Cornwall the day before. The safest escape route, in my humble opinion, is a ferry to the Irish Republic."

"He caught the eight forty Air France flight at Dublin Airport. German passport."

"Name?"

"Klaus Müller."

"I assume you had a look at his prior travel."

Ménard nodded. "He spends a lot of time on airplanes."

"Where does he make his home?"

"Leipzig. Or so he says."

The next photo Ménard laid on the table was of lesser quality. It showed the same man walking over the paving stones of the rue Lepic in Montmartre. The time was 7:32 p.m., about an hour before Emanuel Cohen's murder.

"Is there video of the fall itself?" asked Gabriel.

"*Non*," replied Ménard. "Which is the only reason why I didn't immediately report this matter to the Police Judiciaire. They are, however, looking into the burned-out car in the Haute-Savoie. It's only a matter of time before they make the connection to the art dealer's murder in Geneva." He paused, then added, "And to your Picasso."

"The only way they'll find out about that painting is if you tell them."

"Good point." Ménard returned the photographs to the envelope and handed it over. "Try not to kill anyone, Allon. And call me the minute you have a lead on the whereabouts of either the Picasso or the man who pushed Dr. Cohen down those steps."

"That would be a violation of my agreement with my friend from Swiss intelligence."

Jacques Ménard smiled. "*C'est la vie.*"

————

The sun had set by the time Gabriel returned to the Cheval Blanc. Upstairs, he found Ingrid tossing her clothing into her suitcase.

"Going somewhere?" he asked.

"Cannes."

Gabriel went into his room and began to pack. "I'm quite fond of the Carlton, you know."

"So am I. But I'm afraid it's out of the question."

"How about the Hôtel Martinez?"

"You can't be serious."

"The Majestic?"

"Not a chance, Mr. Allon."

28

Rue d'Antibes

Ingrid had traced the hack of the Geneva Freeport to an apartment building on the rue d'Antibes, the exclusive shopping street that flows through the heart of Cannes's *centre ville*. The small hotel located opposite the hacker's dwelling did not live up to the splendor suggested by its name. Gabriel requested adjoining rooms on an upper floor and in short order was handed a pair of keys and a brochure describing the hotel's amenities, of which there were few. He told the clerk he was a resident of Montreal and showed him a false Canadian passport to prove it. His Danish colleague supplied the required credit card. They planned to stay for three nights, they explained. Perhaps a night or two longer if circumstances required it. The clerk did not foresee a problem, as vacancy was not an issue.

Upstairs, they unlocked the communicating door between their rooms and opened the blinds to the fading afternoon light. Three floors beneath them was the rue d'Antibes. It was one way and scarcely wide enough for a single vehicle. Perhaps fifteen meters separated their rooms from the windows of the opposing apartment building.

"This won't do," said Ingrid.

"I shouldn't think so," agreed Gabriel.

They headed downstairs and went into the shadowed street. Ingrid threaded her arm through Gabriel's as they walked past a parade of luxury boutiques.

"Office doctrine, Mr. Allon. A fancy hotel and a pretty girl."

"I'm afraid we don't make a terribly convincing couple. And our hotel is quite possibly the worst in the *centre ville*."

"But conveniently located, wouldn't you say?"

At the opposite end of the street was an upscale electronics store. Ingrid went inside alone and emerged a few minutes later with a compact high-resolution webcam. They killed an hour strolling the Croisette before returning to the hotel. Ingrid placed the camera in the window of her room and attached it to her computer with a USB cable. Then she drew the blinds and switched off the lights.

Gabriel inspected the image on the screen. "Can you record the feed?"

"Yes, of course. And better yet, I can forward it to my phone."

"Good," said Gabriel. "Because under no circumstances are we eating in this hotel."

"Office doctrine?"

"It is now."

The building was five floors in height, with a pair of boutiques on the ground level. The residential entrance was sandwiched between the two shops. The intercom panel listed eight apartments. The accompanying nameplates suggested that only two of the dwellings were occupied by Frenchmen. Three of the names were English-language in origin, one was Spanish, and one was German. The nameplate for Apartment 3B was empty.

By half past seven that evening, lights were burning up and down the length of the rue d'Antibes. Only four of the eight apartments showed signs of life—two on the second floor and two on the fourth. At 7:42 p.m. the lights in one of the fourth-floor apartments were extinguished, and a moment later a man and woman of retirement age emerged from the street-level door. The rigidity of their bearing suggested they were the Schmidts of 4A. Their attire suggested they were heading out to dinner.

Gabriel and Ingrid waited until nearly nine o'clock before doing the same. They left the privacy signs hanging on their doors and informed the clerk that they did not require turndown service—unnecessarily, as it was not being offered. Outside, they debated where to eat.

"One of my favorite restaurants in the world is in Cannes," said Ingrid. "It doesn't take reservations, and the wait for a table is terrible during the summer. But it's perfect in the off season."

"Am I allowed to know the name of the restaurant?"

"It's a surprise."

The restaurant, La Pizza Cresci, was located on the western flank of the Vieux Port, on the Quai Saint-Pierre. Inside, they were shown to a window table in the main dining room. Ingrid immediately sensed Gabriel's discomfort.

"We can go somewhere else, if you like."

"Why?"

"Because you look as though you've just seen a ghost."

He stared silently out the window.

"Is there something you're not telling me?"

"Search the words Abdul Aziz al-Bakari and Cannes."

Ingrid took up her phone and typed. "Shit," she said after a moment.

"It was a night to remember, I assure you."

"I'm sorry, Mr. Allon. I didn't realize."

"It was a long time ago."

"Let's leave."

"Are you kidding? It's impossible to get into this place."

Ingrid laughed in spite of herself. "I can't take you anywhere."

———

It was a few minutes after eleven when they returned to the hotel. The privacy signs were still hanging from their doors, and there was nothing to suggest that the rooms had been entered during their absence. They watched the two hours of stored video at four times the normal playback speed. The occupants of 4A had returned at 10:37 p.m., but otherwise the building's entrance had seen no activity. By midnight the lights had dimmed in three of the four apartments, but the occupant of 2B was awake until nearly four. Ingrid reckoned they had found their man. Hackers, she explained, did their best work in the dark.

"What about the nameless occupant of the apartment upstairs?"

"It doesn't look to me as though he's in Cannes at the moment. Therefore, I'm betting the hacker is Martineau in 2B."

Ingrid's theory collapsed at half past seven when the apartment's occupant opened the shutters. Madame Martineau was a matronly woman in her late sixties. For any number of reasons, she did not fit the profile of a typical computer hacker.

"I stand corrected," said Ingrid.

The woman left the building at nine o'clock carrying a traditional

French wicker shopping basket. Herr and Frau Schmidt went out a few minutes later, and at nine thirty "Ashworth" from 2A made her first appearance. She was a slender long-limbed woman of perhaps thirty-five with short blond hair.

"What do you think?" asked Ingrid.

"She doesn't look like a hacker to me."

"Neither do I, Mr. Allon. Maybe I should follow her."

"Allow me," said Gabriel, and headed downstairs. By the time he stepped from the hotel's doorway, the woman was a hundred meters down the rue d'Antibes. He closed the gap to about thirty meters and followed her to a café on a small side street, where she breakfasted on café crème and a brioche before making her way to the office of a major British real estate firm. Gabriel went inside and spent a few minutes scrutinizing the available properties. The woman from 2A offered him a business card. It identified her as Fiona Ashworth, manager of the real estate firm's Cannes branch.

Gabriel slipped the card into his pocket and started back to the hotel. On the rue d'Antibes he was surprised to see Ingrid, hastily attired in jeans and a cotton pullover, walking toward him through the bright sunlight. Something in her demeanor made him seek shelter in a pharmacy. She passed it a moment later, her eyes staring straight ahead. Smooth as silk, thought Gabriel. Very impressive, indeed.

———

He purchased a few needless toiletries from the pharmacy and returned to the hotel. Upstairs, he sat down before Ingrid's open laptop and watched the recorded video, beginning at half past nine, when the English estate agent had left the building. Twelve minutes later, while she was having breakfast under Gabriel's watchful eye, the shutters of Apartment 3B had swung open and its nameless occupant had appeared in the window. It turned out he was in Cannes, after all. He had sandy brown hair and an unkempt beard, and looked as though he had had a long night, perhaps several. He lit a cigarette and, expelling a lungful of smoke, gazed left and right along the street. Then he closed the shutters and disappeared from view.

But only until 10:04 a.m., when he stepped from the building's entrance and headed east on the rue d'Antibes. He was wearing a leather jacket and looking down at the phone he carried in his right hand. Gabriel realized now that he had walked past the man a few seconds before he spotted Ingrid.

He rang her mobile.

"I'd love to chat," she said calmly. "But I'm afraid I'm rather busy at the moment."

"Where are you?"

"Have a look out your window."

Gabriel did as she suggested. The man from 3B was approaching from the east. He was carrying a plastic shopping bag in his left hand and the phone in his right. Forty meters behind him, Ingrid was inspecting the merchandise displayed in the window of Zara.

"Did he go anywhere interesting?"

"The Monoprix over on the rue du Maréchal Foch."

"What did he buy?"

"Does it matter?"

"It might."

"Coffee and microwavable Indian food." Ingrid entered the Zara boutique. "After leaving *le supermarché*, he stopped at a *tabac* and grabbed two packs of Winstons."

"Did he meet with anyone?"

"Not a soul."

The man had arrived at the entrance of the apartment building. He jabbed at the keypad with the index finger of his right hand, then opened the door and went inside. Gabriel drew the blinds and sat down at the laptop. The man appeared on the screen a moment later.

"What's he doing now?" asked Ingrid.

"Looking for the Scandinavian woman who's been following him around the *centre ville* of Cannes for the past thirty minutes."

"He never saw me, Mr. Allon. And he never will."

29

Rue d'Antibes

Ingrid probed the defenses of the Wi-Fi networks within range of her computer while the maid tidied up the room. There were twenty-two networks in all, with signal strengths ranging from one bar to four. Most bore the names of businesses along the rue d'Antibes. The rest appeared to be personal. One was called SCHMIDTNET. Another was designated ASHWORTH. There was one network with no apparent name, just a seemingly random series of letters and numbers. Ingrid reckoned it was the one that belonged to the hacker in Apartment 3B.

When the maid had gone, she returned the camera to its place in the window and reattached it to her computer. Gabriel met her downstairs in the lobby and escorted her across the street to one of the boutiques on the ground floor of the apartment building—the one directly beneath 3B. While pretending to shop, Ingrid checked the available Wi-Fi networks with her phone. There were now only nineteen in range, but the networks called SCHMIDTNET and ASHWORTH had gained strength. So, too, had the one with no apparent name.

"Four bars," she said. "That has to be him."

Leaving the boutique, they walked down to the Croisette and took a table at one of the restaurants along the beach. Gabriel ordered a bottle of Bandol rosé, then listened while Ingrid explained what she proposed to do.

"Hack the hacker?"

"Not his computer," she replied. "Just his network."

"Won't he notice?"

"Eventually, I suppose. But it's the only way to determine whether it's safe for one of us to enter the apartment and have a look round. If he's a professional hacker, it will be obvious."

"To you, perhaps. But I might mistake him for one of those idiots who spends his evenings playing video games."

"Which is why I should be the one who goes in there."

"I got a good look at the passcode on the street-level door this morning. I'm fairly certain it's—"

"Five, one, seven, nine, zero, two, eight, six."

"What about the door to his apartment?"

"I'm sure it's just an ordinary French lock."

"Which means you won't be able to open it without a bump key or a hand grenade."

"There's a locksmith up in Grasse who sells bump keys and other unlocking tools."

"You've done business with him in the past, I take it?"

"Monsieur Giroux is a fellow traveler. There isn't a villa on the Côte d'Azur that he hasn't robbed." She opened her menu. "Have you been to this restaurant before?"

"Once or twice."

"Did you kill anyone while you were here?"

"Not that I can recall."

The picturesque town of Grasse, sometimes referred to as the perfume capital of the world, was a half hour north of Cannes at the foot of the French Alps. Monsieur Giroux's shop was located on the Route Napoléon. Gabriel waited in the rental car while Ingrid went inside. She emerged ten minutes later with a set of professional-grade bump keys that, in the right set of hands, would open any lock in Europe in a matter of seconds.

"He threw in a lockpick gun as well."

"Perhaps there's honor among thieves, after all."

They stopped at a nearby hardware store long enough for Ingrid to purchase a screwdriver and a roll of gaffer tape, then started back to Cannes. It was late afternoon by the time they were back in their rooms at the hotel. Gabriel attached the camera to his computer and kept an eye on the feed while Ingrid made her first tentative moves against the nameless network. By eight that evening she was in.

"How?" asked Gabriel.

"It's impossible to explain the process to someone like you."

"A moron?"

"A layman."

"Try."

She spoke for several minutes in a strange and foreign tongue. Derivation function, cryptographic hashing algorithm, wired equivalent privacy, deauthentication frame, medium access control, physical layer protocols, something called "evil twin access points." The upshot of all this gibberish was that she had deceived the network into surrendering its own password.

"Are you still connected?"

She shook her head. "It's not safe for me to be logged on while he's working."

"Did you happen to notice anything interesting before you took your leave?"

"Two desktops, two laptops, four phones, and an alarm system."

Gabriel swore softly.

"It's not a problem. I'll disable the alarm before I go in, and I'll reset it on my way out the door. He'll never know I was in his apartment."

"Unless you happen to bump into Madame Martineau or Herr Schmidt on your way out."

Ingrid looked at the screen of Gabriel's computer. "Or the lovely Fiona Ashworth."

The British estate agent was returning home from her office on the Croisette. She punched in the passcode—five, one, seven, nine, zero, two, eight, six—and went inside. A moment later the lights came on in her second-floor apartment. The windows of Madame Martineau's unit were likewise illuminated. The apartment above hers, however, was in darkness.

"Does he ever turn on the lights?" asked Gabriel.

"Blackout shades. A trick of the trade."

"We can't prove that he's the hacker. Not yet, at least."

"And if he is?"

"I'm going to have a word with him."

"You're not going to lose your temper, are you?"

"Not me," said Gabriel. "I've turned over a new leaf."

Ingrid smiled. "That makes two of us."

———

Shortly before eleven o'clock, with the occupants of the apartment building apparently bedded down for the night, they walked to the

Vieux Port for a quick pizza at Cresci. This time they sat in a darkened corner of the dining room so Ingrid could keep an eye on the feed from the camera.

"Who was the other gunman that night?" she asked.

"I'm sorry?"

"The other assassin who helped you kill Zizi al-Bakari."

"You met him once."

"Really? Where?"

"In Russia. He was the one who helped me get you out of the Range Rover and across the border into Finland."

It was after midnight when they returned to the hotel. Ingrid wrapped the grip of the screwdriver with several layers of gaffer tape and practiced bumping the lock on the door between their rooms. Her brief retirement had done nothing to diminish her skills; she was able to open the door in a matter of seconds. Indeed, she was faster with a bump key than the lockpick gun—and quieter as well.

At 2:00 a.m. Gabriel insisted that she get a few hours of sleep. She stretched out on the bed and wrestled with dreams of Russia until seven thirty, when she woke with a start. Gabriel poured her a cup of room service coffee. She drank some and made a sour face.

"How is it possible to get bad coffee in France?"

"You should have tasted the sludge they brought me a couple of hours ago."

She looked at the shot from the camera. "Anything?"

"Not yet."

She carried her coffee into the bathroom and showered and dressed in a businesslike black pantsuit.

"How do I look?"

"Like the thief who robbed several guests at the Carlton and the Martinez a few years ago."

Gabriel rang room service and ordered another pot of coffee and a pitcher of steamed milk. It arrived twenty minutes later as matronly Madame Martineau emerged from the door of the apartment building, her wicker shopping basket in hand. The Schmidts appeared shortly after nine, followed twenty minutes later by Fiona Ashworth.

"I'm thinking about buying a little pied-à-terre along the Côte d'Azur," said Ingrid. "You didn't keep her card by any chance, did you?"

"Office doctrine dictated that I burn it."

Ingrid, annoyed, tapped her fingernail on the desktop.

"Perhaps you should practice bumping the lock a few hundred more times."

Before she could reply, the shutters of Apartment 3B swung open, and the occupant appeared in the window. As usual he spent a moment searching the street below.

"He's a hacker," said Ingrid. "And he's afraid someone is watching him."

"Someone is."

At length the man withdrew and the shutters closed. Ingrid placed the bump keys and screwdriver in her handbag and shoved a pair of Bose Ultras into her ears. Gabriel dialed her phone on his secure Solaris and established a connection. He could hear the sound of her breathing. Her respiration rate was elevated.

"Where the hell is he?" she asked.

"Right there," said Gabriel as the street-level door opened. The man hesitated in the threshold for a long moment, then set off on an easterly heading. Gabriel opened the blinds and peered into the street. "You may proceed."

Ingrid connected her computer to the man's Wi-Fi network and went after the alarm system while Gabriel kept watch at the window. Two minutes was all it took.

"We're good, Mr. Allon. The alarm is disabled."

Gabriel drew the blinds. "I think I'll go downstairs for a proper café crème."

"Mind if join you?"

"Not at all," said Gabriel, and followed her out the door.

30

Rue d'Antibes

Downstairs, they bade the clerk a pleasant morning and walked out. Gabriel went to the café next door, and Ingrid crossed the street to the entrance of the apartment building. She punched the eight-digit passcode into the keypad on the intercom panel, and the dead bolt opened with a thud.

Entering, she was relieved to find the foyer deserted. She stood stock-still for a second or two, listening, then headed toward the staircase. Her ascent to the third floor was swift and soundless. Apartment 3B was on the left side of the landing. She slid her bump key into the lock and gave it two firm taps with the grip of the screwdriver. The lock surrendered at once.

She turned the latch and slipped into the apartment. The air was stale and reeked of tobacco and curry. Closing the door behind her, she once again stood motionless and listened. The only sound she heard was Gabriel's voice in her Bose earbuds.

"Checking in."

"I'm still here."

"Anyone else at home?"

"It seems not."

"How's the alarm?"

She checked the wall-mounted system panel. The status lights were blinking green. "It appears as though someone has disabled it."

"I wonder who that could have been."

The entrance hall emptied into a central corridor. Ingrid swung to the right and went into the sitting room. It was awash in the radiance of computers. They were arrayed on a long trestle table. With the exception of a threadbare couch, the room was otherwise unfurnished. As Ingrid had predicted, blackout shades covered the windows.

"Seen enough?" asked Gabriel.

"Probably. But I think I'll have a closer look before I go."

She walked over to the trestle table. He was no amateur, that much was obvious. There were six large monitors, three monitors for each of the high-end Lenovo desktops. All six of the monitors showed evidence of a hack in progress, perhaps more than one. His two laptops were open and illuminated with activity. From one of the devices came the sound of two men conversing in English.

Ingrid raised the volume. "Do you hear that? He's listening to someone's phone."

"Time to leave, Ingrid."

"If you insist."

She lowered the volume on the laptop to its original setting and photographed each of the six monitors, along with the screens of the laptops. Just then one of the hacker's phones shivered with an incoming text message. She quickly photographed that, too.

"May I ask what you're doing?"

"Gathering intelligence."

Next to an overflowing ashtray was an old-fashioned steno pad. The hacker, it seemed, was a native speaker of French. Ingrid leafed through the pages, snapping photographs.

"That's quite enough," said Gabriel.

"Let me finish."

"There isn't time."

"It won't take but a minute."

"You don't have one," said Gabriel. "Thirty seconds, maybe. But certainly not a minute."

But even that estimate proved optimistic. The hacker, observed Gabriel, was clearly a man in a hurry. He was once again approaching from the east but had nothing in his hands to show for his brief expedition into the real world. No shopping bags or baguettes, only a phone. If he maintained his current pace, Gabriel calculated he would arrive at the entrance of the building in twenty seconds or less. There was a good chance he would bump into Ingrid as she was leaving. If nothing else, he would spot her as she stepped from the door.

Gabriel could hear her footfalls. "Where are you?" he asked.

"On my way down."

"It's too late. Turn around and head up to the fourth floor. Wait on the landing until our friend is back in his apartment."

The hacker was about twenty meters from the café. He passed within a few inches of Gabriel's table, then headed diagonally across the street toward the apartment building. At the residential entrance he reached a hand toward the intercom panel, but a sudden noise made him swing his head to the left before entering the passcode. Gabriel heard the same noise. It was the roar of a high-performance motorcycle racing along the rue d'Antibes.

A look of fear swept over the hacker's face. He reached for the keypad a second time and in his haste entered the passcode incorrectly. The bike was perhaps fifty meters away and closing fast. Gabriel slid a ten-euro banknote beneath the remnants of his café crème and stepped calmly into the middle of the street. The motorcyclist sounded his horn and applied his brakes, slowing his speed only marginally. Gabriel looked at the hacker and in French shouted, "Five, one, seven, nine, zero, two, eight, six."

This time the hacker entered the passcode correctly, and the dead bolt snapped. Gabriel pivoted toward the motorcycle bearing down on him and saw the helmeted man atop the saddle draw a gun from the inside of his leather coat. The weapon had no suppressor. Silence, it seemed, was not a priority.

The motorcyclist pointed the gun in the direction of the man standing frozen with fear at the entrance of the apartment building. Gabriel held his ground for another second or two, then stepped from the path of the speeding machine and shoved the hacker through the unlocked door. They came to rest in a heap in the foyer. Outside, the motorcycle sped past the building without slowing. The engine note faded and a moment later was gone.

The hacker was sprawled supine on the tile floor. He sat up and rubbed the back of his head, then checked the tips of his fingers. There was no blood.

"Are you all right?" asked Gabriel.

"*Oui*. It's just a bit of a bump." He offered Gabriel his hand. "I'm Philippe, by the way. Who are you?"

"I'm the man who just saved your life."

"And I cannot thank you enough, Monsieur. But how did you know the passcode for my building?"

"Come upstairs," said Gabriel. "I'll show you."

31

Rue d'Antibes

Ingrid was waiting on the landing outside the hacker's apartment. On Gabriel's signal, she unlocked the door with her bump key and screwdriver. Then she stepped aside and gave the hacker a beguiling smile.

"*Après vous.*"

The hacker looked to Gabriel for an explanation and, receiving only a blank stare, went hesitantly into the darkened entrance hall. Ingrid silenced the bleating alarm by entering the disarm code into the control panel. Gabriel closed the door and switched on the lights.

The display had its intended effect. The hacker looked at Gabriel and asked, "Who are you?"

"You may refer to me as Monsieur Klemp."

"You're German?"

"When the mood strikes me."

The hacker's gaze shifted to Ingrid. "And her?"

"My associate."

"Does she have a name?"

"I'm more interested in yours," replied Gabriel.

"I told you, it's Philippe."

"Philippe what?"

"Lambert."

"Are you carrying a weapon, Philippe Lambert?"

"*Non.*"

Gabriel pushed the hacker face-first against the wall and subjected him to a thorough search. He found nothing but a second phone and a billfold. The driver's permit and credit cards all bore the name Philippe Lambert.

"Satisfied?" he asked.

Gabriel handed over the billfold. "What sort of work do you do, Philippe?"

"Digital marketing and advertising. I'm a freelance consultant."

"That would explain why a man on a motorcycle was about to kill you."

"He must have mistaken me for someone else." Lambert paused, then added, "As have you, Monsieur Klemp."

"I think you hacked the Geneva Freeport a few days ago. In fact, my associate is quite certain that you were the one who did the job."

"Your associate doesn't know what she's talking about."

"She traced the source of the hack to your IP address. She also had a look at your computers while you were out this morning. She can show you the photos, if you like."

Lambert managed to smile. "Breaking and entering is a crime in France, Monsieur Klemp."

"So is computer hacking and digital theft."

"Are you a police officer?"

"Fortunately for you, I'm not." Gabriel attempted to slip past Lambert, but the hacker blocked his path. "I would advise you, Philippe, to choose another course of action."

"Or what?"

"My associate and I will leave, and the man on the motorcycle will kill you the next time you set foot outside this apartment." Gabriel went into the sitting room and deliberately surveyed his surroundings. "I really love what you've done with the place. Did you hire a decorator, or did you do this yourself?"

"I don't live in the physical world." Lambert pointed to the computers and monitors arrayed on the trestle table. "I live in that one. It's a perfect world. No disease or wars, no floods or famines. Just ones and zeros." He looked at Ingrid and asked, "Isn't that right?"

She walked over to the trestle table and raised the volume on one of the laptops. The same two men were conversing in British-accented English.

"Macedonian malware," said Lambert. "Cheap but quite effective."

"Who are they?"

"I cannot answer that question, Monsieur Klemp. Not unless you tell me who you really are."

Gabriel exchanged a look with Ingrid, and she sat down at Lambert's computers. A few seconds later Gabriel's image appeared on three of the large monitors. The hacker did not seem terribly surprised by the revelation. In fact, he appeared relieved.

"What are you doing in Cannes, Monsieur Allon?"

"I want to know who hired you to hack the Geneva Freeport."

"And if I tell you?"

"I will intercede with the relevant authorities on your behalf."

"What I need, Monsieur Allon, is your protection from the man on the motorcycle."

"Who sent him?"

Lambert pointed toward the laptop. "They did."

———

Lambert's possessions, such as they were, were already crammed into an overnight bag. A couple of changes of clothing, toiletries, a passport, several thousand euros in cash. He added the phones, the laptops, four external hard drives, and the steno pad. The two Lenovo desktops he wiped clean.

Gabriel kept watch at the window, phone in hand, Ingrid's voice in his ear. She was across the street at the hotel, hastily clearing out their rooms. Shortly before eleven she rang the clerk at the front desk and informed him that she and her Canadian colleague would be checking out earlier than anticipated. The clerk dispatched a bellman to collect their luggage. The valet fetched their rental car.

Ten minutes later it was waiting in the rue d'Antibes, engine running, luggage in the trunk.

Gabriel looked at Lambert and said, "Let's go."

They headed down the stairs to the foyer. Gabriel opened the door and peered into the street. Ingrid, having settled the bill, was waiting at the entrance of the hotel.

"Shall we?" she asked.

They all three stepped into the rue d'Antibes at the same instant and climbed into the waiting car—Lambert in back, Ingrid in the passenger seat, Gabriel behind the wheel. He waited until the car was rolling before closing his door. Ingrid removed the Bose Ultras from her ears and took a long look over her shoulder.

"No sign of him."

"For the moment," said Gabriel, and headed for the Vieux Port. They shot past La Pizza Cresci in a blur, then raced westward along the crescent of golden sand rimming the Baie de Cannes. Gabriel glanced into the rearview mirror and saw a motorcyclist following about fifty meters behind them.

"You were saying," he remarked.

Ingrid turned to have a look for herself. "Could be a different motorcyclist."

"It isn't," said Gabriel. "Same motorcyclist."

———————

During the short drive to the Autoroute, Gabriel performed a series of time-tested maneuvers designed to expose vehicle-borne surveillance, just to make certain there were no misunderstandings. The man on the motorcycle matched him turn for turn.

"Doesn't that idiot know who I am?"

"Perhaps he's heard about this new leaf of yours."

"Rest assured, it's now old and dry and lying on the ground."

"Do you have a gun, by any chance?"

"It's possible I forgot to pack one."

Gabriel followed the westbound ramp onto the Autoroute and pressed the throttle to the floor. Soon they were sailing along at 150 kilometers per hour with the man on the motorcycle in close pursuit.

"What do you suppose he's planning to do?" asked Ingrid.

"If we're lucky, he'll shoot Philippe and leave us in peace."

"And if we're not?"

"He'll kill us all." Gabriel met Lambert's anxious gaze in the rearview mirror. "Which is why I have no choice but to encourage him to shoot Philippe."

They continued west for another forty kilometers across a rugged Provençal landscape dotted with umbrella pine. Then, at the village of Le Muy, Gabriel turned onto the D25 and headed south toward Saint-Tropez. The road was nearly empty of traffic.

"What on earth is he waiting for?" asked Ingrid.

"If I had to guess, he's hoping I'll make a mistake."

"Like what?"

"This," said Gabriel, and swerved onto the D44. It was a narrow, treacherous road that snaked its way through the sparsely inhabited hills north of Saint-Tropez. There was no centerline on the tarmac, and no verge or guardrails. On the right side of the road rose a rocky and unstable ridge. A deep ravine fell away to the left.

Gabriel drove dangerously fast, his grip light upon the wheel, his foot never once touching the brake. Ingrid and Lambert kept watch on the man on the motorcycle. He had no trouble matching Gabriel's speed.

They flashed past a hotel and the entrance of a winery, then scaled the slope of a hill and raced along the rim of a small valley of vine-yards and olive groves. The bike accelerated and closed to within thirty meters of the car's rear bumper.

"It looks as though he's making his move," said Ingrid.

Gabriel glanced into the rearview. For the moment, at least, the assassin had both hands on the controls. "It's not so easily done, you know."

"What's that?"

"Firing a handgun while driving a motorcycle at an excessive rate of speed."

"Ever tried it?"

"The assassin never does the driving. Only the shooting."

"Office doctrine?"

"Absolutely."

"And what does it say about a situation like this?"

"Tell me the instant he reaches his right hand into the front of his jacket."

"Now!" shouted Ingrid.

Gabriel slammed on the brakes and expertly sent the car into a 180-degree spin. The man on the motorcycle managed to avoid a collision only by veering to the left. Airborne, he plunged into the valley below.

Gabriel eased the car into PARK and looked at Ingrid. "He must not have noticed my turn signal."

"Perhaps you should check on him."

Gabriel climbed out of the car and clambered down the slope of the steep hill. The mangled bike was lying in a coppice of oak trees along with a Heckler & Koch VP9 tactical pistol. Gabriel slid the weapon into the waistband of his trousers, then walked over to the assassin. His shattered body had come to rest in the shade of an olive tree. There were, thought Gabriel, worse places to die.

He removed the dead man's helmet. The now-lifeless face was instantly familiar. So was the name on the German passport that Gabriel found in his jacket pocket. His phone was of the disposable variety. It showed several missed calls, all from the same number.

Gabriel tossed the dead man's helmet into a tangle of brush and hurried up the slope of the hill to the car. A moment later he was speeding in the opposite direction on the D44. He gave the phone to Ingrid and the passport to Lambert.

"Do you recognize him?"

"*Oui.*"

"Is Klaus Müller his real name?"

"I wouldn't know."

"What *do* you know, Philippe?"

"He occasionally works for Monsieur Robinson."

"Who's Robinson?"

Lambert returned the passport. "Take me somewhere he can't find me, Monsieur Allon. Then I'll tell you everything."

32

Marseilles

Gabriel returned to the Autoroute and once again headed west. As they were approaching Marseilles, the dead man's phone shivered with an incoming text message. Ingrid looked down at the screen.

"He wants to know whether the flowers have been delivered."

"That would explain the HK nine-millimeter."

"You should have left it at the scene."

"I took it for safety reasons only."

"Whose?"

"Mine, of course. Only a fool would come to Marseilles without a gun."

They plunged into the Prado-Carénage Tunnel and emerged a moment later at the bustling port. It was much larger than its counterpart in Cannes and had a well-deserved reputation for criminality, which was the reason Gabriel had come there. He slid the car into an illegal parking space on the Quai de Rive Neuve and turned to face Philippe Lambert.

"I need some cash."

"For what?"

Gabriel indicated the fishmongers plying their trade in the esplanade on the port's eastern flank. "A thousand should do."

"For fish?" The Frenchman removed a bundle of twenty-euro banknotes from his suitcase and handed it over. "It had better be the finest fish in all of France, Monsieur Allon."

"Trust me, Philippe. You won't be disappointed."

Ingrid watched as Gabriel climbed out of the car and walked over to one of the fishmongers, a gray-haired man in a tattered wool sweater and a rubber apron. A brief conversation ensued and the money changed hands. Then Gabriel returned to the car and dropped behind the wheel.

"Who is that man?" asked Ingrid.

"His name is Pascal Rameau."

"Is he an actual fisherman?"

"Yes, of course. But he has other business interests as well, all of them criminal in nature."

"Such as?"

"Theft, for one. With all due respect, Pascal and his crew are without question the finest thieves in Europe. They pulled a couple of jobs for me back in the day."

"Why did you just give him a thousand euros?"

"Transport."

Rameau was now holding a phone to his ear. He caught Gabriel's eye and pointed to a spot along the quay. Gabriel hit the trunk release and opened his door.

"What about the car?" asked Ingrid.

"One of Pascal's men will drop it at Hertz."

"How thoughtful of him."

Luggage in hand, they set off along the quay. Gabriel purchased a dozen sandwiches at a boulangerie, then ducked into the pharmacy next door for scopolamine patches and tablets.

"I don't suffer from seasickness," protested Ingrid.

"You will if the seas are running two to three meters."

"What about you?"

"I never get seasick."

He led Ingrid and Lambert across the street and onto a jetty stretching toward the center of the harbor. Near the end of the dock was a twelve-meter motor yacht called *Mistral*. The owner of the vessel, a man named René Monjean, was standing on the afterdeck in a Helly Hansen offshore jacket.

"Long time, no see, Monsieur Allon." He shook Gabriel's hand warmly. "To what do I owe the honor?"

"Someone is trying to kill my friend. I need to get him off the mainland as quietly as possible."

Monjean smiled. "You've come to the right place."

Gabriel made the introductions, first names only, then asked about the marine forecast.

"The wind is starting to blow," said Monjean. "But it shouldn't be too bad. I'll have you there in ten hours, twelve at the most."

"Twelve hours?" asked Lambert. "Where are you taking me?"

"Libya," said Gabriel, and went into the boat's small but comfortable salon.

Monjean gave them a quick briefing. "There's a head down below and two berths." He tapped the stainless-steel door of the fridge. "And plenty of beer and wine."

With that, Monjean headed up to the flybridge. As the boat eased away from the jetty, Gabriel offered Ingrid the scopolamine. She opened the fridge instead and pried the cap from a bottle of Kronenbourg.

"What sort of jobs did Pascal Rameau do for you back in the day?"

"The kind I couldn't do for myself."

"Did our captain take part in these robberies?"

"Absolutely. There's nobody better than René Monjean."

"Has he ever pulled a heist in Moscow?" Ingrid drank her beer and smiled. "I didn't think so."

Monjean rounded Île Pomègues, the largest of the four islands at the entrance of the Port of Marseilles, and made for Planier Light. There he turned to the southeast and brought their speed up to a comfortable twenty-five knots. The wind was steady from the north, the seas were moderate. Gabriel and Ingrid drank Kronenbourg on the afterdeck and watched the setting sun while Lambert chain-smoked Winstons. Three times he asked Gabriel to reveal their destination, only to receive three different replies. Gabriel in turn pressed Lambert for additional information on the man he had referred to as Monsieur Robinson. Lambert, cupping his hand over the flame of a plastic lighter, revealed that Robinson's first name was Trevor and that he was the head of security at a small law firm with offices in Monaco and the British Virgin Islands.

"Firm have a name?"

"Not yet, Monsieur Allon."

By half past eight the last light of sunset was gone, and a three-quarter moon shone like a torch in the cloudless sky. The wind picked up, the air turned colder, the swells exceeded a meter in height. Ingrid went into the salon and reluctantly swallowed a dose of the scopolamine and adhered a patch to the side of her neck. Then she unwrapped the sandwiches that Gabriel had bought in Marseilles and pulled the cork from a bottle of rosé.

"Dinner is served," she called out, and Gabriel and Lambert came in from the afterdeck. René Monjean switched on the Garmin autopilot and the AIS collision alarm and joined them in the galley. The unlikely circumstances of the gathering made serious conversation impossible, so they engaged in polite small talk and listened to Melody Gardot on Monjean's onboard audio system. It was a recent acquisition, he explained, part of a major overhaul of *Mistral* he had carried out that winter. He said nothing as to how he had financed the project, and Gabriel, who was certain he knew the answer, didn't ask. René Monjean wasn't terribly particular about what he stole, but he specialized in the illicit acquisition of paintings.

By ten thirty he was back at the controls in the main helm station with a thermos of strong coffee to get him through the night. Ingrid and Lambert took the berths, and Gabriel stretched out on the convertible bed in the salon. Exhausted, he slept until seven. He found René Monjean up on the flybridge in the cold morning air.

"*Bonjour*, Monsieur Allon." Monjean pointed out a rocky island about two kilometers off the prow. "Île de Mezzu Mare. You and your friends will be on solid ground in about a half hour."

Gabriel went down to the galley. Ingrid, drawn by the aroma of freshly brewed coffee, emerged from belowdecks. She sat down at the table and rubbed her eyes.

"For some reason, they hurt like hell."

"It's a side effect of the scopolamine."

"How much longer do you intend to make me stay on this boat?"

"A few more minutes."

"And then?"

"A scenic drive through the mountains."

"Wonderful." Ingrid drank some of the coffee. "Is it my imagination, or do I smell rosemary and lavender?"

"I'm sure it's only the scopolamine."

Ingrid took up the packet and read the warning label. "Eyelid irritation, headache, feelings of restlessness, and problems with memory. But nothing at all about rosemary and lavender."

————————

The bustling port into which René Monjean expertly guided *Mistral* was Ajaccio, birthplace of Napoleon Bonaparte and capital of the occasionally restive French island of Corsica. Ingrid and Lambert had breakfast in a café near the ferry terminal while Gabriel saw to the rental car. By nine fifteen they were speeding along the island's rugged western coastline. Lambert, stretched sideways across the back seat, watched the waves rolling across the picturesque Golfu di Liscia.

"Much better than Libya, Monsieur Allon. But where exactly are you taking me?"

"A village in Haute-Corse. It's near Monte Cinto." Gabriel glanced at Ingrid and added, "The highest mountain in Corsica."

"Exactly what I was hoping to hear."

Gabriel followed the coast road to the seaside resort of Porto, then headed inland and began the long climb into the mountains. Ingrid lowered her window, and the pungent scent of rosemary and lavender filled the car.

"I knew it wasn't my imagination," she said.

"Macchia," explained Gabriel. "It's a dense undergrowth that covers most of the island's interior. When the wind is right, you can smell it out at sea."

They passed through the towns of Chidazzu and Marignana and Évisa, then crossed the border into Haute-Corse. In the next village a young girl pointed at Ingrid with the first and fourth fingers of her right hand.

"Why did she do that?"

"She was afraid you might give her the *occhju*. The evil eye."

"Surely they don't believe that nonsense."

"Corsicans are superstitious by nature. They live in fear of contracting the evil eye, especially from blond-haired strangers like you."

"And if they do?"

"They have to go to the *signadora*."

"Well," said Ingrid. "I'm glad we cleared that up."

Beyond the village, in a small valley of olive groves that produced the island's finest oil, was a walled estate. The two men standing guard at the entrance were well armed. Gabriel gave them a friendly tap of the horn, and the men touched the brims of their traditional *birretta* caps in reply.

"Who lives there?" asked Ingrid.

"The man who will make certain that nothing happens to Philippe."

The road climbed a steep hill and spilled into the next valley, and soon it was little more than a dirt-and-gravel track. Gabriel nevertheless increased his speed.

Ingrid shot a nervous glance over her shoulder. "Is someone following us again?"

"No," replied Gabriel. "The danger lies ahead."

"Where?"

Just then a horned domestic goat, perhaps two hundred and fifty pounds in weight, rose from its resting place beneath the twisted limbs of three ancient olive trees and took up a defensive position in the center of the track.

"There," said Gabriel, and applied the brakes.

The enmity in the beast's deportment was obvious at once. Even Ingrid, who was new to the island, could see that something was amiss. She looked to Gabriel for an explanation. His voice, when at last he spoke, was heavy with despair.

"The goat belongs to Don Casabianca."

"And?"

"We've had our disagreements in the past."

"You and Don Casabianca?"

"No."

"Not the goat?" asked Ingrid.

Gabriel nodded gravely.

"Were you unkind to him?"

"Other way around."

"You must have done *some*thing to upset him."

"It's possible I insulted him once, but he had it coming."

"Honk the horn," said Ingrid. "I'm sure he'll move out of the way."

"Trust me, it will only make matters worse."

She reached across the front seat and sounded the horn. The goat, incensed, lowered its head and delivered four piledriver blows to the front end of the car. The last shattered glass.

"I warned you," said Gabriel.

"What now?"

"One of us has to have a word with him."

Ingrid raised a hand toward the windscreen. "Be my guest."

"If I set foot outside this car, it will be a fight to the death."

"What about Philippe?"

"Impossible. The goat is Corsican. He loathes the French."

Ingrid opened her door and placed a foot on the dusty track. "Any advice?"

"Whatever you do, don't look him directly in the eye. He has the *occhju*."

Ingrid, incredulous, climbed out of the car and addressed the goat in Danish. Gabriel, of course, had no idea what she was saying, but the goat appeared to hang on her every word. At the conclusion of her remarks, the creature cast a malevolent final glance at Gabriel, then retreated into the macchia.

Ingrid settled into the passenger seat with a smile and closed the door. Gabriel pushed the throttle to the floor and sped away before the goat had a chance to change his mind.

"What did you say to him?"

"I assured him that you were sorry for hurting his feelings. I also implied that you would take steps to atone for your conduct."

Gabriel, seething, drove in silence for a moment. "Did he apologize for attacking the car?"

"I didn't raise it."

"How bad is the damage?"

"Bad," she answered.

Gabriel glanced at Lambert over his shoulder. "I'm going to need another thousand euros."

33

Haute-Corse

The secluded villa that stood at the end of the track had a red tile roof, a large blue swimming pool, and a broad terrace that received the sun in the morning and in the afternoon was shaded by laricio pine. Gabriel made entry into the property without aid of a key or unlocking device and showed Ingrid and Philippe Lambert inside. The furniture in the sitting room was draped with white linen. Ingrid threw open the French doors and surveyed the weighty volumes of history and politics lining the handsome shelves.

"Who lives here?" she asked, her neck craned sideways.

"The villa is owned by a British subject."

Ingrid tapped the spine of a biography of Clement Attlee. "That would explain why all of these books are in English."

"It would," agreed Gabriel.

She pointed toward a small landscape by Claude Monet. "And how do you explain that?"

"The owner is a successful business consultant."

"But why did the business consultant with a Monet hanging on his wall forget to lock his front door?"

"Because he used to work for the man who lives in the large estate in the next valley. Therefore, no one on Corsica, least of all a professional criminal, would ever be so foolish as to even think about robbing this place."

Gabriel went into the kitchen and opened the door to the pantry. It was empty save for an unopened bag of Carte Noire and two containers of shelf milk. He prepared the coffee in the French press and warmed the milk in a saucepan on the stove while Ingrid and Lambert freshened up in their rooms. By half past twelve they were all gathered around the kitchen table. Lambert fired up a Winston and his laptops. And then he told them everything.

———

He began his account with an abbreviated version of his unexpectedly sparkling curriculum vitae. Born in an upscale arrondissement of Paris, he was the son of a senior executive from the French financial services giant Société Générale and a graduate of the prestigious École Polytechnique, where he studied advanced computer science. Upon graduation, he chose to postpone a lucrative career in the private sector and instead joined the DGSE, France's foreign intelligence service.

"I worked in the Technical Directorate. Electronic surveillance and other special tasks. We were nowhere near as good as you Israelis, but we weren't half bad, either. I spent much of my time targeting the Islamic State. In fact, I provided technical support for that joint French-Israeli operation you ran after the attack on the Weinberg Center. It was a thing of beauty, Monsieur Allon. Truly."

Lambert left the DGSE after ten years and went to work in the Paris office of SK4, the Swedish-owned corporate security firm. He specialized in network security and monitoring systems for offices and physical infrastructure, and his clients included some of the biggest names in French business. His base compensation package was a half million euros a year, a fivefold increase over his old salary at the DGSE.

"Life was good," said Gabriel.

"No complaints."

"What happened?"

"Trevor Robinson."

It was Robinson, with a call to Lambert's personal mobile phone, who made the initial approach. He said he wanted to discuss a business proposition of considerable sensitivity. He implied that it would be well worth Lambert's while to listen to what he had to say.

"Did he happen to mention the name of the company where he worked?"

"He said next to nothing."

"And you, of course, told him you weren't interested."

"I tried, Monsieur Allon. But he was quite persistent."

Robinson acknowledged that his firm had an office in Monaco and suggested they meet there. Lambert flew down on a Friday evening and checked into the exclusive Hôtel de Paris, where Robinson had reserved a suite in his name. They met for coffee the next morning, continued their discussions over lunch at Le Louis XV, and came to terms while cruising the Mediterranean on the firm's yacht.

"Yacht have a name?"

"*Discretion.*"

"Catchy. What about the firm?"

"Harris Weber & Company."

Ingrid opened her laptop.

"Don't," said Lambert. "I installed the tracking software on the firm's website. It's the best there is."

Gabriel opened his own laptop and found a reference to Harris Weber & Company in a directory of Monaco law firms. There was a street address on the boulevard des Moulins and a phone number, but nothing else. Lambert filled in the rest of the picture, beginning with the full names of the firm's founding partners, Ian Harris and Konrad Weber.

"Harris is British and Weber is from Zurich. They met in the early nineties while working on behalf of the same client and decided to start their own firm. Neither one of them has ever seen the inside of a courtroom. They're in the business of helping companies and wealthy individuals reduce their tax burdens by moving their assets to offshore financial centers."

"And Robinson?"

"He joined the firm in 2009."

"From where?"

"The counterintelligence division of MI5."

"Why did a garden-variety law firm specializing in offshore financial services feel the need to hire a former MI5 officer to handle its security?"

"Because Harris Weber is anything but a garden-variety firm. Its clients include some of the richest and most powerful people in the world. Some of the most dangerous as well. When dealing with such people, it pays to have a man like Trevor Robinson on the payroll."

"Not to mention Philippe Lambert."

"For the record, I am not an employee of Harris Weber. I am an independent contractor with a single client, a company called Antioch Holdings. It's a limited liability entity based in the British Virgin Islands. Antioch pays me several million dollars a year, the vast majority of which remains hidden in offshore accounts. I also have use of an apartment in Monaco and a luxury villa on Virgin Gorda."

"And what sort of services do you provide this client?"

"Nominally?" Lambert shrugged. "Network security."

"And in reality?"

"The same job I did for the DGSE."

"Electronic intelligence collection?"

"*Oui*, Monsieur Allon. And other special tasks."

To understand the nature of those tasks required Lambert to offer a fuller explanation of Harris Weber & Company and the strategies it used to serve its clients. They were, for the most part, the richest of the rich, billionaires many times over who traveled on private jets and superyachts and maintained lavish residences in every corner of the globe. Rarely, however, were they the owners of record of their expensive toys and properties. Instead, they acquired the symbols of their immense wealth using limited liability shell companies created by Harris Weber. These companies were nominally headquartered not in Monaco but in Road Town in the British Virgin Islands, where the firm maintained a small but busy office on Waterfront Drive. A secretary in the office, a certain Adele Campbell, served as the director of these corporate entities.

"At last count," said Lambert, "she controlled more than ten thousand companies, which would make her one of the most powerful businesswomen in the world. The real owners of the LLCs are known only to the firm's lawyers."

Buying homes and other luxury goods behind the cloak of an offshore shell company, Lambert pointed out, was perfectly legal and had numerous advantages, beginning with the tax savings. But it also allowed the superrich clients to conduct their affairs in secret, invisible to the prying eyes of government, law enforcement, and their fellow citizens. This was the world that Harris Weber & Company offered its clients. It was an exclusive world without rules or taxes where the needs of the less fortunate were of no concern.

"Fifteen years ago the total amount of wealth in private hands worldwide was about a hundred and twenty-five trillion dollars. It is now four hundred and fifty trillion dollars, approximately ten percent of which is held in offshore financial centers where it is beyond the reach of tax collectors. Which means the money cannot generate tax revenue to provide better schools or housing or health care for ordinary citizens."

Most of the firm's clients, Lambert continued, came by their fortunes legitimately or through inheritance and were determined to employ every measure legally available to them to avoid the payment of taxes—even if those measures were at best ethically questionable and might well have led to reputational damage if disclosed to the broader public. A significant portion of Harris Weber's clientele, however, earned their money through criminal activity or by stealing it from their citizens. The firm represented nine kleptocratic heads of state, dozens of corrupt government officials, and numerous Russian billionaires who had grown rich through their proximity to the Kremlin. Much of their ill-gotten money was invested in real estate, which they purchased using offshore shell companies.

"Do you know why most ordinary citizens can't afford to live in cities like London or Paris or Zurich or New York? It is because the global superrich are bidding up the prices of real estate with the help of offshore providers like Harris Weber. One client alone, a Middle Eastern potentate who shall remain nameless, purchased more than a billion dollars' worth of commercial and residential property in London and Manhattan while hidden behind a complex web of LLCs and layered trusts created and secretly managed by the firm. And when the potentate decided to sell some of that property at a profit, the transactions took place offshore, with Harris Weber pocketing several million dollars in fees."

The firm grew wildly rich, as did its many business partners—especially the European wealth managers and private bankers who were an invaluable source of clients. Harris Weber promised everyone absolute secrecy, but inevitably problems arose. When they did, Trevor Robinson gave the names to Philippe Lambert, and Lambert lit them up and sucked them dry.

"Phones, computers, medical and financial data. Anything I could lay my hands on. I gave the material to Robinson, and he used it to make the problems go away."

"He blackmailed them?"

"The lucky ones. The ones who didn't get the message he dealt with in other ways."

"Who were they?"

"Anyone who posed a threat to the firm's business or its clients."

"Such as?"

"Tax officials, regulators, investigative journalists, sometimes even the clients themselves."

"What about an art historian from Oxford?"

Lambert hesitated, then nodded slowly. "*Oui*, Monsieur Allon."

"Why was she targeted?"

"Untitled portrait of a woman by Pablo Picasso."

"The painting was a threat to the firm?"

"Not just the firm. The clients, the partners, the banks . . ." Lambert shrugged. "Everything."

34

Haute-Corse

It was Ian Harris, a minor collector with a taste for Dutch portraiture, who originally hit upon the idea. He referred to it, innocuously, as "the art strategy." Not art as an investment, but art as a means of laundering and concealing wealth and, more important, of conveying wealth from its country of origin to offshore tax havens. It was made possible by the art world's long-standing tradition of secrecy. Nearly $70 billion worth of paintings and other objets d'art changed hands each year, most of it privately. Buyers typically did not know the identity of sellers, sellers did not know the identity of buyers, and government regulators and tax collectors knew almost nothing at all.

But exploiting that inherent vulnerability, explained Philippe Lambert, required a facility like the Geneva Freeport, which permitted customers to store their art in climate-controlled vaults rented by anonymous shell companies. Under the lax rules of the Freeport, the shell company was not required to disclose its beneficial owner. He could purchase a $200 million painting at auction in New York or London and avoid all taxation merely by shipping it to the Freeport. Furthermore, the secret owner of the shell company could sell his $200 million painting at a profit within the confines of the Freeport with no tax implications.

"The Freeport always had a shady side to it," said Lambert. "But Harris Weber & Company turned the place into a six-hundred-thousand-square-foot washing machine."

"What was Galerie Ricard's role?" asked Gabriel.

"Ricard was a washerwoman, nothing more. He changed the loads, pushed the buttons, and got a tiny slice of each transaction. But there were always fights about money. He believed he was underappreciated and underpaid."

For all its ingenuity, Lambert went on, the art strategy was quite simple. All it required were two anonymous limited liability shell corporations in the British Virgin Islands, which Harris Weber created for a modest fee. The client would then purchase a painting—at auction or privately through the auspices of a gallery—and immediately ship it to the Freeport, where it would be placed in a vault rented by one of the shell companies. The client would then sell the painting, sometimes in a matter of days or even hours, at Galerie Ricard, under conditions of strict secrecy. The proceeds of the sale would then be funneled into the second anonymous shell company, with the money deposited at one of Harris Weber's partner Caribbean banks. There it would remain invisible to the tax authorities of the client's host country. He was free to invest the money in equities or commodities—tax free, of course—or he could use it to acquire valuable assets such as private jets, yachts, and luxury homes.

As a result of the scheme, several hundred billion dollars' worth of private wealth was funneled offshore and buried beneath layers of corporate shells and trusts. Harris Weber & Company and its stable of ethically challenged lawyers received hundreds of millions in legal fees and commissions. Still not satisfied with their earnings, they decided to further leverage the art strategy by going into the art business themselves. With a portion of their profits, they acquired a small but extremely valuable collection of high-priced paintings, which they used primarily for purposes of money laundering—sham "sales" that generated hundreds of millions' worth of additional commissions and profits. They stored the paintings in the Geneva Freeport under the supervision of Galerie Ricard and managed the collection through an anonymous limited liability shell company based in the British Virgin Islands.

"OOC Group, Limited?"

"*Oui*, Monsieur Allon. It stands for Oil on Canvas. But there were several other shell companies and layered trusts standing between OOC Group and Harris Weber. It would be extremely difficult for anyone to piece together the puzzle."

Unless, of course, a problem arose with one of the paintings in the firm's inventory—a problem that would allow a plaintiff in a legal proceeding to penetrate Harris Weber's records through the process of discovery. This was the situation confronting the firm when Trevor Robinson woke Lambert from a sound sleep early one morning in mid-December. Robinson was on the slopes of Chamonix. Lambert was at the villa on Virgin Gorda.

"And the problem?"

"The Picasso," said Lambert. "Harris Weber acquired it ten years ago in a private sale brokered by Christie's in London. Professor Blake had somehow uncovered details of the transaction, including the name of the buyer."

"Oil on Canvas Group, Limited?"

Lambert nodded.

"But how did Trevor Robinson know what she had discovered?"

"He didn't go into the details. He just wanted me to find out whether the professor really had the goods. I hacked into her phone and computer and grabbed everything, including her version of the painting's provenance. It listed the name of the original owner as well as the name of the rightful heir."

"Dr. Emanuel Cohen."

"*Oui*, Monsieur Allon."

Lambert also discovered the name of the man with whom Professor Blake was having an extramarital affair: Leonard Bradley, a wealthy trader and art aficionado who lived with his wife and three children in a clifftop home near Land's End in Cornwall. Lambert forwarded the information to Trevor Robinson, along with hundreds of intimate text messages and geolocation data pinpointing the likely location of their trysts. It was Lambert's assumption that the former British spy would use the damaging information merely to pressure Professor Blake into amending the findings of her inquiry. Trevor Robinson, however, had other ideas.

"He wanted me to send Professor Blake a text message from Bradley's number."

"And the nature of the message?"

"Bradley needed to discuss a matter of the utmost urgency."

"Mrs. Bradley had found out about the affair?"

"That was the implication."

"What time did Bradley want to see her?"

"Five p.m."

"The cliffs above Porthchapel Beach?"

"*Oui.*"

"What did you do?"

"I sent the text," said Lambert. "And two hours later Professor Blake was dead."

———

Emanuel Cohen died three days later, the victim of an apparent fall down the steps of the rue Chappe in Montmartre. Lambert knew nothing of the doctor's fate. He was hard at work on another matter, an overzealous Norwegian tax official who was targeting one of the firm's most important clients. Lambert gave Trevor Robinson a mountain of compromising material—the Norwegian had a weakness for child pornography—and Robinson gave Lambert his next assignment.

"Hack the Geneva Freeport?"

Lambert nodded.

"Did Robinson tell you why?"

"The problem with the Picasso had resurfaced."

This time, though, the threat was internal. Edmond Ricard had received a lucrative offer for the Picasso that he wanted to accept. The prospective buyer, interestingly enough, was Anna Rolfe, the world-renowned violinist. She intended to store the painting in the Geneva Freeport under Ricard's supervision. He was confident the canvas would remain under lock and key and out of public view for the foreseeable future.

"I assume Harris Weber & Company was opposed to the deal?"

"Vehemently."

"Why didn't the partners simply tell Ricard that the painting wasn't on the market?"

"They did."

"And?"

"Ricard agreed to withdraw from the negotiations. But I was monitoring his phone, and I knew that he had no intention of backing out of the deal. It was to be a trade rather than an outright sale. The Picasso in exchange for works by Van Gogh, Modigliani, and Cézanne. Ricard planned to sell the three paintings and pocket the money. He was confident his partners at Harris Weber would never find out about it."

"Because his partners intended to leave the Picasso in the Freeport forever."

"*Exactement*, Monsieur Allon. As far as the firm was concerned, Ricard's double-dealing was the final straw."

Lambert was confident in his ability to crack the Freeport's network undetected. Nevertheless, out of an abundance of caution, he carried out the hack from a hastily rented apartment in Cannes. Alone in his darkened room overlooking the rue d'Antibes, he was monitoring the Freeport's security cameras when a man with an art transport case entered the stubby office block at 4 Route du Grand-Lancy, home of Galerie Ricard. Fifteen minutes later, after the man had left the building, Lambert made a single keystroke, and six months' worth of Freeport security video vanished into thin air.

"Or so you thought," said Gabriel, and clicked the trackpad on his laptop.

Lambert glared at the screen, then at Ingrid. "How were you able to resurrect it?"

"Quite easily, actually."

They watched as the man with the art transport case stepped from the elevator on the third floor and requested admission to Galerie Ricard.

"What did you think was going to happen next?" asked Gabriel.

"Robinson told me that he was going to remove the Picasso from the gallery before Ricard could complete the transaction with Anna Rolfe."

"Remove?"

"Robinson's word, not mine."

"When did you realize that he had made you an accomplice in yet another murder?"

It wasn't until the next morning, when Lambert read about Ricard's killing in *Nice-Matin*. Alarmed, he rang Trevor Robinson in Monaco and informed him that he was going to take a nice long vacation somewhere far away. Brazil, perhaps. Or better yet, Sri Lanka.

Instead, he barricaded himself in the apartment in Cannes and began grabbing as many files from Harris Weber & Company as he could lay his hands on. His plan, to the extent he had one, was to use the material to ensure his survival when the day came that Trevor Robinson decided that he was no longer of use to the firm.

"That day arrived much sooner than I expected. Fortunately, Monsieur Allon, you were there to prevent me from being killed."

"Don't thank me, thank my associate. She's the one who traced the hack to that apartment in Cannes."

Lambert looked at Ingrid and asked, "How?"

She rolled her eyes. "I only hope you covered your tracks a little better when you hacked into Harris Weber's database."

"I did."

"Find anything interesting?" asked Gabriel.

Lambert picked up one of the external hard drives he had taken from the apartment. "A directory of every shell company ever created by the firm. But I'm afraid it's useless without the names of the beneficial owners."

"The clients, you mean?"

"*Oui*, Monsieur Allon."

"And where would we find those?"

"All of the firm's sensitive attorney-client information is stored offline on an external hard drive. And the hard drive is locked in a safe inside the firm's offices in Monaco."

"How much data are we talking about?" asked Ingrid.

"Three terabytes, at least."

"Does the safe have a door on it?"

"Of course."

"That's a relief," said Ingrid. "Combination or keypad?"

35

Villa Orsati

Philippe Lambert's external hard drives contained more than merely a list of the shell companies created by the law firm of Harris Weber & Company. He had also saved the contents of Charlotte Blake's missing mobile phone—the metadata, the geolocation data, the Internet browsing history, the emails and text messages. They left no doubt that she had been involved in an affair with Leonard Bradley, a wealthy high-frequency trader who owned a substantial clifftop home not far from the spot where she was murdered.

There was also a copy of Professor Blake's provenance for an untitled portrait of a woman, oil on canvas, 94 by 66 centimeters, by Pablo Picasso. It was purchased, she discovered, from Galerie Paul Rosenberg in June 1939 by the businessman and collector Bernard Lévy. In July 1942, one week after the Paris Roundup, Lévy entrusted the painting to his lawyer, Hector Favreau, and went into hiding in the south with his wife and daughter. Favreau kept the painting until 1944, when he sold it to André Delacroix, a senior official in the collaborationist Vichy regime. The painting remained in the Delacroix family until 2015, when it was put up for sale at the venerable Christie's auction house in London. It fetched a mere fifty-two million pounds, in part because of concerns about its past. The buyer was OOC Group, Ltd., of Road Town, the British Virgin Islands. Charlotte Blake, a former employee of Christie's, had a photocopy of the sales agreement to prove it.

But how had Trevor Robinson known of Professor Blake's explosive findings? The most likely explanation was that Robinson had been tipped off by someone, probably in mid-December. Gabriel searched the professor's emails and text messages but found nothing to suggest she had shared the information with anyone. The phone's geolocation data indicated that she had spent the long winter academic break in isolation at her cottage in Cornwall. Her only travel during this period was a three-day visit to London, where, on the afternoon of December 15, she spent ninety minutes at the Courtauld Gallery.

It occurred to Gabriel that Sarah Bancroft, a member of the Courtauld's board of trustees, might know something about Professor Blake's visit to the gallery. He reached her at Isherwood Fine Arts, where she was showing a painting to a prospective buyer. She sounded relieved to hear his voice.

"Please tell me you didn't kill him," she said.

"Who?"

She delivered her answer in a stage whisper. "Monsieur Ricard."

"We should probably postpone this discussion until I get back to London."

"Where are you now?"

In coded language, Gabriel informed Sarah that he had borrowed her husband's villa on Corsica. Then he told her about the ninety minutes that Professor Charlotte Blake had spent at the Courtauld Gallery in mid-December.

"I'm sure there's a perfectly reasonable explanation," she said.
"Like what?"
"Oh, I don't know. Perhaps she wanted to see a painting."
"As far as I can tell, she was in one spot the entire time."
"And you're sure it was the fifteenth?"
"Why do you ask?"
"I was at the Courtauld the same day. Bloody board meeting. Three hours of unmitigated tedium, after which I went home and crawled into my empty bed."
"Is it still empty?"
"Don't even think about it," she said, and rang off.

At one fifteen that afternoon Gabriel unleashed Proteus on Trevor Robinson's mobile phone. In less than an hour, the hacking malware had seized control of the device's operating system. After downloading the former MI5 officer's emails and text messages, Gabriel instructed Ingrid to locate and delete Philippe Lambert's inferior Macedonian malware. Armed with Proteus, it took her all of five minutes.

"Would you mind if I made a copy of this stuff for myself?"

"I would, actually. But you can have this." Gabriel handed Ingrid the HK tactical pistol. "I have to run an errand. Shoot anyone who comes within fifty meters of the villa."

Outside, Gabriel climbed into the damaged rental car and set off down the unpaved track. Don Casabianca's wretched goat was reclining in the shade of the three ancient olive trees. The beast remained there, vigilant but motionless, as Gabriel braked to a halt and lowered his window. He addressed his adversary in French.

"Listen, I don't know what my friend said to you earlier, but nothing about this situation between us is my fault. In fact, this is one of the few disputes in my life where I am entirely blameless. Therefore, I am the one who is owed an apology, not you. And tell your master, the loathsome Don Casabianca, that I expect him to pay for the damage you inflicted on my automobile."

And with that, Gabriel raised his window and rolled away in a cloud of dust. He followed the road over the hill and into the neighboring valley, and a moment later slowed to a stop at the entrance of the grand estate. The two guards regarded the front of the car with expressions of mild bemusement. They did not bother to ask for an explanation. Gabriel's long feud with Don Casabianca's ill-mannered caprine was now part of the island's lore.

The guards opened the gate, and Gabriel headed up a long drive lined with Van Gogh olive trees. Don Anton Orsati's office was located on the second floor of his fortresslike villa. As usual, he received Gabriel while seated behind the heavy oaken table he used for his desk. He wore a pair of loose-fitting trousers, dusty leather sandals, and a crisp white shirt. At his elbow was a bottle of Orsati olive oil—olive oil being the legitimate front through which the don laundered the profits of his real business, which was murder for hire. Gabriel was one of only two people who had managed to survive an Orsati family contract. The other was Anna Rolfe.

Rising, Don Orsati offered Gabriel a granite hand. "I was beginning to think you were avoiding me."

"Forgive me, Your Holiness. But I had to attend to an urgent matter."

The don regarded him skeptically with a pair of black eyes. It was like being studied by a canine. "The urgent matter wasn't that pretty blond woman, was it?"

"The man in the back seat."

"Rumor has it you gave René Monjean a thousand euros to get him out of Marseilles."

"What else does rumor have?"

"A worker at a vineyard north of Saint-Tropez stumbled on a body early this morning. A motorcyclist, no identification or phone. The police seem to think someone must have run him off the road."

"Do they have a suspect?"

The don shook his head. "It's quiet up there this time of year. Apparently, no one saw a thing."

Gabriel wordlessly tossed the German passport onto the tabletop. Don Orsati opened it to the first page.

"A professional?"

"Quite."

"Were you the target?"

"The man in the back seat," replied Gabriel. "He's a computer hacker who works for a dirty law firm in Monaco."

"Who wanted him dead?"

"The dirty law firm."

"What about the pretty blond woman?"

"She used to be a professional thief."

"And now?"

"Hard to say, really. She's still a work in progress."

The don held up the passport between two thick fingers. "Are you keeping this for any reason?"

"Sentimental value, mainly."

"In that case, perhaps we should get rid of it." Don Orsati carried the passport over to the large stone fireplace and dropped it on the stack of macchia wood burning on the grate. "And how can we at the Orsati Olive Oil Company be of service to you?"

"I require protection for the computer hacker."

"For how long?"

"Long enough for me to pull a heist at the dirty law firm."

"And if the heist goes sideways?"

"I'm confident it won't."

"Why?"

"The pretty blond woman."

———————

Gabriel told Anton Orsati the rest of the story outside on the terrace, over a bottle of pale Corsican rosé. He omitted none of the salient details, including the fact that he was working in collusion with two European police forces and the security and intelligence service of Switzerland. The don, who made his living in part by avoiding entanglements with law enforcement, was predictably appalled.

"And when the police ask their star witness, this Philippe Lambert fellow, where he went into hiding after the attempt on his life? What happens then?"

"It is my hope, Don Orsati, that it doesn't come to that."

"We have a proverb here on Corsica about hope."

"And for nearly every other occasion as well," added Gabriel.

"He who lives on hope," said Don Orsati, undeterred, "dies on shit. And he who answers the door to the police lives to regret it. Especially if that person is in my line of work."

"I'm quite certain that's not an actual Corsican proverb."

"Its sentiments are sacred and correct, all the same."

"But he who sleeps," said Gabriel, quoting a proverb of his own, "cannot catch fish. And he who seeks, finds."

"And what exactly are you hoping to find at the law firm of Harris Weber & Company in Monaco?"

"Several million pages of incriminating documents."

"Which will lead to the recovery of the missing Picasso?"

Gabriel nodded. "It will also lead to the prosecution of the firm's founding partners, not to mention a great number of extremely wealthy people who have used unethical or in some cases illegal methods to conceal hundreds of billions of dollars' worth of their wealth in offshore tax havens."

"This might come as a shock to you, Gabriel, but I believe that what a man does with his money is his business, not his government's. That said, I will agree to look after Lambert until the threats to his life have been eliminated. I will, however, expect to be reimbursed for his room and board, not to mention the extra manpower costs for his security."

"He has several million dollars at a bank in the British Virgin Islands."

"A good start." Orsati smiled. "The question is, where shall we put him?"

"For the time being, he can stay with me at Christopher's place."

"While you plan this heist of yours?"

Gabriel nodded.

"Does Christopher know what you're up to?"

"He doesn't have a clue."

"It might be wise to include him."

"Christopher is no longer an employee of the Orsati Olive Oil Company. He is an officer of His Majesty's Secret Intelligence Service."

"And?"

"One of the founding partners of Harris Weber is British, and the firm is incorporated in the British Virgin Islands, which is a British overseas territory."

"Is that a problem?"

"As a general rule, Western intelligence services are forbidden to spy on their own people."

"But you're not spying on the firm. You're simply going to steal its files."

"It's rather the same thing."

"I don't care how good your pretty friend is," said Orsati. "You can't send her into that office alone. You need at least one more person, preferably a professional."

"Anyone come to mind?"

"What about the man who gave you a ride to Corsica?"

"Can you arrange it?"

"Consider it done." Orsati lifted his gaze toward the darkening sky. "When storms roll in, dogs make beds."

"What about goats?" asked Gabriel.

"Is there a problem?"

"He had a go at my car this morning. Someone has to pay for the damage, and it isn't going to be me."

Don Orsati sighed. "Coins are round and come and go."

"So do goats," said Gabriel darkly.

"Not one hair on its head. Otherwise, there will be a feud."

"That's not a proverb, either, Don Orsati."

36

Haute-Corse

The operational planning commenced a few minutes after eight the following morning when René Monjean, after yet another overnight crossing from the mainland, guided *Mistral* into the tiny marina in the resort town of Porto. Gabriel was there to meet him. They put the vessel in order, then climbed into the car and headed eastward into the mountains.

"What happened to your headlight, Monsieur Allon?"

"Vandalism."

"Corsicans," muttered Monjean disdainfully.

"Imagine how they feel about you Marseillais."

"They can't stand us. But then again, Corsicans can't stand anyone. That's why they're Corsicans." Monjean lit a cigarette and eyed Gabriel through a cloud of smoke. "You, however, seem to be quite well connected on the island."

"It pays to have friends like Don Orsati in my line of work."

"And what is your game these days?"

"I'm an art conservator. But in my spare time, I help the police solve art-related crimes."

"That's interesting," said Monjean. "In my spare time, I sometimes commit art-related crimes."

"Stolen anything lately, René?"

"That depends on the ground rules of our relationship."

"One hand washes the other and both hands wash the face."

"What does that mean?"

"It's a Corsican proverb. It means that I will use you as a source or an operative, but I will never breathe a word about you to my friends in the French police. Or any other police force, for that matter. Everything will be entre nous."

"What about money?"

"It doesn't come from singing."

"Another Corsican proverb?"

Gabriel nodded. "I'll pay you whatever you want. Provided, of course, your fee is within reason."

"It would depend on the nature of the job and the value of the target."

"I need you to steal a few documents from a law firm in Monaco."

"How many?"

"Several million."

Monjean laughed. "How am I supposed to carry several million documents out of an office building in Monaco?"

"You're going to copy them off a digital storage device."

"It's not my thing, Monsieur Allon. I steal objects, not data."

"But it's Ingrid's thing."

"The woman from the other night?"

Gabriel nodded. "She's a professional."

"How do we get into the building?"

"Philippe will open the doors remotely. You'll walk in, copy the documents, and walk out again."

"How long will it take?"

"Three or four hours."

"A lot can go wrong in four hours."

"Or four minutes," added Gabriel.

Monjean lapsed into silence.

"Any more questions, René?"

"Just one."

"Fire away."

"How do you know Don Orsati?"

"Someone hired him to kill me a long time ago."

"Why aren't you dead?"

"Luck of the Irish."

"But you're not Irish."

"Figure of speech, René."

"Mind if I ask one more question, Monsieur Allon?"

"If you must."

"What really happened to your headlight?"

There was no embarrassing recurrence of the incident that morning, for once again Don Casabianca's obstreperous goat allowed Gabriel to drive past the three ancient olive trees unmolested. Two of Don Orsati's men were now standing watch outside the villa at the end of the dirt-and-gravel track. René Monjean dropped his duffel bag in the entrance hall and went into the sitting room. His sharp eye was caught by the Monet landscape hanging on the wall.

"Is it real?" he asked Gabriel.

"You tell me."

The art thief leaned in for a closer look. "It's definitely real."

"Not bad, René."

"I have no formal training, but I've managed to develop a pretty good eye for paintings."

"I would advise you to forget that you ever saw that one."

"The owner is a friend of Don Orsati?"

"You might say that."

They went into the kitchen, where Ingrid and Lambert were staring at laptops. Gabriel once again saw to the introductions, but this time they left nothing to the imagination. Ingrid rose to her feet in order to properly shake Monjean's hand, or so she made it appear. The art thief regarded her warily.

"Monsieur Allon assures me that you're a professional."

"He says the same about you. In fact, he says there's no one better than René Monjean."

"He's right about that."

"I think you'll find that I'm rather good myself."

"We'll see."

Ingrid returned the mobile phone she had plucked from Monjean's pocket. "We will indeed."

———

With a total area of just two square kilometers, the Principality of Monaco was the world's second-smallest sovereign country, larger only than Vatican City. Its primary attractions were its historic cathedral, its aquarium and exotic gardens, and, of course, the Casino de Monte-Carlo. Some thirty-eight thousand people lived in the city-state, but fewer than ten thousand were Monégasque citizens. They were protected by a highly professional security force numbering 515 officers, which meant that tiny Monaco had the largest per capita police presence anywhere on earth.

The boulevard des Moulins stretched for just five hundred meters through the heart of the principality and was lined with elegant, butter-colored apartment buildings where sixty thousand euros would buy exactly one square meter of real estate. Harris Weber & Company occupied two floors of the commercial building located at Number 41. On the ground floor was a hair salon—exclusive, of course—and a branch of Société Banque de Monaco. Directly opposite was a café called La Royale.

"It's the perfect place to kill a few minutes while you're getting to know the neighborhood," said Lambert. "But don't worry, the lawyers of Harris Weber would never dream of setting foot there."

The other tenants of 41 boulevard des Moulins, he continued, were medical professionals, accountants, financial advisers, and architects. Visitors were admitted remotely by the tenants' receptionists, but those who worked in the building unlocked the street entrance with their personal cardkeys. The same keys operated the lift, with access to floors carefully restricted. Harris Weber's lobby and reception area were on the fourth floor, but the offices of the founding partners and senior associates were upstairs on the fifth.

"Along with Trevor Robinson's," added Lambert.

"What about the file room?" asked Gabriel.

"It's down on four."

Lambert was logged on to the system. He tapped a few keys on his laptop, and a shot of the file room appeared on his screen, courtesy of Harris Weber's internal security cameras. An attractive young woman was at that moment crouched next to the open drawer of a metal filing cabinet.

"Mademoiselle Dubois. She's one of the secretaries. Anyone in the firm can access the paper files stored in those cabinets, but access to the secure room is strictly limited." Lambert pointed out a vaguely out-of-focus doorway on the left side of the shot. "The lock is numeric and biometric, but I can override it."

"Is there a surveillance camera in that room?"

"Yes, of course. Trevor Robinson trusts no one."

Lambert worked the keys on his laptop, and a small windowless room appeared on his screen. It contained a table, a swivel chair, a desktop computer, a printer, and a double-doored executive safe.

"The computer is air-gapped," Lambert continued. "If one of the senior lawyers needs to review sensitive attorney-client documents, he removes the storage device from the safe and attaches it to the desktop. If he needs to print the documents, he keeps them only as long as necessary. Trevor Robinson handles the shredding personally. If he had his druthers, he'd burn the documents instead. It's just like an intelligence service."

Gabriel pointed out the electronic lock on the safe. "I don't suppose you know the combination."

"I'm afraid not. Whenever someone punches in the passcode, they block the view of the camera, which is by design. Trevor Robinson changes it every few weeks, much to the chagrin of Herr Weber, who has a dreadful memory."

Ingrid had a closer look at the lock.

"Recognize it?" asked Gabriel.

She nodded. "It's American made, secure but vulnerable. Like many electronic locks, the internal actuator can be manipulated from outside the safe with a magnet."

"How powerful does it need to be?"

"A forty-by-twenty-millimeter rare-earth magnet should do the trick. Professional locksmiths call them hockey pucks. They're referred to as permanent magnets because they're so strong. And quite dangerous." She glanced at Monjean. "Isn't that right, René?"

He nodded knowingly. "A colleague crushed a finger using one of those things."

"I hope it was worth it," said Gabriel.

"A blue-and-white Tianqiuping vase." Monjean smiled. "It fetched two million on the black market."

"Any other options?" asked Gabriel.

"A computerized automatic dialer," said Ingrid. "You attach it to the lock and let it run the numbers until it stumbles on the correct combination."

"How long will it take?"

"Hard to say. Could be twelve minutes or twelve hours."

"Can you lay your hands on one on short notice?"

"My friend in Grasse will sell me one, I'm sure."

"Monsieur Giroux?" asked Monjean.

Ingrid frowned. "Perhaps Philippe should give us a guided tour of the entire office."

It began in the fourth-floor reception area, with its stylish furnishings and artwork to match, and concluded in the fifth-floor conference room, where Ian Harris and Konrad Weber were at that moment meeting with a slick-looking creature with a chemically enhanced face and a price-available-upon-request suit. There was no audio, only video. The cameras, said Lambert, were concealed.

"How late do they work at night?" asked Gabriel.

"The firm's office hours are ten to six, but one of the young associates always stays until nine."

"Close of business in the British Virgin Islands?"

Lambert nodded.

"And the rest of the building?"

"It's dead by then. As soon as the last lawyer leaves for the night, Ingrid and René will have the place to themselves. I'll let them into the building and let them out again when it's time to leave."

"How's the Internet here?"

"Rock-solid and surprisingly fast. Your friend has an excellent network."

Gabriel turned to Monjean. "Escape route?"

"The French border is fifty meters to the west of the building, but my preference would be to leave by boat."

"Can you reserve a berth in the port?"

"At this time of year?" Monjean shrugged to indicate it would not be a problem. "You can spend the evening listening to my new audio system while Ingrid and I steal the documents. And then we'll all take a nice midnight cruise together to celebrate."

Gabriel made to reply but stopped when he heard the sound of a car drawing up outside in the forecourt. The driver greeted Don Orsati's security men in fluent *corsu* and then let himself into the villa. He wore a charcoal-gray suit by Richard Anderson of Savile Row, an open-neck white dress shirt, and handmade oxford shoes. His hair was sun-bleached, his skin was taut and dark, his eyes were bright blue. The notch in the center of his thick chin looked as though it had been cleaved with a chisel. His mouth seemed permanently fixed in an ironic half-smile.

"Well, well," he said. "Isn't this jolly."

37

Haute-Corse

In the autumn of 1989, Gabriel reluctantly agreed to deliver a lecture in Tel Aviv to a visiting delegation of officers from the Special Air Service, Britain's elite commando regiment. The topic was the April 1988 targeted killing of Abu Jihad, the PLO's second-in-command, at his seaside villa in Tunis, an operation that Gabriel had carried out. At the conclusion of his presentation, he had posed for a photograph with the members of his audience, wearing a hat and sunglasses to conceal his identity. After the last picture was snapped, the handsome British officer standing next to him thrust out his hand and said, "My name's Keller, by the way. Christopher Keller. I imagine we'll be meeting again someday."

From the moment he arrived at SAS headquarters in Herefordshire, it was obvious that Christopher was different. His scores in the Killing House, an infamous facility where recruits practice close-quarters combat and hostage rescue, were the highest ever recorded. His most remarkable achievement, though, was the time he posted for the Endurance, a forty-mile march across the windswept moorland known as the Brecon Beacons. Laden with a fifty-five-pound rucksack and a ten-pound assault rifle, Christopher shattered the course record by thirty minutes, a mark that stands to this day.

He was assigned to a Sabre squadron specializing in mobile desert warfare, but his intelligence and ability to improvise on his feet soon brought him to the attention of the SAS's Special Reconnaissance Unit. After eight weeks of intense training, he arrived in war-torn Northern Ireland as a plainclothes surveillance specialist. The subtleties of local accents required most of his colleagues to utilize the services of a Fred—the unit's term for a local helper—when tracking IRA members or engaging in street surveillance. But Christopher quickly developed the ability to mimic the various dialects of Ulster with the speed and confidence of a native. He could even switch accents at a moment's notice—a Catholic from Armagh one minute, a Protestant from Belfast's Shankill Road the next, then a Catholic from the Ballymurphy housing estates.

His unique combination of skills did not escape the notice of an ambitious young officer from T Branch, the Irish terrorism department of MI5. The officer, whose name was Graham Seymour, was unimpressed by the quality of intelligence he was receiving from MI5's informants in Northern Ireland and was eager to insert an agent of his own. Christopher accepted the assignment, and two months later he slipped into West Belfast posing as a Catholic named Michael Connelly. He took a two-room flat in the Divis Tower apartment complex on the Falls Road and found work as a deliveryman for a laundry service. His neighbor, with whom he shared a cordial relationship, was a member of the IRA's West Belfast Brigade.

An Anglican by birth, Christopher attended mass regularly at St. Paul's Church, the IRA's favorite house of worship. It was there, on a wet Sunday during the holy season of Lent, that he met Elizabeth Conlin, daughter of Ronnie Conlin, the IRA's field commander for

Ballymurphy. Their brief love affair would end with Elizabeth's brutal murder and Christopher's abduction. His interrogation took place at a farmhouse in South Armagh and was conducted by a senior IRA man called Eamon Quinn. Faced with the prospect of an appalling death, Christopher decided he had no recourse but to fight his way out. By the time he made his escape, four hardened terrorists from the Provisional Irish Republican Army were dead. Two had been virtually cut to pieces.

He returned to SAS headquarters at Hereford for what he thought would be a long rest, but his stay was cut short in August 1990 when Saddam Hussein invaded Kuwait. He quickly rejoined his old Sabre unit and by January 1991 was in the western desert of Iraq, searching out the Scud missile launchers that were raining terror on Tel Aviv. On the night of January 28, his team located a launcher a hundred miles northwest of Baghdad and radioed the coordinates to their commanders in Saudi Arabia. Ninety minutes later a formation of Coalition fighter-bombers streaked low over the desert. But in a disastrous case of friendly fire, the aircraft attacked the SAS squadron instead of the Scud site. British officials concluded the entire unit was lost, including Christopher.

In truth, he had survived the incident without a scratch. His first instinct was to radio his base and request extraction. Instead, enraged by the incompetence of his superiors, he started walking. Concealed beneath the robe and headdress of a desert Arab, and highly trained in the art of clandestine movement, he made his way through the Coalition forces and slipped undetected into Syria.

He continued westward across Turkey and Greece and eventually washed ashore in Corsica, where he fell into the waiting arms of Don Anton Orsati. With his northern European looks and SAS training, Christopher was a valuable addition to the don's stable of Corsican-born assassins. His prophesized reunion with Gabriel occurred thirteen years after their first meeting. Gabriel survived the encounter only because Christopher declined a perfect opportunity to kill him. He returned the favor by convincing the director-general of the Secret Intelligence Service to give Christopher a job. Because the director was none other than Graham Seymour, the man who had sent Christopher into West Belfast, the negotiations went smoothly.

Under the generous terms of Christopher's repatriation agreement, SIS provided him with a new identity and allowed him to keep the small fortune he had amassed working for the Orsati Olive Oil Company, a portion of which he had invested in his maisonette in Queen's Gate Terrace. He acquired Sarah Bancroft soon after. Gabriel had initially opposed the relationship, but in the end he played a decisive role in their decision to marry. The wedding took place at an SIS safe house. Gabriel gave away the bride.

The SIS had also allowed Christopher to maintain possession of his comfortable villa on Corsica. Seated in a deck chair next to the swimming pool, Gabriel explained to his old friend the nature of the crime he was planning to perpetrate in the Principality of Monaco. Christopher, like Don Orsati before him, was deeply troubled by what he was hearing.

"You've placed me in a precarious situation." He gave his glass of Johnnie Walker Black Label a shake, rattling the ice. "Very precarious, indeed."

"With all due respect, Christopher, your entire life has been one long precarious situation."

"But that doesn't change the fact that I am now obligated to inform my superiors about your findings regarding the murder of Professor Charlotte Blake, including the role played by a former MI5 officer named Trevor Robinson. If your hacker's allegations are true, it's going to be a scandal for the ages."

"The allegations *are* true," said Gabriel.

"Prove it."

"I intend to."

"By stealing the names of Harris Weber's clients?"

Gabriel nodded.

"What are you going to do with them?"

"Depends on the names, I suppose."

"Given the fact that Harris Weber & Company is, for all intents and purposes, a British firm, it is likely that many of its clients are British as well. It is also likely that some of them are public figures. People who've made a lot of money. Posh people with grand estates in Somerset and the Cotswolds. You see my point?"

"I don't believe you've made one."

"Those files, in the wrong hands, can do a lot of damage."

"Or in the right hands," replied Gabriel.

Christopher ignited a Marlboro with a gold Dunhill lighter and exhaled a cloud of smoke. It was carried away by a sudden gust of wind that bent the laricio pine trees surrounding the terrace.

"The plan?" he asked.

"Sorry," answered Gabriel. "That's need-to-know only."

Christopher laid a sledgehammer hand on Gabriel's forearm. "You were saying?"

Gabriel complied with the request for an operational briefing.

"How did our old friend René Monjean get mixed up in this?" asked Christopher.

"It was the don's idea, actually."

"In my experience, René doesn't work for free."

"He expects to be paid at some point."

"And Ingrid?"

"She has more money than you do."

"Are you two . . ."

"Are we what?"

"You know," said Christopher.

"I don't, actually."

A female voice behind them calmly supplied the answer. "What your friend wants to know, Mr. Allon, is whether we're sleeping together."

Gabriel and Christopher swung around in their chairs in unison and saw Ingrid standing on the flagstone deck, clad in spandex athletic attire and a pair of Nike trainers.

"I'm going for a run. I'll be back in a couple of hours."

She turned without another word and was gone. Christopher drained the last of his whisky. "Don't I feel like a complete ass."

"You should, you reprobate."

"Does she ever make a sound? And who the hell takes two-hour training runs?"

"Ingrid does."

"Where did you find her?"

"I'll tell you the story tonight on the way to Monaco."

"I'm not going anywhere near Monaco."

"Suit yourself. But if you change your mind, *Mistral* departs the marina at Porto at midnight."

"Have you checked the weather forecast?" Christopher smiled and said, "*Bon voyage.*"

38

Haute-Corse

By the time Ingrid reached the three ancient olive trees, she was moving along at a brisk pace. She paused long enough to bid Don Casabianca's goat a pleasant afternoon—the poor thing really was quite harmless—then turned onto a footpath that carried her up the slope of the hill and into a pine forest. The wind was getting up, promising a rough crossing to the mainland later that night. She wondered whether the Englishman named Christopher Keller would be joining them. She had been tempted to tell him the truth about the nature of her relationship with Gabriel—and about the job she had done in Moscow—but that was not her place. Besides, she had a feeling Christopher had done a dirty job or two himself.

After thirty minutes of sustained effort, she realized that she had no earthly idea where she was. Pausing, she checked her location on her phone and saw that the village was just beyond the next hill. She spotted it a moment later as she stood gasping for air atop the ridge. The bells of the church were tolling two o'clock.

She was careful not to turn an ankle during the descent down the opposing slope and entered the village at an unhurried walk. A single street spiraled its way past shuttered houses to a broad and dusty square. It was bordered on three sides by shops and cafés and on the fourth by the church. The rectory was next door, and next to the rectory was a crooked little house.

She took a table at one of the cafés and ordered a coffee from the indifferent waitress. In the center of the square, several men in crisp white shirts were locked in a hotly contested game of *pétanque*. Two sullen mothers sat on a bench beneath the limbs of a plane tree while their sons chased one another with sticks. Another child, a girl of eight or nine, was knocking on the door of the crooked little house.

The door opened at once, and a small pale hand emerged, clutching a slip of blue paper. The girl carried it across the square to the café. Ingrid gave a start when the child sat down at her table.

"Who are you?" she asked.

The young girl wordlessly handed Ingrid the slip of paper.

I've been waiting for you . . .

Ingrid looked up. "Who lives in that house?"

"Someone who can help you."

"With what?"

The girl said nothing more. Ingrid could not remove her eyes from the child's face. The resemblance was uncanny.

"Who are you?" she asked again.

"Don't you recognize me?"

"Yes, of course. But it's not possible."

"Speak to the old woman," said the child. "And then you will know."

———

By the time Ingrid reached the opposite side of the square, the woman was standing in the doorway of the house, a shawl across her frail shoulders, a heavy cross around her neck. Her skin was pale as baker's flour. Her eyes were pools of black.

She placed a hand to Ingrid's cheek. "You have a fever."

"I've been running."

"From what?" The old woman opened the door wider and beckoned for Ingrid to enter. "Don't be afraid. You have nothing to fear."

"Tell me about the girl first."

"Her name is Danielle. She lives here in the village. One day she will take my place."

"She looks exactly like . . ."

"Like what?" asked the old woman.

"Me," replied Ingrid. "She looks the way I did when I was her age."

"That hardly seems possible. After all, the child is a Corsican. And you, of course, are Danish."

Before Ingrid could reply, the woman drew her into the house and closed the door. A candle burned at the small wooden table in her parlor. It was the only light in the room.

The woman lowered herself slowly into one of the chairs and pointed toward the chair opposite. "Sit," she said.

"Why?"

"A small ritual to confirm my suspicions."

"About what?"

"The state of your soul, my child."

"My soul is just fine, thank you."

"I have my doubts."

And then Ingrid understood. The old woman was the *signadora*, the healer of those afflicted with the evil eye.

Ingrid reluctantly sat down. On the table before her was a plate filled with water and a small bowl of oil. "Refreshments?" she quipped.

The old woman regarded her through the candlelight. "Your name is Ingrid Johansen. You are from a small town near the German border. Your father was a schoolteacher. Your poor mother did nothing but look after you. You left her no other choice."

"Who told you those things?"

"It is a gift from God."

Ingrid gave a skeptical smile. "Tell me more."

"You arrived yesterday morning by boat from Marseilles," the woman said with a sigh.

"So did several thousand other people, I imagine."

"The boat is owned by René Monjean, the Marseillais thief who works for Pascal Rameau. You were accompanied by the Israelite, the one with the name of the archangel. Tomorrow evening you and René will steal some documents for him in Monaco." The woman smiled, then asked, "Would you like to know the passcode for the safe?"

"Why not?"

"Nine, two, eight, seven, four, six." The *signadora* nudged the bowl across the tablecloth. "Dip your finger into the oil and allow three drops to fall into the water."

Ingrid did as she was told. The oil should have gathered into a single gobbet. Instead, it shattered into a thousand tiny droplets, and soon there was no trace of it.

"*Occhju,*" whispered the *signadora*.

"Gesundheit," replied Ingrid.

The cross around the old woman's neck caught the flickering light of the candle. "Shall I tell you when it happened?" she asked.

"I'm guessing that I came down with it while I was in Moscow. The weather was dreadful."

"You were the same age as Danielle," said the *signadora*. "There was a man who lived on the same street as your family. His name was Lars Hansen. One afternoon while you were playing—"

"That's quite enough," said Ingrid evenly.

The old woman allowed a moment to pass before continuing. "You never told anyone, so your mother didn't understand why you began to steal things. The truth is, you couldn't help yourself. You were afflicted with the *occhju*."

"I steal because I enjoy it."

"You steal because you *need* to steal. But I have the power to make the illness go away. Once the evil has left your body, you will be able to resist the temptation to take what isn't yours."

The *signadora* held Ingrid's hand and began to speak mournfully in the Corsican language. A moment later she emitted a cry of pain and began to weep. Then she slumped in her chair and appeared to lose consciousness.

"Shit," whispered Ingrid, and tried to revive her. The old woman finally opened her eyes and said, "Don't worry, my child. It won't stay within me long."

"I don't understand."

"The *occhju* has moved from your body to mine." With her black eyes, the *signadora* indicated the bowl of oil. "Try it again."

Ingrid dipped her finger into the oil and allowed three drops to fall into the plate of water. This time it gathered into a single gobbet. Then the *signadora* performed the test herself and the oil shattered.

"*Occhju*," she whispered.

Ingrid stood. "How did you know about him?"

"Who, my child?"

"Lars Hansen."

"It is a gift from God," said the old woman, and her eyes closed.

39

Haute-Corse

You might have warned me."

"You told me that you were going for a run," said Gabriel. "Not to the village."

"And if you had known?"

"I wouldn't have let you anywhere near her. She's scared me to death on more than one occasion."

They were standing before the French doors in the sitting room of the villa. Ingrid's spandex running clothes were soaked with the rain that was now pelting the terrace. The laricio pine trees were writhing in the gusty wind.

"How is it possible that she knows about my childhood?"

"You're asking me to explain the inexplicable."

"She knows about our plans for tomorrow night, by the way. My God, she even knows the code for the bloody safe."

"I guess we won't need that rare-earth magnet and automatic dialer, after all."

"Better safe than sorry."

"Probably," agreed Gabriel. "But she's never wrong."

A blast of wind rattled the French doors. "Maybe we should wait another day," said Ingrid.

"The rain is forecast to end around eight o'clock. By midnight the skies will be clear."

"What about the sea state?"

"Two to three."

"Is that all?" Ingrid peered into the kitchen. Philippe Lambert was monitoring the late-afternoon activity at Harris Weber, and René Monjean was watching a football match on the television. "Where's your friend?"

"Climbing the highest mountain on Corsica."

"In weather like this?"

"It amuses him."

"It's funny," said Ingrid, "but he doesn't look like a business consultant to me."

"That's because he isn't one."

"Is he coming with us to Monaco?"

"He says not."

"What a shame." Ingrid watched the rain in silence for a moment. "There was a young girl in the village. The one who brought me the note from the *signadora*."

"Danielle?"

"How did you know?"

"We've met," said Gabriel.

"Do you remember what she looks like?"

"The last time I saw her, she bore a shocking resemblance to my daughter."

"Really? But tell me something, Mr. Allon. What does your daughter look like?"

———————

They spent the remainder of the afternoon working their way through the documents that Philippe Lambert had stolen from his former employer. In all, Harris Weber & Company had given birth to more than twenty-five thousand anonymous offshore shell corporations. Most had been created at the behest of wealth managers or the private banking divisions of major financial services firms. Harris Weber used code names to conceal the identities of its partners, all of whom received enormous finders' fees and kickbacks in return for their business. Its largest customers were called Bluebird and Heron, which Lambert believed were probably Credit Suisse and Société Générale. A company designated Nightingale had asked Harris Weber to create and manage more than five thousand shell companies. Lambert suspected the firm was British.

Missing from the data were the names of the superrich individuals behind the anonymous companies, the so-called beneficial owners. Those could be found in the safe at Harris Weber's office in Monaco. Konrad Weber opened it at half past five that afternoon and, after attaching the offline storage device to the air-gapped computer, printed several documents. He placed them in his attaché case, then returned the storage device to the safe and locked the door.

The Swiss lawyer left the office, as usual, at the stroke of six o'clock. Ian Harris was gone by six fifteen, as were most of the senior associates and secretarial staff, but Trevor Robinson hung around until nearly seven. Lambert recorded the security chief's departure, including the thirty seconds he spent waiting for the lift. The surveillance camera in the foyer was to Robinson's left—his good side, thought Gabriel. With his square jaw and ample head of gray-blond hair, he looked considerably younger than his sixty-four years. There was nothing in his demeanor to suggest he had orchestrated the murder of three people to protect his firm and its clients. But then Gabriel had expected nothing less. A retired MI5 counterintelligence officer, Trevor Robinson was a liar and deceiver by trade.

By all appearances, however, Robinson was oblivious to the fact that his mobile phone was now infected with the Israeli malware known as Proteus. It allowed Gabriel and Lambert to listen in on two calls that Robinson placed during the short walk from the firm's office to his apartment on the Avenue Princesse Grace. The first call was to an ex-wife in London named Ruth. The second was to their son, Alistair, who dispatched his father to voicemail. Robinson left a curt message—it expressed neither love nor affection—and cut the connection.

He received an incoming call at 9:05 p.m. while standing on his balcony overlooking the Plage du Larvotto, Monaco's artificial beach. It was Brendan Taylor, the young associate who had drawn the short straw and was working late. Taylor informed Robinson that the Road Town office was now closed and that he was leaving for the night. Robinson asked Taylor whether the door to the file room was securely locked, and Taylor replied that it was. Then he switched off the lights and boarded the elevator. It was 9:10 p.m.

By then the wind was howling through the mountain valleys of northwestern Corsica and clawing at the tiles of Christopher's roof. Of Christopher himself, however, there was still no sign. Gabriel placed several calls to his mobile phone, but there was no answer. A text message received no reply.

"Perhaps we should ring the *signadora*," suggested Ingrid. "I'm sure she can locate him."

"The *signadora* doesn't have a phone."

"How silly of me. But we have to tell someone that he's missing."

"Christopher is a world-class mountaineer and quite indestructible. I'm sure he's fine."

Ingrid went up to her room to shower and change and pack her bag. When she returned, Gabriel offered her a scopolamine patch. "Put it on now. You'll thank me later."

She adhered the patch behind her left ear and swallowed two tablets for good measure. Then she checked the time. It was ten fifteen.

"We'll give him until ten thirty," said Gabriel.

They waited until 10:45 instead. Gabriel placed a final call to Christopher before pulling on his coat. Then he looked at Lambert and said, "Whatever you do, don't try to leave this villa. Otherwise, those two men outside will shoot you and bury you at sea in a concrete coffin."

"Don't worry, Monsieur Allon. I'm not going anywhere."

Gabriel smiled. "You'll hear from me in the morning. Provided, of course, we don't capsize and sink."

He went into the windblown night and dropped behind the wheel of the rental car. René Monjean was sprawled in the back. Ingrid was in the passenger seat. She leaned close to the windscreen as the beam of the only functional headlamp illuminated the three ancient olive trees.

"Do you think something happened to him?" she asked.

"We can only hope."

"I was talking about your friend."

"So was I." Gabriel slowed to a stop as Don Casabianca's goat stepped from the macchia and blocked the path. "I thought we had resolved this situation."

"Evidently not."

"Say something to him in Danish again. He seems to respond to it."

"Should I ask him if he knows where Christopher is?"

"Only if you want him to smash the other headlamp."

Ingrid lowered her window and with a few soothing words persuaded the goat to move aside. Gabriel followed the road to the entrance of Villa Orsati and asked the guards whether they had seen Christopher. They informed him that the Englishman had dined alone with Don Orsati after a difficult ascent up Monte Cinto but was no longer at the estate.

"When did he leave?"

"About an hour ago."

"Did he say where he was going?"

"Does he ever?"

Gabriel was tempted to ask Sarah Bancroft if she knew her husband's whereabouts, but such a course of action would have violated the most basic precepts of his former trade. And so he drove down the treacherous western slope of the mountains by the light of a single headlamp and rolled into the tiny marina in Porto a few minutes after midnight. Which was when he spotted Christopher, still in his Gore-Tex climbing gear, sitting on the afterdeck of *Mistral*, a cigarette between his lips, a nylon overnight bag at his side. He pondered the luminous dial of his wristwatch, then looked at Gabriel and smiled.

"You're late."

"I thought you weren't coming with us."

"And miss all the fun? I wouldn't dream of it." Christopher flicked his cigarette into the oily waters of the marina. "Leave the key in that rental car of yours. And don't worry about the smashed headlamp. His Holiness will take care of everything."

They stowed their bags belowdecks and locked the drawers and cabinets in the galley. Then Gabriel and René Monjean climbed up to the flybridge and fired the engines. They headed due west across the choppy waters of the Golfe de Porto before turning to the north. The sea state deteriorated instantly. Ingrid felt a wave of nausea wash over her and decided to take her chances outside on the afterdeck. She found Christopher relaxing in the cockpit, as though the boat beneath him were gliding across a glassy ornamental pond.

"Feeling unwell?" he asked.

"A little. You?"

"Actually, I'm feeling rather guilty."

"You should, Mr. Keller. You gave us quite a scare."

"I was referring to the incident this afternoon at the pool."

"When you asked Gabriel if we were having an affair?"

Christopher nodded. "The truth is, I knew you weren't."

"Why?"

"Because Gabriel is madly in love with his wife and children. He also happens to be the most decent and honorable man I've ever met."

"And what about you, Mr. Keller? Are you decent and honorable?"

"I am now. But I still have a naughty streak."

"So does Gabriel."

"That he does," said Christopher, and lit another cigarette.

40

Monaco

A bit nicer than Marseilles, wouldn't you agree, Monsieur Allon?"

"Actually, René, I've always had a soft spot for your hometown."

"Too many criminals," replied Monjean.

"I have a soft spot for them, too."

They were approaching the entrance of Port Hercule, the larger of Monaco's two harbors. The luxury apartment buildings lining the waterfront sparkled in the bright morning sunlight. A monstrous superyacht, perhaps a hundred meters in length, loomed over one of the quays.

Gabriel quickly searched the vessel's name online. "It's owned by a member of the Qatari royal family."

"What does he do for all that money?"

"As little as possible, I imagine."

A harbormaster in a whaler-type craft directed them to their berth. It was along a noisy quay lined with shops and restaurants. Gabriel connected his laptop to *Mistral*'s satellite Wi-Fi network, then rang Philippe Lambert in Corsica. Lambert was awake and monitoring Harris Weber's internal surveillance cameras. At half past eight the office was still deserted.

Gabriel raised the volume on the audio feed from Trevor Robinson's mobile phone and brewed a pot of coffee in the galley. Ingrid carried a cup belowdecks, where she hosed herself down in the cramped marine shower before changing into her dark pantsuit. René Monjean emerged from the owner's berth dressed in jeans and a black pullover. Upstairs in the salon, Gabriel advised the French thief to do a bit of shopping while he was getting to know the neighborhood around Harris Weber's office.

"The stores in Monaco are the most expensive in the world," Monjean protested.

"Which means you're sure to find something appropriate to wear to this evening's festivities."

Monjean and Ingrid left *Mistral* at nine fifteen and set off along the quay. Gabriel went onto the forward deck and found Christopher lying shirtless on a cushion, beer in hand.

"It's a bit early in the day for that, isn't it?"

"I'm on holiday on my friend's motor yacht in Monaco. The mid-morning carbonated beverage is simply part of my elaborate cover."

"Might I trouble you to run a small errand for me on the French side of the border?"

Christopher sighed. "What did you have in mind?"

"I'd like you to collect a parcel from a certain Monsieur Giroux. He'll be waiting outside the tennis club in Cap-d'Ail."

"Why can't Monsieur Giroux bring the parcel here?"

"Because it contains a computerized automatic combination dialer and a forty-by-twenty-millimeter rare-earth magnet."

"In that case, perhaps you should handle it, old sport." Christopher closed his eyes. "Those rare-earth magnets are bloody dangerous."

———

Ingrid paused beneath the white awning of the Gucci boutique on the Avenue de Monte-Carlo. "Perhaps we can find you something presentable to wear here."

"Only if we steal it," replied René Monjean.

They moved along the spotless pavement to the next shop. "How about Valentino? They have lovely things for men."

"I prefer Hermès." It was located next door. "Home of the seven-hundred-euro polo shirt."

Ingrid eyed the elegant garment worn by the mannequin in the window. "And the five-thousand-euro cashmere stole."

"I'm sure you can get it for less," said Monjean. "Much less."

"Are you daring me?"

"It would look great with the pantsuit you're wearing."

It would, indeed. But Ingrid had no desire to possess it. She was sure it was only a side effect of the scopolamine. Her eyes were killing her.

"I'll pass," she said.

"Should I pinch it for you?"

"Dressed like that?" She looked him up and down. "They wouldn't let you in the store."

They followed the avenue past the Casino de Monte-Carlo and the Hôtel de Paris, then walked through the Jardins de la Petite Afrique to the boulevard des Moulins. Number 41 was to the right. They sat down at an outdoor table at La Royale, and Monjean ordered two café crèmes in his Marseillais French.

"Have you noticed that there's no dirt in this place?" he asked.

"And no poor people, either."

"There are plenty of poor people. They sweep the floors and change the beds and clean the toilets, but they're not allowed to live here. To tell you the truth, I hate Monaco. It's the most boring place on earth."

"Ever work here?"

"Sure. You?"

"It's possible that I picked a few pockets in the casino. I also had a nice score at the Hôtel de Paris."

"Room safe?"

She nodded.

"How did you open it?"

"Magic word."

"What was inside?"

"A diamond necklace and a hundred thousand euros in cash."

"How much did you get for the necklace?"

"Two fifty."

"Antwerp?"

"Actually, I returned it to Harry Winston on the Avenue Montaigne in Paris. They kindly gave me a full refund despite the fact that I couldn't find my receipt."

"I'll keep that in mind," said Monjean. On the opposite side of the boulevard, a well-dressed man was approaching the entrance of Number 41. "Looks like a British lawyer to me."

"How can you tell?"

"Could be the stick up his ass."

Ingrid nodded toward the attractive young woman approaching the building from the opposite direction. "And here comes Mademoiselle Dubois."

The well-dressed man arrived first. He inserted his cardkey into the reader and held the door open for the secretary—and for the man who emerged from the back of a Mercedes sedan. It was Ian Harris, founding partner of the dirty law firm that bore his name.

"I think I'm going to enjoy this," said Monjean. "I only wish we could steal something from him other than those files."

"They're worth hundreds of billions of dollars."

"Not to me. But it is rather ironic, don't you think?"

"Thieves stealing from thieves?"

"Exactly."

"Poetic justice, I'd say." Ingrid's phone shivered with an incoming message.

"Something wrong?" asked Monjean.

She glanced at the man with gray-blond hair and a square jaw coming along the pavement. "Does he look like a murderer to you?"

"The good ones never do."

Trevor Robinson jammed his cardkey into the reader and went into the building.

"Seen enough?" asked Ingrid.

"*Oui.*" Monjean swallowed the rest of his coffee. "Let's get out of here."

———

At a computer shop on the boulevard d'Italie, Ingrid purchased two palm-sized external hard drives with a combined storage space of sixteen terabytes, more than enough to handle Harris Weber's sensitive attorney-client files. Then she marched René Monjean over to an American clothing retailer near the yacht club and supervised the purchase of a blazer, a pair of gabardine trousers, leather oxfords, a blue button-down dress shirt, and an attaché case.

They returned to *Mistral* shortly after noon to find that Gabriel and Christopher had prepared lunch. They dined on the sunlit afterdeck in the manner of four friends on holiday while monitoring the audio feed from Trevor Robinson's phone. The former MI5 officer was lunching at Le Louis XV with the head of HSBC's wealth management division. The topic of conversation was the prospect of data loss and exposure. Robinson assured the HSBC executive that the firm's most sensitive files were offline and entirely inaccessible.

"There will be no spillage from Harris Weber & Company," he promised. "You and your bank have absolutely nothing to fear."

Ingrid helped René Monjean with the dishes, then repaired to her berth for a few hours of sleep. For the first time in many years, Lars Hansen visited her in her dreams, though this time the encounter took place in a lavender-scented grove of towering laricio pine trees. When she returned home, her mother pointed at her in the Corsican way and screamed, "*Occhju.*"

She woke with a start to find her berth in semidarkness. It was nearly seven thirty. She gave herself a quick rinse in the marine shower, then put her hair in order and dressed in the same dark pantsuit. Next she packed her handbag. Her laptop was fully charged, but she added a power cord nonetheless, along with the two external hard drives. She carried no wallet or identification, only her phone and a wad of cash. After a moment of deliberation, she tossed in her bump keys and screwdriver, more out of habit than anything else. The automatic combination dialer and rare-earth magnet were in René Monjean's attaché case.

Upstairs in the galley, Ingrid poured herself a cup of coffee from the thermos flask. Gabriel was seated at the table, a phone at his elbow, laptop open. From the speakers came the sound of Trevor Robinson's voice. In the background was a low multilingual murmur.

"Where is he?"

"The Crystal Bar at the Hôtel Hermitage. Brendan Taylor is minding the store."

"Did anyone open the safe this afternoon?"

"Ian Harris. He returned the storage device when he was finished."

"Did you happen to see the passcode?"

"No," said Gabriel. "But I'm guessing it's nine, two, eight, seven, four, six."

Christopher and René Monjean were outside on the afterdeck. Monjean looked faintly ridiculous in his blazer and trousers—like a thief pretending to be a businessman. Christopher, in his tailored Savile Row suit, looked like the real thing. Ingrid helped herself to one of his Marlboros. The combination of caffeine and nicotine raised her heart rate and blood pressure, but she still felt unusually serene. There was no tingling in her fingertips, no fever.

She smoked the last of the cigarette and then returned to the salon. Trevor Robinson had left the Crystal Bar and was walking along the Avenue Princesse Grace toward his apartment. Brendan Taylor was playing solitaire on his computer at Harris Weber. The two men spoke at 9:05 p.m. Robinson asked Taylor whether the file room was locked. Taylor told Robinson that it was.

The young associate left the office at 9:09 p.m., but Gabriel waited until nine thirty to dispatch his operational team. Christopher departed *Mistral* first, followed ten minutes later by Ingrid and René Monjean. As they walked along the Avenue de Monte-Carlo, Ingrid allowed her eyes to wander over the costly goods displayed in the shop windows. Once the very sight of such luxuries would have set her ablaze. Now, strangely, she felt nothing at all.

41

Boulevard des Moulins

The two outdoor tables at La Royale were both unoccupied. Christopher sat down at one, ordered coffee and a cognac, struck his Dunhill lighter, leaned a Marlboro into the flame. Only then did he ring Gabriel.

"Comfortable?" inquired his old friend.

"Never better."

"Our associates are headed your way."

Christopher looked to the left and saw Ingrid and René Monjean walking along the pavement on the opposite side of the boulevard. There was not another pedestrian in sight—and no officers of the Sûreté Publique de Monaco, either.

"Are we a go?" asked Gabriel.

"I believe we are."

Ingrid and Monjean paused at the entrance of Number 41. So quiet was the boulevard that Christopher, from his observation post at the café, could hear the thud of the dead bolt. Only then did he take a first nip of the cognac.

They were off to a fine start.

Ingrid and Monjean crossed the half-lit lobby to the building's only lift. There was no need to press the call button; Philippe Lambert, a hundred miles to the south in the mountains of Corsica, had already summoned the carriage. Ingrid gazed directly into the surveillance camera during the slow ascent to the fourth floor.

"How do I look?" she asked.

"Just fine," replied Gabriel. "But who's that unsavory-looking fellow standing next to you?"

"Haven't the foggiest."

The doors slid open and Ingrid followed Monjean into the foyer. A single overhead light shone dimly. On the wall directly before them was Harris Weber & Company's understated logo. Next to it was a glass door and card reader.

"Open sesame," said Ingrid.

A buzzer groaned, a lock snapped.

They were in.

Nothing about Harris Weber's stylish workplace suggested that the firm was involved in the practice of law. Ingrid followed a corridor past a row of empty glass-enclosed offices, then turned to the left. A locked door halted her progress.

"Ready when you are," she said, and the lock gave way.

The room they entered was in darkness. With the flashlight function of her phone, Ingrid illuminated several rows of metal file cabinets. At the opposite end of the room was yet another door.

"Would you mind terribly?" she asked.

Lambert unlocked the door remotely, and Ingrid and Monjean went inside. A table, a swivel chair, a desktop computer, a printer, and a double-doored executive safe with an electronic lock.

Ingrid entered the combination.

"Shit," she whispered.

"Don't tell me," said Gabriel.

Ingrid opened the door of the safe. "Works every time."

She illuminated the interior.

"*Merde,*" said René Monjean.

"What's the problem now?" asked Gabriel.

"Several million euros in cash," replied Ingrid.

"Is there anything else?"

"A rather large pile of physical documents and a twenty-terabyte SanDisk external hard drive."

Ingrid removed the SanDisk and connected it to her laptop.

"How much data is there?" asked Gabriel.

"Three point two terabytes."

"How long will it take?"

"One moment, please. Your question is very important to us." Ingrid connected one of the storage devices she had purchased that morning and initiated the transfer. "According to the little window on my screen, it will take four hours and twelve minutes."

"Which will leave you plenty of time to photograph the rest of those documents."

"It would be my pleasure," said Ingrid, and rang off.

René Monjean was eyeing the stacks of newly minted euro banknotes. "How much do you suppose there is?"

"Five or six million."

"Do you think they would miss a million or two?"

"Probably."

"Not even tempted?"

No, thought Ingrid. Not in the least.

Shortly before 11:00 p.m., the waiter at La Royale informed Christopher that the establishment would soon be closing. He drank a final coffee, smoked a final cigarette, then settled his bill and was on his way. He rang Gabriel while walking along the deserted pavements of the boulevard.

"Time remaining?" he asked.

"Three hours and fifteen minutes."

"An eternity."

"And then some."

"If I stay on this street any longer, the *sûreté* will arrest me for loitering."

"They would be doing the rest of the world a favor."

"Be that as it may," said Christopher, "my detention would come as an unpleasant surprise to my superiors in London. It would also leave us with no one in close proximity to our two colleagues."

"In that case, you should probably find somewhere to spend the next three hours and fourteen minutes."

Christopher walked down the gentle slope of the hill to the Place du Casino and obtained an outdoor table at Café de Paris, the celebrated Monaco eatery that remained open until 3:00 a.m. For the sake of his not-so-elaborate cover, he ordered pasta with truffles and a bottle of pricey Montrachet, then watched as a million-euro Lamborghini, bright red in color, pulled up outside the ornate entrance of the Casino de Monte-Carlo. The cameras of the assembled paparazzi flashed as the owner of the motorcar, a celebrity Spanish fashion designer, entered the casino with an underfed model on his arm.

The waiter appeared with the Montrachet. Christopher, with nothing but time on his hands, was slow in signaling his approval.

When he was alone again, he rang Gabriel with an update on his whereabouts.

"Hanging by a thread, are you?"

"Bored senseless, if you must know. Can I bring you anything?"

"Ingrid and René Monjean."

The connection died as another seven-figure supercar rolled up outside the entrance of the casino. This time it was a Bugatti. A silver-haired man, a beautiful young girl. Christopher glanced at his watch. Nothing but time.

————————

It was after midnight when Ingrid finally finished photographing all of the physical documents stored in the safe. She returned the files to their original positions, then checked the progress bar on her computer. The original time estimate, as it turned out, had been too pessimistic. The operating software now predicted the data transfer would be complete in one hour and thirty-nine minutes, which would have them out the door by 1:45 a.m. at the latest. As far as Ingrid was concerned, their departure could not come soon enough. She was no stranger to lengthy jobs—her last theft had involved weeks of planning and observation—but the take itself nearly always occurred in the blink of an eye.

René Monjean, who was peering over her shoulder, was growing restless as well. "Is there nothing you can do to make it go faster?" he asked.

"What exactly did you have in mind?"

Monjean turned away from the computer and stared at the money. "You're not thinking about doing something stupid, are you?"

"Have you ever seen that much money before?"

"Twice."

"Really? When?"

"My last job. I got five up front and five on delivery."

"What did you steal?"

"Something I shouldn't have."

Monjean closed the door of the safe.

"Wise move, René."

By 12:45 a.m. Christopher had worn out his welcome at Café de Paris, so he paid his bill and headed across the square toward his last remaining refuge, the Casino de Monte-Carlo. Inside, he handed over the required twenty-euro admission fee and purchased five hundred euros in chips, which he promptly lost at the English roulette table. He purchased another five hundred and dropped most of that playing blackjack. Finally, at half past one in the morning, the dealer presented him with a pair of queens. At the instant Christopher split his hand, his mobile phone pulsed, leaving him no choice but to step away from the table and abandon the last of his money.

"As usual," he said, "your timing is impeccable."

"Sorry to put a damper on your evening, but Trevor Robinson just left his apartment."

"Where is he going?"

"It looks as though he's headed to the office."

"At one thirty in the morning?"

"One thirty-two, actually."

"Does he know they're inside?"

"If he does, he hasn't called the *sûreté* yet."

Christopher watched the dealer sweep away the last of his chips. "I assume you've instructed our friends to vacate the premises."

"Not surprisingly, Ingrid would like to finish copying the files."

"And you, of course, told her to leave immediately."

"To no avail."

Christopher set off across the gaming floor toward the exit. "Time remaining?"

"Thirteen minutes."

"Where is he?"

"Headed west on the boulevard d'Italie."

"Any suggestions?"

"Improvise."

42

Boulevard d'Italie

Christopher waited until he had reached the Avenue de Grande Bretagne before breaking into a run. He headed east, past slumbering apartment houses, then scaled a flight of steps that delivered him to the boulevard d'Italie. At half past one in the morning, it was deserted save for a single pedestrian, a fit-looking specimen with gray-blond hair, marching in a westerly direction at a determined clip. Christopher bade the man a pleasant evening in French as they passed one another on the darkened pavement. Then he stopped in his tracks and in English called out, "Excuse me, but by any chance are you Trevor Robinson?"

Robinson walked a few more paces before stopping and turning around. A retired intelligence officer who knew all the tricks, he regarded Christopher with suspicion.

"I am, actually," he said at last. "And who might you be?"

"Peter Marlowe's the name. We met about a hundred years ago in the bar of the Connaught. Or perhaps it was the Dorchester. I was with a client at the time, and he was good enough to introduce us." Christopher thrust out a hand and smiled. "What a pleasant surprise. Fancy meeting you here, of all places."

Approximately three hundred meters separated the offices of Harris Weber & Company from the spot where the firm's director of security stood chatting with a man who claimed to be a business consultant called Peter Marlowe. A pedestrian moving at a normal pace could be expected to cover the distance in three and a half minutes, less if he was in a rush. Which meant that Gabriel, in his makeshift op center aboard *Mistral*, had little margin for error.

He checked the shot from the surveillance camera and saw Ingrid hunched over her laptop. "Time remaining?"

"Five minutes," she answered.

"There's no way Christopher can keep him occupied for that long."

"I'm sure he'll think of something. He strikes me as the resourceful type."

A moment passed.

"Time remaining?" inquired Gabriel.

"Four minutes and seven seconds. But who's counting?"

"I am."

"Rest assured," said Ingrid, "so am I."

He claimed that he was an independent wealth manager who had come to Monaco to meet with a client, a fabulously rich British expat who dwelled in the Odeon Tower, the principality's tallest building. Professional discretion did not allow him to identify the client, and Trevor Robinson, who was clearly anxious to be on his way, did not pursue the matter.

"Forgive me," said Christopher, hoping to prolong the encounter a moment or two longer, "but I can't seem to recall the name of your firm."

"Harris Weber & Company."

"Yes, of course. Offshore financial services, if I'm not mistaken."

"You're not."

"Have a card, by any chance?"

Robinson reached into the breast pocket of his jacket and handed one over. Christopher scrutinized it at considerable length by the yellow light of a streetlamp.

"I have a client who requires a firm with your particular expertise."

"We'd be happy to be of assistance, if we can."

"I'd love to discuss it further. Is there any chance you're free for a drink tomorrow?"

"I'm not, actually."

"Next time I'm in town?"

"By all means." Robinson turned to leave, then hesitated. "Tell me something, Mr. Marlowe. What was the name of your client who introduced us?"

"I believe it was George Anderson."

"I'm afraid I've never heard of him."

"Could've been Martin Elliott," suggested Christopher.

"Doesn't ring a bell," said Robinson, and set off down the boulevard. Christopher waited until he had disappeared from view, then descended the steps to the Avenue de Grande Bretagne. He was relieved to find Ingrid and René Monjean waiting for him in the Place du Casino.

"I hope it was worth it," he said.

"It was," replied Ingrid.

"All of it?"

She smiled. "Every last byte."

They headed down the Avenue de Monte-Carlo to the port and boarded *Mistral*. René quickly untied the lines and clambered up the ladder to the flybridge. Ingrid and Christopher went into the galley and found Gabriel staring at his laptop.

"Where's Trevor?" asked Christopher.

"A few minutes ago he made a call from the landline phone in his office. I wasn't able to monitor his end of the conversation because for some reason he switched off his mobile."

"And now?"

"He's standing in front of the safe."

"Doing what?"

"Filling an attaché case with cash." Gabriel looked up at Ingrid. "Do you have something for me?"

Smiling, she surrendered the external hard drive. Gabriel connected the device to his laptop and a single folder appeared on his screen. Inside the folder were thousands more, each bearing the name of a client. Moguls and monarchs, kleptocrats and criminals. The richest of the rich, the worst of the worst.

"Oh dear," said Gabriel. "This is going to be ugly."

PART THREE

The Contest

43

Queen's Gate Terrace

Ingrid made a backup copy of Harris Weber's files during the overnight voyage from Monaco to Marseilles. She gave one to Gabriel and entrusted the other to Christopher. Together they boarded a midday train to Paris, then caught the 4:10 Eurostar to London. A taxi delivered them to a tony address in Kensington.

"Where are we?" asked Ingrid.

"Home," replied Christopher.

"How lovely."

"Wait until you get a look at his wife," remarked Gabriel.

She was mixing a martini for herself in the kitchen, an attractive woman, stylishly attired, with wide blue eyes and shoulder-length blond hair. She kissed Christopher and greeted Gabriel with obvious affection. Their attractive female traveling companion she regarded with suspicion.

"I'm Sarah," she said at length. "And who might you be?"

"I might be Ingrid."

"Charmed, I'm sure." Sarah smiled coolly and turned to Gabriel. "Mind telling me where you boys have been?"

"Monaco."

"Doing what?"

"Christopher had dinner at Café de Paris and lost his shirt at the casino. Ingrid stole several million incriminating documents from a dirty law firm called Harris Weber & Company."

"Sounds like loads of fun. Why wasn't I included?"

"You can help us review the documents, if you like."

"Several million, you say? How can I possibly resist an invitation like that?" She opened the door of the Sub-Zero. "What shall we have for dinner? Curdled milk, moldy cheese, or something that might or might not have been a bell pepper once?"

"Perhaps we should order in," suggested Gabriel.

Sarah reached for her mobile phone. "For some reason, I'm in the mood for Chinese."

"When have you ever seen me eat Chinese food?"

"Now that you mention it, never." She thumbed through the options on Deliveroo. "I guess that leaves Italian or Italian?"

"Much better."

"What would you like? The veal Milanese or tagliatelle with ragù?"

"I'll let you decide."

"Tagliatelle it is." She turned to Ingrid. "And you?"

"I'll have one of those," she said, and pointed toward the martini. Sarah smiled. "That's the spirit."

———

They worked until the food arrived, worked throughout dinner, and then worked late into the night. The volume of material was enormous, but the dots were not difficult to connect. More than twenty thousand companies and individuals had utilized Harris Weber's services since its founding, and the firm had saved every document and scrap of paper generated by the relationships—including certificates of incorporation, banking and billing records, hard copies of emails, and photoscans of handwritten minutes initialed by the partners themselves. One was a reminder by Ian Harris to send the client in question, a Middle Eastern monarch, a gift on his sixtieth birthday. His Majesty's file indicated he had assembled a global real estate portfolio worth in excess of $500 million, all nominally owned by shell corporations created by Harris Weber & Company. The monarch's corrupt prime minister was also a client.

So were former prime ministers from Qatar, Iraq, Pakistan, Ukraine, Moldova, Australia, Italy, and Iceland. There were hundreds of other government officials as well, some no longer in office, others still holding positions of power. Spain's ruling class seemed to have a particular affinity for Harris Weber's services, as did their counterparts in Argentina and Brazil. The billionaire daughter of Angola's former dictator did a brisk business with the firm. The son of a former UN secretary-general was likewise a client.

The professional sports world was well represented, especially the notoriously corrupt European football leagues, and the entertainment industry contributed several boldface names. One was a reality television star who was famous for being famous and made millions in the process. A music impresario used a Harris Weber–created shell corporation to purchase his superyacht. And when the impresario decided to sell the vessel to a Saudi prince—at a substantial profit, of course—Harris Weber handled the paperwork.

Other clients of the firm included a well-known Italian automaker, the owner of one of the world's largest hotel chains, an Indian textile tycoon, a Swedish steel baron, a Canadian mining magnate, the leader of a Mexican drug cartel, and, curiously, a descendant of Otto von Bismarck. And then, of course, there were the Russian oligarchs. Each owed their extraordinary wealth to Russia's kleptocratic president, and some were undoubtedly holding a portion of his ill-gotten fortune. Gabriel now knew the names of the shell corporations they used to conceal their activities—and the account numbers at the banks that held the shell companies' money.

One of Harris Weber's Russian clients had been in the news of late. It was Valentin Federov, the billionaire investor whose million-pound contribution to the Conservative Party had forced the abrupt resignations of Prime Minister Hillary Edwards and Party treasurer Lord Michael Radcliff. The Russian's file listed no fewer than twelve British Virgin Islands–registered shell companies and twelve corresponding bank accounts, all at dubious Caribbean houses of finance. Interestingly enough, Lord Radcliff, a multimillionaire businessman and investor, was a client of Harris Weber & Company as well.

"You're right," muttered Christopher. "This is definitely going to be ugly."

"Quite," agreed Gabriel.

Lord Radcliff, an avid collector of Old Master paintings who had acquired a number of works through the auspices of Isherwood Fine Arts, was the beneficial owner of four anonymous offshore companies. But one of those entities, LMR Overseas, rented a storage vault in the Geneva Freeport—or so Ingrid was able to establish with a quick search of the document she had plucked from the Freeport's computer network. Driftwood Holdings, one of Valentin Federov's many shell companies, also rented a vault.

So did a shell company owned by the Italian automaker. And the Swedish steel baron. And the Canadian mining magnate. And the founder of Italy's largest fashion house. And the scion of a Greek shipping dynasty. And the chairman of a French luxury goods conglomerate. And the former CEO of the now-defunct RhineBank AG of Frankfurt. In all, some fifty-two wealthy clients of Harris Weber & Company controlled vaults in the tax-free storage facility, as did the firm itself. The shell company it used was Sargasso Capital Investments, which was a subsidiary of OOC Group, Ltd. The nominal director of the company was Adele Campbell of Road Town, the British Virgin Islands. The beneficial owners were Ian Harris and Konrad Weber.

By 4:00 a.m. Gabriel had assembled the most explosive findings into a hundred-page cover document. But what to do with the material? Handing it over to the Financial Conduct Authority, Britain's independent financial regulatory body, was out of the question. The files had been obtained illegally, and the FCA's track record was undistinguished, to say the least. Gabriel concluded that their only recourse was a leak to a friendly reporter. There were one or two outstanding matters, however, he wanted to clear up first.

"Such as?" asked Christopher.

"How did Trevor Robinson know that Charlotte Blake had identified a British Virgin Islands–registered shell company called OOC Group as the current owner of the Picasso?"

"What's the answer?"

"Obviously, Professor Blake told someone."

"Any candidates?"

"Only one."

44

Land's End

"Nice sled," said Ingrid, and ran her hand over the leather dashboard of Christopher's Bentley Continental GT. "All-electric, is it?"

"Lunar," replied Gabriel. "It's cutting-edge stuff."

Smiling, she leaned her head wearily against the window. They were headed west on the Cromwell Road through the gray early-morning light. "I can't remember the last time I slept."

"Try to get some rest. We have a long drive ahead of us."

"*How* long?"

"It's five hours to Land's End. But we have to make a stop in Exeter along the way."

"Inspector Dalgliesh?"

"Peel," said Gabriel. "And he's only a detective sergeant."

"Apple Peel? Banana Peel?"

"Timothy Peel. And trust me, he's heard them all before. He lived next door to me when he was a child. The other boys at school teased him mercilessly."

"Is that why he became a cop?"

"Apparently, I had something to do with it."

"How do you intend to explain me?"

"With as few words as possible."

"In case you're wondering," said Ingrid, smothering a yawn, "I have never stolen anything in Exeter. In fact, I'm quite certain I've never set foot there."

She reclined her seat and closed her eyes. Gabriel switched on the radio and listened to the news on the BBC. The 1922 Committee of Tory backbenchers were scheduled to convene the following afternoon to begin the process of selecting a new leader and, thus, the next prime minister. Home Secretary Hugh Graves remained the favorite but was expected to face a stiff challenge from Foreign Secretary Stephen Frasier and the chancellor of the Exchequer, Nigel Cunningham. Prime Minister Hillary Edwards, during a brief appearance before reporters outside Number Ten, had declined an invitation to put her thumb on the scale. A panel of political experts agreed that a kind word from the unpopular outgoing premier would be tantamount to a kiss of death.

"Do you think it was a coincidence?" asked Ingrid suddenly.

"That Valentin Federov and Lord Michael Radcliff are both clients of Harris Weber?"

"Exactly."

"I've been wondering the same thing." Gabriel drove in silence for a moment. "Have you ever hacked a bank?"

"Never."

"Think you can do it?"

"Are you forgetting that I just hacked the Geneva Freeport?"

"Point taken."

"Looking for something in particular?"

"Not sure. But we'll know it when we see it."

Gabriel waited until he had reached Bristol before ringing Timothy Peel. He intimated that he had identified the killer of Professor Charlotte Blake and made it clear that his findings could not be delivered electronically. Peel suggested they meet in a pub about a mile from the headquarters of the Devon and Cornwall Police. Gabriel, after entering the name of the establishment into the Bentley's navigation system, said he would be there by twelve thirty at the latest.

The pub in question was the Blue Ball Inn in Clyst Road. Gabriel and Ingrid arrived to find Peel seated at an isolated table in the back. He shook Ingrid's hand, took note of her appearance and Scandinavian accent, and then looked to Gabriel for an explanation.

"Ingrid provided technical and other assistance to my investigation."

"Other?"

"I'll get to that in a moment."

Peel produced a detective's notebook and pen and laid them on the table. Gabriel glared at the items with reproach, and Peel returned them to his pocket.

"Who murdered her, Mr. Allon?"

"A German contract killer named Klaus Müller."

"Where is he now?"

"Regrettably, Herr Müller died in a tragic road accident in Provence a few days ago."

"Were you involved in this accident?"

"Next question."

"Who hired Müller to kill Professor Blake?"

"A law firm that's using valuable paintings like the Picasso to launder money and conceal the wealth of some of the world's richest and most powerful people. Müller murdered her with a hatchet to make it appear as though she was a victim of the Chopper. And he would have gotten away with it were it not for you."

"There's still one thing about the case that doesn't make sense."

"Why was Charlotte Blake walking around Land's End after dark?"

Peel nodded.

"I know the answer to that, too."

"How?"

"Her phone."

"Did you find it?"

"Next best thing," said Gabriel.

———

It was not necessary for Gabriel to explain to Timothy Peel who Leonard Bradley was or where he resided. The Bradley home, one of the largest in West Cornwall, had been targeted numerous times by local thieves. A break-in the previous winter had resulted in the loss of several thousand pounds worth of electronics, silver, and jewelry. Peel had tracked down the two perpetrators—they were a couple of numbskulls from Carbis Bay—and had even managed to recover some of the stolen property. Bradley had been most appreciative, as had his wife.

Consequently, Peel was confident that Leonard Bradley would agree to speak to him if he appeared on his doorstep unannounced. Whether Bradley would be willing to discuss his extramarital relationship with the late Professor Charlotte Blake was another matter entirely. The easiest way to secure his cooperation would be to arrange a formal interview. But that would require Peel to go on the record with his superiors, not to mention the boys from the Metropolitan Police who were now in charge of the Chopper investigation. Such a course of action would involve certain admissions on Peel's part—admissions that would almost certainly end his brief career.

And so it was that Detective Sergeant Timothy Peel, at half past two that afternoon, found himself behind the wheel of his unmarked Vauxhall Insignia, pursuing a beautiful Bentley Continental as it sped westward along the A30. Eventually the Bentley pulled into the car park at Land's End, and the passenger, an attractive Danish woman in her mid-thirties, headed into the amusement center. The driver joined Peel in the Vauxhall. He headed toward Porthcurno, the tiny village where Professor Blake's body had been discovered.

"And you're absolutely sure she was involved in a romantic relationship with Bradley?"

"Would you like to read the text messages?"

"I'd rather not. But he's bound to deny it."

"I'm not here to judge him. I just want to know whether Charlotte Blake told him that she had found the Picasso."

"What makes you think she might have?"

"Didn't they teach you anything at detective school, Timothy?"

He turned into a narrow track and headed toward the coastline. "And if she did tell him?"

"I would like to know the reason why. And if it is relevant to our investigation, I will pursue the matter further."

"*Our* investigation?"

"You're the one who dragged me into this."

"But my superiors don't know that."

"And they never will."

"Unless I do something stupid."

"Like what?"

Peel guided the Vauxhall through an open gate and rolled to a stop outside a stately stone manor perched atop the cliffs. "Like this," he said, and climbed out.

45

Penberth Cove

It was Cordelia Bradley who answered the bell. She was a tall, pale-complected woman of perhaps fifty with windblown reddish hair and eyes the color of the cloudless Cornish sky. She remembered Peel from the robbery investigation and greeted him warmly. Gabriel she regarded with astonishment.

"Forgive me, Mr. Allon, but you are the last person I expected to see on my doorstep."

She invited them inside and closed the door. Peel, while standing in the entrance hall, asked whether her husband was at home and had a moment to talk.

"Yes, of course. But what's this about?"

"Mr. Allon is completing a research project that Professor Blake was working on at the time of her murder. He's hoping that Mr. Bradley might be able to help him."

"Why Leonard?"

It was Gabriel who answered, untruthfully. "I found his name and telephone number in her notes."

"That's strange."

"Why is that?"

"Because Leonard and Charlotte were at Oxford together and spoke on the phone regularly. There's no reason in the world why she would write down his number. It was stored in her contacts." She paused, then added, "As was mine."

She led them along a central corridor to a pair of French doors overlooking the sea. Near the edge of the cliff was a separate cottage with walls of glass.

"My husband's office," said Cordelia Bradley. Then she plucked a phone from her pocket and smiled without parting her lips. "I'll let him know you're coming."

The cottage was reached by a manicured gravel footpath. Leonard Bradley, alert to danger, waited in the doorway. He was a slender man with a fine-boned face and dark hair. His clothing was casual but costly. His smile was artificial.

"You've caught me in the middle of a rather complex trade, gentlemen, but please come in."

Gabriel and Peel followed Bradley into the cottage. His office was an architectural showpiece, the realm of an alchemist who magically made money from money. He settled behind his large glass desk and invited Gabriel and Peel to sit in the two modern chairs opposite. They remained standing instead.

An awkward silence ensued. Finally, Bradley looked at Gabriel and asked, "Why are you here, Mr. Allon?"

Gabriel exchanged a long look with Peel before answering. "Charlotte Blake."

"I gathered that."

"The two of you were close friends." Gabriel lowered his voice. "Unusually close."

"And just what are you implying?"

"Let's skip this part, shall we? I've read the text messages."

Bradley's face drained of color. "You self-righteous bastard."

"I am neither, I assure you." Gabriel glanced deliberately around Bradley's magnificent office. "Besides, you know what they say about people who live in glass houses."

The remark lowered the temperature, but only slightly. Leonard Bradley posed his next question to Peel. "Am I a suspect in Charlotte's murder?"

"You are not."

"Is this an official proceeding?"

"No."

"In that case, Detective Sergeant, why are you here?"

"I'll leave, if you like," replied Peel, and started toward the door.

"Stay," insisted Bradley. Then he looked at Gabriel and asked, "Won't you please sit down, Mr. Allon? You're making me terribly uncomfortable."

Gabriel lowered himself into one of the chairs, and Peel sat down next to him. Bradley stared intently at his computer screen, his hand hovering over the keyboard.

"You wanted to ask me something, Mr. Allon?"

"Professor Blake was conducting a sensitive provenance investigation at the time of her murder."

"Yes, I know." Bradley's gaze settled briefly on Gabriel. "Untitled portrait of a woman by Pablo Picasso."

"When did she tell you about it?"

"A few days after she obtained a copy of the sales records from Christie's. They revealed that the painting was in the hands of an offshore shell corporation called OCC Group, Limited. Charlotte wanted to know whether I could discover the name of OOC's beneficial owner."

"And what did you—"

Bradley raised a hand, requesting silence, then tapped his keyboard once. "I just earned three million pounds for my investors on a multitiered currency play. It's the sort of thing I do, Mr. Allon. I bet on tiny fluctuations of the markets and leverage the trades with large sums of borrowed money. Sometimes I hold my positions only for a moment or two. Charlotte thought it was a truly ridiculous way to earn a living." He paused. "As do you, I imagine."

"Glass houses," repeated Gabriel.

The remark brought a smile briefly to Leonard Bradley's face. "We were at Oxford together, Charlotte and I. She was from Yorkshire, and working class to the core. Her accent was atrocious back then. The posh crowd were quite cruel to her."

"But not you?"

"No," said Bradley. "I was always fond of Charlotte, despite the fact that I was considered rather posh myself. And when I bumped into her late one afternoon while walking along the South West Coast Path . . ." He was silent for a moment. "Well, it was as though we were undergraduates again."

"And when she asked for your help?"

"I conducted a routine corporate search into the company known as OOC Group, Limited. And when my search turned up nothing useful, I put Charlotte in touch with an old friend who's more familiar with the world of offshore financial services. I'm afraid she was even less helpful than I was, but they had a good chat nevertheless. Charlotte was raving about her afterward."

"Can you tell me her name?"

"Yes, of course. It was Lucinda Graves."

"The wife of the next British prime minister?" asked Gabriel.

"So they say." Bradley stepped from behind his desk and showed them out. They stood at the cliff's edge for a moment admiring the view of Penberth Cove. "Your first visit to Cornwall, Mr. Allon?"

"Yes," he lied. "But I'm sure it won't be my last."

Bradley gazed westward toward Porthchapel Beach. "Did you really read Charlotte's text messages?"

"I'm afraid so."

"Why was she walking along the coast path after sunset on a Monday afternoon? Why wasn't she in her car headed back to Oxford?"

Gabriel made no reply.

"I thought that would be your answer," said Leonard Bradley, and returned to his house of glass.

During the drive back to Land's End, Timothy Peel engaged in a running discourse on the imminent demise of his once promising career as an officer of the Devon and Cornwall Police. Gabriel waited until the homily had reached its conclusion before assuring the young detective sergeant that his fears were overblown.

"I'm sure it's nothing, Timothy."

"Are you really?"

"Reasonably sure," said Gabriel, amending his earlier statement. "After all, Lucinda Graves is the wife of the next prime minister."

"Does her name appear in the files you stole from Harris Weber?"

"*Stole* is an ugly word."

"Borrowed?"

"No. Lucinda Graves's name does not appear in the files. But all that means is that she isn't a client."

"What else could she be?"

"Harris Weber gets most of its clients from wealth managers at big banks or from smaller firms like Lucinda's. It's entirely conceivable that she's in business with them."

Peel swore softly. "I have to tell my chief constable everything we know, preferably *before* he hears it from Leonard Bradley."

"Leonard isn't going to say anything to anyone. And neither are you."

Peel turned into the car park at Land's End. Ingrid was sitting on the bonnet of the Bentley, her back against the windscreen.

"Where did you get the car?"

"Borrowed," said Gabriel.

"What about the girl?"

"Stolen."

"I suppose she's married."

"No."

"Involved with anyone?"

"I wouldn't know."

"Think she might be interested in having a drink with a handsome country policeman when this is over?"

"Probably not."

Peel unlocked the doors of the Vauxhall. "What now?"

"I'm going to find out whether the wife of the next prime minister is a criminal."

"And if she is?"

Gabriel climbed out without another word and dropped behind the wheel of the Bentley. Ingrid, after sliding off the bonnet, ducked into the passenger seat. Peel shadowed them eastward as far as Exeter, then pulled onto the verge and flashed his headlamps. Gabriel flashed his lights twice and was gone.

It was Leonard Bradley's habit, at the conclusion of each trading day, to pull on a pair of Wellington boots and walk the cliffs alone. The time away from his desk and computers, he told Cordelia and the children, was an essential part of his work. It gave him a chance to clear his head of clutter, to reflect on his successes and console himself over the occasional market misstep, to see around the next corner, to quite literally look beyond the horizon.

Until recently, the sojourns along the cliffs had also provided Bradley with the opportunity, perhaps once or twice a week, to spend a few moments with Charlotte. They would pretend to bump into one another near Porthchapel Beach. And if no one else was in sight, they would steal away to the thick wood near the old St. Levan Church. The hurried encounters, with their impassioned kisses and desperate clutching at clothing, only fed their desire. Yes, their affair had been a long one, but seldom did they actually complete the sexual act. Their problem was logistical in nature. Bradley lived and worked in the isolated manor he shared with his wife and children, and Charlotte divided her time between Oxford and gossipy little Gunwalloe on the Lizard Peninsula. She forbade Bradley from ever calling on her there. Her neighbors, she said, watched her like hawks.

Especially Vera Hobbs and Dottie Cox. If they ever see us together, we'll be the talk of Cornwall . . .

For a long time after Charlotte's murder, Bradley had ventured only eastward, oftentimes wandering as far as the fishing village of Mousehole. Now he headed westward into the glare of the declining sun, down to Logan Rock, over to Porthcurno Lookout, across the car park of the Minack Theatre to the cliffs above Porthchapel Beach. He half expected to see Charlotte waiting there, a wicked smile on her face. "Haven't we met somewhere before?" she used to say. And Bradley would reply, "Why yes, I believe we were at Oxford together." Bradley had been posh and Charlotte had been northern and poor. Posh boys like Bradley did not marry poor girls from the north. They married girls like Cordelia Chamberlain.

He cast his gaze toward the thicket of trees near St. Levan Church and imagined the final dreadful seconds of Charlotte's life. It was obvious that Gabriel Allon and the young detective did not believe that she had been murdered by the serial killer known as the Chopper. She was killed because of her investigation into the Picasso—and Bradley, in one way or another, had had a hand in her death. Now, to make matters worse, he had managed to entangle the wife of the next prime minister in the matter. After carefully weighing his options, he concluded he had no choice but to warn her that she would soon be hearing from none other than Gabriel Allon.

He placed the call while standing on the windblown cliff above Porthchapel Beach, a few hundred yards from the spot where Charlotte had been murdered. Much to his surprise, the wife of the next prime minister answered straight away. "Listen, Lucinda," he said with an air of false indifference. "I know you must be terribly busy at the moment, but you'll never guess who dropped by to see me today."

46

Old Burlington Street

B y the time they reached Taunton, Gabriel's eyes were heavy with fatigue. Bristol was the most obvious place to spend the night, but Ingrid had always wanted to visit the ancient Roman city of Bath, and it was only a few miles out of their way. They walked the honey-colored splendor of the historic center until sunset, then repaired to their adjoining rooms at the Gainsborough hotel and spa in Beau Street. Ingrid connected her computer to her mobile hot spot, checked the download speed, and went to work.

This time her target was BVI Bank, a notoriously corrupt financial institution located across the street from the Watering Hole in Road Town. Owing to the time difference, BVI's employees were still at their desks when Ingrid commenced her attack. One of them, a vice president called Fellowes, unwittingly granted her access to the bank's most sensitive data, including an account linked to LMR Overseas, the shell company owned by Lord Michael Radcliff.

"Oh my goodness," said Ingrid.

"What's wrong?" asked Gabriel from the next room.

"Just forty-eight hours after Lord Radcliff resigned as treasurer of the Conservative Party, he received a payment of ten million pounds."

"From whom?"

"You're not going to believe this."

"At this point, I wouldn't be surprised if you told me that the money came from Winston Churchill himself."

"I'm afraid it's better than that."

"That's not possible."

"You might want to come in here."

Gabriel hoisted himself off the bed and went through the communicating door. Ingrid was seated at the writing desk, her face lit by the glow of her laptop. With Gabriel looking over her shoulder, she pointed toward the name of the company that had paid Lord Michael Radcliff ten million pounds.

It was Driftwood Holdings.

"Valentin Federov?" asked Gabriel.

Ingrid smiled. "Do you know what that means?"

"It means that the Conservative Party official who accepted the million-pound contribution that brought down Prime Minister Hillary Edwards received ten times that amount from the same Russian businessman."

"Does that sound like a coincidence to you?"

"No," replied Gabriel. "It sounds like a conspiracy to remove Hillary Edwards from Ten Downing Street."

"I thought so, too. But why?"

Ingrid downloaded Lord Radcliff's account information to her external hard drive, then copied the data onto Gabriel's backup device. They both managed to get several hours of sleep and by eight the following morning were headed east on the M4. As they were approaching Heathrow, Gabriel rang the main number at Lambeth Wealth Management and asked to speak to the firm's chief executive officer, Lucinda Graves. He was transferred to Ms. Graves's assistant, and the assistant questioned him at length as to the nature of his call. At the conclusion of her inquisition, she took down his contact information but held out little hope that Ms. Graves would be getting back to him anytime soon. The Conservative Party leadership election was scheduled to begin in earnest at 2:00 p.m. If all went according to plan, Ms. Graves's husband would soon be prime minister.

Gabriel rang off and looked at Ingrid. "That went about as well as could be expected." But by the time they reached the London suburb of Chiswick, his phone was ringing.

"You must forgive my assistant," said Lucinda Graves. "As you can probably imagine, I'm suddenly the most popular financier in London."

"To tell you the truth, I was pleased she seemed not to recognize my name."

Lucinda Graves laughed. "I'm only sorry we didn't have a chance to talk at the Courtauld the other night. My husband is going to be green with envy."

"Why is that?"

"He was quite disappointed that you declined his invitation to drop by the Home Office. I can't wait to tell him that you came to see me instead."

"Is that an invitation?"

"Any time before two o'clock would be fine."

"I can be there by eleven."

"It sounds to me as though you're driving."

"The M4."

"Do you know where my office is located?"

"Old Burlington Street in Mayfair."

"Ask a spy a stupid question," she remarked.

"I'm an art restorer now, Ms. Graves."

"There's a Q-Park directly across the street from our office," she said. "My assistant will arrange a space for you."

And with that, the connection died.

"Well," said Ingrid. "That went better than expected."

"Yes," agreed Gabriel. "Imagine that."

———

He dropped Ingrid at a coffee shop in Piccadilly and at 10:55 a.m. guided the Bentley down the Q-Park's narrow ramp. The office block on the opposite side of Old Burlington Street was six floors in height, pale gray in color, and contemporary in design. A woman in her late twenties greeted Gabriel in the lobby and escorted him upstairs. Lucinda Graves was on the phone when they entered her office. She rang off at once and, rising, extended her hand.

"Mr. Allon. So lovely to see you again."

The assistant withdrew, and Lucinda conveyed Gabriel to a seating area where a coffee service rested on a low, sleek table. It was all very formal and rehearsed. Gabriel had the uncomfortable feeling he was being courted.

Lucinda sat down and filled two cups. "Have you seen the lines outside Somerset House? Thanks to you, the Courtauld is now London's hottest art museum."

"I'd love to take the credit, but the Van Gogh was in remarkably good condition when it came to me."

"Did you really play no role in its recovery?"

"I authenticated it for the Italian Art Squad. But that was the extent of my involvement."

"And now you're investigating the murder of that art historian from Oxford?"

Gabriel managed to conceal his surprise. "How did you know?"

"You're the professional. You tell me."

"Either the British government is monitoring my phone, or Leonard Bradley called you after I left his house. I'm betting it was Leonard."

She smiled with considerable charm. Absent the security detail and telegenic husband, she was smaller than Gabriel remembered and altogether ordinary in appearance. Her most appealing asset was her smoky contralto speaking voice. One could easily imagine Lucinda Graves singing torch songs in a darkened cabaret.

She glanced at the large wall-mounted television. Her husband was addressing a knot of reporters outside the Palace of Westminster. "Care to make a prediction?"

"I'm afraid I know very little about the inner workings of British politics."

"But that's not true, is it? After all, you lived in this country for many years after that incident in Vienna, and my husband tells me that you were quite close to Jonathan Lancaster. That was why he was so interested in meeting with you."

"What else has your husband told you?" asked Gabriel.

"That you were the so-called foreign intelligence operative who helped Lancaster when he got into trouble with that Russian sleeper agent who was working at Party Headquarters. Her name escapes me."

"Madeline Hart."

"The worst British political scandal since the Profumo affair," said

Lucinda. "And yet Lancaster managed to survive because of you." Her gaze returned to the television. "Please continue, Mr. Allon."

"The chancellor of the Exchequer will not survive today's balloting."

"Hardly a bold prediction. But who will secure the most votes?"

"Home Secretary Hugh Graves."

"How many will he receive?"

"Not enough to force Foreign Secretary Frasier to drop out of the race."

"It would help to unify the Party if Stephen were to bow out gracefully."

"The only way Frasier will drop out is if your husband allows him to remain at the Foreign Office."

"Never. Hugh intends to make a clean sweep of the Cabinet."

"In that case, he'll have to offer Frasier an exit ramp."

"Such as?"

"A public invitation to stay on as foreign secretary. Frasier, of course, will decline the offer. And tomorrow morning your husband will enter Number Ten for the first time as prime minister."

"Not bad, Mr. Allon. I think I'll suggest it to Hugh."

"I would appreciate it if you kept my name out of it."

"Don't worry, it will be our little secret."

Gabriel drank some of the coffee. "And what about you?" he asked. "What happens if your husband carries the day?"

"I will have no choice but to step away from Lambeth Wealth Management until Hugh leaves office. I only hope his premiership is as long as your friend Jonathan Lancaster's. He's still in the Commons, as you know." She paused for a moment, then said, "His backing would make Hugh unstoppable."

It was an invitation, thinly veiled, for Gabriel to assist in securing Jonathan Lancaster's support for her husband's candidacy. Having no desire to play even a minor role in the election of the next British prime minister, he guided the conversation back to the matter at hand.

"Yes," said Lucinda. "As a matter of fact, I did speak to Professor Blake about the Picasso."

"Do you happen to remember when?"

"Is it important?"

"It might be."

Lucinda aimed a remote at the television, and her husband vanished. "Sometime before the holidays, if memory serves. She rang me here at the office and said she was searching for a Picasso that had been acquired at Christie's by an anonymous shell company."

"OOC Group, Limited?"

Lucinda nodded. "She asked whether I would be willing to use my contacts in the London financial world to determine who or what the OOC Group was. I told her that it wouldn't be ethical."

"May I ask why?"

"Because many of my most important clients do business using shell companies. In fact, it's rather hard to find a wealthy person in London who doesn't."

"So you never met with her?"

"I didn't have the time. December is always one of our busiest months."

"And you never mentioned it to anyone?"

"Truth be told, I did my best to forget that I had ever heard of a company called OOC Group, Limited." Lucinda rose and her assistant magically appeared at the door. "I'm sorry I couldn't have been of more help, Mr. Allon. But it was wonderful to have finally met you. Rest assured, you will have a good friend in Downing Street if Hugh prevails in the leadership election."

"I have no doubt he will," said Gabriel, and started toward the door.

"Have you figured out what it is?" asked Lucinda suddenly.

Gabriel stopped and turned. "I'm sorry?"

"The OOC Group."

"No," he lied. "Not yet."

———————

It was 11:27 a.m. when the flashy Bentley driven by the legendary intelligence operative and art restorer Gabriel Allon emerged from the Q-Park garage in Old Burlington Street in Mayfair. Lucinda Graves knew this because she was standing in the window of her office and marked the time on her mobile phone. She allowed five minutes to pass before dialing a number stored in her directory of recent calls. The man at the other end gave her an update on Allon's movements.

"He just picked up a woman in Regent Street. They're currently headed south on Haymarket."

"Going where?"

"I'll get back to you."

Lucinda reluctantly severed the connection. Another ten minutes went by before her phone rang.

"Well?"

"They just walked into the Courtauld Gallery."

"He knows," said Lucinda, and killed the call.

47

Courtauld Gallery

A most unusual request," said Dr. Geoffrey Holland. "Frankly, I don't see how I can possibly accommodate you."

The director of the Courtauld Gallery was seated behind his desk, a forefinger pressed to his thin lips. Gabriel stood before him like a barrister pleading his case. Ingrid was downstairs roaming the exhibition rooms, a crime waiting to happen.

"I wouldn't ask if it wasn't important, Dr. Holland."

"Be that as it may, we have strict guidelines about this sort of thing."

"As well you should. But in this case, I think there is a compelling reason to make an exception."

"Your pro bono restoration of the Van Gogh, you mean?"

Gabriel smiled. "I wouldn't dream of resorting to such a cheap tactic."

"Of course you would." Holland's forefinger was now tapping a staccato rhythm on the surface of his desk. "And you're certain that Professor Blake was here on the day in question?"

"She arrived at four twelve and left shortly before the museum closed. If I had to guess, she spent the entire time in the café."

"That's hardly unusual. Many of our regular patrons find the café a wonderful place to while away an afternoon."

"But Charlotte Blake was no ordinary patron. She was a world-renowned provenance researcher who was looking for a Picasso worth more than a hundred million pounds."

"Do you really think the video will help you find it?"

"I wouldn't be here if I didn't."

Holland considered Gabriel's answer at length. "All right, I'll make an exception. But it's going to cost you."

"How much?"

"My Florigerio needs a good cleaning."

"*The Virgin and Child with the infant Saint John*? Who's resorting to cheap tactics now, Geoffrey?"

"Do you want to see the video or not?"

"I'd love to."

Holland lifted the receiver of his phone and dialed an internal number. "Hello, Simon. Geoffrey calling. Pull up the video from four o'clock on the afternoon of December fifteenth. I need to have a look at something straight away."

Four twelve, you say?"

"On the dot."

"Do you mind if I ask how you know that, Mr. Allon?"

"I would, actually."

Simon Eastwood, a former Metropolitan Police detective who now served as the Courtauld's chief of security, rattled the keyboard of a computer in his office, and a still image of the museum's lobby appeared on the screen.

"Do you see her?"

"Not yet."

Eastwood set the scene in motion with the click of his mouse. When the time stamp in the lower right corner of the screen read 4:12:38, Gabriel asked the security chief to pause the recording. Then he pointed toward the woman coming through the doorway, wearing a Burberry overcoat and scarf against the December cold.

"There she is."

Eastwood resumed the playback. As Gabriel predicted, Professor Charlotte Blake headed directly to the Courtauld's café and placed her order at the crimson counter. The table she selected was in a deserted corner of the room. After shedding her coat, she pulled a book from her bag and began to read.

It was 4:25 p.m.

"You see," said Geoffrey Holland. "She merely popped into the café for a cup of tea and a scone."

"On the same afternoon that you were meeting with the museum's board of trustees."

"I don't see how that's relevant."

"Do you remember what time the meeting ended?"

"If memory serves, it dragged on until nearly five."

Gabriel asked Simon Eastwood to advance the recording to 4:55 p.m. and increase the playback speed. Charlotte Blake sat with the stillness of a figure in a painting while patrons and employees buzzed like insects around her.

"Pause it," said Gabriel when the time stamp reached 5:04:12. Then he pointed to one of the figures in the tableau. "Do you recognize her?"

"Yes, of course," replied Geoffrey Holland.

It was Lucinda Graves.

Gabriel asked Simon Eastwood to resume the playback at normal speed. Eastwood looked to Geoffrey Holland for approval, and Holland, after a moment's hesitation, nodded his head solemnly. Then they watched in silence as the wife of the soon-to-be prime minister sat down opposite a woman who in a month's time would be dead. By all appearances their conversation was cordial. It concluded at 5:47 p.m. They were the last customers to leave the café.

"May I have a copy of this video?" asked Gabriel.

Eastwood looked at Geoffrey Holland, who delivered his ruling without delay.

"No, Mr. Allon. You may not."

―――――――

Perhaps it slipped her mind," said Ingrid without conviction.

"It didn't. She invited me to her office to pump me for information and then lied to my face. Quite well, I might add. Lucinda Graves is the link between Charlotte Blake and Trevor Robinson. Lucinda is the reason that Charlotte was murdered."

They were walking westward along the Strand toward Trafalgar Square. "When you think about it," said Ingrid, "it would explain a great deal."

"Beginning with the Federov scandal," added Gabriel. "It was manufactured by Lucinda and her friends at Harris Weber in order to force Hillary Edwards to resign. It was a coup directed against a sitting British prime minister."

"None of which we can prove."

"With one important exception."

"The ten-million-pound payment from Valentin Federov to Lord Radcliff?"

"Exactly."

They rounded a corner into Bedford Street and headed toward Covent Garden. Ingrid asked, "How much does Radcliff know about the plot?"

"If I had to guess, he knows everything."

"Which means his lordship is a most dangerous man."

"So am I," replied Gabriel.

"What are you planning to do?"

He pulled his phone from his pocket, composed a text message, and tapped SEND.

The reply was instant.

I'll call you back in five minutes . . .

———————

Christopher's beloved Bentley was wedged into a slender space on the bottom level of a car park in Garrick Street. Gabriel, certain the vehicle had not survived the ordeal intact, hurried down the internal stairwell with Ingrid at his heels. The light on the lower landing, functional an hour earlier, was no longer working. Consequently, he never saw the object—a human fist or perhaps a large-caliber bullet—that slammed into the left side of his skull. He was aware of his legs buckling beneath him and of his face colliding with concrete. Then there was only darkness, warm and wet, and the maddening electronic ringtone of his unanswered telephone.

48

Westminster

The phone at the other end of the call belonged to Samantha Cooke, chief political correspondent of the *Telegraph*. Needless to say, she was perplexed by her inability to reach her old friend. He had been a trusted source in the past, especially during the Madeline Hart affair, which had made Samantha's reputation. Furthermore, it was *he* who had made contact with *her*. His text message implied that he had uncovered vital information related to the Conservative Party leadership election, which Samantha herself had set in motion with her explosive reporting on the Valentin Federov contribution. She had promised to ring him back in five minutes and had been true to her word. And now, inexplicably, he was ignoring her.

Samantha redialed, then, after disregarding the automated invitation to leave a voicemail, dashed off a quick text expressing her urgent desire to speak to him. It included a reference to her present location, which was the Members Lobby of the Palace of Westminster. For all the tension in the air, there was little doubt as to how the first round of balloting would play out. Indeed, Samantha had already written her story, with the exception of the final vote totals. It declared that Chancellor Nigel Cunningham's candidacy had come to an end and that an overwhelming majority of Tory backbenchers wanted Home Secretary Hugh Graves to lead the Party into the next general election. Foreign Secretary Stephen Frasier had underperformed expectations. He nevertheless intended to take his case to the Party rank and file.

It was all cut and dried, thought Samantha, and dull as dishwater. Which was just one of the reasons why she was so anxious to make contact with her trusted source. "I'm Gabriel Allon," he had told her on the occasion of their first meeting. "I only do big."

But why wasn't he answering her calls? She sent another text message and, receiving no response, swore softly.

"Surely it's not as bad as all that," said a familiar male voice.

Samantha looked up from her phone and saw the even-featured face of Hugh Graves. She quickly managed to regain her composure. "My editor," she groaned.

"If he had any sense, he'd double your salary."

"I'm lucky I still have a job, Secretary Graves. These are tough times for the newspaper business."

"And for other British industries as well. But I assure you, the country's future is limitless."

It sounded as though he were rehearsing the speech that he would soon deliver on the doorstep of Number Ten. Samantha was having none of it. "The most recent economic forecasts," she pointed out, "paint a far bleaker picture."

"I think you'll be pleasantly surprised by what the next year will bring."

"With you at Number Ten?"

He smiled but said nothing.

"And what about Mrs. Graves?" Samantha persisted. "Will she be one of your advisers?"

"My wife is a brilliant economist. I would be a fool not to seek her advice. But no, Lucinda would not hold any formal role in my government, were it to come to pass."

"May I quote you on that?"

"Sorry, Samantha. Lobby rules."

The strictures of the Lobby journalism system required Samantha to abide by the minister's wishes. "Can't you at least give me *some*thing on the record, Secretary Graves? After all, if it wasn't for me . . ."

There was no need to finish the sentence. Were it not for Samantha, Hugh Graves would not be wearing the confident smile of a man who knew he would soon be prime minister.

"I look forward to this afternoon's vote," he said. "And I trust that my colleagues will reach the correct decision as to who should lead the Party and the country."

More dishwater, thought Samantha, but it would have to do. "How many votes will you receive?"

"We shall soon find out," he replied, and set off across the lobby.

Samantha sent a transcript of the on-the-record quote to her political desk, then tried once again to reach Gabriel. Her call received no answer. Frustrated, she sent him another text.

There was no reply.

———

The voting commenced when Big Ben tolled two o'clock. The setting, as usual, was Commons Committee Room 14, the largest in the Palace of Westminster. Such was the level of skullduggery during the previous leadership contest that members had to display their Parliamentary passes when entering and were forbidden to carry their mobile phones. The voting itself was conducted with conclave-like formality, though it was a black metal box, not an oversize gold chalice, into which the MPs slipped their paper ballots.

By half past four the votes had been tabulated, and all 325 members of the Conservative Parliamentary Party were crammed into Room 14 to hear the results. They were delivered with all the drama of a weekend weather forecast by Sir Stewart Archer, chairman of the 1922 Committee. Samantha Cooke watched the proceedings live on her phone, then plugged the numbers into her copy and shot it straight onto the *Telegraph*'s website. There were no surprises. Nigel Cunningham was out, Hugh Graves was in control, and Stephen Frasier, despite a surprisingly poor showing, was vowing to fight on.

But where the hell was Gabriel Allon?

49

New Forest

It would be another forty-five minutes before Gabriel would be able to say with any degree of confidence that he was not in fact dead. He reached this conclusion in the New Forest of Hampshire, though this, too, would have been a revelation to him. Hooded and gagged, his limbs immobilized by duct tape, he was largely cut off from the world around him. He was aware of motorized movement—he could hear the drone of an engine and tires rushing over wet tarmac—and could discern the warm presence of a body lying next to him. The faint aroma of female scent told him it was Ingrid.

Precisely how this state of affairs had come to pass remained a mystery to him. He recalled a meeting in a stylish office in Mayfair and a visit to a London art museum, which one, he could not say. The injury to his head had occurred in a fetid stairwell—of that much, at least, he was certain. He had been struck with something heavy behind his left ear, though he had no idea who had wielded the implement. The stickiness along the side of his neck told him the blow had resulted in substantial bleeding. His inability to hold even a simple thought was doubtless a symptom of a severe concussion.

He had always prided himself on his mastery of time. It was one of many peculiar skills he had developed as a child, the ability to declare with stopwatch accuracy when a minute or an hour had passed. Now time slipped through his fingers like water, and any effort to measure its progress set his head to throbbing. Instead, he attempted to recall the purpose of his visit to the office in Mayfair. He had met a woman there, a woman with a pleasing voice. Lucinda was her name, Lucinda Graves. Her husband was someone important. A politician, yes, that was it. The next prime minister, or so they said.

But why had he called on Lucinda Graves, of all people? And what had compelled him to visit a museum afterward? Those were the questions bouncing around Gabriel's suddenly disordered mind when the vehicle beneath him—he assumed it was a transit van—made a right turn onto an unpaved track. Some length of time later, a few minutes, perhaps an hour or more, it crunched to a stop in a bed of gravel. Then the engine died and doors were hauled open. Gabriel, his head throbbing, counted the footfalls of at least four men.

Two pairs of hands seized him, one pair by the shoulders, the other by his legs, and lifted him from the back of the van. Neither of his porters spoke a word as they bore him across the expanse of gravel and into a shelter of some sort. The floor on which they laid him was concrete and cold as the surface of a frozen millpond. "Where's Ingrid?" he tried to shout through the gag, but a sliding wooden door rattled shut, and the shackle of a heavy-duty lock snapped into place.

So, too, did a portion of Gabriel's memory. He had gone to the stylish office in Mayfair, he recalled with a flash of sudden clarity, to ask Lucinda Graves about her conversation with Charlotte Blake.

And he had subsequently paid a visit to the Courtauld Gallery to prove that Lucinda had lied to him. Lucinda Graves was the reason Professor Blake was dead—and why Gabriel was lying hooded and bound on a cold concrete floor. Lucinda's husband would soon be prime minister, and Gabriel would soon be dead. Of that much, at least, he was certain.

———

By six that evening the whole of Whitehall was in agreement that it was a foregone conclusion. The only question still to be answered, went the thinking, was how it would come about. His margin of victory in the 1922 Committee had been considerably larger than the experts and oddsmakers had predicted, suggesting that Tory MPs had been eager to demonstrate fealty to the man who would soon control their political fortunes. They streamed to his parliamentary office after the vote to offer their congratulations and lobby for a seat in his Cabinet. And then they found the nearest reporter and declared—on background and in hushed tones—that it was time for Stephen Frasier to bow out of the race.

The foreign secretary was confronted with the statements during a sometimes-contentious interview on the *Six O'Clock News*. It didn't help matters that the BBC presenter mistakenly referred to Frasier's rival as "Prime Minister Graves." Frasier's shrinking band of loyalists urged him to see the race to its end. But during a meeting with his closest political advisers at seven that evening—details of which somehow leaked to the press—it was made clear to Frasier that he faced an uphill battle. Graves, a tough-on-immigration Brexiteer, was popular with the Party's increasingly populist rank and file, while Frasier, a late convert to Euroscepticism, was regarded with suspicion. The best he could hope for, advised the advisers, was a lop-sided loss. The more likely outcome, though, was a career-damaging thrashing. The wiser move would be to declare a ceasefire for the good of the Party and sue for peace.

And so it was that Foreign Secretary Stephen Frasier, at 8:07 p.m., took the first hesitant step toward bringing about a dignified with-drawal from the field of battle. He did so with a phone call to his rival, personal device to personal device. Graves suggested they meet at his palatial home in Holland Park. Frasier, a lifelong public servant of far more modest means, insisted the meeting take place at Conser-vative Campaign Headquarters instead.

"When?" asked Graves.

"How about nine o'clock?"

"See you then."

"And no bloody leaks," insisted Frasier.

"You have my word."

But by half past eight the news of Stephen Frasier's imminent ca-pitulation was the talk of Whitehall. The news reached Samantha Cooke as she was sinking her teeth into a brie-and-bacon panini at Caffè Nero in Bridge Street. She devoured the rest of the sandwich while rushing over to CCHQ. Hugh Graves was stepping from the back of his ministerial car when she arrived, looking every inch the prime minister. The foreign secretary appeared five minutes later. "Is it over?" Samantha called out, but Frasier smiled bravely and said, "Actually, it's only just begun."

Which was not at all the case, as Samantha Cooke, with a rapid series of phone calls to her trusted sources, quickly discovered. Fra-sier had come to Party HQ to offer his sword in surrender. Graves planned to extend an olive branch in return, a wholly disingenu-ous invitation to stay on as foreign secretary in the new Cabinet.

Frasier, of course, would politely decline the offer and return to the backbenches. It would all be over in time for the *News at Ten*. And tomorrow morning, after receiving the required invitation from the monarch to form a new government, Hugh Graves would stride through the world's most famous front door as prime minister.

Samantha bashed out an update, and by nine thirty it was the lead item on the *Telegraph*'s website. She forwarded a link to Gabriel Allon's number but once again received no response. She was now worried that some terrible tragedy had befallen him. An accident, perhaps something worse. Fortunately, one of his closest friends and associates had by then reached the same conclusion. And at 9:45 that evening, as the rest of official London awaited a puff of white smoke from Party Headquarters, he was in a taxi bound for Garrick Street, the last known location of his Bentley motorcar.

50

Garrick Street

The technology that allowed Christopher Keller to determine the whereabouts of his automobile was nothing more sophisticated or secretive than the Bentley app on his mobile phone. He had used the same software to monitor Gabriel and Ingrid's movements during their visit to Cornwall. He knew, for example, that they had lunched at the Blue Ball Inn in Clyst Road in Exeter, doubtless with Detective Sergeant Timothy Peel of the Devon and Cornwall Police. He also knew that they had spent the night in Bath, probably at the Gainsborough hotel and spa in Beau Street. By eleven o'clock that morning the Bentley was in Old Burlington Street in Mayfair, and shortly before noon it was moved to Garrick Street in Covent Garden. Christopher had no idea why, as all attempts to reach Gabriel that evening had proven fruitless. Even more ominous, it now appeared as though his phone was off the air.

The taxi dumped Christopher outside a Waterstones. He crossed Garrick Street, phone in one hand, the spare remote for his car in the other, and headed down the corkscrew ramp of the garage. He found the car crammed into a corner space on the lower level, its doors unlocked. There was no luggage or computer bags—and no external hard drives containing sensitive attorney-client documents from the law firm of Harris Weber & Company.

Christopher walked over to the metal door that gave onto the internal stairwell. On the tarmac there were dark droplets of something that appeared to be dried blood. He found more droplets inside the stairwell itself, though he had to use his phone to see them because someone had unscrewed the overhead light. This was the spot where they had made their move, he thought. They were professionals, men such as himself. But because this was London, where the CCTV surveillance cameras never blinked, it was all on video.

Christopher hurried over to the Bentley and slid behind the wheel. Five minutes later, after paying the exorbitant charge for a ten-hour stay, he was speeding down Whitehall toward Parliament Square. The political drama unfolding at Conservative Campaign Headquarters had brought Westminster to a standstill. He battled his way along Broad Sanctuary to Victoria Street and continued west to Eaton Square in Belgravia, where, at ten fifteen, he arrived at the home of Graham Seymour, the director-general of the Secret Intelligence Service.

His eccentric wife, Helen, answered the bell dressed in a flowing silk kaftan. Graham was upstairs in his study, watching the news on television. He inclined a cut-glass tumbler of single malt toward the screen. Hugh Graves and Stephen Frasier were standing shoulder to shoulder on the floodlit pavement outside Party Headquarters. Graves was all smiles. Frasier appeared stoic in defeat.

"It seems we have a new prime minister," said Graham.

"I'm afraid we have a much bigger problem than that," replied Christopher.

Graham muted the television. "What now?"

Christopher fortified himself with some of the whisky before attempting to explain the situation.

"What on earth was he doing in Covent Garden?"

"Truth be told, I haven't a clue."

Frowning, Graham reached for his secure phone and dialed Amanda Wallace, his counterpart at MI5. "Sorry to be calling so late, but I'm afraid we have a bit of a crisis on our hands. It seems something has happened to our friend Gabriel Allon . . . Yes, I know. Why did it have to be tonight of all nights?"

Later it would be determined that Amanda Wallace rang the Operations Room at MI5's Millbank headquarters at 10:19 p.m. and informed the duty officer that Gabriel Allon was missing and presumed kidnapped. She then gave the duty officer Allon's last known location, which was a public car park in Garrick Street. He had arrived there at midday in a borrowed Bentley automobile. MI5 was to make no effort to identify the owner of the vehicle, as he was a clandestine operative of the rival service based on the opposite side of the Thames at Vauxhall Cross.

With an array of invasive surveillance tools at his disposal, the duty officer and his crack staff quickly determined that the borrowed Bentley had entered the car park at 12:03 p.m. Allon emerged four minutes later, accompanied by an attractive woman in her mid-thirties. They made their way on foot to the nearby Courtauld Gallery and remained there for a period of forty-two minutes. Leaving, they engaged in an animated conversation as they walked along the Strand. After making the turn into Bedford Street, Allon appeared to have composed and sent a single text message.

They returned to the car park in Garrick Street at one fifteen and were not seen again. The next vehicle to depart the facility, at 1:20 p.m., was a Mercedes-Benz Sprinter transit van, dark blue in color, driven by a large man wearing a dark coverall and a woolen watch cap. He headed across the Waterloo Bridge to Southbank and by three o'clock was approaching the cathedral city of Canterbury. The van's last known location was the Kent Downs, a 326-square-mile nature area where CCTV cameras were scarce. It was the assumption of the MI5 duty officer and his staff that the kidnappers had transferred Allon and the woman to a second vehicle—and that they were no longer in the southeast of England.

But what was Gabriel Allon doing in London in the first place? And where had he gone before his visit to the Courtauld Gallery? An answer to the second question, at least, was easily obtainable. Allon had dropped the woman in Piccadilly at 10:55 a.m. and driven to Old Burlington Street, where he entered a six-story modern office block. The building's most prominent client, interestingly enough, was the wealth management firm run by Lucinda Graves, the wife of the next British prime minister.

It was this intriguing piece of news that MI5 director-general Amanda Wallace, at 11:10 p.m., delivered by secure phone to her counterpart at the Secret Intelligence Service. "The question is, Graham, what was he doing there?"

"Lucinda's on the board of trustees at the Courtauld, if I recall."

"She is, indeed."

"Could have been art related," suggested Graham.

"Perhaps," replied Amanda.

"I don't suppose you've mentioned any of this to the home secretary. After all, he *is* your minister."

"I didn't want to spoil his evening. Evidently, they're having quite a blowout in Holland Park at the moment."

"In that case, I think we should keep it between us for now."

"I couldn't agree more."

Graham rang off and looked at Christopher. "Do you have any idea why your friend Gabriel Allon went to see the wife of the next British prime minister this morning?"

"Lucinda Graves?" Christopher helped himself to another glass of the single malt before answering. "Actually, I'm afraid I might."

51

Blackdown Hills

It was 11:17 p.m. when the wooden door of the shelter finally trundled open and two men entered Gabriel's makeshift prison cell. Bound and hooded, he was unaware of the time, but the number of visitors was easily discernible by the scrape of their shoes over the concrete floor. They seized him by the shoulders and hauled him to his feet. Instantly his darkened world began to spin out of control.

They sawed away the duct tape from his ankles and prodded him to walk, but his legs were unresponsive and he feared he was about to be sick. At last the spinning subsided and he was able to place one foot in front of the other, hesitantly, like a patient walking the halls of a surgical ward. His first steps were on the concrete floor of the shelter, then the gravel of the drive. A gentle rain was falling, and the air smelled of freshly turned earth. There was not a sound to be heard other than the crunch of footfalls. Gabriel's were arrhythmic and faltering, the stagger of a wounded man.

"Where is she?" he tried to ask through the duct-tape gag, but his two handlers only laughed in response. It was his considered opinion, having resided in the United Kingdom for a number of years, that it was the laughter of two Englishmen of working-class upbringing, perhaps thirty to thirty-five years of age. They were both several inches taller than Gabriel, and the hands holding him upright were large and powerful. He wondered whether one of the men was responsible for the dent in the left side of his skull. He only hoped he was presented with an opportunity to return the favor.

Eventually the loose gravel was replaced by the firmer footing of a paved walkway. Then, after a laborious climb up a flight of steps, there was a roof over Gabriel's head and carpet beneath his feet. The two men helped him into a straight-backed chair and removed the hood. Gabriel closed his eyes. The photophobia brought about by the injury to his head made the light painful in its intensity.

He opened one eye slowly, then the other, and surveyed the room around him. It took a moment to appreciate the scale of the place; it was the size of a tennis court. The overstuffed chairs and couches were covered in silk and chintz and brocade, and there was a per-vasive smell of newness in the air. The leather-bound books lining the shelves appeared unread. The gilt-framed Old Master paintings looked as though they had been executed earlier that evening.

The two men who had delivered Gabriel to this place were now standing like pillars beside him. Two more men were seated in a pair of matching wing chairs, and Trevor Robinson, in a dark suit and tie, was pouring himself a whisky at the drinks trolley.

He waved the crystal decanter in Gabriel's direction. "You, Allon?"

Gabriel, his mouth covered by duct tape, made no attempt to reply. Robinson, smiling, returned the decanter to the trolley and carried his glass over to an ornate credenza. It was strewn with the wreckage of two laptop computers, two external eight-terabyte hard drives, and a mobile phone. By all appearances it was Ingrid's

Android device. Gabriel's Solaris phone had been in his coat pocket when he entered the car park in Garrick Street. He reckoned it was now in the signal-blocking Faraday pouch that Robinson held in his free hand.

He nodded in Gabriel's general direction, and one of the men ripped the duct tape from his mouth. The pain was like a hard slap in the face. For the moment, at least, it made him forget the incessant pounding in his head.

"How about that drink now?" asked Robinson. "You look as though you could use one."

Gabriel glanced around the room. "You've done very well for yourself, Trevor. Taking early retirement from MI5 was obviously the right career move."

"The property belongs to a client of the firm. He allows us to borrow it for special occasions."

"Is that what this is?"

"Most definitely." Robinson tossed the Faraday pouch onto an oversize coffee table. It landed with a thud. "After all, it's not often that one gets to entertain a legend."

"Your hospitality leaves something to be desired."

"The bump on your head, you mean? Sorry, Allon, but I'm afraid there was no other way." Robinson indicated one of the two men seated silently in the wing chairs. "It was Sam who did it, if you must know. Sometimes he doesn't know his own strength."

"Why don't you cut the duct tape from my wrists so I can thank him properly?"

"I wouldn't, if I were you. Sam is a veteran of the Regiment. So are the two men standing next to you. They now work for a private security firm based in London. The firm's clients are all extremely wealthy and demand nothing but the best."

Gabriel looked at the fourth man. "And him?"

"Three Para. He spent a great deal of time in Afghanistan."

"That leaves Ingrid," said Gabriel.

"Ms. Johansen is resting at the moment and can't be disturbed."

"You didn't do something stupid, did you, Trevor?"

"Not me," replied Robinson. "But I'm afraid Sam was forced to apply a bit of pressure to loosen her tongue. After that she was very cooperative. In fact, with her help, I was able to recover the documents you stole from our office in Monaco and BVI Bank in Road Town. You now have no evidence to support any claim of financial misconduct by Harris Weber & Company or its clients."

"How did you know?" asked Gabriel.

"About your theft of our confidential files? I didn't," admitted Robinson. "But I surmised as much after having a word with one of my paid assets in the Swiss government. I met with him in Bern the morning after your little heist."

"That would explain your late-night withdrawal of cash from the safe."

"It was money well spent, as it turns out. My source told me that you were the one who discovered Edmond Ricard's body at his gallery in the Freeport. He also said that you were working with Swiss intelligence to track down Ricard's killer and recover the Picasso. Needless to say, I was alarmed by the news, as were the founding partners of my firm. You are a worthy opponent."

"I'm flattered."

"Don't be, Allon. The ice beneath your feet is very thin, indeed. Fortunately for you and your associate, I've been authorized to offer you a settlement package. As your representative in this matter, I strongly advise you to accept it."

"The terms?"

"You will receive ten million pounds, payable to a limited liability shell company that Harris Weber & Company will create on your behalf. In return, you will sign a nondisclosure agreement which will prohibit you from ever discussing this affair. Ms. Johansen will also receive ten million pounds. And then, of course, there's the small matter of the Picasso, which OOC Group, Limited, will return to the heirs of Bernard Lévy at a date to be determined. With no admission of wrongdoing, I might add."

"Tempting," said Gabriel. "But I'm afraid I have a few demands of my own, beginning with the financial aspects. Instead of paying my associate and me twenty million pounds, Harris Weber & Company will donate one billion pounds to the British charities of our choice in order to undo some of the damage your firm has done by helping the wealthy evade taxes. And then, of course, there's the small matter of Hugh Graves, who must drop out of the leadership contest so that Stephen Frasier can become prime minister." Gabriel managed a smile. "With no admission of wrongdoing, I might add."

Trevor Robinson displayed a smile of his own. "Haven't you heard the news, Allon? The foreign secretary threw in the towel earlier this evening. Hugh Graves is scheduled to meet with the King at Buckingham Palace tomorrow morning. Once His Majesty asks him to form a government—"

"Harris Weber will own a prime minister," interjected Gabriel. "Which is why Lucinda Graves phoned you a few minutes after she met with Charlotte Blake at the Courtauld. She was understandably concerned that her ties to your firm would be exposed during any litigation over that Picasso. Therefore, the firm decided to take appropriate measures to protect its multimillion-pound investment in her husband's political future."

"The best-laid plans of mice and men," said Robinson. "And they were nearly destroyed because an art historian from Oxford found a sales receipt at Christie's."

"I'm glad we cleared that up."

"Rest assured, there's a great deal about this affair that you don't know."

"Beginning with your motives. What did Harris Weber hope to gain by making Hugh Graves prime minister?"

"Surely you're not that naive, Allon." Robinson went slowly to the trolley and refreshed his drink. "Your implacable sense of right and wrong is admirable, but I'm afraid it's rather out of fashion at the moment. The truth is, there is no right and wrong any longer. There is only power and money. And more often than not, one begets the other." He glanced at Gabriel over his shoulder. "Are you sure I can't get you something?"

"A pair of noise-canceling headphones would be nice."

"You would be wise to listen to what I have to say. The old order is crumbling, Allon. A new order is rising in its place. We at Harris Weber refer to it as Kleptopia. There are no laws in Kleptopia, at least not for those with unlimited resources, and no one cares about the needs of that great mass of humanity who are less fortunate. Power and money are all that matters. Those without it want to acquire it. And those who have it want to hang on to it at all costs. I'm offering you the opportunity to be a part of that world. Get on the gravy train while you can. If you're not offshore, you're nowhere at all."

"I'll choose my world over yours, Trevor. Besides, a lousy ten million doesn't go very far in Kleptopia."

"Your world is gone. Can't you see that? And if you don't sign that agreement, you and that pretty Danish girl of yours will be gone, too."

"I've given you my terms," said Gabriel.

"Hugh Graves? It's over, Allon. Nothing can stop him now."

Gabriel glanced at the Faraday bag. "Perhaps you should have a look at my phone. You might think otherwise."

"Ms. Johansen claimed not to know the password."

"It's fourteen digits," said Gabriel. "Sometimes even I have trouble remembering it."

Robinson opened the pouch and removed the phone. "Quite heavy, isn't it?"

"But very secure."

Robinson held the phone a few inches from Gabriel's face. "No facial recognition?"

"Are you serious?"

"Tell me the password."

"Show me Ingrid."

Robinson sighed and then buried his fist in Gabriel's abdomen, leaving him incapable of speech for nearly two minutes. He allowed another minute to go by before reciting fourteen numbers.

"Three, two, one, six, five, nine, three, five, one, four, five, four, seven, six."

Robinson entered the numbers and then frowned. "It didn't work."

Gabriel retched before answering. "You obviously entered it incorrectly."

"Recite it again."

"Three, two, one, six, five, nine, five, three, one, four, five, four, seven, six."

Once again the phone rejected the passcode as entered. This time it was one of the former SAS officers who struck Gabriel. The force of the blow nearly stopped his heart.

Robinson was shouting into his face. "Give me the fucking password, Allon! The *correct* password!"

"Listen carefully this time, you idiot. You've only got three more tries before the phone autodestructs."

"Slowly," cautioned Robinson.

"Three, two, one, six, five, nine, three, five, one, four, five, nine, seven, six."

The next blow struck Gabriel in the cheekbone and carried him to the very edge of consciousness.

"Last chance," said Robinson.

Gabriel spat a mouthful of blood onto the luxurious carpet before reciting the fourteen digits in the correct sequence. Robinson, his hand shaking with rage, managed to enter them correctly. The phone vibrated as he stared at the screen.

"Is that my wife, by any chance?"

"Samantha Cooke of the *Telegraph*."

The phone ceased vibrating, then, a few seconds later, pulsed with a text message.

"What does it say?"

"It says you have one hour to accept Harris Weber & Company's generous settlement offer." Robinson slid the phone into the Faraday pouch and sealed the Velcro flap. "Otherwise, you and the pretty Danish girl die."

———

They returned the hood to Gabriel's head and, after a rain-drenched journey over paving stones and gravel, hurled him onto the concrete floor of his holding cell and locked the door. He soon realized that this time he was not alone; someone was lying next to him. The faint aroma of female scent and fear told him it was Ingrid.

"Did they hit you?" she asked.

"I can't remember. You?"

"Once or twice. And then I made a deal with them."

"Good girl. What were the terms?"

"I promised to tell them everything if they would agree to let a doctor examine you."

"In case you were wondering, they didn't live up to their end of the bargain. In fact, they gave me quite a going-over in there."

"The passcode for your phone?"

"Yes."

"I had a feeling."

"Do you really not know it?"

She sighed and then recited it perfectly.

"I could have used your help earlier," said Gabriel. "I had a devil of a time remembering the damn thing."

"How long was the phone out of the Faraday bag?"

"Long enough."

52

Petton Cross

On the western fringes of the Gloucestershire town of Cheltenham stands an enormous circular structure that resembles a stranded alien spacecraft. Known to those who work there as the Doughnut, the building is the home of the Government Communications Headquarters, or GCHQ, Britain's signals intelligence service. Twenty-four hours a day, seven days a week, its officers eavesdrop on sensitive communications around the world. Occasionally, however, they are assigned more mundane tasks, such as determining the approximate location of a mobile phone. This they can accomplish quite easily, provided the device is switched on and transmitting a signal.

Three veteran GCHQ officers were engaged in just such a search that evening. They were well acquainted with the phone in question. It was a secure device carried by the retired chief of Israeli intelligence, a man who over the years had worked closely with his counterparts at Millbank and Vauxhall Cross. As a matter of course, and despite assurances to the contrary, GCHQ tracked his device whenever it popped onto one of the British networks, though all attempts to penetrate its formidable defenses had proven fruitless.

In short order the officers were able to determine that the phone had returned to the United Kingdom two days earlier, that it had ventured as far afield as Land's End in Cornwall, that it had spent a night in the ancient Roman city of Bath, and that it had gone dark at 1:37 that afternoon near Greenwich Park in southeast London. But finally, at 11:42 p.m., the phone awakened from its hours-long slumber and reattached itself to the network. Its stay was brief, slightly less than five minutes, but more than sufficient for the three officers to identify the location of the nearest cellular mast.

It was this small but vital piece of data that the overnight duty officer in Cheltenham, at 11:54 p.m., personally relayed to SIS chief Graham Seymour. Graham, who was still at his home in Belgravia, in turn delivered the news to Amanda Wallace of MI5. The two senior spymasters were in agreement that, for the time being, at least, they should continue to withhold the information from both their prime minister and the man who would soon succeed her, Home Secretary Hugh Graves.

They likewise agreed that this was an intelligence matter and not something that could be left solely in the hands of the police. Still, they could not possibly mount a rescue attempt without first alerting the chief constable of the local territorial force. It was Graham Seymour, shortly after midnight, who placed the call, waking the chief constable from a sound sleep. Their conversation was two minutes in length, unpleasant in tone, and characterized by a distinct lack of candor on Graham's part. He refused to divulge even the barest details about the nature of the emergency and insisted on maintaining full control of the response. He required no assistance, he said, other than an unmarked car and a driver. Much to the chief constable's surprise, he requested a specific officer for the job.

"But he's a junior detective with absolutely no experience in this sort of thing."

"If you must know, Chief Constable, we've had our eye on him for some time."

And so it was that, ninety minutes later, Detective Sergeant Timothy Peel was sitting behind the wheel of an unmarked Vauxhall Insignia, watching a Royal Navy Sea King approaching Exeter from the east. It settled onto the helipad at the headquarters of the Devon and Cornwall Police at 1:47 a.m., and a single black-clad figure emerged from the cabin with a nylon rucksack over one sturdy shoulder. Head lowered, he hurried across the tarmac and dropped into the Vauxhall's passenger seat.

"Timothy," he said with a smile. "So good to finally meet you."

———

He instructed Peel to make his way to the M5 and head north. At two o'clock on a rainy Wednesday morning, the motorway was empty of traffic. Peel was doing ninety, no lights or siren. His passenger was unimpressed.

"Does this bloody thing go any faster?" he drawled.

Peel increased his speed to triple digits. "Mind telling me where we're going?"

"Petton Cross."

It was a nothing little village near the border with neighboring Somerset. "Any particular reason?"

"I'll explain when we get there," replied his passenger, and ignited a Marlboro with a gold Dunhill lighter.

"Must you?" asked Peel.

He smiled. "I must."

Peel lowered his window a few inches to vent the smoke. "It occurs to me that I don't know your name."

"With good reason."

"What should I call you?"

"How about David?"

"David?" Peel shook his head. "Doesn't suit you."

"In that case, you should call me Christopher."

"Much better." Peel glanced at the rucksack. "What have you got in there, Christopher?"

"Zeiss night-vision field glasses, two Glock pistols, several spare magazines of nine-millimeter ammunition, a couple of secure phones, and a box of McVitie's."

"Dark chocolate?"

"But of course."

"I'd kill for one."

He fished the tube of biscuits from the rucksack and handed one to Peel. "Cornwall lad, are you?"

"Mostly."

"Which part?"

"The Lizard."

"Port Navas, by any chance?"

Peel's head swiveled to the left. "How did you know?"

"A friend of mine used to live there. The old foreman's cottage overlooking the quay. An art restorer by trade. A spy in his spare time."

Peel returned his eyes to the road. "My mother and I lived in the house at the head of the tidal creek. We were neighbors."

"Yes, I know. He told me the story one night when we were holed up in a safe house and the telly was on the fritz."

"Where was the safe house?"

"Can't seem to remember. But I do recall the fondness with which he spoke about the little boy who used to signal him with a torch from his bedroom window each time he returned to Port Navas. You meant a great deal to him, Timothy. More than you'll ever realize."

"He made me the person I am."

"We have that in common, the two of us." Christopher lowered his voice. "Which is why I came here tonight."

"What's in Petton Cross?" asked Peel.

"A cellular mast that detected the presence of Gabriel's phone about two hours ago. It is my profound hope that he and his friend Ingrid are somewhere in the near vicinity."

"What happened?"

"They were abducted in London this afternoon. A car park in Garrick Street, very professional. About an hour before it happened, Gabriel paid a visit to Lucinda Graves's office in Mayfair. I was wondering if you knew why."

"Professor Charlotte Blake."

Christopher pointed toward the exit for the A38. "You'd better slow down, Timothy. Otherwise, you'll miss your turnoff."

It was smaller, even, than tiny Gunwalloe, just a handful of cottages and farms clustered around the intersection of four small roads. One led due north. Peel followed it for a few hundred yards, then turned into a narrow lane that carried them up the slope of a low hill. To their right, barely visible over the dense hedgerow, a single red light shone atop a cellular mast.

There was no verge, and no turnout in sight, so Peel slowed the Vauxhall to a stop in the center of the lane. The immediate proximity of the hedgerows required him to shimmy sideways from behind the wheel. In the boot was a pair of Wellingtons, a necessity for police work in rural England. He pulled them on and played the beam of a torch over the hedgerow. It was impenetrable to light.

"Surely there's a gap somewhere," said Christopher.

"Not on this road, there isn't."

"Then I suppose we'll have to go through it, won't we?"

Christopher slung his rucksack over his shoulder and walked through the hedgerow as though it were an open door. By the time Peel managed to extract himself, the SIS man was halfway across the meadow on the other side. Peel clambered after him awkwardly in the Wellingtons and was gasping for air when he finally reached the brow of the hill. Christopher was breathing normally despite the freshly lit Marlboro jutting from the corner of his mouth.

He pulled the night-vision field glasses from the rucksack and, rotating slowly at the base of the mast, searched the land in every direction. A few lights burned here and there, but otherwise this corner of Devon was still sleeping soundly.

At last he lowered the glasses and pointed toward the northeast. "There's a rather grand property a couple of miles in that direction. You wouldn't happen to know who owns it?"

"That's Somerset, sir."

"And?"

"Not my jurisdiction."

"It is now."

Peel held out a hand. "Mind if I have a look?"

Christopher surrendered the field glasses, and Peel scrutinized the property in question. It looked to be about a hundred acres. The substantial redbrick Georgian manor was in exquisite condition. There were lights burning on the lower floor, and a Range Rover was parked in the drive. Behind the main house was a collection of farm buildings. There was also another vehicle, a Mercedes-Benz Sprinter transit van. It appeared to Peel as though someone was sitting in the driver's seat.

He lowered the glasses. "A simple check of the Land Registry will tell us the name of the owner."

"What are you waiting for?"

Peel rang Exeter and gave the duty officer a general description of the parcel of land and an approximate address—a bit north of the old church of St. Michael in Raddington, west side of Hill Lane.

"That's Somerset," replied the duty officer.

"Tell me something I don't know."

"I'll get back to you."

"Quickly," said Peel, and killed the connection.

Christopher was holding the night-vision glasses to his eyes again. "He won't mention any of this to your chief constable, I hope."

"He's a Cornwall lad, like myself."

"Is that a yes or a no?"

Peel's phone pinged with a text message before he could offer a response.

"And the winner is?" asked Christopher.

"The property is owned by a limited liability company registered in the British Virgin Islands."

"Company have a name?"

"Driftwood Holdings."

Christopher lowered the glasses and stared hard at Peel. "Are you carrying a sidearm, Timothy?"

"I am not."

"Do you know how to use one?"

"Quite well, actually."

"Ever shoot anyone?"

"Never."

Christopher returned the field glasses to the rucksack. "Well, Timothy Peel, this could be your lucky night."

53

Somerset

Timothy Peel officially strayed onto the territory of the Avon and Somerset Police at 3:02 a.m., when his unmarked Vauxhall Insignia rolled over the little humpback bridge spanning the River Batherm. To make matters worse, his passenger was giving him a rapid tutorial on the basic operation of a Glock 19 pistol. Peel, who was not authorized to carry or discharge a firearm regardless of the county, had no business being in the same car with it.

"The magazine holds fifteen rounds." Christopher pointed toward the bottom of the grip. "You insert it here."

"I know how to load a bloody gun."

"Don't talk, just listen." Christopher rammed the magazine into the grip. "When you are ready to fire your weapon, you must chamber the first round by racking the slide. A Glock has an internal safety mechanism that disengages automatically when you pull the trigger. If for some reason you feel the need to pull it fifteen times, the slide will lock in the open position. Eject your empty magazine by pressing the release on the left side of the grip, and insert your backup. Then rinse and repeat." He handed Peel the fully loaded weapon. "And do try not to shoot me, Timothy. It will greatly increase your chances of surviving the next few minutes."

"I never realized that SIS officers carried sidearms."

"I'm not a normal SIS officer."

"I gathered that." Peel pointed out the silhouette of a bell tower rising above the meadow on their left. "There's the church of Saint Michael."

"You don't say."

"I was just trying to orient you."

"This might come as a surprise, but I've done this sort of thing a time or two."

"Anywhere in particular?"

"West Belfast, South Armagh, and other assorted garden spots in the province of Northern Ireland." He lit another cigarette. "There's where I acquired this terrible habit. One of several, as a matter of fact."

Peel made a left turn into Churchill Lane and headed north.

"Switch off your headlamps," said Christopher.

Peel did as he asked.

"The sidelights, too."

"I won't be able to see."

"Don't talk, just listen."

Peel killed the lights and reduced his speed. Clouds obscured the moon and the stars, and sunrise was still three hours away. It was like driving with his eyes closed.

"A little faster, Timothy. I'd like to get there before they kill them."

Peel pressed the throttle, and a hedgerow clawed at the left side of the Vauxhall.

"Try to keep the damn thing on the road, will you?"

"What road?"

Christopher looked down at his phone. "You are approaching Hill Lane."

Peel managed to make the right turn without further damaging the Vauxhall and started up the slope of the highland for which the road was named. As they were approaching the summit, Christopher instructed Peel to find a spot to leave the car. He turned through the open gate of a pasture and rolled to a stop. A flock of sheep, invisible in the inky darkness, bleated in protest.

Christopher climbed out of the car and pulled on the rucksack, then barged through another hedgerow and struck out across a pasture. Peel followed after him, the unauthorized Glock 19 in his right hand. The grass was knee-deep, the soil saturated and unstable. Peel's Wellingtons squished noisily beneath him, but somehow Christopher flowed across the pasture without a sound.

They breached another hedgerow and crossed a second pasture, this one populated by cows. A thick wood marked its northern border. Christopher turned to Peel in the pitch-darkness and said quietly, "Please charge your firearm, Detective Sergeant."

Peel racked the slide, chambering the first round.

"Keep your finger on the side of the trigger guard and the weapon pointed toward the ground. And don't say another word unless I speak to you first."

Christopher turned and disappeared into the trees. Peel followed a step behind, both hands on the Glock, the barrel angled safely downward. The darkness was absolute. He could see nothing but the faint outline of Christopher's powerful shoulders.

The SIS man froze suddenly and raised his right hand. Peel stood like a statue behind him, unaware of what had provoked the reaction. There was nothing to see, and the only sound Peel heard was the kettledrum beating of his own heart.

Christopher lowered his hand and resumed his methodical advance. When he froze a second time, he shed his rucksack and removed the Zeiss field glasses. He peered into the darkness for a long moment, then handed the glasses to Peel. They revealed to him the large property he had seen a few minutes earlier while standing at the foot of the cellular mast. The lights were still burning on the lower floor of the redbrick Georgian manor, and the Mercedes transit van was still parked outside the collection of farm buildings. There appeared to be no one behind the wheel.

Christopher returned the glasses to his rucksack and slung it over his shoulders, then led Peel out of the wood and onto the grounds of the estate. Unlike the surrounding pastures, there was no livestock to warn of their presence. A manicured gravel drive stretched from the manor to the outbuildings at the rear of the property. Christopher walked soundlessly along the verge, Glock at eye level, forefinger on the trigger. Peel's weapon remained pointed at the ground.

There were three outbuildings in all, also redbrick and Georgian in style, arranged around a walled central court. To reach the entrance required a journey of about twenty yards across the gravel. Christopher chose speed over stealth and entered the courtyard at a dead sprint with the Glock in his outstretched hand. Peel braced himself for the sound of gunfire, but there was only silence. He entered the courtyard to find Christopher swinging through the open door of one of the three buildings. He emerged a moment later carrying two black hoods, one of which was crusted with dried blood.

Peel snapped a photograph of the van's registration plate, then opened the rear door. An overhead dome light illuminated the cargo hold. Christopher stared at the bloodstains, then closed the door without a sound. A moment later he was creeping across a darkened meadow toward the Georgian manor, a Glock in his outstretched hands, Timothy Peel a step behind.

———————

The table was circular and fashioned of rosewood. Arrayed upon it were a pile of documents, a Montblanc fountain pen, a Faraday pouch, a mobile phone, and a SIG Sauer P320 pistol. Gabriel and Ingrid sat shoulder to shoulder in a pair of matching George VI coronation chairs. Hoodless, they were able to get a look at one another for the first time. There was a large bruise on the right side of Ingrid's face, and her eye was bright red with a subconjunctival hemorrhage. Gabriel was confident he looked far worse. Even Trevor Robinson seemed embarrassed by his appearance.

He walked over to a drop leaf end table and extracted a cigarette from an antique silver box. "I trust you've come to your senses, Allon."

"I don't want your money, Trevor."

"What about the Picasso?"

"I'll get it back one way or another."

"Not if you're dead, you won't." Robinson lit the cigarette and sat down at the table. "Besides, Allon, do you really want to make a widow of your wife because of a painting that happened to belong to some Jew who died in the gas chambers?"

"Are you trying to get on my good side, Trevor?"

"I wouldn't dream of it. But I am interested in helping you reach the best decision for all parties involved." Robinson placed a document before Gabriel and laid the fountain pen atop it. "This gives Harris Weber full power of attorney to handle your affairs related to this matter, including the creation of a limited liability shell company registered in the British Virgin Islands. Please sign where indicated."

"That would be rather difficult, given the fact that my hands are bound behind my back."

Robinson nodded toward one of the men.

"Don't bother," said Gabriel. "I have no intention of signing it."

"Perhaps this will change your mind." Robinson took up the pistol and leveled it at Ingrid's head. "I'm not going to do it in here, of course. That would make quite a mess. But you will watch her die unless you sign those documents."

"Put down the gun, Trevor."

"Wise choice, Allon."

Robinson laid the gun on the table, and one of the men cut the duct tape from Gabriel's wrists. His shoulders were stiff, as if from rigor mortis, and the fingers of his right hand struggled to maintain their grip on the elegant fountain pen. It was the gun he wanted, the SIG Sauer P320. But in his current condition he was not at all certain he could seize it before Robinson. Besides, now that his hands were free, the four former elite soldiers had drawn their SIGs as well. Any attempt by Gabriel to take possession of the weapon, even a successful attempt, would result in a bloodbath.

Robinson was pointing toward the red flag attached to the bottom of the page. "Sign here, please."

"I'd like to read it first, if you don't mind," said Gabriel, and focused his eyes on the document's opening line. It was then that he heard something that sounded like the snapping of a tree limb. For an instant he thought it was only a mirage brought about by his concussion. But the startled reaction of the four professional security men assured him that was not the case.

The one called Sam was the first to raise his weapon. In the cavernous room the sound of the gunshot was deafening. A reply of three shots followed, and three tightly grouped rounds blew a large hole in Sam's chest. The next two men went down like targets in a carnival shooting gallery, but the fourth managed to squeeze off several wild shots before a portion of his head vanished and his legs buckled.

Only then did Trevor Robinson reach for the SIG Sauer and point it once again toward Ingrid's head. Gabriel hurled himself in front of her as several shots rang out. A moment later he saw a familiar face hovering over him, the face of the little boy who had lived in the cottage at the head of the tidal creek in Port Navas. But what was he doing here, of all places? And why was he holding a Glock 19 in his hand? Surely, thought Gabriel, the vision was illusory. It was only his disordered mind playing tricks on him again.

54

Vauxhall Cross

One and a half miles separated the opulent Georgian estate from the pasture where Peel had left the Vauxhall. He covered the distance in his Wellingtons in a little over ten minutes, pausing twice to be violently sick, and drove back to the estate with the headlamps doused. In the blood-spattered drawing room he found Christopher photographing the faces of the corpses. Peel had killed two of the men himself, including the gray-haired man in a suit and tie who had been preparing to shoot Gabriel and Ingrid.

He looked down at the dead man's face. "Who is he?"

"Trevor Robinson. At least he used to be." Christopher snapped a photo of the man, then, after scrutinizing the image, snapped a second. "He's the chap who arranged for Professor Blake to be murdered. None of which you will ever mention to your superiors. After all, how could you? You weren't here tonight."

"I killed two people."

"You did no such thing."

Peel held up his right hand. "And when the Avon and Somerset Police swab me for gunshot residue?"

"I'm quite confident they won't."

"Why not?"

"Because we won't be mentioning any of this to them, either."

Peel stared at the five bodies. "We can't just leave them here."

"Of course we can."

"For how long?"

"Until someone finds them, I suppose."

Gabriel was shoving documents into a black overnight bag. The side of his neck was caked with dried blood, and his cheek was badly swollen. Ingrid appeared to have come through the ordeal with only a single contusion. She was clearing smashed computers and hard drives from a credenza as though oblivious to the carnage around her.

"And what about them?" asked Peel. "Were they here tonight?"

"Don't be ridiculous," replied Christopher.

"Gabriel's blood is in that outbuilding and in the back of the van."

"Not to worry, he has plenty more."

Peel turned to Gabriel and asked, "Did you touch anything?"

He held the Montblanc fountain pen aloft, then dropped it into the nylon bag.

Peel pointed toward the mobile phone lying on the circular table. "What about that?"

"It belonged to the late Trevor Robinson. The remains of my mobile device are in that Faraday pouch." He added both items to the overnight bag.

"Passport and wallet?" inquired Peel.

Gabriel patted the front of his jacket. "And Ingrid has hers as well. There's nothing to prove we were ever here."

"Except for the video from the security system."

"This property is owned by a corrupt Russian billionaire." Gabriel pulled the zipper on the overnight bag. "There is no video."

They switched off the lights and went out, closing the ruined front door behind them. Gabriel and Ingrid tossed their bags into the boot and crawled into the back seat. Christopher sat in front next to Peel. He rolled up the drive with his headlamps doused and stopped when they reached Hill Lane.

"Where to?"

"The Royal Navy air station in Yeovilton. I've arranged for a Sea King to take us back to London."

"Us?"

"You don't really think we would leave you here alone, do you?"

Peel turned into Hill Lane and immediately scraped against a hedgerow. "Request permission to turn on the bloody headlamps."

"Permission granted," replied Gabriel.

Peel met his gaze in the rearview. "Are you ever going to tell me what happened tonight?"

"You saved our lives. And for that, we are both very grateful."

"What did they want from you?"

"The documents we acquired from Harris Weber & Company in Monaco."

"Which would explain why they smashed your computers and phones."

"And the two external hard drives," added Gabriel.

"Too bad you didn't stash a copy on the Cloud."

"Yes," said Ingrid with a smile. "Too bad."

It was approaching 5:00 a.m. when Peel guided the Vauxhall past the sentry post at the naval air station. The Sea King waited on the tarmac, its Rolls-Royce Gnome turboshaft engines whining. It ferried them eastward to the heliport in Battersea, where they climbed into a dark gray van with blacked-out windows. Twenty minutes later, after a harrowing ride up Battersea Park Road, it turned into the garage of SIS Headquarters on the Albert Embankment.

Peel and Ingrid were immediately shown to an underground holding room. But Gabriel, a frequent visitor to the building in his previous life, was allowed to accompany Christopher upstairs to Graham Seymour's magnificent office overlooking the Thames. The SIS chief was seated behind his mahogany desk, the same desk used by each of his predecessors. Nearby stood a stately longcase clock constructed by Sir Mansfield Smith-Cumming, the first "C" of the Secret Intelligence Service. The hands showed half past six.

Graham rose slowly to his feet and regarded Gabriel at length. "Who did that to you?"

"A fellow named Trevor Robinson and four hired goons."

"I knew a Trevor Robinson when I was still at Five. He worked in D Branch. Last I heard he was living in Monaco and making millions working for a law firm that specialized in offshore financial services."

"Same Trevor," replied Gabriel.

"Where is he now?"

"A lovely Georgian manor in Somerset. It's owned by Valentin Federov, the Russian oligarch whose contribution to the Conservative Party brought down Prime Minister Edwards. Trevor was just borrowing the place."

"I don't suppose he's still alive."

"I'm afraid not."

Seymour's eyes settled on Christopher. "Please tell me you didn't kill a former MI5 officer."

"Which answer would you like to hear?"

"What about his four associates?"

"Use your imagination, Graham."

He turned to Gabriel. "Am I to understand that Lucinda Graves is somehow mixed up in this mess?"

"Without question. And so is her husband."

"Says who?"

"The late Trevor Robinson."

"Well," said Graham. "That would present us with something of a problem, wouldn't it?"

———

Among the many amenities contained within the Secret Intelligence Service's riverfront headquarters were squash courts, a fitness center, a rather good restaurant and bar, and a full-time medical clinic. The physician on duty, after a brief examination, determined that her patient had likely suffered a moderate to severe concussion. He was nevertheless able to provide SIS chief Graham Seymour with a detailed description of the unlikely series of events that had occasioned his present condition. He omitted only a single relevant fact, that Christopher had played a minor role in the theft of the sensitive attorney-client documents from the Monaco office of a British-registered law firm. Graham surmised as much by dint of the fact that Gabriel had driven Christopher's Bentley to Cornwall. He was also reasonably confident that Christopher's wife, Sarah, was in it up to her eyeballs. The three of them were thick as thieves.

"What are the chances that the Courtauld Gallery still has a copy of that video?"

"Based on the reaction of the gallery's director," replied Gabriel, "I'd say they're next to zero."

"In that case, you don't have a single shred of evidence to link Lucinda Graves to the murder of that Oxford professor. Nor, for that matter, can you link Lucinda to a conspiracy to maneuver her husband into Downing Street. In fact, you can't prove that such a conspiracy existed in the first place."

"The ten-million-pound payment from Valentin Federov to the treasurer of the Conservative Party would suggest that it did."

"*Suggest* being the operative word," said Graham. "But why bring down Hillary Edwards? What did she do to deserve such a fate?"

"Trevor Robinson declined to answer that question." Gabriel paused. "But perhaps you can."

Graham made his way to the window. The skies above London were beginning to brighten. The Thames was the color of molten lead.

"Not long after the invasion of Ukraine," he said after a moment, "it became abundantly clear to Amanda Wallace and me that Britain's failure to clean up its financial services industry was not just a domestic problem, it had become a threat to global security as well. We are, quite simply, the money laundering capital of the world. Untold billions in dirty and stolen money flow through our banks and investment firms each year, much of it Russian in origin. That money has made a great many people in London extremely rich. But it has also done a great deal of damage to our society. And it has rotted our politics to the core."

"If memory serves," said Gabriel, "you and I once had a spirited discussion about this very topic."

"It was a blazing row, as I recall. And as was often the case, you were right." Graham walked over to his desk and removed a manila folder from the top drawer. "This is a copy of a confidential report that Amanda and I presented to Hillary Edwards last autumn. It recommended strict new anti-money-laundering laws and other reforms to flush the dirty money from our financial system and real estate markets, and from our politics as well. The prime minister, after reading our report, wanted to go even further. So did the chancellor of the Exchequer and the foreign secretary."

"What about Hugh Graves?"

"The home secretary was concerned that the proposed legislation would weaken a key British industry and needlessly anger the Party's deep-pocketed financial backers in the City of London. The prime minister disagreed and informed the Cabinet that she intended to move forward with a first reading of the bill as quickly as possible. Then the story appeared in the *Telegraph*, and she was finished."

"Perhaps you can convince her to reconsider her decision to resign."

"Impossible." Graham looked at the face of the longcase clock. It was a few minutes after seven. "In approximately four hours' time, Hillary Edwards will deliver her resignation to the King at Buckingham Palace. His Majesty will then invite Hugh Graves to form a new government in his name, at which point he becomes prime minister. There's nothing that can stop him now."

"And if His Majesty were to decline to meet with him?"

"It would send our political system into turmoil."

"Perhaps *you* can intervene."

"An even worse idea." Graham offered Gabriel the manila folder. "You, however, are uniquely positioned to help us out of this unfortunate situation."

Gabriel accepted the document. "That leaves the five dead bodies at Valentin Federov's estate in Somerset."

"A regrettable situation," said Graham. "Who do you think was behind it?"

Gabriel smiled. "Surely it was the Russians."

"Yes," agreed Graham. "Ruthless bastards, aren't they?"

55

Queen's Gate Terrace

It had been Samantha Cooke's ambition, having worked the previous evening until 2:00 a.m., to sleep until at least half past eight, which would leave her just enough time to get to Downing Street to witness the departure of one prime minister and the arrival of another. Her phone, however, awakened her at seven fifteen. She didn't recognize the number but tapped ACCEPT nonetheless.

"What on earth do you want?"

"Is that any way to talk to an old friend?"

The old friend was Gabriel Allon.

"I called you about a thousand times last night. Where in God's name were you?"

"Sorry, Samantha. But I was tied up and couldn't come to the phone."

"Care to explain?"

"I'd love nothing more. A car will appear outside your door in a few minutes. Please get in it."

"Can't, I'm afraid. I have to get to Downing Street to cover the changing of the guard."

"There isn't going to be one. Not if I have anything to do with it."

"Really? And how are you going to manage that?"

"You," he said, and the call went dead.

The car was an all-electric Mini Cooper, neon blue in color. The man behind the wheel had the benevolent demeanor of a country parson, but he drove like a demon.

"Haven't we met somewhere before?" asked Samantha as they hurtled along the Westway.

"Never had the pleasure," he replied.

"Davies is your name, isn't it? You delivered me to that safe house up in Highgate a few years ago."

"Must have been my doppelgänger. My name's Baker."

"Pleased to meet you, Mr. Baker. I'm Victoria Beckham."

They flashed through Bayswater in a blur, then careened through Kensington to Queen's Gate Terrace, where they lurched to a stop outside a large Georgian house the color of clotted cream. The driver instructed Samantha to use the lower entrance.

"And by the way," he added, "it was lovely to see you again, Ms. Cooke."

She climbed out of the car and descended the flight of steps leading to the lower entrance. A ruggedly handsome man with bright blue eyes and a notch in the center of his square chin waited to receive her.

"Please come in, Ms. Cooke. I'm afraid we haven't much time."

She followed him into a spacious eat-in kitchen. An attractive woman in her mid-thirties, Scandinavian in appearance, was pouring herself a cup of coffee. Gabriel was seated atop a stool at the granite-topped island, staring at a mobile phone. It was connected to a laptop. Next to the laptop was a pile of documents.

"What happened to you?" asked Samantha.

"I slipped and fell in a car park in Garrick Street."

"How many times?"

He looked up from the phone, then indicated the stool next to him. "Have a seat, please."

Samantha removed her coat and sat down. Gabriel handed her a printout of a story from the *Telegraph*. It was her exclusive on the Valentin Federov contribution.

"Congratulations, Samantha. There are very few reporters who can say they brought down a prime minister. Unfortunately, you didn't get the entire story." He slid a bank statement across the countertop. It was from BVI Bank in the British Virgin Islands. The name of the account was something called LMR Overseas. "Do you recognize those initials?"

"Can't say that I do."

"LMR Overseas is an anonymous shell company owned by Lord Michael Radcliff. If you review the account activity, you will see that LMR Overseas received a ten-million-pound payment from a company called Driftwood Holdings just forty-eight hours after Radcliff resigned in disgrace."

"Is the timing significant?"

"I'd say so. You see, Samantha, the beneficial owner of Driftwood Holdings is none other than Valentin Federov."

"That's not possible," she whispered.

"You're holding the proof in your hand."

She scrutinized the document carefully. "But how can you be sure that Lord Michael Radcliff is actually the beneficial owner of LMR Overseas? Or that Federov controls Driftwood Holdings?"

Gabriel nudged several more documents across the counter. "These are from the law firm that created and administers both of those shell companies. They prove that the real owners are Lord Radcliff and Valentin Federov."

Samantha looked at the letterhead on the first document. "Harris Weber & Company?"

"It's registered in the British Virgin Islands as well, but those documents came from the firm's Monaco office." Gabriel handed her an external flash drive. "So did these. You'll need a team of experienced investigative reporters to help you review all the material."

"How much is there?"

"Three point two terabytes."

"Bloody hell! Who's the source?"

"We received assistance from someone close to the firm. That's all I can say."

"We?"

Gabriel glanced at the Scandinavian-looking woman. "My associate and I."

"Does she have a name?"

"Not one that's relevant to these proceedings."

Samantha pointed toward the man with bright blue eyes. "What about him?"

"Marlowe is his name."

"What does he do for a living?"

"He's a business consultant. His wife runs an art gallery in St. James's."

"Is that so?" Samantha cast her eyes over the documents arrayed before her. "Let me see if I understand this correctly. Lord Michael Radcliff, treasurer of the Conservative Party, accepts a one-million-pound contribution from a pro-Kremlin Russian businessman that leads to his own resignation and the resignation of Prime Minister Hillary Edwards. And then Lord Radcliff receives a ten-million-pound payment from the selfsame Russian businessman?"

"Correct."

"Why?"

"For helping Hugh Graves become prime minister." Gabriel managed to smile. "Why else?"

"I was manipulated into publishing that story? Is that what you're saying?"

"Of course."

"For what reason?"

Another document came gliding across the countertop. It was a memorandum from the directors of the Secret Intelligence Service and MI5, addressed to Prime Minister Edwards.

"I heard rumors of this," said Samantha. "But I was never able to prove its existence."

"I suggest you ring the foreign secretary. Evidently, he was quite keen on the proposal. So was the chancellor."

"And Graves?"

"What do you think?"

"I think Hugh and his lovely wife, Lucinda, probably thought it was a dreadful idea."

"Graves was definitely opposed to the new regulations. As for his lovely wife . . ."

"Is she involved in this somehow?"

"You should probably put that question to the person who told you about the Federov contribution."

"I don't know who the source was."

"Of course you do, Samantha. The answer is staring you right in the face."

She looked down at the documents. "Where?"

Gabriel pointed toward the second paragraph of her original story. "You bastard."

Samantha immediately rang Clive Randolph, the *Telegraph*'s political editor, and in a remarkable display of journalistic skill dictated eight paragraphs of pristine if alarming copy. Randolph, having played a supporting role in bringing down a British prime minister, was in no mood to destroy her chosen successor even before he had settled into Number Ten.

"Not with this thin gruel," he said.

"I've got the goods, Clive."

"Where have I heard that before?"

"I got played. It happens."

"Who's to say you're not being played again?"

"The documents are irrefutable."

"Send them to me right away. But I want a quote, Samantha. A full and complete admission. Otherwise, we wait."

"If we wait—"

The connection died before she could finish the thought.

She quickly photographed the statements from BVI Bank and the attorney-client documents from Harris Weber and, as instructed, emailed them to her editor. Then she reread the memorandum that Graham Seymour and Amanda Wallace had prepared for Prime Minister Edwards. With a call to Foreign Secretary Stephen Frasier, she confirmed that Edwards had intended to move forward with the reforms, with Frasier's full support.

"And what about Hugh Graves?" she asked.

"Do I really need to answer that?"

"He was opposed, I take it?"

"Vehemently. But don't quote me. Background only. Now if you'll excuse me, Samantha, my car is pulling up outside Number Ten. The final meeting of the Cabinet followed by the traditional last photograph. Needless to say, I'm not looking forward to it."

Samantha rang off and returned the memorandum to Gabriel.

"Do you remember our ground rules?" he asked.

"I can characterize the document only. No direct quotes."

She shoved the documents and the external hard drive into her bag and pulled on her coat. Gabriel was staring at the phone again. It was vibrating with an incoming call.

"Shouldn't you answer that?"

"It's not important." He placed the phone face down on the countertop and eased himself off the stool. He was quite obviously in considerable pain.

"What *aren't* you telling me, Gabriel Allon?"

"A great deal."

"You realize that my career and reputation are on the line?"

"You can trust me, Samantha."

"May I ask one more question?"

"By all means."

She looked at the phone lying on the counter. "Who was that call from?"

"Lucinda Graves."

"Why would she be calling you, of all people?"

"She's not."

56

Number Ten

The atmosphere in Downing Street was of a pending public execution. The instrument of death, a wooden lectern, stood a few paces from Number Ten's famous black door. The bloodthirsty spectators, in this case the Whitehall press corps and their colleagues from around the globe, were gathered on the opposite side of the street. The flash of their cameras dazzled Stephen Frasier's eyes as he emerged from his ministerial car. He savored the moment; it was the last time he would ever arrive at the seat of British power as foreign secretary. A part of him was actually looking forward to being a backbencher again. At least that was the fairy tale that Frasier had told himself after bowing out of the leadership contest. He hadn't slept a minute last night. He only hoped it didn't show.

The press were baying for a comment. Frasier damned his rival with faint praise before making his way past the lectern toward the door of Number Ten. As usual, it opened automatically. Rectangular red carpets were arrayed over the black-and-white checkerboard floor in the lobby. A few other members of the Cabinet were milling about like strangers at a funeral.

Frasier's arrival occasioned a smattering of polite applause. It seemed his decision to spare the Party a protracted leadership fight had found favor with his colleagues. Several assured him in coffee-scented whispers that he had been their preferred candidate. He was certain they had told the chancellor the same thing—and that they would soon be falling over themselves to assure Hugh Graves that they had been secretly pulling for him the entire time. Such were the rules of the game. Frasier played it as well as any of them.

Hillary Edwards was laughing at something the minister of health had just told her. It looked to Frasier as though she was glad it was finally over. Her premiership would end the instant she handed her resignation to the King, though she would retain several perks, including her car and driver and her protection detail. Frasier, for his part, would soon be commuting to the Commons on the Tube, with no protection other than his wits and his briefcase. He was looking forward to that as well, or so he told himself.

He made his way over to the prime minister and kissed the proffered cheek. "You deserved better, Hillary."

"As did you, Stephen." She lowered her voice. "If you ever repeat this, I will deny it and denounce you as a liar, but I was hoping it would be you."

"That means a great deal to me."

"Might we have a word in private?" She led him into the Cabinet Room and closed the door. "You look like shit, Stephen."

"I didn't sleep a wink."

"That makes two of us." The prime minister walked over to the chair at the center of the table, the only chair in the Cabinet Room with arms, and ran a hand over the tawny leather. "I'm going to miss it, you know. I'm only sorry I wasn't able to live up to the standards set by some of my predecessors. And if you ever repeat that, Stephen Frasier, I will deny it as well."

"I was always loyal to you, Hillary. Even during the tough times. You made me foreign secretary. I will never forget that."

"Have you heard any rumors about your successor?"

"The usual names are being bandied about, but nothing definitive as yet."

"I'm worried, Stephen."

"About?"

"The foreign policy that Hugh intends to pursue as prime minister. To borrow a line from Margaret, now is not the time to go wobbly. Hugh always said the right things about the war in Ukraine, but I was never sure his heart was really in it."

"Nor was I. But if he tries to dial back our support for the Ukrainians, the Parliamentary Party will rebel, with me leading the charge."

"And me at your side." The prime minister checked the time. "We should probably invite the others in."

"Do you have a moment for a juicy piece of gossip?"

She smiled. "Always."

"I received a most interesting phone call a few moments ago."

"From whom?"

"Samantha Cooke of the *Telegraph*."

"My favorite reporter," said the prime minister icily. "What did she want?"

"She asked whether we had been planning to impose strict new transparency rules on the financial sector. I had the feeling she already knew the answer."

"And what did you tell her?"

"I acknowledged that the bill in fact existed and that it had my wholehearted support. I also might have mentioned that Hugh was opposed to the plan."

"But why is Samantha pursuing that story today, of all days? Why isn't she outside Number Ten with the rest of the rabble?"

"We shall see," said Frasier, and started for the door.

"Stephen?"

He paused.

"Not that it matters now, but I had nothing at all to do with approving that contribution from Valentin Federov."

"You were always very clear about that."

"But you believe me, don't you, Stephen?"

"Of course, Hillary. Why wouldn't I?"

"Because no one else does. I might have been a failure as prime minister, but I am not corrupt. And I did not approve that contribution."

"May I quote you on that?"

Hillary Edwards settled into her chair for the last time. "Please do."

———

The clerical-looking driver of the neon-blue Mini Cooper covered the two and half miles from Queen's Gate Terrace to Warwick Square in just under ten minutes. Lord Michael Radcliff lived in one of the grand Regency houses on the square's northern flank. The bell push summoned a maid clad in a traditional uniform. Samantha said that Lord Radcliff was expecting her, and the maid, after a moment's indecision, invited her inside.

His lordship was standing in the stately center hall, one hand on his ample hip, the other holding a mobile phone to his ear. He lowered the device and regarded Samantha with apprehension.

"I didn't realize we had an appointment, Ms. Cooke."

"We don't. But this will only take a moment."

Radcliff told the person at the other end of the call that a minor crisis had arisen and rang off. Then he looked at Samantha and asked, "Haven't you done enough damage?"

"You're the one who did the damage, Lord Radcliff. Not me."

"What on earth are you talking about?"

"You were the source of the leaked documents regarding the Federov contribution. You're the reason that Hillary Edwards is about to make a farewell speech on the doorstep of Number Ten."

"You seem to be forgetting, Ms. Cooke, that I was forced to resign as a result of the Federov scandal as well."

"But you were well compensated in return, weren't you? Ten million pounds, as a matter of fact. Not bad for a few minutes' work."

Radcliff treated her to a contemptuous smile. "Have you taken leave of your senses?"

She handed him the statement from BVI Bank. He thrust on a pair of half-moon reading glasses before reviewing it.

"This proves nothing, Ms. Cooke. It is merely a coincidence that this offshore company has the same initials as I do."

"But that's not true, Your Lordship." Samantha handed over the documents from Harris Weber. "These prove beyond a shadow of a doubt that *you* are the beneficial owner of LMR Overseas."

He flipped through the documents in silence for a moment, then asked, "Where did you get these?"

"They were given to me by a trusted source. Unlike you, he had the decency to deliver them in person."

"These are confidential documents that were undoubtedly stolen from my attorneys. If you publish anything about them, I shall haul you into court and sue you into oblivion."

She snatched the documents from his grasp. "Perhaps you should phone your libel lawyer. Because I intend to reveal the ten-million-pound payment that you received from Federov later this morning. My story will also suggest that it was part of a plot by Harris Weber and its wealthy clients to ensure that the so-called London Laundromat remain open for business."

"The ten million pounds was related to my work as an international business consultant and investor, not my work for the Party. It was a fee for services rendered, nothing more."

"Payable to an offshore account held by your anonymous shell company?"

"Such arrangements are quite common and perfectly legal. My lawyers and I will be happy to walk you through the paperwork." Another smile. "How does next week sound?"

"If it was all perfectly legal and quite common, why did you lie to me about LMR Overseas?"

"Because wealthy individuals such as myself use anonymous offshore companies for a reason. Acknowledging beneficial ownership of such a company would rather defeat the purpose, wouldn't it?"

"You use anonymous companies, in part, to shield dirty deals like this one from the prying eyes of the press. Fortunately, I have the means of making it public. Something tells me that your fellow citizens won't look favorably upon your business relationship with Federov. In fact, I'm confident your reputation will be ruined after my story appears."

"Which is why I would advise you to tread carefully. Otherwise, you'll be hearing from my lawyers." He slipped past her and opened the door. "Please leave, Ms. Cooke. I have nothing more to say."

"Have you no statement at all?"

"Write whatever you want. But bear in mind, it will have profound consequences."

"I certainly hope so," snapped Samantha, and stormed out of Radcliff's house.

"One moment, Ms. Cooke."

She paused at the bottom of the steps.

"Your story will be wrong for another reason."

"How so?"

"Perhaps we should discuss the ground rules first," said Radcliff.

"Your choice."

"Background only."

"Proceed, Your Lordship."

"The conspiracy to bring down Hillary Edwards went far beyond a single law firm."

"How far?"

"I'll tell you everything you need to know." Radcliff paused, then added, "On one condition."

"What's that?"

"Your story must make no mention of the ten million pounds I received from Valentin Federov."

"No deal."

"If you publish the details of that payment, we're going to spend the next several years tearing each other limb from limb in court. Neither one of us will emerge with our reputations intact. I'm offering you a way out, not to mention the story of a lifetime. What's it going to be, Ms. Cooke? Going once. Going twice . . ."

57

Buckingham Palace

The Mini Cooper was waiting curbside when Samantha emerged from Lord Radcliff's house. Her phone rang the instant she settled into the passenger seat.

"Well?" asked Gabriel.

"We had a rather spirited exchange, to put it mildly."

"He denied everything?"

"But of course. Then, after threatening to sue me to death, he told me the truth."

"Why would he do a thing like that?"

"Because it turns out that his lordship was a bit player in a much broader conspiracy to bring down the Edwards government. And he wasn't going to take the fall alone."

"Did he name names?"

"Quite a few," said Samantha. "But you'll never guess the name of the ringleader."

"Be still, my beating heart."

"Mine's going a mile a minute."

"Have you got the receipts?"

"A recording, actually. Now if you'll excuse me," she said before ringing off, "I have a story to write."

———

Prime Minister Hillary Edwards emerged from Number Ten promptly at ten fifteen and took to the lectern to deliver her farewell address. She had prepared the text without the help of her speechwriters and memorized it during her sleepless final night in Number Ten's private apartment. She made no mention of the scandal that brought down her government or of her successor. Nor did she make any attempt to defend her turbulent premiership, having decided to leave that to the historians and the press. She was resigned to the fact that their verdict was likely to be harsh.

At the conclusion of her remarks, she slid into her official Range Rover Sentinel and left Downing Street for the last time as prime minister. A few tourists gawked at her during the short drive to Buckingham Palace, but there was no show of support. The King's equerry, kilted and adorned with decorations, greeted her in the central quadrangle and escorted her upstairs to the 1844 Room, where His Majesty waited. Their conversation was brief, a few pleasantries, a question or two about her children and her plans. Then she handed over her resignation and it was done. She was left with the distinct impression that the monarch was not sorry to see her go.

The equerry then marched her downstairs to the quadrangle and helped her into the Range Rover. Her phone was lying on the back seat, quivering with a stream of incoming text messages. She assumed they were expressions of support from her Party colleagues, the same colleagues who had unceremoniously cast her out of Number Ten. She would grant herself a few hours' reprieve before responding—time enough, she reasoned, for the sting of her public defenestration to subside. She was not yet fifty and had no intention of retiring from the Commons and fading into obscurity. Memories of the Federov fiasco would soon fade, and she would once again stand for Party leader. There was nothing to be gained by petty vindictiveness.

But as her Range Rover sped along Birdcage Walk, the stream of text messages suddenly turned to a raging river. She reluctantly took up her phone and read the message that was bannered across the top of the screen. It was the MP from Waveney, a steadfast friend and ally.

He must be stopped . . .

There was no indication of who *he* was or why this fellow needed stopping. But subsequent messages quickly unraveled the mystery. Several contained a link to a breaking news story that had appeared while Hillary was meeting with the King. Written by Samantha Cooke, it said that the *Telegraph* had obtained a recording of the prominent London financier Lucinda Graves conspiring with the ousted Conservative Party treasurer Lord Michael Radcliff to bring down the Edwards government. The centerpiece of the plot was the million-pound Federov contribution. It had been made, according to a Party insider, with the specific intention of harming the prime minister.

A prime minister, thought Hillary Edwards, who had just handed her resignation to the King.

She rang Stephen Frasier.

"We shall see, indeed," he said. "I had a feeling it was something big."

"Now we know why Samantha was asking you about the financial reform package. I only wish she had published her story a few minutes earlier. I would have thought twice about resigning."

"Had you done that, Hillary, you would have thrown the Party into turmoil."

"If the messages on my phone are any indication, the Party already is in turmoil. Someone has to convince Hugh to cancel his meeting with the King. He is in no position to accept an invitation to form a new government."

"Nor, for that matter, should His Majesty extend one."

"Talk about turmoil," said Hillary.

"Perhaps you should ring him."

"His Majesty?" she quipped.

"Hugh Graves. If he'll take anyone's call, it's yours."

"What a splendid idea."

Her first call to Graves went straight to his voicemail. When two more attempts to reach him met with the same result, she called Stephen Frasier again.

"Much to my surprise," she said darkly, "Hugh isn't answering."

"That's probably because he's now on his way to the Palace."

"Someone has to tell him to turn around."

"Agreed," said Frasier. "But who?"

———————

For the record," said Christopher as he guided his Bentley along South Carriage Drive, "this is a truly dreadful idea."

"My specialty," replied Gabriel from the back seat.

"Mine, too," seconded Ingrid.

Christopher glanced at the morose-looking young detective sergeant hunched in the passenger seat. "And what about you, Timothy? Don't you have an opinion?"

"I'm not here, remember?"

"Well done, my boy. You obviously have a bright future."

"I *had* a bright future. Now I have no future at all."

"Could be worse," said Christopher. "Just ask Hugh Graves."

According to Radio 4, the prime minister–designate was on his way to Buckingham Palace, unaware, it seemed, of the explosive story in the *Telegraph* regarding his wife's involvement in the Federov scandal. The BBC's presenters were running out of adjectives to describe the unprecedented nature of the unfolding political crisis. Gabriel, for his part, was enjoying the spectacle immensely.

"Make a left turn into Park Lane," he said.

"I know the bloody way," replied Christopher.

"I was afraid you might be trying to take advantage of my diminished mental capacity."

"Your brain seems to be functioning just fine." Christopher shot a glance into the rearview mirror. "But your face could definitely use a bit of retouching."

"It will have to do for now."

"How are you planning to explain that nasty bruise to your wife and children?"

"It's a toss-up between you and the goat. I'm leaning toward you."

Christopher turned into Stanhope Gate and headed eastward across Mayfair.

"Nicely done," remarked Gabriel.

"Care for another injury?"

Ingrid laughed quietly.

"Don't encourage him," said Gabriel.

"I'm sorry. But the two of you are quite funny."

"Trust me, we've had our ups and downs."

Samantha Cooke had joined the BBC's coverage by phone from the *Telegraph*'s newsroom. Under intense questioning from the presenters, she declined to say how she had obtained the recording of Lucinda Graves and Lord Michael Radcliff. She then expressed regret over having published her original story about the Federov contribution. She had been misled, she said, as part of the conspiracy to bring down Prime Minister Edwards.

Her chosen successor reached the gates of Buckingham Palace as Christopher skirted Berkeley Square. Two minutes later, after a dash down Savile Row, he braked to a halt outside a six-story contemporary office building in Old Burlington Street. A gray Range Rover Sentinel waited curbside, watched over by two officers from the Met's Protection Command. The press were gathered on the opposite side of the street, their cameras trained on the building's entrance.

"For the record," said Christopher.

"I heard you the first time," replied Gabriel, and climbed out of the car.

———

The employees of Lambeth Wealth Management had noticed that something was amiss the minute Lucinda arrived at the office. Her edgy mood, they reckoned, was understandable. Her husband was about to become prime minister, thus requiring a suspension of her career. She had already selected a placeholder chief executive and transferred her substantial personal fortune to a blind trust. All that remained was a farewell address to the troops. Knowing Lucinda, it would be as warm as the North Sea in winter. She reserved her seductive charm for Lambeth's moneyed clients. Her employees were more likely to be on the receiving end of her volatile temper. She had grudging admirers at the firm but no close friends. She was feared rather than loved, which was how she preferred it.

Nevertheless, the staff organized a reception to mark the occasion. It was held downstairs on the fifth floor, the engine room, as Lambethians referred to it. The flat-screen televisions, usually tuned to the financial channels, had been switched to the BBC. They were muted while Lucinda spoke—coincidentally, at the same moment Hillary Edwards was delivering her farewell address outside Number Ten. Lucinda's speech was the longer of the two. Afterward she worked the room, an untouched glass of champagne in her hand. Her smile was forced. She seemed anxious to be on her way.

At exactly 10:45 a.m., as Hillary Edwards was handing her resignation to the King, a silence fell over the gathering, and the firm's stunned employees turned to face the televisions. No one dared to raise the volume, but then it wasn't necessary; the breaking news banner at the bottom of the screen was sufficient. Lucinda was the last to notice it. Her brittle smile faded, but the hand holding the champagne flute remained steady.

"Turn it up, please," she said after a moment, and someone increased the volume. The voice they heard was Lucinda's; there was no mistaking her throaty contralto. It was a recording of a conversation she had had some months earlier with Lord Michael Radcliff, the fallen Conservative Party treasurer and a longtime Lambeth client. They were discussing a plan to bring down the Edwards government. The BBC presenters and political analysts had dispensed with any semblance of objectivity and were beside themselves with indignation.

"Will you excuse me?" said Lucinda, and climbed the internal staircase to the sixth floor. The privacy blinds in her office were drawn, which had not been the case when she went down to the reception. The culprit was standing before the window overlooking Old Burlington Street, a hand to his chin, his head tilted slightly to one side. Lucinda managed not to scream when he turned to face her.

"You," she gasped.

"Yes," he replied with a smile. "Me."

58

Old Burlington Street

How did you get in here?"

"You left the door open."

"Get out," Lucinda said through clenched teeth. "Otherwise, I'll have you arrested."

Gabriel smiled. "Please do."

She went to her desk and snatched up the receiver of the phone.

"Put it down, Lucinda. You'll thank me later."

She hesitated, then replaced the receiver.

"A much more sensible play on your part."

She pointed toward the television. "I suppose this is all your doing."

"It was the *Telegraph* that broke the story. It says so on the bottom of the screen."

"Where did Samantha Cooke get that recording?"

"Since there were only two people in the room at the time, I'm betting it was Lord Radcliff. He's a client of your firm, if I'm not mistaken. And when he required untraceable offshore shell companies to conceal some of his more unsavory business dealings, you sent him to Harris Weber & Company. You've been funneling wealthy clients to them for years. And in the process, you've earned hundreds of millions in fees and kickbacks. You're part of the team, a member of the family."

"I'll let you in on a little secret, Mr. Allon. We're *all* part of the team. There isn't a bank or investment house in London that *isn't* in bed with Harris Weber. And the best part is, it's all perfectly legal."

"But Hillary Edwards planned to shut down the London Laundromat, which is why she had to be removed from office. Your colleagues asked you to handle the dirty work. After all, you and your husband had the most to gain." Gabriel glanced at the television. "And the most to lose, as it turns out."

"There's nothing illegal about scheming against one's political rivals, Mr. Allon. We've been doing it on this blessed plot for more than a millennium."

"I doubt the Crown Prosecution Service would agree. Fortunately for you, I'm enormously fond of this country and have no desire to see its political system thrown into chaos. Not when democracies around the world are under siege. Therefore, I'm prepared to be reasonable." He paused, then added, "Which is more than you deserve."

Lucinda closed the door to her office and lowered herself decorously onto her couch. Gabriel couldn't help but admire her display of outward composure. She was miscast as a money launderer, he thought. She would have made an excellent spy.

"Coffee?" she asked.

"Thank you, no."

She poured a cup for herself and turned to face the television. Her husband's Range Rover was at a standstill in the central quadrangle of Buckingham Palace. A protection officer stood next to the rear door, which was closed tight. As yet, there was no sign of the King's equerry.

"Care to make a prediction?" asked Lucinda.

"I'm more interested in yours."

"The equerry will appear in a moment and escort Hugh to the 1844 Room, where His Majesty will ask him to form a government. This minor scandal will blow over in a few days, in large part because the Party backbenchers are quite pleased that the hapless Hillary Edwards is gone. Furthermore, they will conclude that yet another leadership contest will do more harm than good."

"Isn't it pretty to think so," replied Gabriel.

"All right, Mr. Allon. Let's hear *your* prediction."

"Your husband's term as prime minister, if it comes to pass, will be measured in days, if not hours. The Party will select a new leader in short order, and you will face charges of criminal tax evasion and money laundering. In addition, you are likely to be indicted as an accessory in the murder of Charlotte Blake."

"I had nothing to do with her death."

"But you definitely warned your partners at Harris Weber about her investigation into the Picasso. You did so because a number of your high-profile clients were using the art strategy to move their wealth offshore. Trevor Robinson, the firm's head of security, made the problem go away."

"I'm not familiar with anyone by that name."

"Trevor is the one who arranged for my friend and me to be kidnapped yesterday. With your help, of course. You invited me here to determine how much I knew. And when it became clear that I knew a great deal, Trevor and his goons snatched us from a car park in Garrick Street. You undoubtedly assumed that I was dead. Which is why you turned as white as a sheet when you saw me a moment ago."

"You have a vivid imagination, Mr. Allon."

He drew Trevor Robinson's mobile phone from his jacket pocket and dialed. Lucinda's phone vibrated an instant later. "Perhaps you should answer that."

She looked at the number displayed on the screen and declined the call. Then her gaze settled once again on the television, where the standoff at the Palace continued.

"Terms," she said quietly.

"Call your husband. Tell him to leave the Palace and resign as Party leader."

"And if I do?"

"I will make certain that you are never linked to the murder of Professor Blake."

Lucinda was incredulous. "And just how do you intend to do that, Mr. Allon?"

"I have a number of influential friends here in London." Gabriel smiled. "At least that's the rumor."

Lucinda reluctantly took up her phone and typed, then placed it face down on the coffee table. Together they watched the image on the screen, a gray Range Rover motionless in a maroon-colored courtyard.

"Perhaps you should send him another message," said Gabriel.

"Give him a minute. It's not easy to let go of Number Ten. It's all he ever wanted."

"He could have had it were it not for you."

"Were it not for *me*," she replied, "handsome Hugh would never have become an MP in the first place. I made him who he is."

A worldwide embarrassment, thought Gabriel.

Finally, the protection officer moved away from the door, and the gray Range Rover eased forward. Lucinda increased the volume. The BBC's presenters and political analysts were struggling to make sense of the drama unfolding before their eyes.

"You won't forget our deal, will you, Mr. Allon?"

"For better or worse, Lucinda, I am a man of my word."

She rose to her feet, looking suddenly drained. "May I ask you a question before you leave?"

"You want to know what I'm doing with Trevor Robinson's phone?"

Lucinda's eyes were vacant. "I'm sorry, but I'm not familiar with anyone by that name."

"That makes two of us," replied Gabriel, and went out.

The Bentley was parked in a loading zone at the southern end of Old Burlington Street. Gabriel slid into the back seat next to Ingrid, and the car rolled away from the curb. The team on Radio 4 was at a loss for words, surely a first in the history of British broadcasting.

"I assume you had something to do with this," said Christopher.

"It was Lucinda's idea. I just helped her reach the best decision for the sake of the country."

"How?"

"By promising her that she would face no charges in the murder of Charlotte Blake."

Christopher looked at Peel. "Do you think you can manage that, Timothy?"

"That depends on whether or not I still have a job."

"Not to worry. I'll explain everything to your chief constable."

"Everything?"

"Maybe five percent of everything." Christopher turned into Piccadilly and glanced at Gabriel in the rearview. "Are you quite finished?"

"I certainly hope so. I'm exhausted."

"What are your plans?"

"The two o'clock British Airways flight to Venice. If it departs on schedule, I'll be home in time for dinner."

"I'll drop you at Heathrow on the way to Exeter. But what about your partner in crime?"

"She's coming with me."

Ingrid looked at Gabriel with surprise. "I am?"

"When those documents from Harris Weber are made public, several hundred very rich people are going to be extremely angry, including a few Russians. I think it would be a good idea for you to stay in Venice until the storm blows over. If you can behave yourself, that is."

Frowning, Ingrid drew her phone. "I've always been fond of the Cipriani."

Gabriel laughed. "Perhaps you should stay with us instead."

PART FOUR

The Cottage

59

London

The 1922 Committee of Tory backbenchers convened in Room 14 of the Palace of Westminster at two o'clock that afternoon and in a unanimous voice vote elected former prime minister Jonathan Lancaster the new Conservative Party leader. He met with the King at Buckingham Palace an hour later and at 4:00 p.m. addressed a shell-shocked Britain from the doorstep of 10 Downing Street. He promised competence, stability, and a return to decency. The Whitehall press corps, having just witnessed the most turbulent day in modern British political history, was justifiably dubious.

Inside, Lancaster met for the first time with his hastily assembled Cabinet. Stephen Frasier stayed on at the Foreign Office, but Nigel Cunningham, a brilliant lawyer before entering politics, became the new home secretary. Cunningham's successor as chancellor of the Exchequer was none other than Hillary Edwards. Her family's personal possessions, having been extracted from Number Ten earlier that very morning, were carted into her new official residence next door.

The press declared the move a masterstroke on Lancaster's part, and one prominent columnist from the *Telegraph* went so far as to predict that a return to normalcy was possible, after all. He was forced to backtrack a few hours later, though, when his colleague Samantha Cooke published another explosive article, this one detailing the size and scope of the plot against Hillary Edwards. The epicenter of the conspiracy was Harris Weber & Company, a little-known law firm that specialized in offshore financial services. But executives from Britain's largest banks and investment houses, including Lambeth Wealth Management, were also involved. They were motivated by a desire to keep the so-called London Laundromat open for business. So, too, was Valentin Federov. According to the *Telegraph*, the Russian oligarch had taken part in the scheme at the behest of his president, who had used the London Laundromat to bury tens of billions of dollars in the West.

The next morning brought yet another shocking development. This time the news was delivered by the chief constable of the Avon and Somerset Police and concerned the discovery of five bodies at an estate near the hamlet of Raddington. Preliminary ballistics analysis indicated that the victims had been killed with two separate nine-millimeter weapons. Four of the men were former soldiers who made their livings as private security contractors—a description that covered all manner of sins—and the fifth was a former MI5 counter-intelligence officer employed by Harris Weber & Company. More intriguing still was the nominal owner of the property where the incident had occurred: Driftwood Holdings, an anonymous shell company controlled by Valentin Federov. Prime Minister Lancaster, in a brief appearance before reporters outside Number Ten, said the available evidence suggested Russian involvement. With the exception of the mendacious Kremlin spokesman, no one took issue with the statement.

Calls to the Monaco office of Harris Weber & Company received no answer. Neither did a pro forma email, sent three days later, offering the firm's founding partners the opportunity to comment on a story that would soon appear on the website of the *Telegraph*. Written by Samantha Cooke and four other seasoned investigative reporters, the exposé detailed how the secretive law firm had helped some of the world's wealthiest people conceal their riches and evade taxation by using anonymous shell companies registered in offshore financial centers. Armed with millions of sensitive attorney-client documents supplied by an unidentified source, the newspaper was able to peel away the layers of secrecy and identify the real owners of the vaguely named corporate entities. Moguls and monarchs, kleptocrats and criminals. The richest of the rich, the worst of the worst.

Within hours of the story's publication, protesters poured into the streets of capitals around the world, demanding higher wages for workers, higher taxes for billionaires, and justice for autocratic rulers who enriched themselves at the expense of their people. The largest protest took place in London's Trafalgar Square and included a tense standoff with police at the gates of Downing Street. Prime Minister Lancaster, a man of means himself, pledged sweeping reforms of Britain's financial services industry and real estate markets. The remarks briefly sent the FTSE into a tailspin. The City moneymen, fearful the music was about to stop, tut-tutted their disapproval.

Follow-up stories appeared almost daily. One detailed how Harris Weber & Company had helped a Middle Eastern potentate secretly purchase more than a billion dollars' worth of real estate in Britain and the United States. Another explored how the firm used an elaborate scheme known as "the art strategy" to move clients' money from its country of origin to offshore tax havens. A key player in the fraud was Edmond Ricard, the murdered art dealer whose gallery had been located within the boundaries of the Geneva Freeport. Using an internal Freeport document, the source of which was never revealed, the story identified more than a dozen billionaire collectors who stored paintings in the facility. The multibillionaire chairman of a French luxury goods conglomerate, outraged by the disclosure, announced plans to move his enormous collection to Delaware. And when the French government commenced a review of the chairman's most recent tax returns, he threatened to take up residence in lower-tax Belgium. Much to the dismay of his countrymen, the Belgians suggested he remain at home.

A subsequent story revealed Harris Weber's previously unknown connection to an untitled portrait of a woman, oil on canvas, 94 by 66 centimeters, by Pablo Picasso. This time the *Telegraph*'s team of reporters identified their source; it was Charlotte Blake, the Oxford art historian and provenance research specialist who had been murdered near Land's End in Cornwall, allegedly by the serial killer known as the Chopper. Professor Blake had determined that the painting's rightful owner was Emanuel Cohen, a Paris physician who had fallen to his death down the steps of the rue Chappe in Montmartre. The timing of his death, coming just three days after Professor Blake's murder, suggested a possible connection—and foul play on the part of someone. If nothing else, the painting for which Dr. Cohen was searching finally gave the scandal a name. From that point forward, the press referred to it as the Picasso Papers.

The French police immediately opened an investigation into Dr. Cohen's death, and their counterparts in Cornwall quietly lowered the number of killings attributed to the Chopper from six to five. The Sûreté de Monaco, long tolerant of tax evasion and other financial shenanigans, issued a rare pledge of cooperation, but were soon investigating the first known case of homicide in the principality in living memory. The victim was Ian Harris, founding partner of the corrupt law firm that bore his name. He died on the pavement of the boulevard des Moulins after having been struck by no fewer than twelve bullets. Later it would be widely assumed, though never conclusively proven, that the two gunmen had been dispatched by an angry client.

The rest of the firm's lawyers wisely shredded their files and went into hiding. Konrad Weber returned to his native Zurich, where he was soon the target of a wide-ranging investigation led by FINMA, the Swiss financial regulatory agency. He met his end on the Bahnhofstrasse beneath the wheels of a Number 11 tram. A hand to the back, and down he went. No one saw the man who pushed him.

———

Nearly lost in the daily deluge of disclosures were the Graveses. Hugh tried briefly to cling to his seat in the Commons but was told he faced expulsion if he did not resign. He did so with a written statement, thus avoiding a nasty confrontation with the Whitehall press corps. In a special by-election held just six weeks later, the Tories surrendered a seat they had held for more than a generation. Still, the margin of Labour's victory was sufficiently small that the political team at Party Headquarters held out hope that the next election would result in a respectable trouncing rather than a complete and utter annihilation.

Lucinda fared little better. A return to Lambeth Wealth Management was out of the question, for Lambeth was forced to close its doors after being abandoned by its clients. She sought work at other investment houses—several of which had taken part in the plot to maneuver her husband into Downing Street—but not even the wealth management division of Deutsche Bank would touch her. Determined to salvage her reputation, she hired London's top crisis-management firm, only to be advised that it would be best if she and her husband disappeared. Her high-priced criminal lawyers thought it a fine idea.

They sold off the grand houses in Holland Park and Surrey—to anonymous shell companies, of course—and vanished so quickly that it was almost possible to imagine they had never existed in the first place. Where they went was anyone's guess. There were purported sightings in the usual places, Mustique and Fiji and the like, but no documentary evidence to support the claims. A wholly unsubstantiated theory circulated that Lucinda had met with the same fate as Ian Harris and Konrad Weber. Another rumor implied that she had stashed more than a billion pounds in the Cayman Islands. This one had a ring of truth, as the *Telegraph* was soon to discover. The actual amount of Lucinda's offshore holdings was closer to a half billion pounds, all of it held by shell companies.

When at last the Graveses resurfaced, it was in Malta, a favorite port of call for scoundrels and tax evaders the world over. The prime minister, a client of Harris Weber & Company, issued the couple Maltese passports in record time and was a frequent visitor to their luxurious seaside villa. Lucinda found work as a rainmaker with one of Malta's most corrupt banks. Hugh, having nothing better to do, began work on a novel, a steamy thriller about a British politician who seeks power at any cost and loses his soul. A once fabled British publishing house purchased the work sight unseen for four million pounds.

The reinvention of Hugh Graves as a literary figure—not to mention the appalling size of his advance—ignited a firestorm of criticism in the British press. The minor scandal was soon overshadowed, however, by the brutal murder of a twenty-three-year-old woman from the Cornish village of Leedstown, by all appearances the Chopper's latest victim. With the Metropolitan Police still in control of the investigation, Detective Sergeant Timothy Peel, having returned to duty after a brief leave of absence, was free to pursue a private matter. Someone, it seemed, had stolen his sailboat.

60

Senen Cove

The cottage stood at the end of Maria's Lane in the hamlet of Senen Cove. It had four bedrooms, a modern kitchen, and a spacious sitting room that Gabriel, after a painstaking survey of the alternatives, claimed as his studio. The favorable publicity surrounding his recent appearance at the Courtauld Gallery had resulted in an avalanche of lucrative requests for his services. Regrettably, a financially lopsided prior commitment, made under duress during a boozy lunch at Claridge's, required his attention first.

The work in question, *Madonna and Child*, oil on canvas, 94 by 76 centimeters, by Orazio Gentileschi, arrived at the cottage in the back of a Mercedes transit van. Gabriel extracted the painting from its shipping crate and secured it to a large studio easel. A cool sea breeze, blowing through the open windows, vented the noxious fumes of his solvents. Nevertheless, at Chiara's insistence, he agreed to wear a protective mask for the first time in his long career.

He rose at dawn each morning and worked without a break until midday. The children, after gamely sampling the local pub fare, prevailed on their mother to prepare proper Venetian lunches instead.

Afterward Gabriel would hike along the South West Coast Path to the tiny port of Mousehole, where he had stashed the ketch. The dangerous rip currents and swift tides of the Cornish coast posed a welcome challenge to his seamanship. The long walks back to the cottage in Senen Cove shed five pounds from his already slender physique.

Returning home late one afternoon, he was surprised to see Nicholas Lovegrove sitting on the terrace with Chiara, a glass of wine in hand. He had traveled all the way to Cornwall, he claimed, to check on the status of the Gentileschi. The true purpose of the visit, though, was to interrogate Gabriel about the Picasso Papers scandal. Gabriel told Lovegrove as much as he could, which was next to nothing.

"Come on, Allon. Show a little leg."

"Suffice to say, Nicky, you played a small but vital role in preventing Hugh Graves from becoming prime minister."

"I gathered that. But how?"

"One thing led to another. That's all I can say."

"And the Picasso?"

"The flight data on Harris Weber's executive jet would suggest that the painting is in the British Virgin Islands. The authorities there are searching for it now."

"Kicking down doors, are they?"

"Hardly."

"It's a shame the painting slipped through our fingers," said Lovegrove. "Still, I have to admit, I rather enjoyed our little escapade. Especially the time I spent with Anna Rolfe." He turned to Chiara. "She really is quite extraordinary, don't you think?"

Gabriel interjected before his wife could answer. "Perhaps we should discuss the Gentileschi instead."

"How soon can you have it ready?"

"Unless I can squeeze it into my carry-on luggage, it will have to be finished before we leave for Venice."

"The sooner the better."

"Where's the fire, Nicky?"

"Isherwood Fine Arts."

"Come again?"

"It seems your dear friend Sarah Bancroft has a buyer. Very hush-hush. Anonymous shell company. That sort of thing."

"How much did she get for it?"

"Eight figures."

"Plus dealer's commission, I suppose."

"But of course."

"So you and my dear friend Sarah Bancroft will each earn in excess of a million pounds on the sale," said Gabriel. "And I will make a lousy fifty thousand."

"You're not trying to renege on our arrangement, are you?"

"A deal's a deal, Nicky."

Lovegrove smiled. "How refreshing."

———

The geography of the west Cornish coast was such that twice each afternoon Gabriel walked through a crime scene. The car park at Land's End where Charlotte Blake had left her Vauxhall Astra. The overgrown hedgerow where her body had been found. The stately stone manor where her lover, Leonard Bradley, lived with his wife and three children. It was inevitable, then, that Gabriel and Bradley should meet. It happened late one afternoon near the Tater-du Lighthouse. Gabriel was headed back to the cottage after leaving the ketch in Mousehole Harbor. Bradley was mulling over a particularly profitable day of trading.

"Allon," he called out. "I was hoping I might bump into you."

The remark caught Gabriel by surprise. "How did you know I was in the neighborhood?" he asked.

"I heard the rumor at the chippy in Senen Cove."

"I would be grateful if you didn't repeat it."

"It's rather too late for that, I'm afraid. It seems you're the talk of Cornwall." They set off together along the coast path. Bradley walked with his hands clasped behind his back. His pace and manner were deliberative. Finally, he said, "You misled me the afternoon you and that detective came to my home."

"Did I?"

"You said it was your first visit to Cornwall. But I have it on the highest authority that you and your wife lived for a time in Gunwalloe, of all places. But you also deceived me about the nature of your investigation. You already knew the truth about OOC Group, Limited, when you came to see me."

"I knew most of the truth," admitted Gabriel. "But not all of it. You gave me the final piece of the puzzle."

"Lucinda?"

Gabriel nodded.

"Is she responsible for Charlotte's death?"

"She played no role in her murder. But, yes, Lucinda is to blame for what happened."

"Which means I am as well."

Gabriel was silent.

"I have a right to know, Allon."

"You sent Charlotte to Lucinda Graves with the best of intentions. You mustn't blame yourself for her murder. It was just . . ."

"Bad luck?"

"Yes."

Bradley slowed to a stop at Boscawen Cliff. "Magical, isn't it?"

"I've always thought so."

"There's a lovely cottage on the market near Gwennap Head. They're asking two for it, but I know for a fact it can be had for one and a half."

"I'm not in the market at the moment. But thank you for thinking of me."

"Will you and your family at least join us for dinner one evening? Cordelia is a wonderful cook."

"It might be a bit awkward, don't you think?"

"We're British, Allon. We specialize in awkward dinner parties."

"In that case, we'd love to."

"How about Saturday night?"

"See you then," said Gabriel, and set off along the footpath.

———————

He arrived at the cottage thirty minutes later to discover that Irene had locked herself in her bedroom and was refusing to come out. It seemed she had heard a report on Radio Cornwall about the most recent murder and had put two and two together. The child's mother, already at her wit's end, seemed pleased by the development. She was reading a tattered copy of *The Thin Man* outside on the terrace. Gabriel told her about his encounter with Leonard Bradley—and about the dinner invitation. His wife informed him that they had other plans.

"No," he said. "No, no, no, no."

"I'm sorry, darling, but all the arrangements have been made.

Besides, it's the least you can do." Chiara shook her head slowly with reproach. "You were so very rude to them."

And so it happened that on a warm and windy evening Gabriel found himself behind the wheel of a rented Volkswagen estate car, headed in a southwesterly direction across the Lizard Peninsula. Irene, convinced they would soon come upon a madman armed with a bloody hatchet, was apoplectic. Raphael, his nose in an advanced mathematics textbook, was oblivious to her ravings. Their mother, in the passenger seat, was serene and ravishing.

"You *will* behave, won't you?" she asked.

"I promise to be my usual charming self."

"That's what I'm afraid of."

They arrived in Gunwalloe to find the Lamb and Flag ablaze with light. Gabriel eased into the last remaining space in the car park and killed the engine. "At least there are no photographers this time."

"I wouldn't be so sure about that," said Chiara, and climbed quickly out. Flanked by his children, Gabriel followed her into the pub, where most of Gunwalloe's two hundred residents cheered his arrival. Not surprisingly, it was the organizer of the party, the irrepressible Vera Hobbs, who confronted him first.

"I knew it from the moment I laid I eyes on you," she said with a mischievous wink. "You were hiding something. It was plain as day."

Dottie Cox from the Corner Market was next. "It was those beautiful green eyes of yours that gave you away. Always moving, they were. Like a pair of searchlights."

Duncan Reynolds wasted no time on pleasantries. "Quite possibly the rudest man I've ever met."

"It wasn't me, Duncan. It was only a role I was playing at the time."

The old railman swallowed some of his beer. "I suppose you heard about poor Professor Blake."

"I read about it in the papers."

"Know her?"

"Didn't, actually."

"Wonderful woman. And quite beautiful, if you ask me. Reminded me of one of those women—"

Vera Hobbs cut him off. "That's quite enough, Duncan, dear. Otherwise, Mr. Allon will never come back again."

He consented to deliver a few remarks, which concluded with a heartfelt if uproariously funny apology for his past conduct. Afterward they feasted on traditional Cornish fare, including pasties fresh from Vera's oven. When the party finally ended at midnight, several men insisted on escorting the Allon family to their car because of the threat posed by the Chopper. This sent Irene into another spasm of panic. Gabriel found it a welcome reprieve from her usual fretting about melting ice caps and submerged cities.

"Was it my imagination," said Chiara when the children had fallen asleep, "or did you enjoy that immensely?"

"I have to admit, I did."

"Irene and Raphael love it here, you know."

"What's not to love? It's very special."

"It's the perfect place to spend the summer, don't you think?"

"We can always rent a cottage for a few weeks."

"But wouldn't you prefer to have something of your own?"

"We can't afford it."

Chiara didn't bother with a retort. "There's a lovely cottage near Gwennap Head that just came on the market."

"Leonard Bradley says it can be had for a million and a half."

"Actually, I was able to talk them down to one point four."

"Chiara . . ."

"The cottage is extraordinary, and there's a separate building where you can set up your studio."

"And work my fingers to the bone to pay for everything."

"Please say yes, Gabriel."

He glanced over his shoulder at his daughter. "What about the Chopper?"

"You'll think of something," said Chiara. "You always do."

61

Port Navas

It would be another week before Gabriel completed the restoration of the Gentileschi. He shipped the painting to Isherwood Fine Arts, which sold the work to something called Quantum International, Ltd., for the princely sum of ten million pounds. Sarah Bancroft leaked details of the sale to Amelia March of *ARTnews*, along with the name of the celebrity conservator who had knocked the canvas into shape. Sarah also agreed to give the celebrity conservator a slice of her lucrative dealer's commission. He wired a portion of the funds to a Marseilles-based thief and invested the remainder in a five-bedroom cottage near Gwennap Head in deepest West Cornwall.

They took formal possession of the property on a Wednesday afternoon in late August. Chiara spent the remainder of her holiday planning a wholesale architectural renovation that would push the final cost of the project well past the original asking price. Gabriel, for his part, lined up several private commissions that would keep the Allon family financially afloat.

But each afternoon he hiked the South West Coast Path to the tiny port of Mousehole and sailed his old wooden ketch in the treacherous waters off the Cornish coast. During one excursion the weather turned suddenly violent, and he was fortunate the vessel did not smash herself to pieces on Logan Rock. That evening the Allon family dined at the home of Cordelia and Leonard Bradley. The occasion was saved from perfection by news of yet another murder, this one in Port Isaac. Poor Irene spent a sleepless night of terror in her parents' bed. Gabriel's Beretta, which he had carried into the country with the assent of SIS chief Graham Seymour, rested on the bedside table.

The following morning, their last in Cornwall, was spent packing their bags and preparing the Gwennap Head cottage for the coming winter. Gabriel left behind the studio easel and supplies he had acquired for the Gentileschi restoration, then set off on foot toward Mousehole. Fair play required him to return the ketch from whence he had purloined it. Chiara and the children planned to collect him quayside in Port Navas, provided, of course, that Irene could be talked out of her room. From there they would proceed to the Hilton Hotel at Heathrow's Terminal 5. They were booked on the morning's first flight to Venice.

The precise timing of the operation, though, was held hostage by the fickle nature of Cornwall's winds and tides. Gabriel crossed Mount's Bay in just under three hours, but unfavorable conditions slowed his journey around Lizard Point, and the sun was beginning to set by the time he finally reached the mouth of the Helford. He rang Chiara and gave her an update on his position and estimated time of arrival. With Raphael's help, she coaxed Irene into the car and started east.

The outgoing tide was running hard and fast, slowing Gabriel's progress further still. He dropped his sails at Padgagarrack

Cove and made his way upriver under power. Port Navas Creek, flat and calm in the gathering darkness, received him like a trusted friend. He aimed the prow toward the stone quay near the old foreman's cottage and, wishing to prolong the journey a moment longer, reduced his speed to a crawl. That was when he spotted the flare of a torch. Smiling, he flashed his running lights twice in reply.

Permission to come aboard."

Gabriel frowned at Peel's black policeman's footwear. "Not in those things, you don't."

Peel left his shoes on the quay and stepped over the lifeline. "Is there anything to drink on this vessel?"

"Is that an official inquiry, Detective Sergeant?"

"I could use a beer, that's all."

"It's possible there's some Carlsberg in the icebox."

Peel ducked into the cabin and emerged with two dripping-wet bottles and an opener. He pried the cap from one and handed it to Gabriel. "You didn't run her aground or smash into anything, did you?"

"I had a couple of close shaves, but I was able to pull her back from the brink."

"I had a rather close shave myself recently. A nasty piece of business in neighboring Somerset." Peel opened the second Carlsberg. "But thanks to your friend Christopher, I came through it without a scratch."

"And when the story broke about Charlotte Blake and the Picasso?"

"I played dumb, didn't I?"

"My name come up?"

"Not at the headquarters of the Devon and Cornwall Police. And my colleagues from Avon and Somerset have no idea that you and Ingrid were ever in that manor house. It's as if it never happened."

"Is it really, Timothy?"

He drank some of the beer but said nothing.

"Can you ever forgive me?" asked Gabriel.

"For what?"

"Allowing you to be placed in a situation where you were forced to take two human lives."

"It wasn't your fault, Mr. Allon. It was your friend Christopher's doing. Besides, the men I killed weren't exactly pillars of the community, were they?"

"Neither were the men that I killed. But I paid a terrible price nonetheless. Killing people ruined my life, Timothy. I would hate myself if it ruins yours."

"How much does Chiara know about what happened?"

"The basics."

"Does she know that you threw yourself in front of Ingrid?"

Gabriel shook his head.

"Bravest thing I ever saw."

"But you won't mention it to her, will you? I'm in enough trouble as it is."

"Don't worry, Mr. Allon. It will be our little secret." Peel glanced at the old foreman's cottage. "Just the way it was when I was a kid. You looked after me back then. And now I'll look after you."

"I didn't realize I needed looking after."

Peel gave a knowing smile. "Did you or did you not purchase that rather large property at Gwennap Head?"

"Wherever did you hear that?"

"I stopped for a pasty at the Cornish Bakery the other day. Vera

Hobbs told me everything. I only wish that I could have come to the party at the Lamb and Flag."

"I could have used your help. They gave me quite a going-over."

"It's probably better if we keep our distance for a while. But I plan to be a frequent visitor to your Gwennap Head estate."

"It's a cottage, Timothy."

"A very large cottage," said Peel. "With one of the greatest views on earth."

Gabriel gazed at the silver-black waters of the tidal creek. "This one isn't so bad, either."

Peel made no reply. He was looking down at his phone.

"Not another one," said Gabriel.

Peel shook his head. "A minor inconsistency with a case I'm working on. A burglary ring operating out of Plymouth. We arrested one of its members yesterday morning, and he promptly gave up the rest of the crew."

"And the inconsistency?"

"The exact number of jobs they pulled. They've confessed to twenty-three separate burglaries, but only twenty-two of them were reported to the police."

"Which one wasn't?"

"A house on Tresawle Road in Falmouth."

"What did they steal?"

"A rare coin collection. Apparently, they got a couple thousand quid for it."

"Have you spoken to the occupant of the house on Tresawle Road in Falmouth?"

"He hasn't returned my call."

"I'm not surprised." Gabriel took a pull at the beer, then shook his head slowly. "Didn't they teach you anything at detective school, Timothy?"

62

Tresawle Road

H is name is Miles Lennox."

"Sounds like a serial killer to me."

"It's a perfectly fine name."

"For an axe murderer," said Gabriel.

"Hatchet, Mr. Allon. The Chopper uses a hatchet." Peel turned into Hillhead Road and streaked across darkened farmland toward Falmouth. "And I'm sure there's a perfectly reasonable explanation for why he didn't call us after his coins were stolen."

"There is," said Gabriel. "He didn't call you because he didn't want you to discover his collection of bloody hatchets."

"It makes a certain amount of sense, I have to admit. He also happens to fit our profile. Right age, right height and weight, right marital status and occupation."

"Rare coin collector?"

"Lorry driver. He works for a beverage distributor."

"Which gives him a perfect excuse to drive around Cornwall and Devon looking for young women to kill."

"We're not there yet."

"We will be in about five minutes."

"More like three," said Peel as they reached the fringes of Falmouth. He worked his way eastward across town and rolled to a stop outside a terraced house in Tresawle Road. It was two floors in height, with a gray pebble dash exterior. A light burned behind the lace curtains of the sitting room window.

Peel switched off the engine. "I should probably call the boys from the Met. It's their case, after all."

"Probably," agreed Gabriel. "But it will do wonders for your career if you make the collar yourself."

"I need backup."

"Not for a routine burglary inquiry. Besides, you have backup."

"You?" Peel shook his head. "Not a chance, Mr. Allon."

Gabriel offered him the Beretta. "At least take this."

"Put that thing away."

Gabriel returned the weapon to the small of his back. "Slap the cuffs on him while you're introducing yourself. And whatever you do, don't turn your back on him."

Peel climbed out of the car and headed up the garden walk. The door opened to reveal the very face of death. Peel displayed his identification and after a moment's hesitation was granted permission to enter the premises. Gabriel heard nothing to indicate there was a struggle within.

Finally, his phone rang. "You'd better be on your way, Mr. Allon. Things are about to get pretty busy around here."

Gabriel slipped out of the car and set off along the darkened street. He heard the first sirens as he rounded the corner into Old Hill. Chiara called him a moment later.

"Mind telling me where you are?" she asked.

"Falmouth."

"Any particular reason?"

"Change of plan. And tell that daughter of ours not to worry," said Gabriel. "I took care of that little problem."

Author's Note

A *Death in Cornwall* is a work of entertainment and should be read as nothing more. The names, characters, places, and incidents portrayed in the story are the product of the author's imagination or have been used fictitiously. Any resemblance to actual persons, living or dead, businesses, companies, events, or locales is entirely coincidental.

There is indeed a civil parish called Gunwalloe on the western coast of the Lizard Peninsula, but it bears little resemblance to the place that appears in *A Death in Cornwall* or three previous Gabriel Allon novels. Sadly, there is no Cornish Bakery, no Corner Market, and no public house known as the Lamb and Flag. The rest of the remarkable region is, for the most part, accurately rendered. Deepest apologies to the Devon and Cornwall Police for the deplorable conduct of Detective Sergeant Timothy Peel, but I required a literary mechanism for inserting a prominent Venice-based art restorer into a British murder investigation.

The restorer in question could not possibly have left a Bentley in a car park in Garrick Street, because no such car park exists. There is indeed an art gallery on the northeast corner of Mason's Yard, but it is owned by Patrick Matthiesen, one of the world's most successful and respected Old Master art dealers. I am happy to report that the theft and recovery of *Self-Portrait with Bandaged Ear* by Vincent van Gogh, one of the Courtauld Gallery's most cherished possessions, took place only in the universe inhabited by Gabriel Allon and his associates. The iconic painting was stolen in a daring smash-and-grab robbery in the opening pages of *The Rembrandt Affair*. The perpetrators were never identified, but I suspect that one of them was none other than René Monjean.

The surrealist Picasso portrait depicted in *A Death in Cornwall* is fictitious, as is its provenance. Therefore, the painting could not have been sold at Christie's in London for fifty-two million pounds. The venerable auction house was the target of a lawsuit filed in 2018 over the sale of Alfred Sisley's *First Day of Spring in Moret*. Art dealer Alain Dreyfus paid $338,500 for the painting in 2008, only to discover that it had once belonged to the French Jewish collector Alfred Lindon. Before fleeing Paris in August 1940, Lindon placed his entire collection in a vault at the Chase Manhattan Bank on the rue Cambon. The paintings eventually fell into the hands of Reichsmarschall Hermann Göring, a frequent visitor to Paris during the Occupation. The rapacious Nazi gave eighteen of Lindon's paintings, including the Sisley landscape, to a corrupt art dealer in exchange for a single work by Titian.

The Musée du Louvre has in fact hired a renowned expert on the wartime French art market to purge its collection of looted paintings, but I'm confident she would have declined Gabriel's request to create six fabricated provenances for six forgeries. There are indeed art galleries operating inside the Geneva Freeport, but none bear the name Galerie Edmond Ricard SA. I granted myself a certain amount of license regarding some of the Freeport's more arcane rules and regulations, but on matters of importance I adhered to the truth. There are an estimated 1.2 million paintings stored in the Freeport, including more than a thousand works by Picasso. Nearly all of the Freeport's clients rent their vaults using anonymous shell companies to conceal their identities. A collector can purchase a painting at auction in New York and avoid all taxation simply by shipping the work into the Freeport. If the collector elects to sell his painting within the Freeport, he will face no tax liability. Typically, the money changes hands offshore, anonymous shell company to anonymous shell company, making the transactions largely invisible to tax authorities and law enforcement. The paintings themselves are then moved to a new vault.

Many of the Freeport's superrich customers undoubtedly reside in Monaco, regarded by many European governments as a haven for tax evaders and money launderers. Visitors to the tiny principality can dine at Le Louis XV or play English roulette at the famed Casino de Monte-Carlo, but they will search in vain for a law firm called Harris Weber & Company, for no such entity exists. There are countless firms like it, though, including Mossack Fonseca & Company, the now defunct offshore services provider at the center of the 2016 Panama Papers scandal.

Like my fictitious Harris Weber, Mossack Fonseca created and administered thousands of anonymous shell companies to help its clients avoid taxation and conceal their wealth and possessions. It did so, in many cases, at the behest of banks, more than five hundred in all. They included Credit Suisse, Société Générale, and HSBC, which, according to Pulitzer Prize–winning investigative journalist Jake Bernstein, purchased dormant shell companies from Mossack Fonseca in bulk. It was because of the banks' previous association with the firm that I felt free to mention their names in the same breath as my fictitious Harris Weber. Furthermore, none of the three institutions are exactly pillars of the global financial community. US regulators fined HSBC a record $1.9 billion in 2012 for laundering more than $881 million for the Mexican and Colombian drug cartels. Société Générale, for its part, reached an $860 million settlement with the Justice Department in 2018 for bribing Libyan officials and manipulating the benchmark LIBOR interbank lending rate. And Credit Suisse? Well, what more needs to be said?

Five years after the Panama Papers scandal, the same group of reporters—the remarkable International Consortium of Investigative Journalists—released an even larger trove of documents they dubbed the Pandora Papers. Obtained from fourteen separate offshore providers, the paper trail revealed that 130 individuals regarded as billionaires by *Forbes* magazine had offshore accounts. So, too, did some 330 government officials and heads of state. They included Jordan's King Abdullah, who used an extensive network of shell companies and bank accounts to secretly purchase $80 million worth of luxury real estate in Malibu and Georgetown—glittering additions to an international property portfolio that already included extensive holdings in the United Kingdom. Never mind that, according to a recent regional survey, His Majesty's people are among the poorest in the Arab world.

The Pandora Papers also raised uncomfortable questions about the source of several large contributions made to Britain's Conservative Party. It was not the first time the Tories' fundraising had faced public scrutiny. As the *New York Times* reported in May 2022: "It is no secret that wealthy Russian industrialists have given heavily to the Conservative Party over the years." Nor is it a secret that politicians from both of Britain's two main parties welcomed the flood of tainted Russian money that poured into London after the fall of the Soviet Union. The bankers, wealth managers, lawyers, accountants, and estate agents welcomed the Russian money, too. And why wouldn't they? Many grew enormously rich as a result.

Only recently has the British government acknowledged that it was unwise to open London's door to organized criminals and robber barons from a corrupt petrostate ruled by the likes of Vladimir Putin. In a stunning report released in July 2020, the Intelligence and Security Committee of Parliament found that Russia had engaged in a prolonged and sophisticated campaign to undermine Britain's democracy and corrode its institutions. The Kremlin's weapon of choice, of course, was money. Among the report's more alarming findings was that several members of the House of Lords were in business with pro-Kremlin Russian oligarchs. The names of the lords were redacted from the public version of the report, as were the names of the British politicians who had accepted contributions from Russian sources.

The report also used the unflattering word *laundromat* to refer to London's financial services industry, long regarded as the money laundering capital of the world. Britain's own National Crime Agency declared recently: "Although there are no exact figures there is a realistic possibility that the scale of money laundering impacting the UK annually is in the hundreds of billions of pounds." So pervasive is the problem, concluded the NCA, that it "has the potential to threaten the UK's national security, national prosperity and international reputation." Financial journalist Nicholas Shaxson, in his 2018 book *The Financial Curse*, described the UK's reputation as follows: "Britain is the country of first choice for every kleptocrat and dictator in the world." But the so-called London Laundromat could not function, as Shaxson documents in painstaking detail, without the archipelago of tax havens that sprung up in the remnants of the British Empire—tiny island territories with limited financial controls that effectively "hoover up" the world's dirty money. The Pandora Papers linked 956 offshore companies to government officials, but two-thirds of those entities were registered in the same offshore financial center: the British Virgin Islands.

In February 2022, days after Russia's invasion of Ukraine, Prime Minister Boris Johnson introduced legislation to impose transparency on Britain's opaque property market, declaring, "There is no place for dirty money in the UK." The journalist and corruption specialist Misha Glenny compared the proposed reforms to "shutting the stable door after the horse has bolted." Six months later, with the London Laundromat still open for business, Johnson announced his resignation, bringing to a close a turbulent premiership plagued by personal and financial scandals too numerous to mention. His successor, Liz Truss, survived for all of forty-four days before being forced out of Downing Street in a revolt that one Cabinet minister likened to a coup d'état. In all, there have been five Conservative prime ministers since Labour surrendered power in May 2010. During the previous period of Tory dominance, which lasted a remarkable eighteen years, there were two: Margaret Thatcher and John Major.

During a testy confrontation with an executive from my fictitious Harris Weber & Company, Gabriel Allon dryly suggests that the firm should donate a billion pounds to British charitable organizations to atone for helping the wealthy avoid paying their fair share of taxes. Sadly, the figure, while substantial, would represent little more than a rounding error to the estimated total of uncollected taxes globally. The truth is, no one really knows how much money is flowing through the invisible offshore world—or how much money has been unethically or criminally diverted from national treasuries.

The growing disparity between rich and poor, however, is plain to see. The richest 1 percent now control more than half the world's privately held wealth, which in 2024 was estimated to be $454.4 trillion. The World Bank estimates that 9.2 percent of Earth's inhabitants, or 719 million human beings, live on just $2 a day, the measure of extreme poverty. In the United States, the world's richest country, 11.6 percent of the population, or 38 million people, are poor. In the United Kingdom the figure is a shocking 20 percent.

But how to explain the superrich multibillionaire who hires a firm like Mossack Fonseca to shave a few million from his tax bill? Or the kleptocratic thug who stashes his money in an offshore bank account, or in a piece of posh London real estate, while his impoverished people struggle to feed their children? "Perhaps what drives them all," wrote British investigative reporter Tom Burgis in his 2020 book *Kleptopia*, "is fear: the fear that soon there will not be enough to go round, that on a simmering planet the time is approaching for those who have gathered all they can unto themselves to cut free from the many, from the others. There's only one side to be on if you wish to avoid destruction: theirs. You are with the Kleptopians or you are against them. The Earth cannot sustain us all."

But the planet, simmering a few years ago, is now burning, and millions of desperate people are on the move in search of a better life. In developed countries, they are straining resources and exacerbating political tensions. Many businesses welcome them, though, for they are a source of cheap and exploitable labor—human capital, in the lexicon of the wealth extractors, willing to do punishing and dangerous work that native-born citizens are not. They pick fruit and vegetables in the blazing sun, they toil in blood-drenched slaughterhouses and meatpacking plants, they wash dishes and clean rooms in luxury hotels, they care for the sick and the dying.

In many cases, the migrants have fled a country ruled by a kleptocrat with offshore bank accounts created for him by the London Laundromat—the same machine that has helped countless billionaires, the richest of the rich, conceal their immense wealth and evade taxation. Hidden by shell companies and layered trusts, these members of an increasingly powerful global plutocracy dwell in a parallel universe, accessible to only a select few. Fine art confers upon the superrich a patina of instant sophistication and respectability, even if they have neither. Which might explain why so many of their ilk have chosen to stash their multimillion-dollar paintings in the Geneva Freeport so as to deny the tax collector his due. What more needs to be said?

Acknowledgments

I am eternally grateful to my wife, Jamie Gangel, who listened patiently while I worked out the plot of *A Death in Cornwall* and then skillfully edited my first draft. My debt to her is immeasurable, as is my love.

David Bull, whose name appears in the third chapter of the novel, was once again an invaluable source of information on all matters related to art and restoration. Maxwell L. Anderson, who has five times served as the director of a North American art museum, including the Whitney Museum of American Art in New York, provided me with a window on some of the more unsavory aspects of the business of art.

My Los Angeles superlawyer Michael Gendler was, as always, a source of wise counsel. My dear friend Louis Toscano made countless improvements to my typescript, as did my eagle-eyed personal copy editor, Kathy Crosby. Any typographical errors that slipped through their formidable gauntlet are my responsibility, not theirs.

Harper president and publisher, Jonathan Burnham, who has the misfortune of also serving as my editor, provided me with an insightful and erudite set of notes on topics ranging from classical music to Venetian cuisine. A heartfelt thanks to the rest of my remarkable team at HarperCollins, especially Brian Murray, Leah Wasielewski, Doug Jones, Leslie Cohen, David Koral, and Jackie Quaranto.

Like the fictitious Gabriel Allon, I am the father of twins. Mine are named Lily and Nicholas, and as always they were a source of love and inspiration throughout the writing year. They have much in common with Irene and Raphael, especially their intelligence, their innate kindness, and their senses of humor. At the time of this writing, however, neither had adopted an animal from the World Wildlife Fund or fallen into hopeless despair over the prospect of melting ice caps and submerged cities. In the Silva family, those characteristics have been assigned to the figure of late middle age who toils behind a locked door, listening to music that annoys those around him.

About the Author

DANIEL SILVA is the award-winning, number-one *New York Times* bestselling author of *The Unlikely Spy*, *The Mark of the Assassin*, *The Marching Season*, *The Kill Artist*, *The English Assassin*, *The Confessor*, *A Death in Vienna*, *Prince of Fire*, *The Messenger*, *The Secret Servant*, *Moscow Rules*, *The Defector*, *The Rembrandt Affair*, *Portrait of a Spy*, *The Fallen Angel*, *The English Girl*, *The Heist*, *The English Spy*, *The Black Widow*, *House of Spies*, *The Other Woman*, *The New Girl*, *The Order*, and *The Collector*. He is best known for his long-running thriller series starring spy and art restorer Gabriel Allon. Silva's books are critically acclaimed bestsellers around the world and have been translated into more than thirty languages. He lives with his wife, television journalist Jamie Gangel, and their twins, Lily and Nicholas.